SEASONS OF PLENTY

SEASONS OF
PLENTY

The Tabitha Jute Trilogy
VOLUME 2

Colin Greenland

HarperCollins*Publishers*

HarperCollins*Publishers*
77-85 Fulham Palace Road,
Hammersmith, London W6 8JB

Published by HarperCollins*Publishers* 1995
1 3 5 7 9 8 6 4 2

A catalogue record for this book
is available from the British Library

ISBN 0 00 224208 7

Set in Ehrhardt and Univers Light by
Rowland Phototypesetting Ltd,
Bury St Edmunds, Suffolk

Printed in Great Britain by
HarperCollinsManufacturing Glasgow

This book is for all those who knew there
was more to tell and told me so.

CONTENTS

Prologue   *page* I

PART ONE
The Heat of the Moment   5

PART TWO
The Fruit of Experience   107

PART THREE
Cold Light Fades   207

PART FOUR
New Blood   299

The world is so full of a number of things,
I'm sure we should all be as happy as kings.

Robert Louis Stevenson,
'Happy Thought'

PROLOGUE

When the guards on Asteroid 000013 started whimpering and licking each other, Dog Schwartz, to do him justice, was the first person to notice.

Everybody was always doing Dog Schwartz justice. People had done him justice in this jurisdiction, and that jurisdiction. The judge on Integrity 2 had pronounced Dog Schwartz fixed in transgression mode, and he had been around a bit since then.

Dog Schwartz was familiar with life in penal institutions from New Malibu to Ganymede. 000013 was bleaker than most, which was not surprising, it being an Eladeldi penitentiary. 000013 was a big rock with a long, looped, lonely orbit. All there was on the rock was a basic dome, a bunkhouse of sleep racks, and in the middle a big hole in the ground where Dog Schwartz and his fellow penitents spent day after abbreviated asteroid day breaking the big rock of 000013 into smaller rocks.

Dog Schwartz was called Dog because someone had once said he looked like one, a big jowly Terran-type dog, a St Bernard or a bloodhound. He didn't mind the name. He accepted the respect it obviously conveyed. But he was touchy about his appearance. In civilian life he would choose colourful clothes, and even managed to impart a hint of flair to his prison greys.

When you talked about dogs on 000013, though, you meant the guards, because the guards on 000013 were all Eladeldi, who look far more like dogs than any human ever could. Eladeldi, it is conventionally agreed, look like some sort of big blue hairy mutant monster terrier standing on its hind legs.

Today they had started behaving like dogs too.

Dog Schwartz rested with his big hands on his huge thighs. He stared at them all, up on the perimeter. 'Look at them,' he said quietly to his mate. His voice was surprisingly light and high, a rather pleasant tenor.

Dog Schwartz's mate, whose usual name was Monk, took the wedge he was holding out of its crack in the rock and looked. The Monk gave a dirty chuckle, which was the only kind of chuckle he knew how to give.

'Fleas,' he said.

They had been mates, Dog Schwartz and the Monk, for ages. Fate, or nature, or something equally big and bad had thrown them together here, and in many similar places. Dog Schwartz and the Monk his companion were the sort of men you were bound to find in prison, whatever species was in charge.

Dog Schwartz may have looked somewhat like a dog, but Dog Schwartz's mate Monk looked nothing like a monk. Monk was short for Monkey: the Gunky Monkey it was in full, because of the state he always managed to get himself into, no matter how many times the guards sent him back through the ablute after work, or before it, for that matter. The Monk was small and sticky. Grease of all kinds seemed to converge from the far-flung corners of the Solar System with the express purpose of adhering to the hands of the Gunky Monkey.

The Gunky Monkey was good with his hands. What the Gunky Monkey liked doing best was taking things to pieces and putting them together again, to see if they would still go. In general, if they had been alive beforehand, they wouldn't; but if they hadn't been, they would. The Monk could fix most things, one way or the other. And he never left anything unfinished that he started, one way or the other.

Dog Schwartz shook himself and wrinkled his nose and pulled his right ear fiercely. 'Fleas,' he scoffed. 'Look. Look at them. They can hear something.'

That was, indeed, the way it looked. The perimeter guards at the top of the pit all had their ears up, and their heads back, as if they could hear some signal out of space, some terrible screech undetectable by their human prisoners.

The Monk showed his teeth, which were brown, where they were not green. 'Whatever it is,' observed the Monk intently, 'they're not liking it.'

At the bottom of the pit, the younger of the two guards dropped his Enforcer with a clang. He shoved up against the elder guard and started nuzzling him.

Dog Schwartz straightened up, rolling his shoulders. 'Get it,' he said aloud, meaning the gun, meaning Leglois, who was nearest. But Leglois was immobile as usual. Fear immobilized Niglon Leglois. Fear of everything.

The elder guard barked, sharp and deep. The younger guard grabbed up his weapon with fumbling paws. The elder guard lifted his head and shouted at the prisoners to resume work; but his speech was unclear, his will divided.

Prisoners on all worlds sense such things as others sense a change in the weather. On 000013, which hasn't got any weather, they sensed them even more readily. They did not resume work. Numb with labour and fatigue, they continued to stand and stare at the guards.

The elder guard kept shouting. The younger one had begun to bark now, urgently, piercingly. Any minute now the warning would come from on high, and then if work did not begin instantly, the shooting would.

Dog Schwartz lifted his hammer as if Monk was still holding the wedge in place; as if he was just about to strike it.

Skittering on the shiny rock, the perimeter guards came racing round the lip of the quarry. Why didn't they shoot? It was as if they had forgotten how to use their weapons. A stir went through the prisoners. The Eladeldi were harsh and zealous in their administration of the law, and in their obedience to Capella, whose law it was. Yet now they seemed as if they had completely lost touch with the law, and with Capella too.

Bulkily, Dog Schwartz was beginning to sidle towards the nearest ramp as the first guards hurtled from it. The guards ran by him, converging on the pit floor detail; but not to reinforce them. They were running to the old guard as if for protection, yammering at him in protest, begging him to stop the noise. The prisoners began to laugh and jeer.

Dog Schwartz stepped up on the ramp and addressed himself to a descending guard, one of the last.

The guard was on all fours. He shied from the big alien figure suddenly blocking his path.

Dog Schwartz went into a crouch. He held his rock hammer out to the side. 'Here, boy,' he said.

The guard snapped at him. He cowered, reaching clumsily for the ultrasonic whip at his belt.

3

Dog Schwartz lifted his hammer and smashed the Eladeldi's skull, together with his neck, left shoulder, and a good part of his back.

Suddenly the pit was full of roaring.

The big man took a moment to preen before spinning balletically in the low g and smashing another guard and another. 'What ho, Monk!' he bellowed in delight. 'Well, well, well!', while the smaller man pitched in with a half-dozen others, stabbing a pinioned figure with his wedge, rolling and skipping in the dirt. Even Leglois had come to life now, and was throwing rocks hectically.

It was no contest. Up above the furry blue officers were running in circles round the compound, whining and howling as if the whole known and trusted universe had upped and died on them. They put up no fight at all against the suddenly swarming inmates, but retreated through the main lock into their shuttle, where they skulked for days, still howling. Meanwhile Dog Schwartz and the Gunky Monkey and Niglon Leglois and all their friends and enemies ate and drank everything they could eat and drink and broke everything they couldn't.

It was only later that the biggest rock anyone had ever seen flew up out of nowhere, and the woman in the long black leather coat offered to take them all away.

PART ONE

The Heat of the Moment

1

This story is about Tabitha Jute, and how she went on a long journey.

My name is Alice, and I'm very interested in stories. Captain Jute used to tell me stories, when I was just a barge. Some of them were stories about her, and how she had come to be my Captain; and some were stories about her and me, about places we had been and jobs we had done together. There was quite a lot I didn't understand. You don't, when you're a barge.

Then Captain Jute, who had driven nothing but barges and tenders and scouters all her life, suddenly came into possession of a starship; and so, in a sense, did I.

Now of course a machine, however advanced and adapted, can't really imagine how it feels to be a person. But I spoke with Captain Jute a good deal at first, and this is how she described what it was like for her, taking over Plenty:

It was like waking up one day to discover you've inherited a gigantic palace. A palace with more rooms than you can possibly count. A room for everything you can think of. A flying room. A swimming room. A treasury where you actually can roll in money. A different bedroom for every night of the year, with one so secret only you can find it, so no one can ever come and tell you to get up, or hurry up, or tidy up. A banqueting hall with a continuous feast for all your favourite friends. A dungeon with continuous tortures for all your favourite enemies. Thousands, millions of rooms, rooms with stories of their own, rooms with people already living in them, some of them, with their own ideas about what's what. People with their own languages, their own needs, their own dreams. And other rooms with things in you can't identify, wild animals and strange machines, indefinable moods and obscure diseases. And the whole palace is flying through space.

That was my job. That was why Captain Jute had taken me out of the wreck of the barge and plugged me into the starship: because I knew how to fly it. At least, I could fly it. I didn't really know how to do it any more than you know how to walk, or gallop, or ooze, or whatever it is you do.

This story starts where the journey began, at Asteroid 000013, and it finishes with the end of the journey, the arrival, which was no kind of end at all, of course, only another beginning. Like most journeys it went much further and took much longer than it was supposed to, even on the soft clocks of subjective time. Neither was I supposed to be so isolated for so much of it – but if everything happened the way it was supposed to there wouldn't be any stories.

I'm afraid you may think Captain Jute doesn't come out of this one terribly well; though of course she didn't begin terribly well either. Goodness knows how many statutes and territories and proprietary rights she violated when she helped herself to that haunted vessel; how many lives she disrupted, how many businesses she ruined. Perhaps if she had paid more attention she might have made a better showing; or perhaps she was only ever clinging by her fingernails anyway, way out over the edge, as usual.

2

At the green dome it was chaos. People of all species were bustling in and out, whistling, shouting, arguing and gesticulating. They were dragging out the old cryonic freezers, the life support machines and environmats, and rolling in automatic trucks of flight control gear, drums of ducting and cable. Little kids were running around with their arms outstretched, making zapping noises at each other.

Smiling as she now found herself having to all the time, smiling at everybody, seeing nobody, Tabitha Jute waded through the usual gang of gawkers and starspotters and into the foyer. Her finger went automatically to tap her wristcom, before she remembered the sensitivity of the mikes here.

'How's it going, Alice?'

'UP AND DOWN AND ROUND AND ROUND,' said a disembodied voice.

It was not at all bad, the new vox. The techs had thought she was crazy when they realized she was asking them to reproduce the acoustics of a Bergen Kobold cockpit in a 200-metre dome. Captain Jute knew it would never be quite the same, but it was a warm voice, human, female, English, ageless, endlessly burdened, endlessly reliable. The Captain laughed. It was Alice all right.

She went past a pile of crates onto the floor of the chamber, acknowledging everybody's greetings. 'Brilliant,' she told them, meaning it now. 'This is all right, this is.'

She went to the helm and sat down in her big chair. She could not forbear to pat the persona unit at her side. 'Brilliant, Alice . . .' Her coffee had arrived, fresh and hot and strong. 'Oh, right, cheers.' Sipping it too eagerly, wincing, the Captain surveyed her bridge.

Over to the right were a pair of cargo drones lowering a bank of monitors from the gallery: brand new Patays, top res 500 mil, still shedding curls of packing foam. Over to the left they were installing stabilizer parallax mesoscopes – beautiful gear, a K's worth of it; gear she had carried a hundred crates of once, from Domino Valparaiso to the cargo bays of a glistening climax mall on Telos 10. Now it was hers.

Captain Jute ran her hand across the tab palettes of her console. They warmed at her touch, spreading patterns of light like coloured oils under smoked glass. She marvelled. 'Where's this stuff come from?'

'THIS IS PLENTY,' said Alice. 'EVERYTHING IS HERE.'

It was the slogan on the orbital's logo, familiar from flyers, ads and signal satellites: a sparkling pantomime swirl of fruit and coins and playing cards spilling from a stylized mound that was something like a tortoiseshell, though those who had actually worked in Plenty's mucky caves and corridors said it was a bin bag.

'Everything is here, somewhere,' said Mr Spinner, smiling over his eternal clipboard.

Mr Spinner had been first officer on a Shenandoah grain freighter.

His purser had chanced to be dragging him around the sin-pits of Plenty during a stopover, and he regarded it as very much his good fortune to have been on board when the station took its first, unexpected, unscheduled flight. Now Shenandoah was in crisis, like everybody else. Mr Spinner's freighter was probably being looted this very minute at Funnel Plat; but Mr Spinner was here, making himself useful. The lights of the bridge gleamed on his bald head. 'The voyage of a lifetime,' he told the AV interviewers. 'The first human voyage to another star.'

Where they should actually go had been the subject of some debate. There was no shortage of suggestions. Cruisers and scouters full of carpetbaggers and representatives had been at them as soon as Plenty materialized in the Belt. Messages were backed up at every com port: questions, demands, bribes, threats, inducements, offers of co-operation. The apocalypse was come, apparently. The Capellans had fallen; Eladeldi everywhere were running around biting their own tails; behind Jupiter the Seraphim were gathering their silent black ships. People in the Belt rather fancied Captain Jute's enormous escape vehicle.

The Captain lounged in her chair. She was drinking a tube of Trajan Special Reserve. She lifted the tube in the air. She was going to speak. Everyone shut up and looked at her.

'This stuff really is quite good,' she said.

Everyone besieged her, shouting. 'Okay!' she laughed. She flashed a humorous dark glance around the excited humans. 'Okay. Alice? What's her range?'

'A GREAT DEAL OF THIS IS STILL QUITE OBSCURE, I'M AFRAID,' the persona replied from the labyrinth of the alien programming. 'PERHAPS WE SHOULD GO TO TITAN BEFORE WE SET OFF.'

The master codes that had woken the Frasque drive had come from someone on Titan, the knowledgable told each other.

'THEY MIGHT BE HELPFUL,' supposed Alice.

More likely they'd want the ship back for their employers, Tabitha thought. Who were either Frasque, who ate people, or Seraphim, who redesigned them. Automatically the Captain looked at the patched wall of the control room, where the last Frasque had come bursting in; and then at Xtasca the Cherub, hovering nearby. Xtasca was a Seraphim creation. It was already translating Frasque charts. Its little red eyes gleamed faintly as it worked the console with its tail.

No, no one was crazy about Titan. Everyone was hungry for the stars. They had been stuck around Sol ever since they first ventured into space, thanks to the Capellans' policy of cultural preservation, or intensive farming, as it might more properly have been called. It was time to leave.

'One at a time now –'

'Von Maanen's Star,' said Karen Narlikar, an ex-trucker like Tabitha.

A tech in Neptune shell ear-rings was hopping up and down. 'No, no,' she said. 'BD+59.1915B. Really. It has this amazing corona.' She pushed through the crowd and thrust a crumpled stack of printout at the Captain.

The Captain took it, pretended to look at it. 'You want to know what I think?' she said. They did. 'Sirius. I saw a thing about it once. Warm worlds – what's that place with all the beaches? That's there, isn't it?'

'So are the Eladeldi,' grinned another tech.

Mr Spinner looked at his fingernails. 'Well, I should suggest Lalande 21185,' he said. 'If she's got the range.' He showed his teeth, stiffly. 'We can go to all these other places on the way back.'

An ironic and pleasurable shiver ran around the company. It was pure bravado, setting off in a weird thing like this, not knowing what it was capable of, not knowing how long you would be gone, or if you would ever return.

If you would survive.

'Let's not go mad,' said Xtasca then, at the console.

Captain Jute looked. The Cherub had accessed an image of a star. Its image was shrouded, as if shining through a thick fog of information in all kinds of inaccessible codes and frequencies.

'Proxima Centauri,' the Cherub said.

'It's logical,' conceded Mr Spinner. Most things about the Cherub were, if you could just work out how.

'Proxima,' said Captain Jute, starting to gloat again. Proxima fucking Centauri! At last. Leaving screaming Capellans and yelping Eladeldi and scheming Seraphim in her dusty wake.

And mum and dad, she said to herself. And everybody else. Everybody.

'No, let's not go mad,' said Captain Jute. 'Just let's go.'

She was so excited and proud she couldn't even feel how scared she was. A stardrive, a Frasque stardrive. How the hell did it work? How the hell did the Capellan drive work, that she had been using all her working life? Well, you had a persona to run it; and Alice was configured for both.

'Are we fit for Proxima, Alice?'

There was the briefest pause while the persona examined the capacity of Plenty.

'I CAN'T SEE WHY NOT, CAPTAIN.'

'PROXIMA CENTAURI,' said all the speakers, amid cheers.

'Is that where we're going?' asked a lanky young man.

'That's where we're going,' said Captain Jute. She flexed her fingers, looking idly at her nails, feeling the corners of her mouth drawing irresistibly upwards.

'Alice? Estimated journey time?'

'NOT YET ESTIMABLE.'

'Well, roughly. Extrapolate it.'

'WHAT VALUE FOR HUMAN PERCEPTION INDEX?'

'One,' said the Captain. 'Infinite. What do you mean, what value?'

'NO RANGE HAS BEEN ESTABLISHED IN INTERSTELLAR HYPERSPACE,' said Alice. 'NO PRECEDENT, CAPTAIN. I AM SORRY.'

Behind her voices were murmuring, 'Palernia, Palernia.'

'Palernia orbits Proxima, Captain,' said Mr Spinner.

'So it does, Mr Spinner,' said the Captain. 'Will somebody go and find some Palernians? A whole five, yes. And don't all stand behind me like that.'

They had found a big screen to put up for her. It was going on the far wall, bolted straight into the matrix. Ultimately it would be possible to run anything on there, live or processed, input from any monitor on the bridge, or anything Alice came up with. Externals they could get too, they believed, though it would be quite a job.

Every time the Captain looked at the wall she thought about the deep-frozen Frasque that had come jerking and shrilling out of it. In death, the ichor of their twiggy bodies had spattered the chamber like white pus, like semen. The floor was still sticky. The techs and console jockeys trampled over it happily, treading cigarette ash everywhere. It made her feel sick, though, when she thought about it.

The Palernians were delighted at her announcement. The five capered happily about, kissing one another and everybody else with great wetness. 'Haaoome!' they mooed.

It was time she took a look at the docks. Tabitha couldn't believe how many things there were to think about. She signed to Mr Spinner, who summoned a lift for her. 'Don't let anybody bother Alice,' the Captain told him, looking pointedly at the techs already drifting towards her vacant chair.

'IT'S QUITE ALL RIGHT, CAPTAIN,' said Alice, and she started to remind Captain Jute once again about the principles of parallel computation, and that everything on that little grey plaque inserted in the machine beside the chair had already been backed up with quintuple redundancy, and that in fact the capacity of the little grey plaque had already been far exceeded in generating the entity that was talking to her now.

'So I can take you with me,' said Captain Jute.

'IF YOU FEEL THE NEED,' said the persona politely.

Captain Jute ejected the persona and stuffed it in her bag, among all her other junk, sunglasses, socket spanner, spare knickers. If it hadn't been for that little grey plaque, Bergen serial 5N179476.900, persona name Alice, none of us would be here at all, she reflected, to justify her pointless act. If it hadn't been for 5N179476.900, and a batty old corpsicle called Hannah, Plenty would be still in Earth orbit; and we would be zombies in the gardens of Charon, with Capellan larvae feasting on our brains.

In the foyer she noticed a sign of the cryo company that had previously occupied this dome. '*Sleep of the Just,*' it read. '*Destiny suspended with dignity.*'

'That can go,' said Captain Jute.

At once people started climbing up to tear the signs down. 'Don't damage them!' cried a fat human with prominent teeth. 'Those will be valuable one day!'

On the lift was a Thrant, a beautiful male with gold eyes, limbs like a z-ball player. It acknowledged her with a twist of its feline head. There were quite a few on board, she'd noticed. She hoped they weren't going to be a problem. Thrant and Perks, she thought, bloody hell. Perhaps they'll eat each other. You couldn't worry about something like that.

Proxima fucking Centauri! she thought.

Saskia Zodiac, in a pair of blue silk pyjamas, sat on Tabitha's bed. Beside her was a tray of breakfast, looking remarkably ravaged. Saskia had a surprising appetite for one so very, very thin.

Saskia was practising some tricks. She did the Stocking Run Finesse, the Three Chip Drop, the Frog Baffle. The frog, a tiny orange one, sat on her palm and chirped briefly before disappearing. Saskia felt sad. For the rest of her life, whenever she performed the Frog Baffle she would miss her brother. They had always practised together, before a show. Each had been as good as a mirror to the other; to anyone else who saw them too, for they were, when dressed, identical.

The last of the Zodiac clone stretched then, luxuriating in the splendid bed. With a sigh, she produced the frog again, then wiggled the fingers of her free hand at the serving drone.

'You're not watching,' she told it.

The drone flickered twelve little jewel-like lights and tweeted inter-rogatively.

The Captain came home to collect her coat. It was a long black leather coat she had picked up somewhere, in some abandoned apart-ment or after some party. It wasn't new. In fact it was pretty shabby. The sleeves were a bit short, and the pockets were too small to put your hands in properly. But she liked it, and wore it everywhere. It flapped and swung in the artificial gravity as she and her conjuror lover raced down Morningstar Drive to the Midway Lifts. Saskia won easily.

Bearing the pair of them, the lift pod crawled slowly but steadily down through the giant central cleft that divided Plenty from stem to stern, from the Mercury Garden above to the roof of the cavern of docks below. People of all species were busy everywhere, toiling with their own hands or directing machines. Dead areas without air or power had already been sealed off with polyfilm generators or cement. In the road tunnels they were cutting back the vegetation, clearing away the worst of the damage done when the station suddenly left its orbital mooring.

The further the lift descended, the hotter it seemed to grow. The Captain pressed the acrobat against the wall of the pod, kissing her juicily. 'I ought to have a car,' she said.

Saskia flexed her neck complacently. 'You're the Captain,' she said. 'You ought to have a fleet of cars.'

'No, I ought to,' Tabitha said. 'What do you think I ought to have?'

The question seemed to irritate her companion. 'Oh god, I don't know,' she said, climbing negligently up the wall. 'Marco used to go on about cars,' she said. 'A big one,' she suggested, 'with lots of flashing lights.'

The Captain reached up and stroked her slender calf. It was funny to remember sometimes how young she really was. 'I'll ask Dorcas,' she said. She had once worked for Dorcas's sister, in a menial capacity. 'She's good at finding things.'

The lift had a working com. She called Dorcas on it. 'Listen, can you get me a car? A big one,' she said, looking at her companion, 'and a driver. Yes. Yes, someone else can do the work for a change.'

They arrived in the docks, that gloomy, confusing warren of machinery and parking berths that occupies the lowest tiers of the station, like the misshapen bottom of the tortoiseshell. In the passenger transit section people who believed they might yet have homes and a hope of reaching them continued to cram departing spacecraft. Captain Jute could barely understand. She hadn't had a permanent address since she was a girl. Her only home had been her barge, the *Alice Liddell*, and that had been disintegrated.

The crowds had thinned considerably, the Captain noted. She summoned one of the departure robots, a simple spaceline seat assignment model, built for ticketing warm bodies into ships. It rolled towards her, its antennae twirling as it went through the process of recognizing her.

'Your report,' said the Captain.

'Disembarkation 86.3% complete,' intoned the robot.

'Let's get them all out of here,' said the Captain, looking round the forlorn faces with their mismatched luggage and tattered souvenirs. 'Don't keep anyone hanging about here any longer than you have to.'

'Herself, she means,' said Saskia, not altogether inaccurately.

Saskia Zodiac too was in permanent exile. She was a refugee, a sole survivor, passing for human. She would never return to the experimental wing of Abraxas where the Seraphim had grown her and her doomed siblings. Since her escape, with Xtasca the Cherub and her last brother Mogul, she had been permanently on the road, or on the run, with Marco Metz's criminal cabaret. Saskia had no particular place to be, unless it was with Captain Jute.

Captain Jute looked through a window into a separate chamber. A hairy blue figure in a prison guard's uniform was prowling up and down, rubbing its shoulder along the walls.

'What's this?' she asked the robot. 'Who have you got there?'

'He came up with the last shipload from 000013,' said the robot. She touched the door open and went in.

The Eladeldi threw himself at the Captain's feet, whining pitifully. 'No,' she said, stepping back. 'No cops!'

The robot hummed, checking its categories.

They had put off all the cops on board, right after the clutch of surviving Frasque. Cyclops helmets flickering resentfully, the executives of suspended laws had been dropped onto the penal colony, while the less salubrious residents and the upcoming convicts jeered and pelted them with rocks and shoes.

Mr Spinner had not been happy about this exchange of personnel. 'Don't you think we've got enough criminals already?'

But the Captain had been in a giddy mood. Perhaps she was under the spell of her own early career as a juvenile delinquent. 'No!' she said gladly. 'You can never have enough criminals!'

Saskia had concurred. 'Criminals are so interesting. We used to be criminals,' she had told the expressionless first officer, 'Marco and Mogul and Xtasca and me.'

Tabitha had kissed her and fondled her long hard head. 'We're all criminals now,' she said.

They rode on down to the floor of the docks, into the din of clanking and squealing and thundering. Through the stern door, the view was of brown rock bleached by floodlight glare: the surface of Asteroid 000013, in the grip of the tractor beams of Plenty. Beyond, eclipsing the waiting stars, the watching ships went to and fro, more than ever of them now, waiting for the ugly great vessel to disappear.

'All ashore that's going ashore,' boomed the departure robots.

*   *   *

16

In a VIP suite secluded from the hubbub of the transit lounge, the last twilight executives, offworld tax shamans and black-listed data surgeons, prepared to abandon the shadowy orbital that had served them so well. Consultants were making tight-lipped, sweaty deals with each other for survival suits and armaments, while their assistants ran to and fro, securing them places on the last Caledonian Lightning.

In the corner, apart from the commotion, a male human tailored in smart but neutral grey stood watching everything through little rimless spectacles. Unlike the others he had no luggage, no equipment and no visible signs of panic; his assistant, if that's what she was, crouched beside him on a leash.

A skeletal woman clutched his arm. 'Henderson, you're not staying?' she said. Her eyes were huge, thyroid, lavishly rimmed with the black of stress.

The man called Henderson nodded, briefly.

'You're crazy,' she said. 'I always knew you were crazy.'

The man cocked his head, nonchalantly.

Somebody called, the woman shrieked and disappeared back into the throng, shouting orders.

The man watched, and stroked his companion.

A Vespan woman, an arms dealer, bulky as a rhinoceros, swayed up to him. 'Kersh,' she rumbled. 'You gone think this place gone factually fly?'

'It's done all right so far,' said the man called Henderson, and also Kersh.

She surveyed him, panting and rolling her humbug eyes. 'Kersh, you gone already gone!' she pronounced as she walloped away, slapping her bulbous brow and voiding air from several bladders at once in jovial disgust.

A yellow human man ran in front of the man in grey, his fist full of credit chips. When he saw who it was, he gave every sign of terror and froze in a guarded posture. 'Nick!' he said, in a voice that warned of violence. 'I can pay you the money! As soon as we get picked up, Nick, I promise!' As he spoke his hand was automatically trying to hide the chips, thrusting them into the pocket of his orange-lined sports jacket.

The man called Henderson, and Kersh, and now Nick, smiled and waved an indulgent hand at his interlocutor's self-betraying action. 'Keep it,' he said. 'Invest it for me.'

The yellow man's jaw dropped open. He was so startled he forgot to be menacing, or persuasive, or even in a panic. 'You're *going?*' he said. 'With that *woman?*'

The woman on the leash did not react. She knew the yellow man did not mean her.

The yellow man was so startled he started to laugh. He laughed derisively, showing jewelled teeth. 'Nick, you really are a crazy man!'

The man shrugged. He looked almost pleased with himself. The soft glow of the biofluorescents shone on his sober red tie, his clean white shirt. The Lightning driver, tired and morose, came on the com to say departure would be delayed. The arms dealer was stuck in the jetway.

With a tug like giant magnets in sudden repulsion, the asteroid was released. Imperceptibly at first, the alien ship began to ease into motion. Slowly the stars started to drift from the edges of the dock mouth to the middle.

It was twenty subjective minutes later that the klaxon started up. Simultaneously Tabitha's wristset began to peep: a call from the stern door.

'This is the Captain,' she said. 'What is it?'

'Freimacher Charisma, Captain,' replied the observer. 'Coming in fast.'

Captain Jute whistled up a hoverjeep, which sped them to the spot. She stood up, leaning on the windscreen, staring across the blackened landing apron through the filmy force curtain. You could see the incoming vessel now with the unaided eye, a black shape against the black. It was hurtling towards them, head on.

'What the –?'

'Identify,' bleated the security system. 'Identify!'

Captain Jute waved her hand. 'Let it in,' she commanded. The crowd gaped at her. She had a premonition, nameless yet. She could not have told you why she was obeying it.

At the very last instant on the edge of possibility, the stern door force curtain opened a slit, and the Charisma, a drab brown Belt ship with mining company insignia, came sliding through in a magnificent suicidal roll. As the pilot finally lost control it pancaked into the apron in an explosion of shattered undercarriage. Three fire drones raced up spraying foam while black smoke began to billow from the wreck and the cockpit blew.

Inside a lone figure stood up: a gaunt, shaven-headed woman wiping her hands, pulling the control leads from the sockets in her temples. Disdaining the rescue machines, she vaulted over the edge of the cockpit and walked towards the approaching jeep.

Tabitha leapt to the floor and ran to her, yelling, 'Dodger!'

'Wotcha, gel,' said the blackened newcomer, standing her ground, surveying the infernal vista of the alien space dock. 'I suppose you stand a good chance of getting on corporate rostering around here,' she said.

'Dodger! Dodger Gillespie!' There was no one in all the worlds she would rather see.

3

Corporate rostering. It was an old joke, from another life. Long years of contract driving, Vassily-Svensgaard packets and Shinjatzu Toiseach Double K's, from Phobos to Autonomy, St Morag to Lhasa. Soap and seaweed, cement and solarfoam, tonnes and kilotonnes. The battery dorms they called henhouses and the Eladeldi hiring halls, and long laughing nights in the pleasure quarter of San Pareil!

Dodger was smirking, her upper lip curled at one side. It was as much expression as you ever saw in her lantern features. She was rolling her habitual ciggy.

'You didn't think you could leave me behind, did you?'

'God, Dodger, it's good to see you.' Suddenly Tabitha was bursting with pride. She flung her arms wide, lifting her face to the black vaults, the floodlights, the blast shields and smoke-encrusted gantries of the docks. 'You like her?'

'Your friend in the pyjamas?' said the crashlanded pilot. Her sockets glinted red in her skull, reflecting the flame as she lit her fag. 'She's gone off somewhere.'

Captain Jute looked back at the jeep. It was empty. Saskia Zodiac had slipped away in the confusion. Perhaps she had had enough of things exploding recently.

'Not her,' said Captain Jute. 'Plenty. My ship!' She wanted to jump up and down. She was always a kid again, around Dodger.

A crowd had formed. 'Everybody,' the Captain announced, 'this is Dodger Gillespie, the best woman who ever spliced a vector!' She lifted Dodger's right hand and shook it, like a referee acclaiming a prize fighter. Tapers whirred. AV cameras were nosing towards the hissing wreck. People were trying to put blankets round Captain Gillespie and waving Geiger counters at her.

Tabitha whistled up the jeep and they climbed in.

'You'll have a chance to talk to her later,' she promised them, as the reporters broke into a run. 'She's not going anywhere!'

The lift drew them slowly up the Cleft towards the bridge. In the tunnel mouths of the passing levels Dodger could see lights and darkness; stalactites and supermarkets; children playing in the over-flow of a broken water main. Here, close at hand, was a team of explorers getting into harness, shouldering their tacklebags and coils of fluorescent orange rope. They raised their goggles and waved. The Captain waved back.

'It's a fucking starship?'

'It is,' said Captain Jute, in the voice of a gameshow host, 'a fucking starship!'

Dodger curled a nostril and blew smoke out of the corner of her mouth. She looked up out of the window at the gloom overhead. 'Why didn't they use it?'

'I don't know,' said Tabitha, dismissively. 'Who knows why the Frasque did anything?'

Her old friend looked at her. She was almost laughing. 'What are *you* doing with it?' she asked, entirely rudely.

'It's a long story.'

Marginally more seriously, Captain Gillespie asked: 'Do you know what you're doing?'

'Of course I don't,' said Tabitha. 'Alice knows,' she said, as a Christian would say, God will provide. She pressed her hand to the bag slung over her shoulder.

Inside the green dome everyone came to see the intrepid space pilot. She shook Mr Spinner's hand and winked at the girls leaning over the gallery.

Captain Jute started looking in her bag. 'Alice,' she said aloud, 'this is Dodger. My oldest friend.'

'WE'VE MET BEFORE, CAPTAIN GILLESPIE,' said the persona, 'ON UCOPIA PLAT, WHEN I WAS A BARGE. YOU CAME TO CAPTAIN JUTE'S SHIPWARMING PARTY.'

Dodger revealed her famous teeth. She pointed a thumb at the banks of equipment, the ranks of flickering control decks. 'You're running this on the persona from that old Kobold?'

Captain Jute finally unearthed the plaque and slotted it in its reader. 'Vastly adapted and improved, aren't you, Alice?' she said.

The function light came on. 'SO ARE WE ALL, I HOPE,' the ship observed, 'SINCE THOSE DAYS.'

Dodger Gillespie laughed and laughed. She didn't stop laughing until she started coughing. She took a grip on the Captain's upper arm as if needing support. 'Only you, Jute,' she coughed, swearing.

Tabitha took the helm. They were coming up to escape speed. On the big screen hung a fuzzy image of yellow Saturn, apparently dead ahead.

'What about it, Alice?' asked Dodger Gillespie. 'You fancy a quick spin to Proxima Centauri, do you?'

'I DOUBT IT WILL BE QUICK, CAPTAIN GILLESPIE,' said Alice. 'AT THE MOMENT WE ARE ASSUMING A SUBJECTIVE TRAVEL TIME OF FIFTEEN MONTHS, PERHAPS THIRTY. HYPERSPACE ON AN INTERSTELLAR PLANE INVOLVES TRANSITS AND ELISIONS OF TEMPORAL CONTINUITY UNLIKE ANYTHING YOUR SPECIES HAS ENCOUNTERED YET. SOME OF WHAT I AM BEGINNING TO CALL THE CONSECUTIVITY EQUATIONS OF THE FRASQUE ALREADY SEEM TO SUGGEST FASCINATING IMPLICATIONS – '

'Alice,' said Tabitha forcefully.

'YES, CAPTAIN?'

'Full speed ahead, Alice,' said Tabitha.

'YES, CAPTAIN,' said the starship.

Captain Gillespie gave a chuckle, leaning on the arm of the big blue chair. 'Christ, gel, take it easy.'

'She's fast, Dodger,' said the Captain. 'Aren't you, Alice? Charon to Venus in two hundred hours.'

'233 HOURS, 16 MINUTES, 51.24 SECONDS.'

Dodger's fag had gone out. She fished for her lighter. 'You've never had anything half this size . . .'

The Captain was watching the blurred face of Saturn sliding by, swirling like clotted gold. 'Venus to the Belt in a day,' she said.

'29 HOURS, 43 MINUTES –'

All around the makeshift bridge screens started snowing, readouts rolling. On the gallery a monitor slid from its cradle with a twang of snapping wire. A pair of mechs hurried along the catwalk towards it, crouching low, holding on with both hands.

'All I'm saying is, you want to get the feel of her before you push the limits.'

'I'm getting out of here!' said the Captain, locking eyes with her, and Dodger saw something in her gaze that was more than madcap; something from deep in Tabitha Jute's astronautical soul that said, *Before they come and take this away from me.*

Then the space about them inverted, as if they and all the personnel and equipment around them were to be forced through the neck of an infinitesimal funnel, and the air turned a deep electric blue. It fractured in rectangular planes like stacked blocks of insubstantial ice. A high-pitched squealing noise had been sounding forever, tirelessly, like the whistle of some celestial kettle. The sound drilled on and on, subdividing and multiplying until the eardrums and eyeballs of everyone aboard threatened to burst with it; until at the last moment it burst itself, into a thousand separate notes spiralling and wiggling away like a firework cascade of demented mesons, and the gates of infinity opened up and let the great ship lumber through.

The fanfares and cheering were so loud no one could hear Alice's official announcement. They had skipped. They had entered the cosmic overpass and would have no more sight of true space for a year, or maybe two! The windows of the Earth Room and the skylights of the Mercury Garden now showed only a pale dull stippled nothingness like frozen smoke; and things tasted different, somehow, though no one was ever able to describe exactly how.

Captain Jute sat back smiling a smug post-orgasmic sort of smile, oblivious to the hubbub all around. She touched a tab, trimmed a set of straying axis co-ordinates, bedded down the thrust. 'There we are, Alice,' she said. 'Steady as she goes, Mr Spinner.'

'Steady it is, ma'am.'

Dodger Gillespie watched her a little while, impressed. The kid

22

was a star. She seemed to have got a good desk crew too, people who'd happily spend all their waking time for the next year knitting up the infinite strings unravelled by the alien programming. She touched the cuff of her shirt to her cheek and found she was sweating.

'You need a drink,' she said.

'No,' said Tabitha. 'I need a lot of drinks. We're gone, yeeee-aaahh –! ' and with that she did jump up and start to yell, and every-body else started yelling again even louder, leaning on each other and holding cotton wool to their bleeding noses. People pressed presents on her, bottles and powders and precarious slices of cake.

The party was in full swing when Dodger Gillespie finally persuaded her to come away. She had to take her by the arm and pull her out of the crowd. Even then she wouldn't leave without her plaque.

'You know Rory's?' asked Dodger, on the way to the exit.

'Who's Rory?' said Tabitha.

'You'll see – if he's still in business.'

Dodger's tone made it plain she had no doubt at all he would be. The question was, could she remember the way? Things didn't always stay where you left them, on Plenty.

Perhaps that was why Tabitha had decided to carry the old plaque everywhere she went.

They passed across Eden Dale Dome, turning off before they reached the aqueduct. Beyond, in the remote regions aft, lay the great reservoirs, the assault courses and bleeping virtual infernos of the Caverns of Disorder. Captain Gillespie was astonished by the vegetation that had suddenly proliferated during the hive's maiden voyage. Sheets of grey flock like Spanish moss hung from the low roofs of the foot tunnels; slow tides of honeysuckle and red Martian weed rolled up the walls in all directions, searching for the delinquent sun.

In the empty shafts beyond West Asgard, shanties were accumulating, precarious platforms of corrugated plastic and sheet foam and aluminium siding. People climbed up and down ladders carrying wardrobes and rusty appliances. They were refugees, building a new life among the salvage; the dispossessed of Asteroid 000013 finding their own level. Nested high and low in the cellular walls like starlings in cliffs, they called out to each other and wagged their ragged black flags.

'Look at them,' said Dodger.

Tabitha did. 'They're all right,' she decided.

'It's ages since I was here,' Dodger said. She shifted on the seat of the lift pod. 'You really don't know the Trivia?'

'What trivia?'

'Rory's bar.'

'I never came here,' said Captain Jute shortly. 'I haven't really had time to look around yet.' She was getting annoyed with admitting it, over and over again, to interviewers and fans and busybodies. To Tabitha Jute, Plenty had always been somewhere to avoid, somewhere you would only get into trouble; and she had, sure as spitting.

The lift turned a corner and passed into a narrow shaft. The Captain saw her face reflected against the dark sliding by. 'I look like shit,' she said, rubbing dirt off the glass and giggling weakly. She did look a bit deranged. She had lost a couple of kilos and her hair was still patchy where the acid spit of enraged Capellans had burned it away. She picked at the bald spots.

'Where do you want to live?' she asked.

'At the Trivia,' said Captain Gillespie.

The Trivia was where it always had been, above the corner where Prosperity and Peacock met Green Lantern Road. 'That's how it got the name,' Rory always told people. 'Three roads. It's Latin. It doesn't mean insignificant at all, actually.'

Rory liked to boast that his establishment was the one original bar in the whole grubby, low-rent station that had stayed open through the hijack and all the subsequent turmoil. When the drive started up, not a glass was broken, so Rory and his regulars claimed. FASTER THAN LIGHT? someone had written up behind the bar. WE ALWAYS WERE.

Tabitha Jute and Dodger Gillespie came in from Peacock, up a twisting flight of narrow steps, under a lopsided arch and into a small whitewashed courtyard. Everything was curved. There was a central lamp standard festooned with auxiliary cables, and an old-fashioned pedal-operated drinking fountain. Across a tiny red-tiled patio rimmed with a tiny fence were doors of red wood and glass dark as molten toffee. Within, lights and shadows cavorted, and music played loudly.

Captain Jute was disoriented. She felt for a moment she must be on a planet, on Earth somewhere even, Greece or Morocco. She remembered the smell of grass and sand, spice and sewage, redolent in hot dry air.

She looked up. Carpets hung over the railings of a balcony. Behind the railings drab green plastic shutters shut in private rooms. Above, instead of blue sky, was an oval ceiling of raw grey matrix, pale as concrete.

'Captain!' cried Rory, from behind the bar. 'This is an honour!'

He was plump and perspiring, with a little thatch of wispy blond hair and eyes of baby blue. He had the cheeks of a drunkard and the forearms of an old sailor, and a big apron that wrapped around him twice.

His premises were much bigger than you'd have thought, coming in that way. In the alcoves of a bubble node chamber were gathered humans, aliens and artifacts, all in a state of delirious celebration, which redoubled when Captain Jute stepped in. Dodger Gillespie too, the latest sensation! Everybody had heard the story of her dramatic arrival. Other spacers jostled to shake their hands, vying to buy them one of the peculiar cocktails that were such a feature of the establishment, Gin Rummies or Quicklime Splits.

'What'll you have, Captain?'

'Beer.'

Rory scratched his pate. He had more beers than he could count. 'What kind?'

'Whatever's nearest.'

He passed her a foaming glass, waving away her credit. 'On the house! On the house!' he said. 'Don't insult me with your money, I won't have it. Have you seen the Window?' It was another famous attraction apparently. At the moment it showed a sunny Terran vista: the sparkling Seine, the slender, silver-dappled piers of the Pont des Arts. As sunny vistas went, it was a bit scratchy.

It was strange how quickly everything had changed. Already the era of Capellan rule seemed ancient history, universally deplored. Captain Jute found herself beset by a number of humans in cardigans and knitted ties, who seemed anxious to tell her how they themselves had been active in community organization at a local level, without reference to Capella or its minions, the Eladeldi. 'When any of the big blue mutts came sniffing around, we said Yes, Controller, No,

Controller, and after they'd gone we went back to doing things exactly the way we'd been doing them all along!' They sniggered excitedly and nudged one another. 'Fair's fair, Captain,' they said. 'We're a different species. It wasn't their place to tell us what to do.'

'One Law for the Ox and the Ass is Oppression!' a young man declaimed loudly. 'That's in the Holy Bible!'

It was some time before Tabitha understood they were making a representation to her to form something they called an Administrative Council, 'with you in the chair, Captain, naturally'. And when she asked what the purpose of this council would be, they told her they didn't want power, they were sick of people having power – they just wanted to 'make sure everything was running properly, and everybody does their fair share.'

'What do you think, Dodger?'

Dodger was leaning away from the conversation. She was tall and thin, and could lean a very long way away when she chose. 'Christ, gel, don't ask me.'

'Well, some very fundamental things need doing straight away,' said the young man who had tried to interest the Captain in the principles of livestock regulation. 'Dividing the Night from the Day, for one!'

Captain Jute, who had never thought much of that particular distinction, drank deep. 'If that's what people want,' she said. She could see faces in the crowd she would much rather be with; no one she knew, yet. 'I don't know, do we need a council for that, though?'

They started to explain to her about consultation and sustaining the community. They would talk and talk until she got tired. She knew they would end up doing what they wanted, whatever they called themselves, and whatever she said. Their sort always would strive to set the world to rights, any world.

Dodger Gillespie was chatting up a fat young woman, somebody's wife by the look of it, not that that was the sort of thing Dodger ever minded. In the Window a colourful flight of hot air balloons was going over, all of them coloured in panels of red and yellow and green and white, all of them twirling slowly.

Captain Jute kept trying not to yawn. At last she got up. 'If you want to do it,' she said, 'do it. Let me see a plan.' Already she was thinking of a way out of it, people who would look after it for her. Dorcas would know someone.

The embryonic Council pushed back their chairs, thanking her respectfully. They would involve some of the others, they said, nodding at the Alteceans, the Thrant bashing away at the ancient pinball machine, just to make sure everything was fair, and their first meeting would be tomorrow – which was to say –

'In fifteen hours' time,' said the biblical young man, clasping his watch like a life support device. 'Fifteen hours by my watch. My watch is right.'

'Let me know,' said Tabitha. Other people were on top of her now. Jesus, there was no end to it.

One was a woman in a glytex gel dress and a headset with power fins. Too late Captain Jute realized her companion had a camera and was pointing it at her. 'This is Geneva McCann for Channel 9,' said the first woman, 'and I'm here at the famous Trivia bar talking to Captain Jute. Captain, may we congratulate you on a successful skip.'

'Yeh,' said Tabitha, drinking concentratedly.

The woman wouldn't leave her alone. 'We know, most of us,' she said, 'what subsolar hyperspace is like. What can we expect to see in hyperspace out between the stars?'

The Captain turned in her seat, looking for the loo. She saw in one booth a huddle of Alteceans drinking what were apparently Trepan Trebles. 'Ask them,' she said. 'They've been there.'

Geneva McCann went on by. Her powerful hipwork in a crush had been a considerable asset to her career.

'Gentlemen, you are from the planet of, let me see if I can pronounce this, Altecea, have I got that right?' She dazzled them with her smile. 'Geneva McCann, Channel 9. We'd like to ask you, what can we expect to see in hyperspace?'

The Alteceans took their snouts out of their bowls and snuffled moistly into red-spotted handkerchiefs. 'Gnothing,' they huffed. 'Up top up down gnothing.' It was the same news from all the other extra-solarians, that hyperspace is the same infinite and insipid nothingness however far you go.

Tabitha Jute escaped into a bunch of spacers and started at last to have fun. At one point she was standing on the table, playing *We Shall Overcome* on a battered harmonica. In the Window, over the rooftops of Paris a flight of twirling windmills had succeeded the twirling balloons. Geneva McCann was talking to a Vespan, who said:

'Us, Capella done gone let move around. You, they leave put.' He slapped the bar with his flipper to illustrate his point and leaned towards her with his googly eyes. 'What Capella gone think of this trip?' he asked, lugubriously.

Geneva McCann spread her hand on her bosom, appalled at the thought. 'Oh my goodness . . .' she said, then flashed a smile and an automatic laugh.

From up on the table Captain Jute saw Saskia Zodiac arrive. She shouted to her, greeted her with a full clinch and a large and powerful kiss.

'I've got your car,' the acrobat shouted in the Captain's ear.

'Now we can go to the ball,' the Captain told her merry chums. She introduced Saskia to Dodger Gillespie, who eyed her. 'You're not having her,' she added.

'Listen to her,' said Dodger to Saskia. 'The Gal who stole the world.'

4

It continued very hot. The surplus vegetation burgeoned, blocking the stairwells and festooning the terraces. The Palernians grew itchy and bit one another. The Perks seemed to have gone to ground, vanishing down the crawl tunnels into regions uninhabited and unexplored.

In the inhabited quarters people clustered together, flowing to and fro as though in the grip of invisible currents. Most residential premises remained vacant, but in the chambers of commerce lights glowed constantly, comforting as campfires on a darkened prairie: the bars and the hologyms, the Chilli Chalet, We Serve Every Level.

Still, as the Administrative Council had foreseen, there were hours on the subjective clock when people slept, and more and more they were coinciding. Whole districts would fall asleep together, as if a soporific gas had been released or some stubborn circadian reflex triggered, a transspecial subsonic drone resonating through the hive, summoning each passenger to bed. Traffic would dwindle, coms fall silent. In the lull, amid scenery altogether chthonic and grotesque, it was easy to imagine one had somehow been transported into a corner of a medieval afterlife, the Inferno at three a.m.

Montgomery Cleft was deserted, its sepulchral archways given up to shadows. High up the port wall, limned by the merest trace from a biofluorescent tube on the landing, a small group was climbing the walkways, stepping over the tangles of snagtooth vine. There was a man and some sort of woman. He carried a small blue holdall. She carried a body.

They were going to an apartment he had picked. There was nothing particular about it, nothing at all characteristic. It was just a place to set things up, a place to put bits and pieces together.

'Next one up,' said the man.

The woman followed, snorting quietly beneath her load. Her big prehensile feet in their thick ply sandals crushed the tendrils of the vine.

In the bleak apartment the man stood with his hands in his pockets, looking around. Sparse, utilitarian furniture gave the place a temporary, provisional look; black square holes in the plaster disgorging stiff tassels of coloured wire – everything, even the blue holdall he set down on the floor: everything spoke of transition.

The man wore a neutral but immaculate grey needlecord suit and small rimless glasses. He had had many names, few of them for very long. His name at the moment was Grant. He was Grant No One, Grant Nothing.

There was a slot through the wall into another chamber which had a window, with a view of another wall of apartments across the ravine. They were all empty. No one was upstairs either, he had checked that in person, walking along the dim corridors and pushing doors open on abandoned possessions and accumulating dust.

'Yes,' he said. He made the monosyllable sound as though some question had been answered, some principle proved.

The woman watched him without blinking. A tick stirred in her pelt and one ear gave a twitch. Her name was Iogo. She was a Thrant. The body on her back was a dead cop.

'All right,' said the man. 'Put him down.'

The woman deposited the dead cop on the floor, on his back.

He was awkward, especially with so much metal in him, but she did not seem to find him heavy. She hunkered down on the floor between the cop and the mattress, her long arms stretched out in front of her, palms upwards. Her dress was plain, deep red, scoop-necked. Her posture pulled it tight around her muscular hips. The claws of all her twenty fingers had been trimmed short, and her tail docked.

The man noticed she was looking up at him with wide eyes, wary of his silence. A blue leather holdall stood on the floor between them, unopened. For the moment Grant Nothing had forgotten whether it was his or hers.

'Yes, well, now then,' he said.

Hitching the knees of his trousers he squatted down easily and unzipped the holdall. The material of his suit moved beautifully across his back and limbs.

Out of the holdall he took a slab of beige plastic like a tablet of wax. It had the bland, anonymous look of custom processing, and no identifying numbers.

From some hidden recess in the back of the tablet, Grant Nothing unreeled two leads. He slipped one into the com point on the wall. The other terminated in a smart plug, which he introduced delicately into a socket on the dead cop's breastplate, like a surgeon inserting a probe into a ventricle.

The tablet peeped.

The woman made a small snuffling sigh.

While the tablet was mapping the cop ROM Grant Nothing opened the mouth of the bag wider and lifted out with both hands a white viscose shirt on a hanger. Holding it by the hook he went through the slot in the wall into the second room.

He crossed to the window and looked down in the amber light, down the cleft to the road at the bottom. Grant Nothing had always been fond of this district because it looked like everywhere else, generic urban orbital, grubby, brutally impersonal. Everything was rockfoam and plastic, and the air stank of cheap petrol.

He returned, passing the woman where she crouched with her sleek head and mute upturned muzzle. 'We need,' he announced, 'to look at some things.'

He hung the shirt from a picture hook someone had put up, and slipped the edge of one sleeve between his index and middle fingers.

The shirt was identical to the one he was wearing, with his grey needlecord suit and raspberry-coloured silk tie.

The tablet peeped again.

'There are some things,' said Grant Nothing as he made a preliminary selection of possible access codes, 'that we need to take a look at.' He lined up his command and entered it, hooking a tricky little Celestina infinite retry on its tail.

If you had asked him how things had changed on board the station since they had kissed the Earth goodbye, Grant Nothing would have given a dry, deprecating laugh.

It was all gone. All the merchandise that used to pass through his pale, smooth hands when Plenty was in orbit, the preferential odds and personal profiles nestling in corners and folds of the Tangle data net which people would pay so highly to have extracted or destroyed: gone. Gone when the Frasque drive had shivered into action and severed all his contacts at a snap.

One person was responsible.

Grant Nothing and his companion could have disembarked at 000013, could have secured a place on any ship; but he had decided to stay put. The situation, however unpleasant, was unique. It was a challenge.

The possibilities, of course, were tremendous.

The tablet peeped. Access. He was in.

Iogo moved away suddenly from the mattress and took up the same posture against the wall, down on one knee with the other pressed in the valley between her breasts, her long arms lying on the floor. She seemed to be tensing herself, as if her identity were somehow in jeopardy here; as if the very blankness of walls and floor threatened to pull her apart.

She gave another sigh and wrapped her arms around her head.

'What?' asked her companion sharply.

Iogo put her head out from between her arms. 'Smell,' she said. Her voice was guttural, small in the apartment, as if it came unwillingly from her.

Grant Nothing looked directly at her then for the first time. 'You'll soon change that,' he told her pointedly.

A noise from the street below drew him back into the other room. There was one of the horrible little taxis hurtling along the empty roadway, headlights violating the darkness. He could hear its passengers, drunks, braying with laughter. One of them had a trombone, and was attempting to play it.

What was the price, wondered the man called Nothing, of their jollity? On what security was it based? What knowledge would ensure it, what other knowledge turn their boisterousness to fear and make them scurry into the shadows?

Iogo the Thrant followed him on all fours. She sat on the floor, nuzzling her shoulder. Her gooseberry-coloured eyes watched her master steadily. She was disliking being close to a corpse. She grumbled, in a soft, preoccupied way, in her nose.

On the com, Grant Nothing had connected with the emergency system of a defunct security firm still slumbering in the net. Now he mimicked its hierarchy codes, its cybernetic heraldry, and generated himself a temporary suite.

The ablute was not working. The man fetched his woman a bowl of water from the tap.

'Dead men make good guardians,' he said.

Iogo did not want this guardian. She wanted to be alone with her man. Though the walls here were smooth and hard and nothing grew, she would stay inside the walls, and stay forever rather than go out there again alone.

'Take the mattress into the other room,' said Grant Nothing. He was supplying his suite with a station security inspector, who had an imperative request under Eladeldi authority to view the extinct cyborg's wanted file.

When the names arrived he blocked major vehicular offences, then triggered the virus. The block he copied to an address where he kept an industry standard multibase search program. The security firm defences saw the data go and slammed down the shields around the temporary suite. Trapped neatly inside them, the bogus inspector continued talking to the cop, propped up behind the desk, so to speak; but it was a shell now only, starting to repeat itself, and Grant Nothing was gone.

'Sixteen point two seconds,' he said.

Iogo understood nothing but the pleasure in his voice. She was glad he was happy. She could overlook the corpse, if it made him happy. While she was with him, and he was happy, she could forget there was no sun. When he looked down at her, he seemed to fill her eyes. When his face was turned away, she knew he was still looking at her inside.

The beige tablet opened up the wanted file and asked which case Grant Nothing would like to view, alphabetically by suspect.

JUTE, he typed. TABITHA.

At this hour, as at every hour, the lights were bright and the music cheerful in the Eden Dale Chilli Chalet. The counter staff were working hard, following the Fifteen Steps to Perfect Service as assiduously as Brahmin monks their mantras. Visible behind them, the kitchen crew stirred the boilers, checking the timers and adding the regulated quantities of dried oregano and basil with almost super-mechanical accuracy. A supervisor authorized a green light for the convoy of trucks that was just arriving, hauling their loads of fresh mince up the gradient of Platinum Canyon.

Passengers and crew, everybody ate at the Chilli Chalet. No matter which level you went to, a Chalet awaited you, just the same as on Earth and on Luna and in the sky. The same ads were dancing luminously on the tabletops, even the ones for supplies and services no longer available on board. Tekunak Charge Catering Division would maintain the ads in all their restaurants, they promised, because the customers liked them. Those seductively spinning spectres of scuba gear and cut glass clocks reminded people of home. They liked the jingles, and sang along.

'Pardon me, ma'am. Geneva McCann, Channel 9. Where are you from?'

'From Earth, originally.'

'How do you like the journey so far?'

'Oh, it's so much better now there aren't so many people here. We've got a much bigger place now.'

'What about your husband, sir, are you enjoying yourself?'

'I'm all day on the golf range in the Crystal Cave,' he told her, chewing mightily. 'It's like a flying holiday camp, this, isn't it?'

Whoever she spoke to, Geneva heard few complaints. 'It's the ultimate cruise!'

'What about the surroundings? Do you feel at home here?'

'The Frasque were allright. Nobody would admit that before, but it was true. The Frasque were doing better by us than Capella.

It was the competition, that's what the bigheads couldn't take.'

'Oh Walter you shut up about your old Frasque now.'

'Were you able to speak the language, Walter?' joked Geneva.

The couple had a teenager with them, who was slumped over his food in the most slovenly way. He laughed, held up his fork like a trident and started to whistle squeakily through his teeth.

'Norval!' His mother flapped her napkin at him, while Beth got the close-up. 'Norval!'

'Don't you think you'll ever regret your decision to come along?' Geneva pressed them.

'I don't fancy anyone's chances much, not without the Capellans. It'll be all wars at home now, you know, like it was before.'

The servers smiled, their teeth pristine. A shaggy Altecean in a paper coat mopped ponderously around the unoccupied tables. Robot gnats zipped about, sucking up crumbs and splashes, spiking every shred of onion.

The passengers had no qualms about sacrificing a year or two of their lives; indeed they had the highest expectations of the rest of their journey. 'It'll be great,' said a man in a djellabah. 'A wonderful education for the children.'

'He likes that Havoc Cavern, don't you, Norval, where they have all the games? Flying around shooting each other and I don't know what.'

Norval started grinning at Geneva in a way that didn't look very suitable for a family show, so she signalled to Beth and strode across to another table, where a big man in a purple and yellow shirt with a black beard and ponytail was attacking a mound of chilli.

'Excuse me, sir, Geneva McCann, Channel 9, and how are you enjoying the trip so far?'

'S'all right,' said the man, attending to his appetite.

This was not promising. And his companion, who had been completely hidden behind his bulk as she approached, was frankly disgusting. He looked as if he'd been deep fried himself, in sump oil.

'Do you believe the Tekunak promise that there will be no shortage of food?' she said pointedly to the man in the colourful shirt, and moved nicely aside, away from his friend, so Beth could get in for a good shot of their overflowing plates.

The big man looked up at her then, twitching his nose as his great jaws rolled. 'This is Plenty,' he said, in a high, mild voice. 'I'm surprised you haven't heard, really. You can get anything you want.'

The door whizzed open and a gaggle of people with toilet seats around their necks burst in. 'Party!' they shouted. 'Party in the Earth Room!'

The staff stared, not quite knowing if they should laugh or not. Managers appeared, watching, as the partygoers burst out again, almost overturning Father Le Coq in the doorway, pelting each other with stolen sachets of Z-Cal sweetener.

'We ought to go to that party,' the big man said, conversationally. His filthy companion smirked. 'They wouldn't let us in.'

'They won't let you in,' asserted the big man, shrugging his shoulders. 'I'm surprised they let you in here.'

The little man smiled as if he thought he had been complimented. His friend spread his elbows, forking in glistening meat. 'Me, I'm an old friend of the Captain's.'

Beth scoped some background. The Chilli Chalet company colour scheme featured a palette of warm oranges and reds, with the furnishing accent on easy-clean tile, natural wood and velour. A blonde human in a gingham skirt was refilling the sweetener dispenser, while the cleaner steamed in the heat. A party of customers rose, saying, 'Well, I thoroughly enjoyed that.'

Outside, Father Le Coq accosted them. He hoped to command their attention with a handful of cards, brightly coloured in felt-tip and bearing pictures cut out of magazines: faces of models; consumer luxuries; phases of the Moon. These were his maps, his talismans. 'My brethren, my sistren, as we creep behind the curtains of the cosmos you better watch and pray. We are in the Outer Darkness and every little sin, every little error could carry you away into another dimension!'

The preacher wore a long mauve jacket, tight black trousers with fraying bottoms, an ancient embroidered waistcoat with many greasy stains and cigarette burns. The top of his head was bald, but his side-whiskers were long and bushy. His urgent eyes were magnified by round spectacle lenses in a gold wire frame. They seemed to bulge out at you, swarming all over you with moist outrage.

'The Di-men-sion of Dam-na-tion!' intoned the preacher, horribly. He whipped out another rectangle of cardboard and held it in his captives' faces, feet wide apart, swaying slowly and mesmerically from side to side. 'Lift yourself up I say and put yourself in the hands of Brother Jesus.'

Le Coq was the preacher of Maison Zouagou, the Tabernacle of Dreams. His hands were heavy with many bulky rings of gilt and silver and plastic. As he shuffled his cards, dramatically, like a fortune-teller, you could see he was a lost soul himself in those overarching streets. For all his talk of the cosmos, he had no idea of his own whereabouts.

His captives were not listening. They were pointing off across Eden Dale Dome, watching a small shiny black figure flying past a distant row of buttresses. 'Look at that, ma! A Cherub!' The Cherubim were the experimental offspring of the Seraphim: humans redesigned for space. They had heard there was one aboard, seen it on AV. Still they had never expected to spot it themselves. 'Everything's here somewhere . . .'

The homegoing diners got into their taxis and were whisked away. The preacher flung his righteous imprecations after them, echoing down the tunnels of the mall.

'Pray to Capella to redeem your sorry ass!'

In the unfinished apartment two figures sat breathing gently in the orange dark. On the floor beneath the window a cube of soft white light sat squarely on the beige tablet, scintillating with turquoise letters.

By now the imaginary inspector was eaten out with virus. Fragments of it were flapping loose about the net, bouncing around, tying up any nosing investigation response routines in rapidly shrinking rags of garbage. Meanwhile in the room the angular blue-green sequences of captive data wriggled and bred.

Iogo watched them. She wanted to know what the man was doing, but she did not want to ask. If he did not want to answer, he would not be happy she had asked. If she made him unhappy, he would make her unhappy.

She looked at the display and then at him. She sighed through her nostrils and wiped her cheek on her shoulder. She saw him look at her and assess her doleful curiosity. She saw him judge her as he sat there, deciding what to give her in reply.

'Come here,' he said.

36

She went to him and ducked her head for him to fondle behind her ears. 'We're pulling Tabitha's tab,' he said.

Grant Nothing felt pleased with himself. He had done a good day's work. The former truck driver and people's heroine had indeed been responsible, as rumour had it, for that recent bout of mayhem in the docks, when a ship had left with cops shooting after it, and caused hundreds of thousands' worth of damage.

Better yet, that was not the only item against Captain Jute's name. On the dead cop's list she was also wanted for corporate security infringement, aggravated assault, abduction and kidnapping, driving without due care and attention, maintenance defaults, licence violations and resisting arrest. She had made the locals cross enough to pull her file from her Jurisdiction of Issue, which turned out to be Mars, Schiaparelli. They had her down for a sizeable unpaid fine for affray, breach of the peace and degrading interspecies harmony.

All interesting material. All useful stuff, when you were getting to know somebody.

While the data sorted itself neatly away in memory, Grant Nothing held out his hand to his companion, who licked it with her small dry tongue.

'It's quite a past she's got, Iogo,' he told her. 'What kind of future, I wonder.'

Iogo knew who Tabitha was. She knew her man was a hunter, with a thousand invisible weapons, and the human woman, Captain Tabitha Jute, was his quarry. His destined prey.

Iogo had never seen the Captain in the flesh. She knew her from the AV screen, her smiling teeth and pack queen stance of hands on hips, long coat thrown back. Sometimes in low tunnels she thought she could feel the woman's spirit like a great black bird flying soundlessly overhead, the spread of its wide wings invisible in the darkness.

She heard the majestic murmur of her man's pride. It called to her, loudly, commanding her to witness. It needed her to see him read the Captain woman's track in the flickering blue letters; to watch while he laid out the cords of his vast invisible catching net.

Iogo laid her head on his knee. The room was hot. The smell of the dead cop was becoming more complex, more insistent. The myriad processes of his putrefaction were forming another sort of display, another claim on her attention. To the part of her that lingered on the veldt of a small brown world somewhere in the recesses of

Cassiopeia, that smell said, Make a wide detour. It warned that the stharauq would be along soon, squabbling with the gobblers and the flies over the remains of whatever it was. It broadcast an olfactory symphony of poison and predators. It spoke of sadness, and howling in the night.

But this was not the veldt. There was no grass, no bruised green sky, no stands of brumin trees or waterpits. There was pallid grey plaster and concrete over thick caked alien ejecta. The scents on the piped winds were hot and rotten, chemical, menacing. Iogo would stay where she was, and remember what to ignore, and when to keep still.

In the outer room, watching the shapes the dirty amber glow of the Cleft threw on the empty walls, Grant Nothing couldn't remember whether he had slept yet tonight or not. Beneath him the unnumbered streets spiralled like the galleries of some subterranean labyrinth. It was as hot, certainly, as living in a fissure of a volcano. It was as hot as living on the lip of Hell.

'Iogo. In here.'

Grant Nothing was not a gambler. Gambling involved a deliberate abdication of control, and was therefore entirely unattractive. He dealt only in known quantities, specified sums. He saw no reason ever to play a game you did not know you were going to win.

Any suggestion that the entire journey was a gamble, with incalculable risks for an obscure prize, would have struck him as irrelevant. His interest was in the usurper of his orbital, not in any hypothetical landfall. There was much to prove, much to gain. Today's crop, carefully husbanded, would germinate.

In the multiplying shadows now two nervous systems were attempting to annex one another, two paired souls striving as if to occupy a single body. Grant Nothing gripped handfuls of Iogo's coat and slid between her legs. Those gigantic pampas thighs that could have crushed his spine parted for him once again. He clawed his fingernails together across the sensitive hollow of her throat, making her grunt deeply and thrust her pelvis at him. The reek of her filled the empty apartment, large and fierce and wild.

5

People had begun to venture in organized groups to the abandoned malls. They would meet at the top of Wingwater Canyon to go through their jungle drill with their guide. 'Stick close to me now, ladies and gentlemen.' His voice was loud, his weapons impressive. 'Please remember, there's no need, I repeat, no need to stockpile. There is plenty for all.' The chainstore prospectors would smile tensely at the witticism and turn on their strimmers. Into the overgrown corridors they would force their way, to return later lugging nets full of towelling dressing gowns and bottles of wine.

Penetrating a new chamber on one of these expeditions, they encountered another party trapped among the greenery. They were almost all women, in worn coats and battered hats. The guide, a former Belt mining foreman, scrutinized them through his visor. Was somebody trying to poach on his claim? 'Where are you from?' he demanded suspiciously.

The one who seemed to be the leader stepped forward. Her tights were tattered and her good shoes were ruined. Still she gripped her handbag and faced undaunted this huge, scarred, unshaven individual. 'Surrey,' she said firmly.

'Little Foxbourne,' said another of them, more faintly. She blinked at the staring scavengers. 'Does anybody know it?'

They were tourists, members of a Women's Institute, who'd come up on a saver-day Orbital Break and lost their way in the tunnels. Some of them had husbands or children with them. Apart from heatstroke and fatigue they were all well, though confused. They were nonplussed to hear the station was now deep in hyperspace, on its way to another star. 'Well, I don't know,' said one, in a tone of affront. She seemed to think the inconvenience of it was deliberate, a gigantic practical joke. She glared at the trees as though she expected an AV compère in a ruffled shirt to spring out of them, crying 'Gotcha!'

A five of Palernians adopted them, putting them all to bed in one big room. They danced sympathetic dances for them; served them tea and presented them with large bouquets of flowers, perhaps an unfortunate gesture under the circumstances.

Channel 2 loved the whole thing. Marge Goodself told the viewers: 'We're jolly glad we came.' She looked good on camera, heroic and brave. 'We're certainly getting our money's worth!' she said.

Afterwards she grimaced as she put her bouquet out of sight. 'We could have done without these,' she said to Laura Overhead, in the next bed. 'I for one have seen enough flowers to last me quite a while.'

'They're doing their best,' said Laura, in a hushing voice. Laura never liked anybody to be upset, ever, for any reason.

Natalie Shoe crumpled another paper tissue. 'Where are we going?' she asked peevishly, for the twentieth time. 'Where are they taking us?'

Her husband Norman patted her hand vaguely. 'Have another lemonade, love,' he said.

'We're going to Proxima Centauri,' said their little daughter Morgan. 'They come from there.' She pointed at their woolly hosts, wobbling about with their trays of liquorice and acorn cake.

As she began at last to understand they would not be home for the Michaelmas Fayre, Natalie's eyes filled with tears.

'What's your planet like, then?' Laura Overhead was asking the Palernians. 'Is it nice?'

Palernia! That succulent orange world, with its rich bom fields and rubicund orchards, its sumptuous vales and echoing dells that open one into another forever and ever, all along the soft massifs of Walkaway and Curdcombry where the three suns glow on the tottering heads of pudding pikes and the laden boughs of porphyria trees! Palernia – home of tasty turtlebat and foxfin parrot, McWelkin's Tumbling Sheep and toffee marmoset, field fish and bloatberry – why had they ever left it? Capella had said come and they had come, hundreds of them, bouncing and gibbering and comforting one another with their spittle, all across the nasty grey waste to a system with only one stinging sun and loud, sharp, hateful planets where everything was made of metal and filled with fire. They wept and hooted and rubbed their faces in distress. They put their paws in their mouths and thought of their long exile in the concrete corridors of Mntce and they wailed for the old folks they had left behind on that artificial moon. Then they remembered. They were going home! Home! 'Haaooome!' They were going to see again the bom glades and the marmosets whose bones snapped in your mouth like sugar, and the sex ponds of Hapchopple with their glutinous slides and personal wattle nibblers! Everything would be well and all their new friends would be happy and they would break the spaceship into little pieces and never leave home ever again!

In Plenty's orbital days, the Earth Room had been the first place first-time visitors made for, before they found the casinos and sex bars and pistol ranges. Some, the less demanding, stayed to sit and watch the blue globe of Terra. Through the panoramic windows they tracked the white swirls of storms far below, following the broadcasts of weather stations on their headsets. They liked to spot individual shapes, buildings and boats, among the orbital Tangle, identifying them by their silhouettes.

In the first weeks out, the Earth Room had been the Party's favourite place. They loved the way the doughy grey void 'outside' would suddenly flash purple, or go all crazed and moiré across the bow. Sometimes one could almost smell it: a remote, actinic discharge of energy, a mighty event somewhere out in Actuality. It smelled like lightning. The Party would scream and cheer. 'Fireworks!' Whatever was happening, wherever it was, they were all glad to be out of it.

Gradually, the fractious hypermedium had settled to a cold grey soup of indeterminacy. The last evidence of objective reality had been a series of faint, broken lines floating vaguely about on the starboard beam, like creases in fine gauze or flaws in a mirror. Some of them seemed to forget, and drift into the ballroom through the glass. When the bridge announced these were traces of Neptune and its moons, gradually receding in real space, everyone had tried to take pictures of them. Then the Girandole boys had discovered Peacock Park and sent to say it was much more fun, and everyone had gone there instead. Only a few boring people had insisted on remaining to mourn, and watch the imaginary lines dissolve completely – 'for if there's no one to see them, they won't be there, you know.'

Today in the Earth Room, as for a long time now, there was nothing to see. The view was featureless and bare as an undrawn chart. Dodger Gillespie sat alone on the red plush banquette. She sat with her legs apart and her jacket beside her. In her head she was watching a movie. Lauren Bacall was asking Walter Brennan, 'Was you ever bit by a dead bee?' Walter Brennan was clutching his ears, looking at Lauren Bacall in alarm. Captain Gillespie scratched the back of her neck. She was wearing wrangler boots, canvas trousers and a muscle shirt. She was hot and bored.

Magnified by the hollow tunnel, the ghostly purr of an engine came to her ears.

Captain Gillespie paused the movie and jacked out. She listened. Moment by moment, the sound was growing louder.

She watched the distant portals of the deserted ballroom. In a moment, she saw something enter between them.

It was a little red car.

Captain Gillespie leaned forward on her elbows.

Coming towards her at speed across the floor was a station service buggy that had been appropriated, customized, and resprayed a fire-engine scarlet. Its new owner had graced it with twin whip aerials and enormous mudguards too wide for the territory, all battered now and dented. At the wheel was a brown young man in a bulky pair of datashades and a black diagonal zip-front shirt.

Captain Gillespie stood up. She picked up her jacket and slung it over her shoulder.

With an abbreviated screech, the little red car stopped, right at Captain Gillespie's feet. The driver was already on his feet, pushing up his shades and sticking out his hand.

'Ronald,' he said.

That wasn't her so she supposed it must be him. 'Gillespie,' she said. His hand was hot.

'Check,' said Ronald. He sounded almost injured, as though she had done wrong to identify herself. 'You're famous,' he added. She saw his eyes pass over her tits and fix covetously on her sockets.

Dodger threw her jacket in the back of the buggy and climbed in after.

'You be integral back there?' he said, turning on the tapedeck. 'You like music?' A noise started, like a garbage compactor making a meal of a cement mixer. 'Moloch Metal,' grinned her driver, flipping down his datashades.

She bared her teeth at him in the mirror. 'That's fine,' she said, though no one, however amped, could possibly have heard her. She took out her makings and started to roll a fag.

* * *

42

The little red car went down Meadowbrook, which was actually a dull brown road tunnel with a scummy-looking canal along it. The walls were sprayed with arcane symbols and cryptic slogans. ZONE DAG ESCAPE, they proclaimed. KJ STACK HERE.

Captain Gillespie leaned over the back of the driving seat and pitched her voice above the shearing metal. 'What is it you're all doing?'

He turned his head to answer. 'Listening to the walls,' he said.

'What can you hear?'

'Vibrations,' he bellowed. He seemed to have to lift his shades to speak. 'Like, there's . . . charged states . . . analogue . . . resonate . . . harmonically.' He grinned happily. 'Integral,' his lips said.

'I see,' she said, though it was hardly true. 'And the Cherub's in charge, is it? Can you turn that down?'

'It's her project,' said Ronald, obliging her. At the same time he had to ask her about her sockets. 'You get movies on them?'

'No,' she said. 'Only brass band music. Go on.'

'The Cherub can read the extra code the Seraphim gave Alice,' Ronald explained. 'We match it to the vibrations in the walls.'

For some reason it was slightly offensive, the familiar way he said 'Alice'.

'Check,' he went on, picking up speed on the empty road. 'The thing is to match the places where it's happening with whatever the persona is doing. Map 'em and callibrate 'em. It's integral! It's actually a whole new science.'

Overhead, the roof closed in. A dusty bundle of cable ran along it, branching at the junctions. Ronald said, 'So how long you known the Chief, anyway?'

How long? Dodger Gillespie remembered Silverside Plat, a hiring hall, a little pale brown girl with a cord of Mandebra colours round the shoulder of her uniform. A new fledgling just waiting for a wise old bird to take her under her wing.

'Since before you were born, Ronald,' she said. 'We used to fly Mitchums out of Vortigern for Shigenaga Patay.'

'Oh, right,' said Ronald. In a moment he said, 'Check: I didn't mean the Captain. I meant the Cherub. Xtasca.'

Captain Gillespie looked out at the scenery. 'I've seen it,' she said.

'So you just coming to check, check?'

'Maybe,' she said. It was dead as Luna down here. They were

deep below the occupied caverns now, negotiating potholes. The springs of the buggy were groaning a song of protest. It sounded like something that might have been on Ronald's tape. 'You call it her,' Dodger remarked.

'Yeah, well, sorry, shit,' said Ronald, comprehensively. 'She's my boss, check? You can't work for somebody and keep calling them it!'

Captain Gillespie felt unenlightened. 'I've had employers you could,' she said. Cherubs were machines, whatever they called themselves. Anything that could swim in hard vacuum was a machine, to her way of thinking.

Where they finally stopped, it was as hot as an oven. Stunted scrub poked out of cracks. Somewhere, water was trickling. Ronald had brought helmets for them both. Captain Gillespie tried her lamp. She saw flaky matrix, a mass of low foliage, tangled and pale. She saw crushed beer tubes, and small yellow blobs in clusters. Perk shit. She saw Ronald standing waiting with a duffel bag on his shoulder. His teeth shone in her lamp beam, but his eyes were still covered.

'You okay, Captain?' he said.

She had seen a sign a couple of kilometres back, above the broken barrier, a relic of orbital days. YOU ARE NOW ENTERING AN UNRECLAIMED AREA, the sign had proclaimed, with terse disclaimers of responsibility for loss, injury or death.

Captain Gillespie grunted. She dropped her dog-end and trod it out.

The boy called Ronald led her to a large hole in the floor. It was like a split in old wood. 'Check, I go first,' he said.

Captain Gillespie motioned him on, not speaking. While he was making the descent she looked around, taking deep breaths. She hoped there would be enough air down there. She had never been keen on the insides of places.

Ronald and Captain Gillespie lowered themselves a short way on staples that had been driven into the wall, then walked in single file, through tunnels where they had to bend almost double to walk at all. The back of Dodger's thighs started to ache. Her foot struck a loose fragment of matrix and she stumbled.

Ronald turned his head, blinding her with his lamp. 'You okay there?' he called. 'This is something, check?'

44

Dodger was too winded to answer. She had thought she'd been into some obscure corners of this overgrown wasps' nest. Now she knew she'd barely begun. The air smelled gritty and dead. She coughed and spat between her feet.

Then there was a noise ahead, a regular, mechanical noise. Could it be the sound of a truck or a car, filtering through from some civilized cavern? No, it was here. It was the soft putting of a slide flask generator, feeding power to a work site. Captain Gillespie rounded a bend and saw the end of the tunnel, and beyond, a haze of white luminance.

It was a large, lofty chamber, a confusing, irregular hollow of curved shadows and light, as if a mass of bubbles had burst in the liquid matrix and left a space of intricate concavity. Scaffolding had been erected against one wall, clamped to its horny ridges, and young men and women, Vespans and humans in brightly coloured clothes, were working on it by the light of industrial floods. There was a robot hoist holding a cradle to the wall, where a large patch of the surface had been cut away.

Ronald put his hand on Captain Gillespie's shoulder. 'Welcome to the Mine!'

The chug of the generator made it hard to be sure she was hearing properly. 'The Mind?' she said.

He nodded. 'Check.'

Dodger was perfectly bewildered.

She switched her lamp off and followed Ronald to the scaffold. There was a chorus of lazy, good-natured greetings. 'Ronald, get your bum back up here.' Nobody greeted Captain Gillespie, which was fine by her. They looked at her sidelong, pretending not to. She looked up at the cradle.

In the cradle was a shiny black metallic creature. It had a big head and tiny hands. In its hands was something that looked like a rack of five parallel soldering irons.

'Hey, boss,' said Ronald.

The creature put its head over the edge of the cradle and looked down. It regarded him, and then her, with tiny circular eyes that lit up red.

'Hello, Ronald. Hello, Captain Gillespie,' it said, politely but quite audibly.

Dodger laughed.

It was the weirdest thing that had ever spoken to her. It looked like a giant bean-shaped black foil balloon with the head of an outsize human foetus and the face of a doll. It had chubby little baby arms and dimpled little baby hands. Captain Gillespie could see where the two of them, herself and Ronald, were reflected on its forehead.

'Hi,' she said.

'I shall be ready to speak to you in twenty-eight seconds,' said the Cherub. It spoke with the voice of a precocious child, insolent, precise. Its eyes dimmed slightly as it returned its attention to its instrument.

Dodger felt sweaty and dull, and dismissed.

'Sure,' she said.

Dodger Gillespie climbed on the scaffolding with the workers. Beneath the horny surface of the wall they had exposed a dark and glistening slab. It was deep red, and resinous.

'Looks like Turkish Delight,' said Captain Gillespie.

'Silicon analogue,' said a young human woman with her arms caked in white dust to the elbow. She had white hair and thick brown eyebrows. She smelt of sweat and chalk. She was wearing a full-length apron, brown leather leggings and a nose stud, nothing else. Dodger gave her an appreciative look.

The stuff inside the wall was warm and dense, and slightly undulant. Overhead, a pair of Vespans were sinking probes in it.

'A quasi-crystalline medium, Captain Gillespie,' said the Cherub. 'Inbuilt. Highly active, here. Calico, what do you make of this?'

While the boy called Calico was looking at the site of Xtasca's interest, Captain Gillespie climbed up to the cradle.

The Cherub had no legs, she saw. It had red eyes and a tail.

She asked it: 'Can I talk to you now?'

The Cherub raised its sweet shiny face to her and lifted its little arms.

Captain Gillespie reached down and picked it up. It was heavy, and warm, and resilient. It felt like a large baby re-upholstered in aluminium foil. As she straightened her back, she discovered it was still plugged in, by the tail.

Down below them, on the floor of the cave, something stirred. Dodger looked, and saw a dull steel dish a metre across, like an

46

outsize flat eggcup. The surface of it was glowing with patterns of light. They were switching, flicking. The dish rose vertically off the floor, spun briefly, and flew up to the cradle.

Xtasca unplugged its tail, extended it, and cast it like an angler casting a fly. The plug on the end of the tail homed directly into a socket in the well of the dish; then it reeled the Cherub across, backwards out of Captain Gillespie's arms, into its eggcup seat.

The flying saucer rocked in the air like a toy boat on a wave.

'Pleasure,' said Dodger.

They went into a shallow alcove where a man was sitting over a stack of wave analysis gear. 'Who are they all?' Dodger asked.

'Conductivicists,' said the Cherub. 'Crystallurgists. Musicians. This is Larry.'

Larry was playing a wrist-mounted board with a headset. 'Larry used to be a recording engineer,' the Cherub said. Larry reached across the table to shake Dodger's hand.

'Honour to meetcha, mam,' said Larry. His voice was deep and lazy.

'Who's the blonde?' asked Captain Gillespie.

'That's Jone,' said Larry.

Hearing her name the dusty woman in the apron looked down from her elevation. She met Dodger's eye, but didn't wave or smile or speak.

'What can we do for you, Captain?' the Cherub asked, politely.

'That's my line,' said Dodger. 'Captain Jute sent me to help you.'

The Cherub looked at her. Its eyes glowed dimly. Then it said, 'No. You help the Captain. She will need you.' And with that it turned and flew away back to the wall, to help the Vespans resite a probe.

'Strewth,' said Dodger. 'What about a cup of tea as long as I'm here?'

Watch by watch the bridge crew wandered about, arguing with each other in desultory voices. They congregated now at this station, now at that, recording the progress of the alien vessel. Young men and women in polyester shirts or washed-out tees with software brands palely emblazoned on the chest would bring her instructions scribbled on the backs of pizza menus, which they called 'procedure updates'.

Captain Jute was still having difficulty remembering anyone's name. They all seemed to decorate their desks with toys and trinkets, coloured stickers with cheery jokes on. Service drones rolled ceaselessly up and down the aisles, collecting litter and dispensing food. The air was stale and smelt of cigarettes.

The business of navigating Alice's short-circuit of the space-time continuum was essentially pretty abstract. What they had to do was model the spatial probability of the ship's target region, a thousand kilometre sphere around Proxima. The mesoscopes generated conjectural four-axial co-ordinates and flashed back hypothetical recovery margins, ten thousand times a second. Only when all of them reached identity could the ship expect to emerge from the void of its own absence.

Up in the gallery, younger devotees collected data from the astroscopes to feed to the mesoscopes. Actually they spent most of their time watching the crew, discussing their performance, chucking cigarettes about, trying to get people below to notice them. Captain Jute found them, if anything, more depressing than their seniors on the floor.

Tabitha Jute sat back in her big blue chair of tensile foam and tubular steel, with one leg up over the arm. She was wearing her black leather coat and slate blue jeans, motorcycle boots and an exclusive dark blue designer shirt with a lace-up front. Her hair had grown in white where the acid had been. She had had the patches made into a pattern with fine silver wire woven into her curls.

On her console, the Captain was watching a movie. There was a dark room, with a teenage girl sitting in a rocking chair. Behind the girl, in an arched doorway, there seemed to be an out-of-focus figure standing, looking in. On the soundtrack synthetic strings were going crazy.

'CAPTAIN,' said an aerial voice. 'THE PROFESSOR IS HERE.'

'You asked to see me, Captain.'

Captain Jute inspected the dapper figure in the three-piece suit who stood before her leaning on a shooting stick.

'Professor Xavier,' she said.

'David,' he said, lavishly.

She considered. 'No,' she said. 'Professor. It suits you.'

'As you wish,' said the Professor expectantly.

48

'You know about the Frasque.'

He shrugged elaborately. 'No more than anyone,' he said.

Captain Jute put her knuckles to her chin. 'Where did they come from?'

That pressed the Professor's Play button.

'The origins of the strange species known as the Frasque are still shrouded in mystery. Scientists believe they were natives of an old star.'

She imagined it, a big bloated red giant, skirted with a planetary system of ash and coal.

'Certainly, this might explain the general desiccation and attenuation of their extraordinary bodies.'

Captain Jute had been looking at the movie. 'The scientists?'

'The Frasque,' he said, not missing a beat. 'It's probable that they came into the solar system as refugees, dogging the Capellans like camp followers after scraps.' The Professor patted his permanently windswept hair. 'Some suspect they may have been previous victims of Capella, their vital substance eaten out aeons ago.'

'And all their technology?'

'Stolen, undoubtedly. Looted from eviscerated civilizations.'

The Captain nodded, tapping her chin on her thumbs. 'Alice? What do you think about this?'

'THE HISTORY IS CONJECTURE,' said Alice, 'AS PROFESSOR XAVIER WOULD BE THE FIRST TO ADMIT. YOU KNOW THE HOME STAR IS IN THE SHIP's MEMORY, CAPTAIN, ACCORDING TO XTASCA's TRANSLATION.'

'Have you identified it?'

'NOT CONCLUSIVELY. THERE ARE MANY STARS IT MIGHT BE, IF IT IS ONE WE KNOW. WOULD YOU LIKE TO REVIEW THE FIVE MOST PROBABLE?'

'Later.' The Captain was remembering the Frasque that had got on the *Alice Liddell*, the walking tree that had invaded her boat and crushed Saskia's brother. She completely regretted whatever impulse it had been that had made her send for Xavier.

'Do you know where I earned my white card, Professor?' she asked, her eyes straying back to her movie. 'On a Saturn convoy. A Frasque convoy.'

'Yes, Captain,' said Xavier, keen to assure her he knew this elementary fact. 'It was on Channel 3.'

'They had human ships, human crews,' said Captain Jute. 'They could make themselves understood, when it suited them. Melissa Mandebra could speak their language. She always was a bit of a swot, apparently.'

'It's a pity we couldn't have kept those few you unearthed,' said Professor Xavier then, lifting the end of his shooting stick and pointing it at the patched breach in the wall. 'There easily could be one or two, still, you know, hiding in the bowels of this vessel. With your permission, Captain, an official expedition –'

'You know what's wrong with these films?' said the Captain. 'They all know there's a maniac with a chainsaw somewhere in the building, and the lights don't work, and they haven't got any weapons, and what do they say? "Let's split up."'

Was that a flicker of contempt on Xavier's well-bred features?

'Well, Captain,' he said mildly, 'many of us would be very pleased if you'd bear it in mind. With the right camera crew, we could really open people's eyes to the truth about this amazing vessel that we're all travelling in. Even you could learn a thing or two, I wouldn't wonder!'

'Secrets with which humankind was never meant to meddle,' she said, watching her screen. If he went and found any more Frasque, she promised herself, she'd joint and roast him for them.

The Professor had barely left when Dodger Gillespie returned. 'Xtasca says she'll check in later,' she announced, throwing herself into a vacant chair.

Tabitha Jute raised her eyebrows. '"She"?' she repeated.

'Well . . .'

Tabitha studied her old friend. 'I thought you were going to give them a hand,' she said.

Captain Gillespie hung her hands loosely over her knees. 'She's not hiring,' she said.

Tabitha grimaced. She hit a key. The movie disappeared. Her monitor now showed the same graphic as the big wall screen, a rainbow-coloured graph overflowing with deviations. She thought it looked like a grid of white bread with purple and yellow jam dripping off it. INTEGRATION INDEX, said the legends. TORQUE SUB-LIMATION FACTOR. For an instant the big screen was over-whelmed by a spiralling maelstrom of fractals; then the original graph returned in four identical versions, each in one quarter of the screen. At the helm, the Captain's monitor continued to reproduce everything faithfully.

'Yeah . . .' said the Captain. She had just caught sight of Mr Spinner, coming back on duty. She glanced at the persona unit. 'Alice?' she said.

'YES, CAPTAIN?'

'Are you okay for the moment?'

'PERFECTLY, THANK YOU, CAPTAIN.'

'Mr Spinner? I'll leave you to it, shall I?'

She was already ringing for the car.

On their way out of the control room they passed someone, a console jockey, reading a faded blue paperback. It had been read many times before, obviously; its pages were soft, its spine collapsed. On the cover was a painting of a sleek silver fashion mannequin sitting in an unlikely position at the controls of an antiseptic-looking scoutship. She was thrusting out her extraordinary bosom, crooking her little finger over the keypad. Her make-up was immaculate.

Captain Jute nodded at it. 'Read that one, have you, Dodger?' she asked ironically. The reader, woken from her trance, blinked at Captain Jute uncertainly. 'I bet it's good,' said the Captain to her, showing her teeth.

'You forgot your plaque,' said Dodger Gillespie.

'Yeah, I know,' said Tabitha. She glanced back unwillingly at the helm. 'She'll be all right,' she said.

A pair of Thrant were coming into the foyer. The female, Captain Gillespie knew, was Tabitha's chauffeuse, Soi. Soi had a peaked cap and a blue-grey tunic that matched Tabitha's jeans, and a pair of jodhpurs slit to accommodate her tail.

The male Captain Gillespie had not seen before. He was wearing a charcoal grey jerkin so unassuming it had to be armoured, blue tights and soft leather boots. His condition was superb. Physically, he and Soi were very similar, with heads like russet panthers and powerful limbs.

'Is he your bodyguard?' asked Dodger Gillespie.

'You can be my bodyguard,' said Captain Jute. She had perked up now she had been released. 'Where are we going?'

*   *   *

51

So they went to the Yoshiwara, where the Party was now in its seventh subjective month, having forsaken Peacock Park for this quarter of brothels, where it had become the fashion to drink white wine and anoint your mucus membranes and lie on caressers with great piles of people and allow complete strangers to interfere with you in the most intimate ways possible, and many that turned out not to be, while music throbbed and sparkled and the fountains turned every colour in the spectrum and Topaz, completely naked, fell into one and climbed out laughing and fell into another one, and people were smearing each other with whipped cream substitute and body oil laced with thril, though Captain Jute restrained herself and kept quite a lot of her clothes on and was really very well behaved, while from time to time Captain Gillespie thought of the Cherub's instruction, and wondered if this counted as helping, because Tabitha Jute was definitely happy, everyone was happy, except the Yoshiwara madams, who sat in their boudoirs and consoled each other. All this pleasure was not good for business.

6

Though Plenty was underpopulated by comparison with its orbital days, still Saskia Zodiac found the passengers intolerable. Gallivanting pleasure-seekers, chortling Palernians, the incurably stupid who thought her fame gave them the right to handle her and ask personal questions in public – people, people, so many people; and never the one she longed for.

The physical absence of Mogul Zodiac was a wound still in Saskia's heart, an air leak in the fragile envelope of her identity. In their last hours together they had quarrelled, delirious and exhausted in the mutant mangroves of Venus. How bitter that memory was; how unassuaged by the sight of his beloved body sinking to rest at last in the greasy and omnivorous swamp.

Hannah Soo had remembered Mogul, sort of, but Hannah was gone, interred on the same planet from a greater height. Xtasca certainly remembered Mogul, from before his cloning, probably; but Xtasca had no interest in the past, only in the gigantic alien conundrum into the very veins of which it tunnelled, rapt as the crawling infant it somewhat resembled.

Mogul Zodiac's lone mourner had distracted herself awhile with Tabitha Jute. She had adored her, clung to her, fixed herself tremulously on her while she learned the hard fact that the universe would, perversely, continue, with other people in it. She loved Tabitha still, usually, when she saw her. Tabitha was so busy these days, with so many other people constantly after her attention.

Saskia felt now she understood the Seraphim experiment that had given life to her and Mogul, Goreal, Zidrich and Suzan. How useful it would be if every applicant could be provided with a Tabitha Jute of their own to listen to their suit.

The artificial acrobat wandered through the abandoned casinos of Sugar Grove, between the shrouded islands of the baccarat tables. She trailed her shapely feet through drifts of colourful debris, broken glass and spent chips – like mosaic pieces from a palace wall.

In the dusty arcades she passed along the lines of silent fruit machines. Here and there she would touch their circuits with a spark wand, waking for a moment some interrupted routine. 'Bonus life . . .' whispered the machines, in the voices of enticing young Thai women. 'Credit boost . . .' Saskia would perch on their consoles, listening carefully. She knew these primitive engines of probability sculpture must be her cousins, and were giving her coded messages she would one day understand.

She came one day to a white pavilion of plastiboard and porcelite. Dead pink tubing over the door spelt out the name of J.M. Souviens. There were no windows. Saskia cracked the lock and found a plinth half a metre high and a metre square with soft seats around it. The roof was full of machinery: AV equipment, it looked like, and a thousand projectors.

She sat in one of the seats. There was a hiccoughing sound and a tall green flame two metres tall suddenly started dancing on the plinth. Saskia jumped up in surprise.

'J.M. Souviens gives you the keys to golden years and treasured memories,' murmured a warm voice from nowhere in particular.

Saskia sat down with one hip on the edge of the deck and looked up at the flame. It was a hologram. It bobbed and jiggled invitingly.

'You're a modelling shop,' she said.

'Come open up the past's great lock and for a while turn back the clock,' said the voice.

'I haven't got a clock,' she said.

'Step back in time and walk again that sunny path down Memory Lane –'

'Without the rhyme, can you do it?'

The kiosk skipped ahead in its routine. 'The more information you deposit, the better the detail you can get,' it told her. 'Our range of options starts with tableau packages at ground zero rates and builds –'

'I haven't really got much information, though,' said Saskia. 'There was the Garden, where I lived with my brothers and my sister and the funny little animals and the little black fairies – only really they were Cherubim, of course. Xtasca might have something from then, but if she has, she's never said.

'And then there was Contraband and Marco Metz and oh, Schiaparelli and Callisto and San Pareil, all those places. They all looked the same to me: the inside of a van, the inside of a venue, the inside of a cheap hotel. Nobody took pictures. The only person who might have had –'

She stopped suddenly, an entire thought sequence occurring instantly in her head.

'I know what I want to see,' said Saskia Zodiac.

The J.M. Souviens chain of modelling shops were the sort of place people went to watch their weddings, their holiday skiing on Olympus, their grandchildren taking a balloon dip into Jupiter. 'J.M. Souviens offers a flexible menu of viewer controls,' said the green flame. 'See how a zoom brings you in real close!' It was a Nero Corban Ariel Six, a helpful but generic sort of persona with all the emphasis on the imaging end.

Saskia brought discs and tapes. 'In fact there's quite a lot of material,' she told the flame while the machine digested them. 'I suppose it was early on in the journey, when people were still very excited. And Tabitha was there,' she reflected. 'The cameras would all come out, everywhere she went.'

Saskia adjusted her veil, the folds of her long black dress. 'When you're ready,' she said.

*   *   *

The miniature scene that appeared on the holodeck showed a glass torpedo with a dead old woman inside. The old woman was wrapped in a bag of quilted satin. There was an ornate voicebox under her chin, and frost in her nostrils. Her lips, made up a severe plum red, were slightly open; her blind eyes stared upwards, immobile. The glass torpedo lay poised on a cargo dispatch ramp, nose down. Below the old woman's head a glass hatch was a square of star-flecked black. Into it, while Saskia watched, swam a green pea magnified to the size of a football.

'That's quite good,' said Saskia, standing up. 'Have we got anything to eat?' She looked around the pavilion as if she expected an usherette to emerge from some unseen room, carrying a tray of popcorn.

The old woman's name was Hannah Soo. Hannah had been their manager, in the days of Marco Metz and Contraband. She had been dead for as long as Saskia had known her. She had been kept here on ice by Sleep of the Just; microwaved for meetings.

Hannah's last days, working alongside Alice in the tangles of the alien programming, had finally exhausted her failing brain. On the soundtrack the acrobat could hear the signal of her personality lapsing into random noise. 'Big on Ganymede . . . Tell Banjo no animal acts. The contract never arrived, you see, you see . . .' Now Hannah Soo was to be buried in space, at her request, high above the poison planet.

She had been more than ready, Saskia remembered, gazing at the dead woman fondly. She had become very attached to Hannah in the last days of her suspension. Hannah had been like a mother to them, Saskia supposed, to her and Mogul and Xtasca and Marco and Tal. Saskia had come to respect Hannah Soo the way she imagined Captain Jute respected Alice.

The arc-lights gleamed on the glass torpedo as the viewpoint slid up and back.

Saskia saw herself among the mourners. The tears on her cheeks glistened tenderly; the dark circles around her eyes had been softened to violet, by the standard enhancement programs of J.M. Souviens. This was Hannah's second funeral, but only Saskia's first. She remembered, she had been thinking at that moment what a very sad thing it was, and wishing Mogul could have had one, and all the others who had died.

Captain Jute was holding a bottle of champagne tied to a ribbon. 'I'm not going to let you go,' Saskia heard her tell the corpse. 'You still owe me money.'

It was a joke. Everybody laughed with embarrassment, and laughed again louder when Hannah's voicebox replied dreamily: 'There isn't any money, sweetheart. JustSleep took every last penny.'

There was organ music playing, a sombre toccata and fugue. It was Xtasca, hovering high over the scene. The Cherub was wearing an enormous hat.

'What?' Saskia jumped out of her seat. 'That's not right.' Quite upset, she reached into the cube of doctored light and tried to brush the intrusion away.

The funeral grew pale and transparent and the green flame reappeared in the midst of it. It bobbed deferentially to Saskia, as if uncertain what error had been made. 'J.M. Souviens apologizes for any distress caused by omissions or inaccuracies . . .' it whispered.

'I don't know where you got that hat from,' she said sharply.

'The more memory you use, the more reliable the picture,' the pavilion advised her hopefully.

Saskia searched the net. She brought more information. The dusty air above the holodeck filled with awkward figures, curious faces, flowers. Saskia sat eating ginger biscuits while the Cherub played Bach, followed by some Chinese jazz. Once again a miniature Tabitha Jute said she ought to go and get her mouth organ, and was dissuaded. Once again she smashed her bottle on the nose of the torpedo. Alcoholic foam flew and compressed air hissed and everybody called goodbye as Hannah Soo's glass coffin went whizzing down the ramp.

Sliding through a teflon chute into the void, Hannah called out: 'Alice? Alice, I think I'm falling . . .'

'Follow her,' Saskia said. She sat forward, watching for the minute white star of incandescence that finally blinked when Hannah's coffin fell into the atmosphere of Venus.

This time, something had changed. Perhaps it had been there all along; or perhaps one of the new tapes contained something crucial, that had made the difference.

There was a ship there. You could scarcely see it, but it was a ship.

'Freeze,' Saskia said. A distant alarm had begun to sound, in the back of her brain.

She tossed back her veil. 'Let me see the ship.'

It looked less like a ship than a flaw in space, a bubble in the void. It was hanging back, silent, anonymous. Even magnified until its slender outline filled the field, it showed no features. Its skin was perfect mirror black, like Xtasca.

The alarm in the back of Saskia Zodiac's brain started to deafen her.

'Are you sure that was there?'

'J.M. Souviens apologizes for any distress caused by omissions or inaccuracies . . .'

'Never mind, of course it was.' Saskia sat back, her pulse racing. 'Save and quit,' she said.

She sat staring at nothing, eating ginger biscuits until she had finished the packet. Then she pulled up her sleeve and called the Captain.

She let it ring and ring. There was no answer.

She tried the bridge. A young man in a headset mended with Sellotape answered. He appeared to be picking his nose. 'Well,' he said, gazing around, 'she's not here at the moment –'

'Can you reach her for me?'

'Just a moment.' He tapped some keys. 'Nope,' he said. He didn't seem perturbed.

'You can't reach the Captain?' expostulated the acrobat. 'Suppose we hit something.'

The crewman blinked. 'Well, that's not actually possible,' he said, in a tone that was almost particular enough to be patronizing. 'You see, we're not occupying any actual space, not any actual continuous dimensional space anyway, so unless we materialize suddenly the co-efficients of all the vectors can't ever actually –'

Saskia made a noise in her throat and switched him off.

Little letters appeared on her wristcom screen. 'Try Trivia,' they spelled.

Saskia rang the bar. Rory was busy. A woman with a Wisp hovering beside her said: 'They went home. Hours ago.'

Suddenly the Wisp flew straight at the camera. It hung there squinting at her, opening and closing its sticky little hands. Its owner laughed, gaspingly, and reached to reclaim it. 'Do give her our love,' she said, petting its flat bald head.

The conjuror hung up convulsively. She hated those squirmy little toys, the way they played with their owners' hair and muttered in their ears. They seemed to her like horrible caricatures of Xtasca, cut-price imitations knocked out cheap by some orbital factory.

At the apartment there were people all over the place, as usual. She recognized Karen Narlikar and Zoe Primrose, and Topaz, who called out: 'She's on her beach.'

Kyfyd the Thrant, who liked to be called Kenny, tried to bar her way. 'Someone een theer,' he told her, putting his head on one side, showing her the tip of one incisor.

She flapped at him impatiently and went in.

All along the Captain's beach, tall palm trees held their shaggy heads up to a brilliant blue sky. In the distance, to what might have been the east, there was a promontory with interesting purple rocks and a tiny lighthouse; to what should have been the west, the beach curved gently away to infinity. The rest was wonderful, scintillating, lazily breaking ocean.

Tabitha Jute had grown her hair. It was cut in a perfect sphere, ten centimetres out from her head. She had nothing on. Nor did her partner.

He was a darker brown than she, his skull shaved to the merest frizz, a small gold ring in the lobe of his visible ear. His back was magnificent, his buttocks smooth and heavy.

Hearing the door, the Captain looked round. Then she patted her companion's waist. 'Time you were gone, Don,' she said.

Don lifted his head, looking across her body at the newcomer. He gave her a small slow wave. Starting to rise, absent-mindedly brushing his thighs as if he thought the sand might actually cling to him, he gave Captain Jute a slow kiss. 'Will I see you later?' he asked.

'If I want you,' she said, 'I know where to find you.'

He stroked her face. 'Bye, Don,' said the Captain.

He stood. 'It's not Don,' he said. 'It's Dan.'

She rolled onto her front and laid her cheek on the virtual strand. 'Whoever,' she said pleasantly.

The sand felt almost real. She couldn't remember when she had last lain in real sand, and heard real waves breaking softly, so close.

The man was gone. Saskia approached in her long black dress. The breeze lifted the edge of her veil.

'What are you wearing that thing for?' said the Captain. 'Take it off. Alice,' she said.

'YES, CAPTAIN.'

'Turn the sun up.'

The environmat grew instantly hotter.

'You've got Alice in here now?' queried Saskia.

'It's easier,' said Captain Jute. She reached up and took her lover by the wrist. She pulled her down and kissed her pointedly.

Saskia looked her in the eye. She looked at the floor. There were no footprints where she had trod. 'Sand,' she said, unenthusiastically.

'It's not real sand,' said Captain Jute.

Saskia Zodiac worked her long toes into it. 'It itches,' she said. 'Why don't you do a bed?'

Tabitha grimaced. She grasped Saskia's ankle.

Saskia had had enough of illusions for one day. 'Let's go in the bedroom,' she said, 'like real people do.'

'I don't want to,' said the Captain, rolling onto her back. 'I don't want to go out there,' she sighed.

'Do a bed, then,' said the acrobat. 'Alice? Do us a bed.'

Alice was much more exclusive these days, rarely speaking to anyone but the Captain. 'CAPTAIN JUTE DOESN'T REQUIRE A BED,' she said.

'But I do.'

'I DO APOLOGISE, MS ZODIAC,' said the persona. 'KEEPING THE CAPTAIN HAPPY IS A STANDING ORDER.'

'Takes precedence over all other protocols,' murmured Tabitha.

'I want a bed,' said the acrobat.

'Oh, go on, do it then,' moaned Captain Jute. 'Stop bothering me. Only reason I come in here,' she went on, as Saskia unlocked the setting and delicately tapped the adjustments, 'is to get away from people bothering me.'

Beneath her, the sand fused. It coalesced. It all turned cushiony, like a big lax butterscotch-coloured inflatable.

'Hey, this is nice,' said Tabitha. She stroked it with her hand. The floor had grown a nap like a fine alpaca blanket.

Saskia came dancing across to her, bouncing on point like a

ballerina. She lowered herself gracefully and turned her back, arms raised above her head.

Captain Jute unzipped the mourning dress. Saskia Zodiac's shoulder blades were curves of ivory. The Captain's hand looked almost black against them.

Tabitha's tongue lapped like a wave. Saskia cried out. She clawed like a Thrant. She cried out in undiscovered languages of despair. She had lost something neither Captain Jute nor anyone else would ever be able to give her back.

Afterwards they lay in the shallows, feeling the imaginary sea sluicing their loosened thighs. Alice made some ships and they watched them go by. There were wonderful schooners with hundreds of snow-white sails; gleaming black ocean liners tall as skyscrapers; Spanish galleons flying the skull and crossbones.

'I always wanted to be a pirate,' said Captain Jute. She had sent for daiquiris, and was getting drunk and melancholy. 'On Integrity 2 with the Rejects: I really used to enjoy the way people looked at us. They were actually afraid of us. Because we wore nasty lurid colours and sharp haircuts they were convinced we were going to rob and maim them.'

She lolled her head back on her shoulders, lifting her bare breasts to the motionless sun. 'We were the Terror of the Walkways,' she said dreamily.

'I know,' said Saskia. 'You told me.'

She was searching for tissues. 'You don't take that bag everywhere any more,' she observed.

'Well, I don't bring it in here,' said Captain Jute immediately. But her companion was right. She couldn't, at that instant, recall when she'd last had her bag, or where she'd put it down. It gave her a funny feeling, as if she'd actually lost something important, which of course she hadn't. She didn't need to carry things around any more. Anywhere she went, people would give her what she needed. 'Drone,' she said. 'Tissues. And some more ice.'

Watching the service drone wallowing doggedly across the re-modelled sand, Saskia Zodiac pulled on her panties. She retrieved her black dress and turned it right side out.

She told Tabitha: 'There were Seraphim hanging around at Hannah's funeral.'

Apocalypso music, sulky and full of ominous basslines, came

drifting from somewhere beyond the palm trees, as if there were a heavy party over there.

'How do you know, petal?' asked Captain Jute.

'J.M. Souviens showed me the black ship,' Saskia said. She clutched her dress to her as if she had forgotten what to do with it. 'The *Seraph Kajsa*,' she said.

Captain Jute hadn't the first idea what she was talking about. 'Alice,' she said, 'did you get that?'

'YES, CAPTAIN,' said Alice.

'What was it?'

'THE *SERAPH KAJSA* CROSSED OUR 73RD ORBIT OF VENUS,' said the vigilant persona.

'How close?' asked the Captain.

'NEAREST APPROACH 1.889KM,' said Alice. 'I HAVE IT LOGGED.'

'Well, have you,' the Captain said tartly. 'Thanks for the information.' The Seraphim were far away. She had left the Seraphim behind. But she didn't like the thought of that ship being there, and Alice knew and even Saskia knew, and nobody had told her. She peered over her shoulder, looking for the scratches on her back. She thought she wanted to snatch the dress from the experimental woman and fling it away; to hold her slender body tight once more and force another orgasm from her. The cruelty of her impulse frightened and silenced her. She felt as if something had passed from the environmat in that moment, flying out of the brilliant air.

She watched Saskia dress with elegant, preoccupied gestures. She needed to say something, didn't know what. She said, 'Are you having fun?'

The thin magician regarded her. 'Yes,' she said. 'Aren't you?'

'Yes,' said Captain Jute, resentfully.

'Well good,' said Saskia, stooping to give her a farewell kiss. The Captain caressed the white hands that lingered on her shoulders.

'I shall need to get some stuff from Alice,' Saskia told her.

'What?'

'Only some memory.'

Tabitha brushed at her hair. 'Of course,' she said.

For some reason she felt unnerved. What did Saskia want Alice's memory for?

It seemed a pledge of affection to demonstrate trust, not to ask.

'Alice? Saskia wants to talk to you.'

'HELLO, SASKIA,' said Alice.

'I need to search some memory, Alice,' said Saskia. 'I'll call you when I'm ready.'

Captain Jute knew then, somehow, it was her brother Saskia was after. Mogul. A strange sensation came over the Captain then, a flatness, like a kind of defeat. 'You can call her on the bridge,' she said. 'Tell the duty officer to give you a cubicle. All right? Saskia?'

The acrobat kissed her again, and departed.

In the absence of Eladeldi, the Vespans had really come on. They were running the body part bingo and the extreme assault courses, and presiding over the Perk fights with an august, paternal benevolence. The Vespan Tiltsnirip Tilpnotuel, known as Tilt, was typical. He looked something like a walrus and something like a camel made of brown and green rubber, and he sported ulsters in broad window-pane check and velvet waistcoats adorned with great swags of gold chain.

'The Meteorite! He a little scrapper, ladies, gentlemen, so as put Banshee down in thirty-two seconds!'

In his flipper Tilt clutched a great wad of paper tickets and a battered old credit meter.

'Under-handicap, he gone up next week, last bout, very last bout at this odds. Oh yus.'

He smiled engagingly, filling Godfrey Bills with trust. How could such a gangling, bulbous, floppy creature possibly be trying to trick you? Somebody must win; why should it not be them this time? 'What do you think?' he asked his companion, Dagobert Moon.

Mr Moon looked at Tilt's champion. 'I like the spiked leather gloves,' he said, reflectively.

'And the matching muzzle,' Mr Bills pointed out. His credit chip was already in his hand. The long neck of the Vespan dipped to inspect it.

'Fifty, sir? One hundred? You can't gone lose this opportunity.' Tilt's face creased and puffed out with animation. 'You dan't gone insult the Meteorite with less than one hundred,' he urged them both in the loud, brassy voice of a well-intentioned uncle. Catching the infection of his warmth, Bills half-believed the bookie was offering them money, not the other way around.

Mr Moon spotted the referee, an elderly, vague-looking human gentleman. 'He doesn't look as if he'd spoil anyone's fun,' said Mr Bills, optimistically.

'Not if they felt strongly about it,' said Mr Moon. He had an interest in fun; other people's, mainly. He rarely felt sure he was having fun himself. He was not sure how to recognize it if he did, except that it seemed to involve parting with irrational sums of money, to people like him, or Tilt the Vespan.

In the flat glare of the floodlights the Perks paced the white-chalked ring, sinewy as weasels. The Meteorite suddenly took exception to some stray provocation. He arced his slender feathery neck, spitting and snarling, making the front row of the crowd take an involuntary step backwards. The level of conversation rose at once with the expectation of violence.

The Meteorite's opponent was, according to the embroidery on the back of his purple nylon dressing gown, the Mo-Lok. The Meteorite had no gown: he was naked but for the gloves, jockstrap and tight taped ankle supports. Both principals were backed up by their tribes. Each was surrounded by a corps of young males and females in various attitudes of admiration. Babies crawled or tottered about with their eyes wide, their paws stuffed absent-mindedly in their mouths. A fearsomely scarred old male stood with his hands on his skinny knees, muttering advice in the Meteorite's ear. The Mo-Lok chewed a jalapeño pepper.

Over the heads of the crowd Tilt was signalling to another of his own kind. Their heads bobbed like senile old humans paying each other kindly regards. 'Do listen,' he bid the two humans, whistling softly through his enormous teeth. 'Nobody gone catch the Meteorite!' He spoke as if confiding some secret of profound wisdom to them alone.

'Oh, well, that's all right then,' muttered Mr Bills, already feeling as if he had done something quite foolish.

Mr Moon puffed out his cheeks and narrowed his eyes. His feet tapped an impatient rhythm on the floor.

The referee raised a finger, and there went the bell.

At once the aged trainer sprang the catch on the Meteorite's muzzle, while the Mo-Lok flung his dressing gown into the dust. His body had been shaved. The muscles of his long low belly pumped pinkly, shocking in their nakedness; his chest bristled with grey spikes of stubble. He opened his little mouth and screamed.

63

'Chi-chi-chi-cheeeeee!'

The Meteorite did not delay for niceties. He leaped on the Mo-Lok with both feet, grabbing at his face. The crowd yelled and whistled, clapping and cheering. The Meteorite aimed a savage swipe at the Mo-Lok's cheek. The Mo-Lok bent his neck in a sharp vee, saving his eye by a fifth of a second. He snapped at the Meteorite's arm. The Meteorite kicked him in the chest. Both fell down.

The referee saw nothing objectionable in any of that. The crowd approved of it all, heartily. The vaults of the empty dock rang to their cries. Surging this way and that together, the two tribes of Perks squealed and screeched their heroes on. Overhead they brandished their totems: a radiator grille from a vacuum tractor; the ragged old pizzle of some Denebian wildebeest.

Tilt flapped his lips, exhaling pointedly. He took a small stylus from a recess in his pouchy head where he had stowed it. Watching all the while the course of the fight with one snailshell-brown and unblinking eye, he started making calculations on his meter. Mr Moon observed, closely.

The Meteorite picked his foe up and smashed him to the floor. He dug his claws into his exposed belly. The air was hot and moist, thick with tobacco smoke and testosterone. The Mo-Lok kicked the Meteorite off him. The Meteorite kicked the Mo-Lok in the head. 'I say!' said Mr Bills weakly. Excitement was making him nervous.

The bell sounded. At once the combatants turned their backs on each other with formidable disdain. Young Perk females rushed to groom them. Thoughtfully the referee moved some fragment of litter out of the ring with the side of his boot.

'It's very noisy,' said Mr Bills to Mr Moon, with some difficulty. 'I wonder how the bookie can bear it,' he said, nodding at Tilt. 'Very sensitive ears, Vespans,' he said.

To it, again! The Meteorite leapt. The spurs on his anklets raked blood from the Mo-Lok's ribs. The Mo-Lok writhed in pain. Hats flew. The hot ammonia stink of embattled Perks was enough to make your head reel.

'Crooo, croooo, croo! Chi-cheeeee!' Second blood! A lucky swipe from the Mo-Lok laid a shallow cut down the Meteorite's shoulder. The combatants squawked and hurled insults at each other. The Mo-Lok showed his bottom. They grappled. The spectators were yelling their heads off. The front row leaned into the ring, connoisseurs of the Groin Lunge, the Full-Hand Twist.

Another fall for the Mo-Lok. Before he could well lash back at the nimble, capering Meteorite and land another bite, it was the end of Round Two.

For a moment it looked as though the principals would not comply, but their tribes rushed into the circle and dragged them out. The females licked their champions' wounds. The white-furred old female on the Meteorite's party brought out a bottle of gin, which he swigged as though it were a fruit cordial. The referee blew his nose.

Tilt nodded. 'A full-heart fight, oh yus.' He made that guttural, sucking noise they make so often, expressing satisfaction. Mr Bills gave his partner a look of confidence and pride.

The referee was consulting his watch. The bell chimed. Round Three.

The Meteorite hopped up out of his corner, spraying gin around. The Mo-Lok shook his head like a wet whippet. The Meteorite started to crow and whoop and spring up and down. The Mo-Lok took a stance.

The Meteorite hurled himself upon him bodily. 'Ooh, you can see why they call him the Meteorite!' said Mr Bills.

But Mo-Lok was not there. He had flickered aside, to land three fast bites on the Meteoritic buttocks. The Meteorite shrieked, trying to wrap his wiry arms around his opponent; but the Mo-Lok again slipped free, darting between his bandy legs.

'Gern, yer bastard!' roared Mr Moon suddenly.

Blood jetted across the floor. The crowd parted for it. The Mo-Lok lined up his claws like razors and slashed a great X across the Meteorite's torso, as if crossing him out. The Meteorite howled with rage and seized the Mo-Lok; but the Mo-Lok ducked under the assault and came up with his teeth fastened in the Meteorite's throat.

The uproar was immense. Mr Bills was shouting earnestly and high for his favourite. 'Come on, Meaty, hit him!' The Meteorite kicked mightily and struggled; but the Mo-Lok had hold of one of his spurs, and though the blood welled and splashed through the fingers of his little hand, he did not let go but started to bend the leg backwards, snapping its narrow bones.

Now the Meteorite's spine was like a stretched steel hawser. The Mo-Lok snaked his head around to show his fans the crimson gobbet of flesh before he spat it from his mouth. He broke the Meteorite's arms. He jumped on the Meteorite's taut spine. He kicked the Meteorite's jaw, smashing it. He kicked it again and again. Then he was down on all fours once more, gnawing at the Meteorite's purple, pulsing gizzard.

The referee stood up and shuffled into the ring. Stooping, he took the Mo-Lok by the right hand and wearily hoisted him upright. The crowd exulted. Even the Meteorite's supporters seemed impressed. They made a tribute of their jeering complaints, the beer tubes and old shoes they threw at the victor as the referee walked him solemnly around the circle. Mr Bills stood there aimlessly, feeling betrayed.

The Mo-Lok grinned and bowed, cuffing himself playfully over the head. He broke away and scampered back to urinate on the broken form of his opponent.

His whistling tribe reclaimed him, lifting him up on their shoulders and gambolling around. The cubs pestered him, cheeping, until a greying one-eyed male waded in and cuffed their heads for them. Meanwhile the elder females on the losing side unrolled big grey bin liners and started to scoop up the matted remains of their hero, and Mr Bills's.

'Oh yus,' said Tilt, licking the side of his hand. He dipped his head to Mr Bills, looking sidelong at Mr Moon. Moon had given Tilt nothing, but he had Bills's money, along with many other people's; and his competitors too were making a profit, apparently, for all their cow-eyed, doleful headshaking. The referee was returning from a conference with one of them, pushing something into his pocket.

Mr Moon pushed his hands deep in the pockets of his fur coat. 'Fixed,' he said.

'Oh, I don't know,' said his companion miserably. 'I don't think so, was it?'

He looked at the congregation of Perks clustering round the lofty Vespans. The feral little creatures were climbing up the coat-tails of their indulgent shepherds, bathing ecstatically in the invisible vibrations of well-being the bloated entrepreneurs seemed effortlessly to bestow on their whole species.

Bills and Moon turned and started to climb the stairs, back towards the shop and a nice cup of tea. Still they could hear the bookmakers' calls behind them as they climbed. 'Ladies sirs!' they cried. 'This now gone be great fighting between the Black Rat and Crusher!' Their voices buffeted the air like tubas fortissimo. 'Oh yus, plenty much more fighting for you!'

7

After work the Little Foxbourne women liked to have dinner at the Chilli Chalet above Peacock Park. 'It's silly to cook,' they would say, watching the menu holos cycle, 'when it's so nice here.'

'And it's quite reasonable, really,' Laura Overhead would admit. She meant you to understand that a Chalet was not the sort of place she would have chosen at home, but perfectly acceptable under the circumstances.

'Very reasonable,' pronounced Marge Goodself. 'And very clean.'

They all agreed with that. 'Very clean.'

'Oh yes.'

In the Chilli Chalet the waiters smiled. They looked so nice in their smart uniforms with their hair brushed and gleaming, their neckerchiefs tied just so. The girls had red paper frills on their heads and the boys sharp creases in their trousers. They scurried to and fro with their trays of plates and ketchup bottles, never colliding, never getting tired or cross.

Natalie Shoe looked out of the window. 'I hope Billy's all right,' she said. Billy was Mrs Shoe's labrador, condemned to languish outside while his mistress ate lasagne.

'Now Billy's quite alright,' Mrs Goodself told her. 'Why don't you just get on with your food and stop worrying about Billy.'

(They had all acquired dogs, the Little Foxbourne women. Marge Goodself's was a lurcher called Gorgon. He had appeared on AV with her. 'As soon as he saw me, he decided I was the one he was going to come home with,' she said, rubbing the top of his powerful skull. 'It was love at first sight, wasn't it, eh? Silly old thing. Aren't you. Aren't you. Yes you are.')

Dotty Wallace dabbed her lips with a red-checked paper napkin. 'She was about again last night,' she said. 'One of the managers said when they woke up some of the chairs had disappeared.'

'Chairs?' The women shook their heads and tutted. They had all heard of her, this dark young woman who broke into people's apartments to steal their things.

'Did anyone see her, Dotty?'

'Oh no, she was too quick for that.'

'Norman always said this place was full of thieves,' said Natalie Shoe. She looked around the dining area, as if the culprit might even now be at the salad bar, helping herself to the serving tongs. 'People steal from the empty shops.'

Marge Goodself lifted her chin and touched her resilient coiffure. 'If they were empty, Natalie,' she pointed out, 'you couldn't steal from them.'

'She'll have the mirror out of your handbag,' Natalie said balefully, and blew on her tea.

'I don't know what she does with it all,' said Dotty Wallace. 'Tapers, microwaves, furniture. I can't believe she can sell it all. I mean, people have got those things, haven't they.'

'Of course they have, dear,' said Marge. 'But you know as well as I do, some people have never got enough. Aren't I right, mm?'

Around the tables, heads were nodding. Some, the women agreed, were never satisfied. When you were away from home, you couldn't always find the things you were used to. But you made do, didn't you? You made do.

'This is a dangerous place. We all have to stick together and look after each other.' Marge tilted her chin at one of the waiters. 'Now come here, dear, and tell me what that armband means.'

The young boy turned his arm proudly so they could see the red band with its gold design. 'This is my Employee Distinction, mam. It means I served five hundred customers last week, with no errors, no complaints and a better than two per cent spill ratio.'

Marge pressed his cheek with her fingertips. 'I'm sure we ought to give you a special tip for that,' she said.

The waiter responded with a manly smirk and a modest wave of his upright palm. 'No thank you, mam, we don't accept them,' he said, though he did produce his company credit meter. 'Instead we operate a charity support system, this week highlighting the Help the Hostages campaign for veterans of Eladeldi Prison Asteroid 000013.'

The Little Foxbourne women knew all about charity, having benefited from it themselves in the early days. They had set out with little more than the clothes they stood up in. Now they had nice jobs and homes all together in Clementine Chambers, this side of the aqueduct. Their own little community. Just like home, in fact, except for the giant stalactites of petrified Frasque spit.

'Ah yes, those poor, poor prisoners,' said Marge Goodself. 'She's probably one of them, you see, this Mystery Woman of yours, Dotty.' She smiled and held out her credit to the lovely young man, while all the rest started digging in their bags.

Up under the very top of the lumpy dome of the good ship Plenty was the amphitheatre called the Mercury Garden. Though there was nothing to be seen now through its great skylights, all the passengers agreed, it was The Place To Go. They thronged the bars and chattered and laughed at the tables around the podium and whirled each other showily across the famous dance floor, which was made of stainless steel. The considerable areas of dereliction had been screened off with giant silkite curtains, so they wouldn't spoil the atmosphere.

The Mercury Garden was more popular and much more prosperous now than it had ever been in orbital days, not least because it had been the scene of one of Captain Jute's adventures. The Captain herself, however, had not set foot there all journey; not until tonight.

As the car arrived, AV crews swung in, tapers whirring, while crowd control drones with rakes extended kept people from surging onto the red carpet. In front of doors big enough for an aeroplane hangar uniformed attendants lined up in a gauntlet of welcome, over which one of the Vespan directors loomed like a tottering pyramid of gourds in a crimson blazer.

'Christ all bloody mighty.' Captain Jute was in a bad mood. She didn't want to go to the Mercury Garden. She had never wanted to go to the Mercury Garden.

'Buck up, dear,' said Dorcas Mandebra, smiling graciously at the crowd.

The Captain fingered her sunglasses. She exhaled gloomily. 'There they are,' she said.

'Who's that?' asked Karen Narlikar, looking round.

'The wannabes,' said Zoe Primrose, Captain Jute's p.a., sitting next to her in the back.

'Oh, them.'

They were always there, wherever she went, in their long black coats. They had had their hair blackened and permed into globes. Some of them even had the silver wire woven in, in the same patterns. They hopped up and down and waved at her. 'I blame the parents,' said Captain Jute.

'Oh-oh, here she comes,' Karen said; and she did, trotting up with Beth and her taper even as Soi buzzed the car doors open.

'Geneva McCann, Captain, Channel 9. On behalf of all the passengers and crew let me welcome you to –'

Tabitha gave her a withering smile, patted her arm and walked straight past her. Kenny the Thrant and Zoe Primrose scampered after. Looking back, Kenny shook his head at the Channel 9 front woman and gibbered warningly.

Geneva ignored him, trying to run after the Captain and resorting to a zoom when the drones prevented her, along with all the squealing fans. The Captain was shaking hands with people. 'Well, it looks as if Captain Jute just can't wait to see the show!' Geneva told the viewers at home. 'Geneva McCann, Captain, Channel 9!'

Then with an ear-battering fanfare the doors slid open, and deep orange light and syrupy music spilled out to engulf everybody. Over thick carpet the Captain sailed into the great amphitheatre, following a bowing maître d' into the arena and up a flight of stairs to the best table, directly in front of the flat-topped pinnacle of matrix that served as a stage. Nearby diners rose and applauded. Others only murmured together, watching her avidly as if she and her party were surely the evening's real entertainment.

The place was packed tonight, because she was here. The tables were full of paying customers smoking hookahs and drinking frothy things with straws in. A speaking face advanced, receded. Somebody put a beer in front of her. She began to drink it.

Karen was grumbling about the fans, the Tabithettes, the Juties. 'If they really cared about you,' she said, 'they'd leave you alone.'

'They're all right,' said the Captain, automatically. 'They're no problem.'

She glared suspiciously at the empty stage.

The seats were large and comfortable, with built-in visor headsets. Captain Jute put hers on. The stage jumped into close-up. The tiniest adjustment made the image whizz around all over the place. She winced and took the set off.

She looked around her at her party. The girls were all agog, tense with anticipation. The Thrants sat at a separate table, sipping tiny glasses of purified water. Everybody kept looking at her covertly.

Then the awful music swelled to a thrilling blare, and the lights went down. In the blackness a spotlight lanced down from the ceiling and spread a brilliant white pool on the stage. A disembodied voice welcomed everyone and announced their host, Mr Entertainment, the King of the Mercury Garden, ladies and gentlemen, Marco Metz!

Captain Jute spilled her beer. Dorcas leaned over and patted her hand. 'Don't be scared,' she said.

'I'm not!' she moaned. 'I'm not scared! There's nothing to be scared of. The whole thing's fucking stupid, that's all. I said I don't want to know and I don't, there's no bloody point. I can't see what bloody point you think –'

But her words were lost in rapturous applause, yelps and whistles.

Marco Metz was a bigger star now than he'd ever been. His show at the Mercury Garden was an institution. People went back night after night. Captain Jute had heard about it from the girls, on the bridge, in the Trivia, before finally banning all mention of his name in her presence. She instructed Alice to screen all her channels, wherever she was, and delete his appearances. Broadcasts would be interrupted by swirling lakes of colour and loud guitars. Every time it happened, inevitably, it made her remember him.

He had been in a critical condition when they brought him up from Venus. Tabitha had seen him carried on board, noted his broken right leg, his mangled arm, his unpleasant colour. She couldn't help starting to feel sorry for him, the piece of shit. Not even the poison planet could keep Marco Metz down.

The comeback started before he regained consciousness. Before her funeral his manager, Hannah Soo, drew up her last ever contract, with Channel 9, guaranteeing exclusive rights in return for the best medical care aboard. They were sketching out the coverage even while the first shred of ruined flesh was being trimmed away, the first crystal implants inserted.

In his post-op interview the nascent superstar looked pale and drawn. He spoke candidly of his hopes and fears. 'The Captain and me, Geneva,' he said, 'we're very important to each other. I guess I shouldn't talk about it.' He shrugged modestly, winced exquisitely. Somehow the gesture expressed his indispensability, his valour, his appalling pain. It was a good moment; Beth had slowed it a fraction, lingered on it.

Geneva McCann asked: 'Has the Captain come to see you yet, Mr Metz?'

'I have to rest. Tabitha knows that.'

'We understand the Captain has refused to speak to you, sir,' said Geneva McCann.

Marco pouted. 'We have our problems,' he said, huskily. 'I wouldn't deny that. Captain Jute's a very particular lady. Demanding,' he said, moving his good shoulder suggestively between the sheets.

They carried an exclusive on the unbandaging of his new hand. He showed off the musical induction glove, which was integrated, and played with captivating unsteadiness *Love is Everywhere* and the opening bars of *Good King Wenceslas*. He appeared with Dr Irsk, his artificial arm around her bulbous form. 'Dr Frankenstein,' he called her. 'Only kidding. The woman's a genius.'

Some months he spent convalescing, recuperating, exercising. From the top of the wall bars he waved, with the bravest of smiles. He cultivated numerous admirers, especially women, especially women with money. Rumours of other prosthetic improvements were in circulation.

His return to performance, to the stage, was delayed. His contract was negotiated and renegotiated until Channel 9 threatened to dump him. Then, with a bound, he was back. 'I need the live contact,' he said, inhaling deeply. 'The smell of 'em,' he said, gutsily. 'And I know it's sentimental of me, Geneva, but I kinda feel I owe it to them. There comes a time when you have to pay your dues,' he told the camera.

Watching it on the news, several of his former nurses laughed derisively.

Now Marco Metz appeared in the spotlight, opening his arms to them all. 'Thank you! Thank you very much –!'

His sculpted white suit perfectly set off his glorious tan, and the black glove on his right hand. He knew the Captain was in tonight.

He saluted her, dedicated his show to her. He commended her to them all: 'The brave and fearless, the beautiful . . .'

The Captain ignored her racing heart, tuned out her ears. The words of the King of the Mercury Garden were quacking, booming sounds that succeeded one another, got muddled in each other's echoes, and died. The thril she had taken before coming scurried through her emotions, hurrying them across the overlit synapses of her nervous system.

A synthetic orchestra played excitedly. Marco Metz stroked his black glove with his left hand. Chords of golden honey rippled through the air. People applauded even more madly.

'Thank you very much, ladies and gentlemen . . .'

She had forgotten how desirable he could look. Repressed it completely.

He played something sticky and rich, full of fancy trills and triplets. Coloured lights filled the stark stage with shapes and shadows. He sang in a deep strangulated voice about brotherhood in space and time.

They had loved it when Capella had taught them to sing it. They loved it still.

Marco Metz put one foot in a small spot as though dipping his toe in a pool of water. His shoe shone like polished metal. It was polished metal. It was his right foot, completely rebuilt. He did some energetic and fluid heel-and-toe steps, then spun the prosthesis through 360° on its ankle. More applause.

'He always was a footloose man,' said Saskia Zodiac.

She was sitting on the table with her legs crossed. She was eating kabli chana and her drink was balanced on her ankles. She wore sealskin trousers, a mauve shantung blouse, and in her earlobes little studs of lapis lazuli. It was amazing how masculine she looked in those clothes, especially with her hair tied back.

'When did you get here?'

The acrobat smiled archly and touched a slender finger to the Captain's lips. Her nose was like a white wax candle. Her eyelids were porcelain. The eyelashes lowered sensuously, lifted. They were dusted with the merest hint of electric blue.

She leaned down and examined the Captain's pupils; then planted a spicy, greasy kiss on the Captain's mouth.

'You mustn't be afraid,' she said.

'I'm not – fucking – scared.'

Everybody watched Mr Entertainment. Now he sang about the Groves of Palernia and danced in rippling green light while he fingered a wistful bucolic motif. Now he sang *Goodbye, Blue Sky*, a chirpy little anthem that had enjoyed a lot of popularity in the first weeks of the voyage. The audience loved his every shimmy and sway.

'Corny,' said the Captain.

Dorcas Mandebra indicated Tabitha's discarded visor with her finger. 'Put your headset on,' she mouthed.

The Captain put her headset on. Instantly he was before her, looking down at her, as though only a few metres divided them. A sheen of sweat glistened on his brow. There were deep lines she didn't remember beneath his liquid brown eyes and down the sides of his mouth. His ordeal on Venus had aged him, scoring marks of suffering on that incongruously noble face.

Tabitha took the headset off, put it back on. Now he was performing a medley on the theme of Flight, sweeping around the stage as though the glove was towing him through the air. He had the moves all right; better now he had lost some weight.

It was a shame. It was. It was a shame he was a piece of shit.

A large green parrot appeared. It circled him, flying with impossible slowness. The audience clapped.

Captain Jute sat up, feeling quite peculiar. The parrot was Marco's alien sidekick, Tal. But Tal had been burned to a smear of grease on the floor of Captain Jute's own cockpit. She pushed up her headset and looked at Saskia.

Saskia had nicked Zoe's visor. She seemed unperturbed. Captain Jute lowered hers over her eyes again.

The parrot was sitting on Marco's shoulder, nestling against his cheek, cute as a cartoon. It was a replica of Tal, perfectly crafted. Captain Jute could see every feather. The thing was a hologram, made of light.

Marco pretended to pet it and swayed from side to side as they sang a duet, he and the illusory bird, in flawless unison, about hearts and wings. You could see the little gizmo in the corner of Marco's mouth that took care of the double-tracking.

During the last verse the parrot left its perch and flew once more around its master. On its next pass it took the cuff of his right sleeve in its spectral beak, then flapped back to the shoulder where it had been sitting, pulling the sleeve up after it to reveal the arm of neoprene and tungsten steel, its jewelled bearings flashing in the spotlight.

They had seen that mechanical marvel fifty times before; still they clapped. Captain Jute was now feeling distinctly dizzy. The bird was a hologram. If it wasn't physically there . . .

'Thank you so much, ladies and gentlemen,' Marco was saying. 'How do you like my new toys?' He whirled the foot and the hand in opposite directions at superhuman speed. 'Good, aren't they?' he called out. 'You know how much they cost?'

As one the legion of the faithful shouted the response: 'An arm and a leg . . . !'

The Captain heard the girls laugh, and Kenny snicker.

She put back her head. Magnified, the Mercury Garden skylights threatened to swallow her into the colourless emptiness of the meta-cosmic void. Below, the music battered, multi-tracked, relentlessly dramatic, total. Tabitha longed for a rinky-tink piano, a cold water wail of cornet. Out of the corner of her eye she saw other figures coming on now, assembling for some kind of big set piece.

She could leave. Everybody would laugh about it forever; but she could, just, walk, out.

'This is the bit,' said Karen in her ear.

The Captain looked.

The stage had been transformed, into a mock-up of the cockpit of some kind of vehicle, with flashing lights and mirror everywhere. Besides the star and his artificial bird there were two identical skinny figures in identical blue and silver spacesuits, and a wobbly black doll on a plate, obviously being worked by remote control from some-where. The twins were clutching one another in terror while the bird and the black doll zoomed around in choreographed swoops representing panic. Marco commanded centre stage, his false arm draped around what looked as if it was supposed to be some kind of periscope. He was singing: 'Contraband is on its way! Contraband will save the day! while the set tipped from side to side and yawed around him.

Captain Jute felt Saskia Zodiac's hand reach down and take hold of hers.

The pilot of Marco Metz's peculiar vessel was a busty young woman in a strange décolleté jacket with decals all over it. She was wearing tights. She seemed to be having difficulty controlling her

75

craft. She kept putting the back of her hand to her forehead. The audience adored her, loudly.

Captain Jute must have called out, or manifested some distress, for she felt Kenny come to her side, nosing aggressively. She shoved him away. She was watching.

On board the imitation ship there came a sudden bang, with sparks and smoke. The improbable pilot cried out and jumped up from her seat, throwing up her hands. She had mirror chrome nail polish on. She skipped across to Marco Metz and draped herself round him. 'Oh, Mr Metz!' she cried in a high-pitched voice. 'Whatever can we do?'

At the other end of a tunnel a thousand parsecs long Captain Jute heard Karen Narlikar sniggering. Dorcas was pushing a pot of thril discreetly along the table to her, Zoe was summoning a waiter for another beer. Tabitha took no notice. She sat through it, through the whole of the rest of it, like an unplugged machine.

When the applause was done and the lights went up, she still sat there, unmoving.

Saskia leaned over and lifted the visor from her head. She brushed the Captain's hair back with her hands, smiled and kissed her lightly.

They were looking at her, Zoe Primrose and Karen Narlikar and Dorcas Mandebra. Their eyebrows were arched, their teeth and fingernails expectant. 'Well?' demanded Dorcas.

Captain Jute glanced at her bodyguard, who was standing beside her chair, knees bent, shoulders forward. His mouth was open, showing his fangs, his inky tongue.

'Fetch him,' she said.

The rest of the gang rustled and murmured. This was a satisfactory move, apparently.

She said: 'Give me a beer.'

Saskia caressed her shoulders, showed her the beer that was already in front of her. She picked it up and drank it.

Then Marco was there. He was wearing a protective cape. Two women were wiping his face with a towel. He waved them off, leaned across the table. He was going to take her hand. A thousand tapers were whirring and Marco Metz was taking her hand.

He had deceived her, cheated her, cut her up and down and sideways sixty ways to Neptune. He was going to kiss her cheek unless she moved her head, now.

She moved her head.

'Tabitha,' the King of the Mercury Garden was saying. 'Captain. You should have told me you were coming. I only got the word literally two seconds before I went on.'

He was perfectly groomed, smug as ever, sleek with fame. He was coasting on the fatigue of having just completed a two-and-a-half-hour multimedia extravaganza. Marco Metz meets the Captain! He takes her hand! It was the climax of tonight's performance.

There were people at the bottom of the stairs, management, reporters, wanting to come up, trying to poke their cameras closer. Kenny was virtually snarling at them. Zoe was feeding them some kind of statement, saying how much the Captain had appreciated the show.

Captain Jute still had not moved her hand. Marco took his away, grabbed the towel from his women. 'Come on, hell, what did you think?' asked Marco, towelling away.

He was embarrassed. He did well to be embarrassed. He had obviously been making an effort, trying to play down his own heroism and glorify her counterpart with lots of big stagy gestures of admiration, but the parts as written didn't allow him much leeway.

'Kenny enjoyed it,' said Captain Jute. 'Didn't you, Kenny?'

Kenny's long eyes glinted.

'Hi, Sas,' Marco said to Saskia. 'Tal's working just great, isn't he? And don't they love it? Oh boy. Like the hand?' he said, swinging his attention back to the Captain. He played a little trill of something sweet, making it wow like a mouth organ, and gave her a melting smile. He was slick as a sandshark, slick all the way down. Nothing stuck to him. 'And the leg?' He pulled up his trouser leg, showing her shiny metal. 'Vanadium steel, zircon bearings. And the glove, sixteen extra circuits, no extra weight.' He was babbling. When he pressed a button on his wrist his right sleeve slid up again, gathered on a hidden wire. She looked at the cluster of telescopic tubes and capillaries that fed into his elbow. 'One hundred fifty-six hours of surgery,' he said proudly. 'They got a good deal.'

Captain Jute stood up. She sensed her entourage regrouping, with subtle motions of hand and head, focused on her, on the pair of them. The evening's excursion required resolution.

The entertainer stepped closer to her. She had forgotten how short he was.

'Can we go somewhere, talk?' he suggested in an undertone. 'I know I've been neglecting you, I admit that, sure, only the show –'

He waved impatiently towards the stage, not looking at it. 'I wanted to see you, only –'

He bowed his head, as though in the grip of emotions too strong for him. Then he raised his eyes, looking at her moistly from beneath his long black lashes. He said: 'I kept away from you because I didn't want you to feel guilty, about leaving me that way. I wanted to give us time,' he said. He put his real hand on her sleeve. 'I've missed you, Tabs,' he said, longing in his voice. 'Believe me. God how I've missed you.'

The Captain lifted her jaw.

'What did you call me?'

He was muttering, waving his hands about. She turned, beckoned brusquely to the people Kenny was holding at the bottom of the stairs.

Uncertainly they came up, the Vespan in his blazer, the maître d' in his silver dinner jacket, and a young woman with big breasts looking rapt and frightened. 'Captain, this is really the most tremendous honour,' said the woman in a squeaky, breathy voice.

Captain Jute looked at her. She looked very familiar. It was the woman who had played the pilot.

She turned from her to Zoe Primrose.

'Who's in charge here?'

The Vespan lumbered forward, nodding, his face folding in and out obsequiously.

'The show's coming off,' she said.

There was an outcry.

'Off,' she said. 'Closed. Over.'

'Hey, Captain, listen, we need to talk about this,' Marco was saying in a deep soulful voice.

Tabitha Jute put her hands in her pockets. 'Take him away,' she said.

Kenny moved in on him then, hard. The entertainer clutched the railing with his real hand. 'You don't like the show? You don't like it?' he said angrily. 'We can change it, pull in a couple extra numbers –'

He stifled a cry of pain as Thrant claws started to prise his fingers free.

Marco's co-star whimpered. The manager made a woeful bubbling noise, and everybody else clutched their possessions.

'Anything you want!' cried the King of the Mercury Garden, as Kenny hustled him back towards the dressing rooms. 'Final say on the script – hey, Captain! A personal appearance, maybe, what would you say to that?'

On the way home the gang were laughing, celebrating the way the little man had squirmed, the way she'd dealt with him. 'It was a very crappy show,' said Dorcas Mandebra firmly.

'It was,' said Captain Jute emphatically. 'He's a crappy performer.'

'You've done everybody a favour,' Karen declared.

Along Montgomery they were cutting back the vines. People pushing infants in pushchairs pointed and waved at the car.

The Captain squeezed Saskia's hand. She had taken more thril, and felt as if she had become a thin, quick film of something fluid, sliding rapidly across the surface of everything. She had to speak quickly, to get things across. She said to Saskia: 'You've been seeing him, then.'

The conjuror shrugged. 'Once or twice,' she said distantly. 'He wanted my opinion on the show.'

It wasn't something Captain Jute felt like hearing. 'You didn't tell me that,' she said.

'You wouldn't let anyone mention –'

'Didn't you tell him it was a piece of shit?' asked the Captain.

Saskia took back her hand. She looked out of the window.

The Captain fiddled with the buckle of her belt. 'You didn't fuck him, did you? You really shouldn't fuck him. Ever. Blokes like him.'

Suddenly she had taken on the role of the young cloneling's mentor, forgetting Saskia Zodiac had known Marco Metz all her life and had sexual congress with him on several different worlds.

'It's like when I was on contracts, back in the old days with Dodger and them, and I was driving this crapped-out Lugger with dirty points, and it kept missing on me. I had to take it in at Grissom Plat. Well, the guy there tried to bullshit me, the way they always do in those places. He said it needed a complete new electrics job, two weeks minimum, only he'd do it one if I went with him to this little place he knew –'

There was a chorus of derisive groans. Karen said, 'Yeah, we all know that little place . . .'

Captain Jute smiled behind her sunglasses. 'I didn't know what was wrong with the thing,' she said, ''cause I didn't know anything about electrics, but I knew damn well I was going to learn about electrics then, so those fuckers couldn't pull that kind of shit on me.'

Saskia looked at the dingy green light that bumped and flowed along the tunnel wall.

'You talk about yourself all the time,' she said.

8

Despite the intense and unremitting heat, many useful public works were completed at this time. The power was reconnected to Clark Kent Fork, and the persistent pressure leak in the forward quarter known as Pearly Gates sealed at last. At the celebration party many prominent hedonists re-emerged, including Marmaduc Flecheur de Brae. They had spent, they claimed, several weeks in a secret palace beneath Asgard Boulevard, where pleasure droids of tireless construction and infinite adaptability were to be enjoyed.

In Peacock Park the Foxbourne WI organised a fête, with races for the little ones. The Palernians loved it, though it wasn't clear whether they fully understood what was going on. They grew overexcited and started breaking up the handicrafts stall, pulling off their clothes and pelting each other with toilet roll covers and jars of jam. Only Marge Goodself knew how to control them. 'Now is that the way to behave?' she demanded, striding towards them over the Astroturf in her sensible shoes. A few sharp words from her and the Palernians would fall back to huddling in their fives, rubbing each other's faces and weeping big noisy tears of remorse. When next Marge clapped her hands and blew her whistle, they came running to line up for the sack race, yodelling plaintively. They sounded like geese trying to imitate dolphins. 'Quiet please, everybody,' said Marge, with a ferocious smile.

Tabitha Jute emerged one day to find Muzak playing in the Morningstar foot tunnels. Sweetly humming strings invited her to fly them to the Moon and listen to the Lullaby of Broadway. 'Who ordered this?' she demanded. 'I didn't order this.' For the next ten days she obliged everyone in the district to go about their business to the sound of Sump Rock: muddy blues with the guitars slowed to a bad-tempered crawl while the bassline hammered viciously along like a maniac banging on a drainpipe. Works by Primordial Slime featured prominently.

'This isn't flying,' Captain Jute told Alice. 'It's civic management or some godawful thing like that.' She couldn't understand the Council meetings now, when she went, though they all reckoned she should authorize everything for them. 'It's not even work,' she grumbled. 'Talking about crap.'

'YOU USED TO LIKE TO TALK, CAPTAIN,' said Alice.

'Talk to you, yes, that's different.'

'OR TO MS ZODIAC.'

'She's never here,' said Captain Jute. She was feeling selfish. And why not? Why shouldn't she put herself first for once?

'OR CAPTAIN GILLESPIE.'

'I haven't got time!' said the Captain, getting out of bed. 'You could do it all for me, Alice,' she said, as she dressed. 'Fix you up with a droid extension, you could run around and do it all. You'd be much better at it than I am.'

'I'D BE MORE THAN HAPPY, CAPTAIN.'

'No,' said Tabitha. 'It's got to be me.'

Today she had a delegation of Alteceans complaining about a soap opera one of the channels was re-running. They expected her to be familiar with it, and when her ignorance was exposed, showed her on the monitor in her office, endless clips of people arguing in some sort of offworld junkyard. Their spokesman kept tapping the screen with a scaly red digit, indicating a member of his species in a shapeless yellow bonnet and dirty crocheted cape. 'Honly Gnalteshean haracter on AV here,' he told her. 'Ang hee a trangsves'gnite!'

Captain Jute rubbed her eyes. The heat was intolerable, with all that fur congregated around her desk. She thought she would choke. She scratched the Altecean spokesman under the chin, the way they liked. Nobody else could tell the difference, she wanted to say, but she knew that would offend them even more. 'You should make your own programmes,' she said. 'Let's go and have a drink.'

She took them down to the Trivia. 'It was an Altecean that taught me to fly,' she told them. It was what she always said to Alteceans. 'Did you know that? Who's for a pint of Old Paralysis?'

In the Trivia Window Saturn's rings were whirling like a rainbow-coloured buzzsaw. Nothing like the real thing, thought the Captain, but people seemed to prefer it; all except the redoubtable Rory, who frowned and shook his head. 'I think we should have something nice to look at for a change,' he said decisively, and punched up a cloudy day at a green field where a number of men in white clothes moved around at great distances from one another, making ritualistic passes with lengths of wood and a little red globe. 'That's more like it,' said the barman with satisfaction. 'Old Trafford.'

In the corner sat the Last Poet, with his coterie. 'The Seraphim,' he proposed. 'Cooking with DNA.' He held up his wineglass as he spoke, drawing attention to its spiral stem. 'Running our DNA through their sterile fingers like skeins of silver noodles.'

Captain Jute bought a vast quantity of drinks, then slipped away. Below the Earth Room there was a stairway which led to a circular door in the hull. In zero-g's and a tether suit, you could go out for a walk.

The Captain stood among the eroded, featureless hillocks and shelving plates that were the skin of her world. It was very much like standing on the surface of a planet. With no scale, no perspective, Plenty shrank to an island of shiny grey rock, in a sea of grey cotton, beneath a sky of grey nothing.

It was strange that such a desolate prospect should be so peaceful; that an environment so dead and empty and inert should be refreshing, like a breath of pure, clean air. Here there were no shadows, no movement, no sound – no sense whatsoever that the rocky island was a ship, that the cotton sea was a pan-dimensional projection of actuality, or that the vacuous sky was in fact the suspended realm of hyperspace tearing past at a speed sufficient to bridge the galaxy.

Captain Jute checked in with Alice. 'What's happening, Alice?' she asked.

'XTASCA IS MAPPING SOME MORE OF MY ORIENTATION CENTRE,' said the persona. 'I CAN CONFIRM THAT THE STRONGEST PHOTO-RESPONSIVE TRACT SEEMS TO BE DIRECTLY ASTERN, BUT WITH THE STAR IMAGES INVERTED AND TRANSPOSED PORT TO STARBOARD.'

'I'll be in later.' Captain Jute wasn't really listening. She put her hands in her pockets and gazed off into the infinite blankness that seemed to yawn all around. Technology had always bored her; alien technology and the people who seemed to understand it. Let them be there when she needed them, that was all she asked.

'You can see Proxima Centauri?'

'DISTINCTLY, CAPTAIN.'

Tabitha stared into the murk. 'I wish I could.'

'Captain? Hello?'

It was another voice, a human, breaking in. Her secretary had found her already. 'Yes, Zoe, what is it?'

'Time for your visit to the Air Plant, Captain.'

The MivvyCorp Air Plants deep in the heart of Plenty continued to flood the alien edifice with their product. Vast glass lungs spread through the canyons of the ship like branching trees. Tabitha Jute stood inside a big tube, up to her waist in ferns that trembled constantly. Kenny crouched nearby, filing his claws. They were going on a trip into one of the unoccupied regions of the ship. The tour was, as usual, a preliminary to some kind of appropriation pitch.

The Captain wore an inspection suit with the helmet down. She was talking to a man from MivvyCorp in shorts and a plastic raincoat. She had already forgotten his name. He was showing her a handful of wet khaki moss.

'Every mouthful of air on board comes wafting out of these little chaps. This one produces more oxygen than all the other species put together.'

The man squeezed the dripping flora until it oozed between his fingers. Now it looked just like runny shit. Tabitha's head felt like a block of wood. It was even hotter in here than everywhere else. Moisture hung in the air like fog.

The official ushered his visitors on. A bee buzzed dozily past. 'Oh yes, we get a lot of those. Butterflies too. Very pretty.'

They came to a lock in the tunnel wall. The man warned the Captain to watch her step in the all-pervading slime.

Inside the lock a guide in MivvyCorp livery stood up to greet the Captain. She was young; her eyes were shining, her face was aglow with reflected fame. Tabitha smiled the smile. She let the girl derive even greater honour from helping her put the oxygen equipment on, then made sure she helped Kenny too, who had brought his own and didn't need any help.

'All right there, Ken?' she radioed. 'Watch your step there, you see? It's a bit slimy.' It amused her to needle him sometimes, making him crane his head forward and cough with irritation. She raised her hand to the guide. 'You go on in,' she said. 'And you,' she said to the MivvyCorp man. 'Go on.'

Kenny panted noisily into the mike as the Captain stepped forward. She took hold of his ear through the envelope of his helmet and shook his head like a faithful dog's. He followed her, flicking on his visor as they squeezed through the plastic sphincter into the airless dark.

The guide led them down a partitioned corridor. To either side abandoned offices lay like boxes full of silence, their desks still littered with unread documents. The Captain's breathing sounded loud in her ears. Her light picked out the square, blocky shapes of equipment: consoles, scramblers, photocopiers. The place resembled the catacomb of some extinct civilization, cells for the worshippers of a rectangular god festooned with cables.

'I don't know that I want to do anything with all this,' said Captain Jute. On all fours Kenny jumped up on a desk, tail curved over his back like the handle of a jug. Dust flew. The Thrant scanned the room before jumping down again and loping silently off into the dark, hunting phantoms.

The air official's voice filled Tabitha's helmet, intimate, invasive. 'We could supply this whole sector for just a 0.7% increase in our power allocation.'

The Captain's beam fell on the dull red sarcophagus of a cola dispenser. She went over to look at it.

'Why?' she said. She had no intention of authorizing it, but she was interested in what he would say.

'All this space could be put back to work.' He was holding out a clipboard. Its face glowed, aqua cool in the darkness.

Tabitha shone her torch into the space under the dispenser spout. There was a large dehydrated spider in the cup socket, its legs cramped into a ball.

'What for?' she asked.

'Tekunak would like it, for one. They need some space for expansion.'

The Captain went out on the balcony and shone the light straight up. Giant gobs of dripped matrix hung slack and yellow, like webbed fingers dangling overhead. The expansion of the Chilli Chalet parent company must be what was on the report of the Commerce Committee meeting, she thought. Reports, reports. She could have people to watch them for her, full time. People never got fed up of talking about things.

'They're going to be running the Sundae Joint too now, as you know.'

Kenny came slinking out to join them. Captain Jute nodded at the clipboard. He took it from the man, sniffed it, shone an invisible beam at it, then brought it to her. On it architectural diagrams changed softly, dark blue rectangles organizing and reorganizing themselves. She fingered its smooth and perfect surface.

The official and the guide smiled at each other. 'Everyone has to be fed.'

Tabitha had wondered sometimes where they got the meat. Everything was here somewhere. Maybe there was a gigantic herd of cattle, roaming on the plains of the 153rd Level.

'I hear you're still poisoning Perks,' Tabitha said.

'You'd have to ask the Stores Committee about that, Captain. I do know some of our end-of-line outlets have been having rodent problems.'

'Perks,' she said.

'I believe that's right . . .' said the MivvyCorp man, his voice dropping in a show of tact.

She gave him his clipboard back.

'Leave them alone,' she said.

Captain Jute knew she should thank the pair for the tour and give them some meaningless promise, but she was dead on her feet. There was good crystal waiting in her apartment. She snapped her fingers. Her bodyguard climbed down from the railings of the balcony and led the way back to the car.

'Is it Sunday?' she said. 'It feels like Sunday.'

He lolled at the opposite end of the seat, his visor still on. It was impossible to guess what he was thinking, but she was sure it could not be anything nice. Captain Jute was tired of her bristly shadow. After a day being minded, she carried the reek of him clinging in her clothes, in her hair. She turned and looked out of the window of the limousine. Their shadow raced along the tunnel wall, keeping pace with them.

Far away to starboard, at the end of Rocking Horse Road, in a building in a cavern where all the other buildings were dark and empty, in a suite with the number 5 on the door, an aged, aged man sat watching fish in a tank.

There were two fish, one red and one kingfisher blue, with long frail triangular fins and delicate silver tails. They reminded the old man of flat round toffees wrapped in brightly coloured paper.

The room where the fish swam and the old man sat was full of candlelight. The walls had been painted purple and yellow and red, at his instruction, and decorated with silver stars and fluorescent orange flowers. Incense burners stood about, and mirrors with velvet scarves hung over them. Music was playing, at a deafening volume.

The old man wore a greasy headband of bottle green suede. Pendants and chains and turquoise beads hung around his withered neck. He sat in a big tub of a mobile chair, his head braced upright. His emaciated left hand was clamped in a silver metal tube on the rim of the chair.

In his good right hand the old man clutched a dropper bottle of dark brown glass. He exhaled, hard, like a crocodile contemplating its pleasure.

The com burbled. A light on the rim of the old man's chair registered the fact; otherwise the ancient creature never would have noticed.

With the little finger of his right hand, the old man opened the com. 'Hello?' he said, forcefully but with scant attention.

'Hello, Uncle Charlie,' said a voice: young, human, male.

A blissful smile cracked the chin beneath the grey moustache.

'Grant!' the old man wheezed. 'How you doing, boy?'

'Fixing it up, uncle,' said the caller, with marked self-assurance. 'Getting it together.'

The old man laughed: a horrifying performance, had there been anybody but the fish there to see. Uncle Charlie laughing was like somebody dying from asphyxiation.

'You know we're going to Proxima Centauri now, Uncle Charlie?' said the caller.

Uncle Charlie seemed to think this was some kind of joke. 'Hee-

hee-hee!' he squeaked, tempestuously. 'You'll be the death of me, man . . .'

'Oh, I hardly think so, uncle,' said his caller urbanely.

The geriatric squinted. 'You still want your stuff, Grant?' he asked, with a silly smile on his reptilian face. 'You ain't calling to tell me you don't want your stuff any more?'

The unseen caller tutted indulgently, which made Uncle Charlie laugh until his lung meter shivered into the red.

'I'm thinking of rationalizing your situation there, uncle,' said the man Uncle Charlie called Grant. 'I think we can do much better for you now, things being as they are.'

Explanations were not forthcoming. The two men patently knew each other of old, and between such intimates much may be conveyed by nuance, without a definite attributable word.

The conversation over, the old man took several minutes to notice he was still holding the bottle in his dead hand. When he did, slowly, painstakingly, he unscrewed the cap, and withdrew the glass dropper. Tilting his head back he lifted the dropper in his right hand, steadily, carefully. There was the soft whine of servos as his chair adjusted to his new position.

With tremulous concentration the old man dispensed one drop of colourless fluid into his left eye, then one into his right. He shut both eyes tight and sucked air through his teeth.

Motors whined again as the silver brace on the old man's left forearm rose off the rim of his chair on some sort of repeller field. It wiped the back of his left hand slowly across his eyes.

'Good stuff,' the old man muttered to himself.

It was a ritual response, automatic as a cleric's grace after food, reinforced by a century of repetition. If you had asked him, Grant's Uncle Charlie probably would not have known he had spoken.

The antiquated relic rubbed the glass of the tank with his fingertip, trying to attract the fish. 'Tweet, tweet,' he mumbled.

The fish veered slowly to and fro, ignoring him. Perhaps they were unaware of him. Perhaps he was like God, immanent, omnipotent in the room, but invisible to the fish. 'The hand that feeds,' he said.

The old man put the dropper slowly back into the brown glass bottle. Determinedly he pressed his thumb and fingers together again, flattening the rubber bulb.

The chair whirred again, tilting him forward.

Anchoring his left arm, the old man reached out over the tank with the dropper in his good right hand.

A drop of colourless fluid splashed into the water.

For a moment, nothing happened. Then one of the fish, the red one, flapped. It did not stop, but flapped harder. It seemed to be in some distress. The blue one swam towards it, and around it in a tight circle.

Then the two fish flew at each other. They began to fight. They fought with their mouths, tearing at each other's fins.

The old man watched in smiling rapture. His right hand wavered, as if pointing out the fish to some invisible witness. His lips moved, but he did not speak.

In the water the fight rolled and flared, scarlet red and kingfisher blue tumbling over and over and round and round like scraps of Chinese silk in the clear water. Through the haze of incense a sharp stink began to rise in the room.

At last one fish, the red one, sank exhausted to the bottom. It lay there flopping feebly. Tiny streamers of blood, like transparent tendrils of red weed, drifted up from its ragged fins. The blue fish continued to blunder about the tank, dazed or indifferent.

The old man grinned wide. His teeth were made of metal. He pressed a button on the arm of his chair.

Along the hallway, down the stairs and across the landing, two nurses sat at a table counting pills. They were talking about *Sharp Practice*, an AV hospital drama that was on every day, in the 'afternoon'. Because of the shift arrangements here, there was always someone who had missed an episode and needed to find out what had happened.

'So what's Marilyn going to do,' the first nurse asked, 'about Clive?'

'She told her mother,' said the second nurse, 'and she said she's very fond of him and everything, but she really doesn't think she can marry him.'

'That's a shame,' said the first nurse. She thought Clive was really gorgeous. She would have leapt at the chance to look after the noble, haunted Clive and his autistic daughter.

The second nurse packed pills into a triangle and tipped them into a plastic phial, which she capped. 'Well,' she said, 'Marilyn might be just saying that. She might be just saying it because it's her mother.'

Their own mothers were not on board. They had not spoken to them for eighteen subjective months now. They did not know that they would never speak to them again. The first nurse went rattling on without a pause. 'But what about Clive and the woman with the broken arm, you know, the skiing accident?'

'Oh, she's in a coma,' said the second nurse. 'Didn't you know? She had her op, and she still hasn't come round. And now Clive is feeling really guilty. And Dr Marshall is on his back because he was the one that took the decision, after the car crash –'

'What car crash?' asked the first nurse.

At that moment the old man in Suite 5 pressed his button.

In the dispensary no signal sounded, but jerkily the second nurse put down her phial of pills and got to her feet, scraping her chair backwards across the plastic floor. 'Hell,' she said, and seemed as if she would have said more, could she have found the voice. Passing her colleague, who said nothing herself but carried on counting pills, the second nurse, whose name was Rix, left the room.

Nurse Rix crossed the landing and climbed the stairs. Her starched white skirt swishing, she went down the hallway where the patients lived. She passed Suite 1, where Consuela had stopped banging her foot against the wall and started moaning about Frankie again. She passed Suite 2, where Gloria would be eating. Whatever else was happening, Gloria would be eating. She would undoubtedly be in need of cleaning up again; but Nurse Rix was unable to take care of that at the moment.

Nurse Rix passed Suite 3, where the door was open. Another of her remaining colleagues was inside, changing Mr Gules's hook-ups. Nurse Rix was well aware she could have done with a hand; but she was not free to give her one.

Nurse Rix passed Suite 4. Here too, the door was open. Jammed in the doorway, Kathleen Beaufort sat, fast asleep. Her Wisp slept too, coiled in her lap.

Kathleen had been pulling at her cardigan again, picking at the wool and unravelling it. She had started on the other cuff now, Nurse Rix noticed. Kathleen knew space, and knew the station was now in flight. She hated her lovely rooms and kept trying to escape by dragging her chair into the hall; but her medication had taken hold and she slept where she sat. At another time Nurse Rix would have put her back to bed among the roses; but Nurse Rix had a prior duty.

Now Nurse Rix arrived at the door of Suite 5. This door, as always, was firmly closed.

She rang the bell.

The door whizzed open.

Inside Suite 5 the aged, aged man sat slumped forward in his mobile chair, staring into the massed flames of a dozen candles.

Nurse Rix focused her will and shouted in his ear. 'Uncle Charlie – music – could you turn it – down, please.'

The old man's braced left arm shot out, trapping the nurse. His good right hand fondled her bottom.

Nurse Rix stood with her legs clamped together, leaning stiffly forward, as if to dissociate herself from his invasion. 'Music,' she shouted again. 'You'll – wake Kathleen.'

The old man showed her his metal teeth. There was instant, resounding silence.

'Did I send for you?' he asked the nurse. His voice was high, nasal and slurred.

'Yes, Uncle Charlie. You know you did.'

'Right . . . Right . . .' The old man swayed his head, making his necklaces stir and rattle softly. 'The fish fell over, nurse,' he said.

His chair spun him back to face the aquarium.

'Another one, Uncle Charlie?' said the nurse. She had lost count of the fish that had died in that tank.

Uncle Charlie cackled.

Her implant took Nurse Rix across the room. It made her plunge her hand in the tank and pull out the dead fish. It turned her to face him.

Her lips worked, like a primitive android's. 'Where – would – you – like – me – to – put – it?' she asked. The words came separately from her like beads on a wire.

Uncle Charlie laughed and laughed. His personal plumbing zipped and bubbled with moist glee. 'She always looks as though she'd like to do me in,' he told the blue fish. 'It's like, heavy . . .' He spoke in a squeaky voice. 'What? What? Can't get into that scene at all.' He cackled again, rocking in his chair.

'You talk a lot of rubbish, Uncle Charlie,' said the nurse tonelessly. 'We're all very fond of you here. We're all your friends.'

Uncle Charlie let her put the dead fish in the disposal. He pressed his face to the side of the tank where the survivor swam tirelessly round and round, bumping against the glass. 'Pisces, right?' he murmured, sniggering and shaking a bony finger. 'Bad karma . . .'

The door whizzed open again and a Vespan woman came in, ducking her enormous head. She plodded into the room, her white coat swaying around her.

'Good morning, Doctor Irsk,' said the nurse.

The doctor's voice was deep and sad. 'Good morning, nurse,' she said. 'Good morning, Uncle Charlie.'

Uncle Charlie snorted. His floppy old mouth worked as if he was tasting something disgusting. The music came on again, at the same volume as before.

Dr Irsk took a wand out of her pocket, pointed it at Uncle Charlie's AV and silenced it. She checked his blood pressure, directing the nurse to adjust an enzyme valve too small for her great flippers. 'Good, good today,' she boomed, puffing up her pouches and rolling her eyes. 'Now a visitor going come up to you, Uncle Charlie,' she announced.

Uncle Charlie's visitor was the big man who had come to see him once or twice before. He was very big, and his clothes made him look even bigger. He was wearing baggy drawstring trousers with random rainbow patterns all over them like a child's finger-painting, a blue shirt with pink roses on and a drape jacket that looked as if it had been made out of a pair of curtains. He wore a black beard and a ponytail, which he continually preened. He said, 'Hello, Uncle Charlie. How are you keeping?'

Uncle Charlie was glad to see him. 'Dog! Right!' He laughed soundlessly. 'Proxima Centauri!' he said, as if it were the punchline to a shared joke.

The man called Dog sat on the arm of a chair. His great thigh flattened like the ham of a cow. He cocked an eyebrow at the nurse and the doctor.

'Don't gone get him all excited,' warned Dr Irsk.

'Ooh, tell that to her,' said Uncle Charlie, leering at the departing nurse.

The doctor left too, and the door closed. Then Uncle Charlie's visitor leaned towards him, examining him.

The old man's pupils were enormous. His nostrils were like two black tunnels, his skin a map of smashed capillaries. His plastic lungs were pumping away merrily. The fluids running in and out of his body were clear and bright. He might live another hundred years.

The man called Dog fumbled his big hand in the pocket of his vivid jacket and pulled out a transparent plastic wallet with what looked like a large number of credit chips in it.

'What the people need, basically, Uncle Charlie,' he confided, 'at this moment in time, at this precise moment in time, is some nice drugs.'

Uncle Charlie gave a sly smile, as though he had caught his visitor out in an absurdity. He spoke in a soft and silly voice. 'You don't need drugs, Dog,' he said.

Dog rolled his formidable shoulders. 'Speak for yourself,' he said truculently.

'No, man,' whined the ancient patient, 'you don't get it. Dig: everything is like that already.'

He spoke as if revealing a principle of the universe. There was a brief pause before Dog said indulgently: 'Like what, Uncle Charlie?'

'Like – everything,' declared the aged one, and he grinned his inane metallic grin. 'Look,' he said, rolling up to the fish tank. 'Watch this, Dog. You'll like this, it's good.'

9

'The purpose of marriage,' said the Good Doctor, holding his frothing glass up to the golden light, 'is procreation. The progenerative union of opposites.'

'The umbrella and the sewing machine,' mused the Last Poet. 'Doolittle and Higgins. The Owl and the Pussycat.'

The Best Judge lay back in his chair. 'Dialectic,' he stated solemnly. 'Prosecution, defence.' He nodded at them round the table, beneath which he rather felt he might be slowly slipping. 'Thesis, antisithith. Tithisith.' The Judge waved his hand in the air, trying to conjure the words from his mouth. 'Sin,' he managed, with a puzzled hiccough.

The Trivia philosophers were having a lovely time. They had

orchids in their beards and champagne in their bellies. There was nothing like a nice wedding, even if it was only Mavis's.

'Which one is Mavis, again?' asked the Last Poet.

'You know,' said the Best Judge. 'The one with the Wisp.'

'Sits over there.' Mavis Forestall, a regular, had a favourite booth near the bar, where she liked to sit swapping mordant comments with her airborne pet. Leaning to point to it, the Good Doctor almost went head over heels, and had to be hauled back into his seat by his companions.

The groom, a hunky mech called Sven, was forgiven his uninteresting provenance, his shiny green suit, his muscles. 'He's obviously fabulous in bed,' imagined the Last Poet.

'Certainly nothing between the ears,' decided the Best Judge.

'The stimulation,' said the Good Doctor, 'of procreation.'

'Needs no stimulus,' the Best Judge opined, looking at the children who were running in and out of the tables, bumping into one another and squabbling. 'Carries on regardless.'

The Captain was to conduct the ceremony, there in the bar. The whole place was decorated with flowers! Rory kept peering resentfully up at them as though he thought they might drop horrible insects down the neck of his polo shirt.

It had been Mavis's idea, of course. Mavis was in pink, a long pink satin sheath dress that made her look, as the Good Doctor had said several times already, like a stick of peppermint rock. Her mouth was even pinker and sweeter than her dress, and she and her cronies had been up since half-past four doing her hair. 'Goddess divine,' drawled the Last Poet.

The goddess's chosen one was grinning this way and that, chewing gum, accepting the congratulations of people he had never seen before.

'Stimulus ubiquitous,' said the Best Judge, leering at the bridesmaids. 'Matrimony is acquiescence,' he said, approximately.

'The finishing touch,' said the Last Poet. 'The gilt on the gingerbread.'

'On the lily,' said the Good Doctor, shaking his head.

The Last Poet sat up straighter. 'The gingerbread,' he asseverated.

The Best Judge judged. 'The lily and the gingerbread,' he declared, magnanimously.

'The Puss and the Alleycat,' supposed the Good Doctor, who had forgotten what they were talking about. 'The bride and the bridegroom . . .'

His companions raised their glasses. 'The bride and bridegroom!'

There seemed to be people here of every shape and size, people from every district, all the potted towns of Plenty. Eeb the Altecean, Mavis's maid of honour, was giving the younger bridesmaids piggyback rides, two at a time, up and down the stairs. Dagobert Moon was here in his fur coat, and his inseparable companion Godfrey Bills in his long fawn mac. No one was gladder than Mr Moon to be out from under the insipid reign of Capella. He had accumulated all the known printed pornography on board and controlled its distribution from a cave above Prosperity. Pale, thoughtful Mr Bills had brought some magazines along in plastic bags, under his coat, in the capacity of marital aids.

The women from Little Foxbourne, not usually seen on these premises, were here in their new hats, and busy passing comments. 'Where did she get that dress?' asked Mrs Overhead.

'Filene's basement,' said Mrs Goodself, with the air of one who knows.

Natalie Shoe held her left elbow in her right hand. 'This whole ship is a basement if you ask me . . .' she remarked to her glum-looking husband.

The Window was showing an infinite field of wheat streaming past, like the view from a crop-spraying helicopter spiralling through a cereal orbital. Meanwhile Mavis's Wisp was humming the Wedding March in a high, irritating whine. Eeb trumpeted and the Best Man flapped at the Wisp with his gloves, but it avoided them easily and farted in his face. Mavis wriggled and laughed fit to burst a seam. Everybody was pressing drinks on Sven, who was not refusing them.

Rory stood behind his bar like a castellan behind his battlements. 'It'll end in tears,' he predicted. 'All this fuss and palaver.'

The Captain clapped him on the shoulder. 'Just keep running that bill, Rory,' she told him. The dour landlord seemed unmoved. He ate another handful of cheese and onion crisps.

Tabitha Jute had never officiated at a wedding before. It was well within her powers, she reckoned. She had had a toot of crystal before she came, just to make sure she would enjoy the proceedings. She wore her black coat open, pinstripe trousers, and a black and gold waistcoat with nothing under it. There was a peaked cap with gold braid jammed down on her bushy head.

She leaned against the bar, listening to whoever managed to squeeze their way past Kenny and through to her. One arm stayed round Saskia Zodiac, the other hoisted her invariable pint of beer. Saskia was saying little, preferring to fold the cocktail napkins into tiny origami birds and animals and give them away to little children. Occasionally she would glance over at Mr Bills, high-shouldered and preoccupied among the festivities. Perhaps he reminded her of someone.

Zoe Primrose was wearing a headset, keeping in touch with the bridge. At the same time she was surveying the crowd, judging its temperament as one might judge the speed of a river before diving in. 'Do you think it might be time, Captain?' she said at last.

The Captain had to cup her ear to hear her amid the noise. Someone was playing peals of church bells on a keyboard and snatches of ribald song kept breaking out.

'You might as well do it,' Saskia said, 'before everybody gets too drunk.' She herself was eating pecans at a great rate but drinking nothing, toying with the same small blackcurrant cordial she had had since they arrived. Her stack of napkins had run out and the children were beginning to fight. Mr and Mrs Shoe's little daughter Morgan had been at the sherry and was reeling around in circles, looking flushed and giddy.

The Captain inspected the principals. Mavis was talking loudly, holding another cigarette for the Wisp to light for her. Separated from her by the crowd, Sven had his collar up and his hands in his pockets, entertaining a knot of admiring bridesmaids.

Letting go of Saskia Zodiac, Captain Jute got Zoe to get Sven's attention, though he was no distance away. 'Here,' she said when he turned to look at her. 'Come here.' She reached out and pulled him to her, reeling him in with an arm around his shoulders.

'Oh my god, it's showtime,' bellowed Mavis as she came stumbling after. People clapped and hooted.

Kenny began to clear a circle around the three of them. Saskia slipped up onto the bar and sat there cross-legged. Rory eyed her suspiciously. The Wisp hovered, holding Mavis's glass and cigarette. 'Doesn't she look happy?' it squeaked.

'I suppose she is,' said the acrobat, remotely.

'Of course she's happy,' said Rory with some energy. 'She's pissed. Look at her,' he said, while the keyboard sounded a thrilling fanfare.

In the Window, the golden sea of grain streamed on, exhilarating, dizzying in the sheer breadth of its fecundity.

The Captain was still leaning against the bar. She had her arm round Sven. She looked at Mavis. She said: 'You want him?'

Mavis bent at the knees and waist. She clenched her fists and made pumping motions with her elbows. 'Yes!' she said throatily. 'Yes! Yes! Yes!'

The Captain gave the groom a sloppy shove in her direction. 'You got him,' she said.

Mavis screeched, plastered herself to Sven and jammed his mouth with her own. Poppies suddenly sprouted amid the wheat. The crowd were laughing, some protesting. The Little Foxbourne contingent tutted, tapping their fingers on the buttons of their coats. With an air of one who senses he has suffered a slight, the Best Man started to make his speech, waving the ring about. What had happened to the ceremony? 'That's it,' said the Captain, smiling fiercely. She picked up her pint and drained it, and ordered another.

'Acquiescent enough for you, are they?' the Good Doctor asked the Best Judge, laughing. The Best Judge muttered, not opening his eyes.

'A man with a maid,' said the Last Poet. He was watching the grappling Mavis and Sven, framing them with his thumbs and index fingers. The Wisp swooped into the shot, to hover above their combined heads like an over-obvious symbol. 'And cyborganic Cupid,' said the Poet, and he put his cigarette in his mouth and patted his pockets at random for a pencil.

Complaints were growing more vehement as it became clear the Captain did not intend to say anything more. Tabitha threw back her head. She shouted: 'What do you expect, Shakespeare?'

People shouted back 'Yes!' and 'Speech!' and 'Dearly beloved, we are gathered together –!'

Captain Jute shook her head slow and hard. Her cap fell off.

Her stance tantalized them. They shouted encouragements at her, mixed with boozy derision. Mavis, coming out of the clinch, realized something was happening, or rather not happening, and she joined in with the slow handclap.

Captain Jute folded her arms. She grinned at the discontented celebrants. She let their blandishments and abuse break over her. She shook her head again, slowly and emphatically, narrowing her eyes. Morgan Shoe was off in a corner, being sick. The Wisp was circling the premises like a remote attack module. Sven was stamping his foot and whistling through his fingers, with Mavis wrapped around him, writhing against him from behind. The noise was becoming intense. Rory took a J-cloth and wiped the bar with firm, demonstrative strokes.

Then just as the protest was peaking, the first souls about to decide she really meant it and move to console themselves with a refill, Tabitha whipped out her harmonica and blew a wild raw blues riff.

The cheers were uproarious. The Wisp screeched like a country fiddle and the keyboard started to honk, and they were off.

They kept it up for a couple of hours, playing all sorts, *Wild Turkey Stomp* and *Stabilizer* and *Seven Nights Drunk*. Godfrey Bills danced with the best of them, waving his hands at the ceiling, while Dagobert Moon sat at a table and scowled. 'It's impossible to hold a sensible conversation!' the Good Doctor objected through the din to the Best Judge, not noticing his companion had fallen asleep.

The churches on board were annoyed that none of them had been asked to solemnize the wedding. Uninvited, one turned up, in the person of Father Le Coq. In his embroidered waistcoat and carbuncular rings he stalked about, uttering pronouncements of doom.

'Mistress Satan, how does she do,' he growled in his most gorgeous, most luscious tones. 'She do most nicely, missy, thank you!'

One of the bridesmaids squealed as he pinned her with his eye. 'You ask me, my sister, who do I mean by Mistress Satan? Who do I mean?'

He rolled his glance around the thinning crowd, frowning dubiously at the Wisp, which put out its tiny pointed tongue. 'Who do I mean, I mean nobody but Mistress Mystery, sisters, runnin' here, scurryin' there with her big black bag. Whoever seen her? Have you? You? You, sister, you? No?'

Le Coq shook his gleaming bald head, pantomiming dumb innocence. 'Nobody seen her! Nobody! Because that Mistress Mystery Woman ain't nobody but Mistress Devil, sisters, the Whore of Babylon, the Unseen Enemy! I tell you, my sisters, that Devil Woman is the enemy of us all, because she is the enemy of Mother Mary and all the Holy Saints of Capella! Now this is the Rooster telling you!'

The bridesmaids clustered round him, teasing him, stroking his greasy jacket, touching his face, cooing. Emerging from their fingers the Rooster's mouth opened wide. 'Brothers and sisters, you stand in need of salvation! Or your immortal souls will be stole by the lady with the big black bag!'

Evangelists and sales people had never been welcome in Rory's establishment. He folded his fleshy arms on the bar and stuck out his bottom lip. 'I don't think I want your kind in here,' he said loudly.

Le Coq pranced towards him, making a long step forward and bringing his hips down low. He stuck out his arm, pointing at the array of beer pumps. 'Mr Landlord, stop up your barrels! Put the cap on tight on your gin and your rum and your whisky . . .' He pronounced the names of the spirits with precision and hate. He waved his big black finger. 'Fill no more glasses I say, Mr Landlord, until you can fill them with the Wine of Brother Jesus, that intoxicates not the body but fills the spirit with inspiration and new heart!'

Now he was up towering amid the women, his long arms around their shoulders. His antique spectacles flashed, his grin was electric, brilliant.

Rory was unimpressed. 'Go on, get out of it,' he said.

The Captain sat at her table, laughing. She stroked Saskia's arm. 'He's great, isn't he?'

Saskia Zodiac seemed unamused. She propped her long chin on her hand. She asked Captain Jute: 'And what do you think about this Mystery Woman?'

The Captain took a drink. 'People should keep their hallucinations to themselves,' she told her consort.

Of course, the preacher overheard her. He turned, shaking his bracelets, ignoring the hunched shoulders and bare teeth of Kenny the Thrant, the gestures of Zoe Primrose, tapping urgently at her headset. The Rooster hopped from foot to foot like a dervish, his long mauve jacket puffing out scents of incense and old blood.

'Captain, turn this ship about! You are heading onto the rocks of de-struction and deva-station! You lead us all in peril of our souls! Turn again to the holy light of Capella, that shines in the heavens to call us home –'

Le Coq waved at the smoke-stained ceiling of the Trivia as though that baleful star had suddenly become visible through the floral decorations. 'Sistren, brethren –' His big hands embraced the bridesmaids, drew them rustling together. 'Capella will forgive you, children, she calls you . . .'

Somebody put a wreath of flowers about his neck. They seized the Rooster by the arms, gave him a plastic coconut, and whirled him off in a drunken conga, across the wine-drenched floor and out into Green Lantern Road. The last they saw of him he was calling for Holy Cola.

And so the throng dispersed, scattering to favourite recreations, or to bed, or both. The philosophers withdrew in reasonable order, Poet and Doctor supporting the insensible Judge. Rory held the door for them, bidding them a stern farewell as they decanted themselves into the street. The Last Poet tried to kiss him and almost got a kick in the backside. Rory was always banning those three, and they were always crawling back in.

The portly landlord stood, arms folded, and surveyed the lucrative wreckage of his domain. He saw the Captain sitting next to Sven, her face close to his. He saw her skinny girlfriend come drifting past. 'Such jollity,' she said. Rory looked at her uncertainly, her pale brow, her distant eyes. She was speaking to the Captain's p.a., getting her to call the Captain's car.

Tabitha Jute had forgotten the huge starship, the epic trek to Proxima; the politics and peacekeeping. In her mind, she was back in the old days, nursing a superannuated barge from dock to dock. 'I bet you could tune a girl's jets for her,' she told the muscular mechanic.

Sven stood with his shoulders back, his thumbs in his belt loops, his hands like two brackets supporting the payload in the front of his trousers. 'Always carry all my own tools,' he purred. Sven was doing some forgetting of his own.

The remaining spectators whooped and cheered as Captain Jute put a hand on the bridegroom's chest, leaned forward and kissed him on the mouth.

'Oh dear oh Lord,' said Rory.

The Captain's hands roved the slopes of Sven's pectorals. She had her knee on his chair, between his legs. She bore down into the kiss as if it were a championship event, and she the people's favourite.

Sven's bride was laughing shrilly. She stood with her knees together and her feet apart, as far apart as the peppermint rock dress would permit. She leaned forward with her right hand spread stiffly across her lap and her left beating the air with helpless laughter. Someone gave her the last of the champagne and put an arm round her shoulders, coaxing her away. The Wisp bobbed after his mistress like a tiny, ugly balloon.

Saskia Zodiac watched, abstractedly, from the door, and thought about her brother. She thought how he would have enjoyed the whole event. He would have had some quick, cruel comment to make on it, articulating their feelings for her.

Captain Jute lifted her face from gnawing Sven's and saw Saskia standing like a sentinel beside the door. 'Do you want some?' she asked her friend. 'No? I'll see you later, then, ah!' she shrieked, as Sven thrust his hand inside her waistcoat and made a very public, and emphatic, grab. She grappled with him in return. Thus entwined, attended by mirthful acolytes, they tottered out to the car.

Saskia touched her lips with the tips of her fingers. She was considering the possibility of randomizing Mogul's vocabulary again, having stabilized it now beyond recognizability into, perhaps, predictability.

The preoccupied acrobat disappeared with her usual suddenness, and no one saw her go.

It was not the end of the day's drama. There were people waiting outside the Captain's apartment, human men and women, some with children. They were dressed in clean pastel leisure suits, safety helmets, elbow and kneepads. There must have been a dozen of them. They were blocking the gate.

Kenny loped over to check them out. 'Who are those bozos?' said Sven, reaching for the door button.

'You stay here,' the Captain told him, pressing his thigh.

She put on her cap, got out and confronted the group. 'Yes?'

They were angry, upset. 'I don't know if you're interested, Captain,' said a heavy, white-haired man with energetic sarcasm, 'but they're killing kids now, down in that Havoc Cavern.'

There was a story about a battlegame, people fighting with real weapons. 'We don't mind if they kill each other,' said a woman. 'But my sister's boy is dead.'

The man stood there with his fists clenched, the picture of right-eous helplessness. He looked like a hippopotamus suddenly. They all looked like hippopotamuses. Tabitha felt herself strobing.

'If you don't want them to go down there, you shouldn't let them,' she said. God, if her seventeen-year-old self could hear her now.

'We can't keep them away!' said the woman.

'That's not my fault,' said Captain Jute. They were all around her, the good citizens, in her face. She climbed on the bonnet of the car. 'Look, I'm sorry about the kid,' she told them. 'But this is Plenty! It's dangerous! I told you when we left it would be dangerous. You have to look after yourselves here! I can't do it for you.'

There was no point. If they hadn't understood it yet, they never would. They would go on complaining whatever you did, expecting the universe to make exceptions for them, demanding to be protected from alien germs, from their neighbours, from their own children. 'Oh, get out of here!' she told them. 'Go on!'

They all started at once then. Captain Jute stopped listening. She stepped up onto the roof of the car. 'Kenny,' she said.

While Kenny did his job she stood there on the car watching, her feet apart, her left hand on her hip, clenched into a fist.

When the last protester was finally dislodged from her entrance and chased away, the Captain climbed down. She said to Soi: 'If they're going to start doing things like this, we're going to have to get some help.'

Kenny bounded up, grinning, showing his navy blue tongue. Captain Jute ruffled his fur in congratulation. He wore it long now, just like her.

Soi opened Sven's door for him. He got out, squinting. 'What's that Havoc place?' he asked them. 'That sounds like a good place.' He looked appreciatively into the courtyard, taking in the fountain, the trees. 'Hey, this is a really nice place too,' he said, and put his hands in his pockets.

Captain Jute took them out again for him. She had a use for them.

Eighteen levels below Eden Dale Dome, in an unnamed, unused chamber, Xtasca's investigations came to a crux. All the principal conductive pathways they could trace seemed to convene here. It was an obvious com control chamber. They were preparing it for conversion, lining up net nodes, linking in the bridge, Alice, CB and

AV channels and surveillance cameras. Red ducts would carry power cables, blue or grey ones coms.

The chamber was hot, and still smelled distinctly of old fire. The floor was gritty, uneven, running with a thin film of water. Tall islands of strap metal shelving stood here and there, overflowing with tools and components. A pick-up hoverplat loaded with a pneumatic drill and a bank of laser combs stood parked next to a low yellow pump truck. They looked like battered metal fauna come to drink at the waterhole.

Captain Gillespie looked up through the growing maze of ducts and chainlink fencing. High overhead the pink vaults were being measured for tap grids. Marbled and glistening, the unshielded analogue looked oddly like raw flesh. Xtasca the Cherub floated there, among the scaffolding.

No one else was around. Some of Xtasca's people had gone to get another pump; others were at lunch, or goofing off somewhere, racing buggies over Shangri-La.

'I REMEMBER MUSIC,' murmured Alice. There were speakers, but no cameras.

'Frasque modulations,' Xtasca's prim little voice came floating down. 'Amplitude seventeen.'

Dodger Gillespie had once seen a Frasque close to, at Byzantium Earthside. It had looked less like an imperialistic spacefarer than a withered thorn tree. It was a naked four-armed scarecrow, three metres tall, made of knobbly, roughly bundled twigs. She had watched it skate across the dock with the swiftness of some horrible overgrown insect; seen its mouth full of teeth like black pegs, seeping a constant sappy drool.

'Fifth-layer deposits show highest activity,' observed the Cherub to the ship.

'OLD MEMORY.'

'Pre-War?'

'HIVE ORGANIZATION. BASIC WORK AND SURVIVAL ROUTINES. MAINTENANCE PROCEDURES,' suggested Alice.

It was hard to believe she had once been a Bergen Kobold persona.

Captain Gillespie exhaled a thin stream of smoke and ground her fag end underfoot. She did not really know why she was here. Protocol was, you never went on another pilot's bridge without invitation. Did that apply, though, this far out? She felt there was another, deeper reluctance that made her not want to hang about up there, where the science of navigation sublimed into pure maths. Most of what the Cherub said went over her head, granted, but at least it seemed to be paying attention. And it had some very tasty staff.

High above she saw light glint off silver chrome as Xtasca inserted its tail thoughtfully in a crevice in the wall. 'Can you feel anything when I do this?'

Long seconds passed.

'A SORT OF – TICKLE . . .' said Alice.

Captain Gillespie saw a pair of butterflies come tumbling out of nowhere, blown on some sternward zephyr. They were brown as cocoa, with little spots of pale butter. Delicate flimsy petals, they danced away among the shelf islands. She put her head around the corner to watch them longer. There was a figure there in a long black leather coat with the collar turned up, taking something off a shelf.

Dodger shouted in surprise.

There was a flash of a smooth pale brown face, a split second of startlement; then the intruder took to her heels.

She ran after, disoriented, knocking into the shelves, scattering bits of equipment. She had a name on her lips, but her tongue refused it. She ran for the gate, cursing as the fugitive launched herself over the fence. God, the girl was slippery.

She chased her out of the chamber, into an overgrown tunnel. Unseen branches slapped her in the face. There was the sound of receding footsteps, quick, nimble. The echoes made them seem to come from all around.

Something zipped past her at speed in mid-air: Xtasca on her saucer. Its slipstream blew dirt in Dodger's eyes. Snagged by trailing shoots she followed, plunging on.

The Cherub was at the next junction, sitting in mid-air with its hands hung out in front of it like a helpless infant looking for a towel. It didn't know which way to turn.

'You go that way, I'll try down here!' Dodger shouted. She didn't know if the Cherub heard, or would take any notice. She ran on for a way, but the tunnels narrowed and there was nothing, no one. The only sound was laughter: an AV soundtrack, leaking through a crevice from civilization.

Captain Gillespie went back to the big cave and leaned on the wall, sweating, breathing hard. In a moment Xtasca arrived from another direction, alone. Its little red eyes glowed angrily in the darkness.

Xtasca checked the shelves. 'There was a binary modulation meter here,' she said. 'It's gone.'

'Yeah, well.' Dodger started to roll herself a cigarette. 'So's she.' She made it sound final; as though there was no point in even talking about it.

The Cherub was unscrewing her tail and screwing in another. Dodger knew by now she was not an artifact that would ever take a hint.

'Bollocks,' she said. It was not clear whether it was an expression of rejection or resignation. 'Did you see her, Alice?' she asked loudly.

'SEE WHO, CAPTAIN GILLESPIE?' replied the blind persona.

The Cherub's new tail was banded steel flex. It flexed, supporting a terminal probe that, once activated, gave out a deep green glow. Xtasca swept the probe in precise quartering arcs across the wet floor.

Dodger clucked her tongue, impressed.

In the green light a footprint shone, lemon yellow. Ahead there was another. Together the space pilot and the Cherub followed them, back into the tunnels.

The trail continued. Here were toeprints only, where the thief had crept beneath the giant crabvine. There was a clear print, pointing under a low archway. The pursuers scrambled through, and clambered down into another cave.

There were more footprints there, running along a gnarled ridge of matrix like the root of an ancient tree. And then they disappeared. One moment they were there; the next they had faded, leaving only the submarine glow of the probe.

Lights flashed on the Cherub's saucer, whirling dizzyingly around like a Catherine wheel.

'What's going on?'

'It's all gone,' said the Cherub. The lights stabilized, angular and glittering.

'What's gone?'

'All her data, completely erased. Without trace.' The Cherub's voice was a flat whirr. 'How bizarre.'

Captain Gillespie looked around, but there were fifty possible holes by which the intruder could have fled, and that was only the ones you could see. Why did she feel relieved?

On the way back into the chamber the little black space creature rode with its large head bent forward, pondering furiously. Its red eyes flickered as its supercharged brain toiled, making unguessable calculations.

'She was there,' it said, the sibilants buzzing. 'She was audible. The air was disturbed. Her mass registered, her heat index was distinct.'

Dodger Gillespie pulled out her pouch of makings.

'You saw her, though, eh,' she said. She chewed her lip, thinking of the glimpse she had had: the crescent of coffee-coloured cheek, the thick mass of curly black hair. Necklaces of what looked like circuit components, threaded on wire.

The Cherub floated unexpectedly close. The mirror sheen of its chubby gut reflected Dodger's disconcerted expression.

'I must get on with my work,' it whispered.

'Search over, then?' asked Dodger Gillespie; but it was already gone.

She climbed back up to Glory Cut to see if anyone was about. The road was deserted, all the lights out.

Captain Gillespie smoked her cigarette. She wondered about hallucinations, about the things you started to see if you stared out into space too long.

A breeze stirred in the tunnel, picking up dust and debris. She flicked her lighter at a poster on the coarse matrix wall. BIG FIGHT, it said. HAPPY VALLEY MO-LOK V. TUGPIT TIGER. The bout was some weeks off, yet the paper was already parched and grimy.

Dodger Gillespie pocketed her lighter. Still pondering, she gazed absently into the darkness. There was only blackness and hot, heavy air; then the sound of an engine, and a curved shape, black against black: a bend in the tunnel ahead, becoming visible as light flowed slowly round it, growing, strengthening, picking out more and more of the tunnel wall.

A ghostly rattle of boogie came echoing to her as a lone pick-up jolted into view, headlights on full beam. It was some of Xtasca's crew returning with the big pump. When they saw her standing at the side of the tunnel they sounded the horn, revved the engine, turned the music up full blast.

'Dodger!'

'Captain D!'

Dodger plucked out her roll-up, hiding an unwilling smirk. 'Silly buggers,' she muttered.

She went out into the middle of the road and stood there with her hands in her pockets, her shoulders hunched, her face averted in mock pain from the onrushing lights. There were stars out there somewhere, gigantic, burning, dancing an ancient stately dance with their delicate consorts of rock and gas and verdure and ocean, Proxima and Palernia and who knew how many others? Captain Gillespie imagined them shining, twinkling in expectation. Within a year or so, subjective, the hot thick mind-numbing hyperspatial fog would clear, and the windows of the Earth Room fill with the light of a new sun.

Till then there was nothing else, really, that mattered a toss.

PART TWO

The Fruit of Experience

1

The story continues, as the journey continued. On we swept, through the non-existent into the unknown. We were so far beyond the mundane realm we hardly felt its call upon us.

There is, in every long journey, this limbo – 'neither here nor there' – when the original prevailing reality fails. The departure can no longer be called to mind, while the destination remains too far off to detect. 'Entering Oklahoma,' I once heard one of the Sanczau pilots call it.

He had crossed the North American continent, on Earth, several times by land. In the middle, he said, were plains so empty every tree you see is a surprise; any smudge of distant cattle an event. 'Entering Oklahoma.' The coast you have left behind is lost in a muddle of disorientation, tangled cities and poor sleep. The purple mountains whose appearance will herald your arrival are beyond the horizon. You drive all day and all night, and dawn still does not disclose them. The pneumatic tyres hum, the black tarmac road rolls beneath you, other vehicles pass constantly, wheeled ones like your own; but your surroundings cease to signify anything but your own endurance.

How much worse the plight of our star voyagers, living like beetles in a rock, seeing nothing but their own unvarying décor, month after month, year after subjective year. On a planetary surface, or any conventional Euclidian plane, the traveller uses space to measure time: the length of shadows; stops on a route; hours between stations. In the interstices of physical structure accessed by the grammatical geometries of Frasque particle syntax, there is no space, so nothing to see at all. Outside Plenty was only the drab lifeless hull of the ship itself, a prohibitive environment for even the most ironical of parties, the most unambitious of strolls, the most clandestine of assignations.

2

The Administrative Council of the Good Ship Plenty now included representatives, volunteered or co-opted, from most of the principal districts, businesses and other interest groups aboard. Captain Jute arrived late for the Wednesday plenary, and Zoe Primrose, relinquishing the chair, filled her in. A spokeswoman from Technicians and Mechanics was just finishing her update on the Integration, which was the popular name for what Xtasca the Cherub was apparently trying to achieve: all onboard circuits, installed and inbuilt, all coms and bridge and life support, connected into one megasystem. 'Total synergy by landfall,' the woman promised, her face alight with millenarian rapture.

There were dozens of questions. A sharp-faced young white man started asking about what he called 'security advantages'. 'So much of what happens on this ship isn't properly monitored,' he announced, speaking directly to the Captain. 'People could get hurt. When things aren't organized properly, that's when people get hurt. Some of the people on this ship are asking for trouble.'

She remembered this one. His name was Rykov. An alumnus of HighGround, the Eladeldi Space Force academy, he was an obvious control junkie. He used every issue as a platform to demand she clamp down on crazies.

Mr Rykov looked showily around the chamber. 'Is there a representative from Havoc Club here?'

It was a sarcastic question, and raised a ripple of amusement. Representatives on the Council from the warplay enclave had been few but memorable. They had all been human, biologically speaking. The first had sat there in a headset, playing DETH BLAST and LIQUIDATION all through the meetings, grunting excitedly every time he racked up another replay. He had soon disappeared. His replacement, provided after repeated demands, had been a braying clown with some kind of brain damage – Havoc's idea of a joke, presumably.

The last time someone had been in attendance from the Caverns of Disorder had been several subjective months ago, and he had been drunk and foul. During a speech by a prominent Altecean he had got up, pulled out his penis, and urinated down the steps of the chamber. Tabitha had had not to laugh. Rykov and some of his chums, on the other hand, had been unequivocally delighted at the excuse for throwing the creature out.

Rykov was in full flow now. 'Let's not forget the specific objections coming from bridge crew and personnel of all major AV node stations –' Excited voices began to chip in. 'The people of New Madagascar are completely in agreement –'

'New Madagascar and the rest of the sternward communities –'

'37.85% support amidships and growing –'

'The objections, *Captain Jute* –'

The little shit had a knack of snapping out her name in a voice like a prison warder, drawing attention to her just at the moment she was starting to space out completely. Dark glasses didn't help.

'– to letting a rabble of drug addicts and electricity abusers occupy one of the largest cell complexes –'

'I think we've heard this song, Mr Rykov,' said the Captain. It was the first thing she had said for some while, and made everybody pause, waiting to hear what she would say next.

'I could do with a beer,' she said.

Members tutted, sighed, chuckled snidely.

'Anybody else fancy a beer? Professor? Mr Rykov? No? Anyone? Drone!'

A service drone rolled into the chamber. 'Beer for me,' she told it.

The drone flashed a pattern of lights at her, whirred, stopped.

She cursed. 'Stupid thing. Has anyone got an empty?' she asked. Someone threw one. She caught it, almost. 'Damn. Drone? There, look, over there: beer. Me.'

The drone scanned her, ran up a series of zeros.

Members murmured, laughing. The Captain cursed again. Zoe was rising from her seat. 'I'll go, Captain.'

Captain Jute squeezed her arm. 'Thanks, Zo.' She stretched. 'If there are no more questions, let's hear Professor Xavier.'

Tapers hummed as the telegenic professor rose, to speak for the Working Group on Topography, he said, which wished to present a new scheme based on the conductivity discovered in the ship so far.

'Thanks, Zoe, great,' the Captain said loudly to Zoe Primrose, returning with her beer. She drank deep, then stuck out her feet and threw back her head. 'Do go on, Professor, forgive me for interrupting.' She pressed her fingertips together, focusing on him.

'The point is, Captain, thank you so much,' said Professor Xavier, with unfailing obsequiousness, 'the more we discover, the more it makes sense to describe this ship, Plenty, in terms of a giant brain, with its own principal lobes, cellular construction, neural routing arrangements and so on.'

The Captain drank her beer and watched a rotating graphic, which was very swish, actually. The familiar lop-sided tortoiseshell shape sectioned itself in different colours, isolating this area and that.

Xavier ran his hand through his hair, as if stroking his own brain in unconscious mimicry. 'Though asymmetrical, the ship as you all know consists of two rough hemispheres, divided by the Midway Cleft. Now that corresponds to what cerebral anatomists know as the Longitudinal Fissure, while Happy Valley, you see, Captain, here, that is very much the equivalent of the Central Fissure, only brought forward somewhat, increasing the size of the Parietal Regions here and here . . .'

It was when she realized they were talking about renaming every single bloody tunnel that she started to laugh.

Xavier looked at her, drawing in his brows and baring his teeth as if in acknowledgment of an unforeseen awkwardness. 'You see some problem with the new system, Captain?' he asked, rubbing his chin.

'Oh no, Professor. It's brilliant. Inspired. A brainwave, you could say.'

The Working Group laughed appreciatively.

Xavier blathered on for a bit, digressing and illustrating, before it became clear they were pressing her for a decision. Christ.

'What about Xtasca?' she said. 'Zoe? Can you get her, please?'

Zoe put the Cherub on their screens without delay. Legless, it lay among a thousand monitors in a hammock of cables spun out from the socket at the base of its own spine. Reflected lights splashed and sparkled all over its skin. It waved its hands in gleeful clutching gestures, like a baby watching a fountain.

'Xtasca,' said the Captain. 'What do you think about all this?'

The posthuman infant blinked at her, opened its rosebud lips of jet. '*Names are inefficient*,' it said. '*Numbers are sufficient. Any accessible location can be described by seven digits or fewer. The computations are not really very complicated.*'

'Thank you, Xtasca,' said the Captain heavily. 'Very helpful.' The woman from Tex-Mex, she noticed, was nodding with satisfaction. Her own head was starting to hurt. This was a familiar condition to her. It told her she was still alive.

'Alice?'

The persona was present, because the Captain was. It answered, after a small delay. 'ALL SYSTEMS CONTAIN ERRORS, CAPTAIN.'

Tabitha screwed up her eyes. 'Is that a yes or a no?'

'It's a yes, obviously,' said Rykov rudely. 'The present system is crap. It's complete chaos.'

'We don't think that's the case,' called the Chilli Chalet spokesman. 'With respect, Captain, surely, the persona is warning us against the enormous amount of exploration and expenditure this project will inevitably entail.' By now the procedural junkies were twitching with withdrawal, glaring at Captain Jute, impatient for her to contain this disorderly conduct.

Captain Jute folded her arms. 'You decide, Alice.'

'THE FRASQUE HAD NO NAMES FOR ANY PART OF THIS VESSEL,' said her incorporeal subordinate.

'Well, we're not Frasque, I hope!' said the representative for Little Foxbourne brightly.

'So let's do it,' said several people. Intently, suspiciously, they watched the Captain. The decision had come to stand for something, clearly, around the chamber. Even former pilots and tech worshippers seemed not to approve of the idea of delegating it to a selfaware construct.

'KEEPING PEOPLE BUSY KEEPS THEM HAPPY,' Alice observed.

Tabitha was getting bored. She had staked everything on a decision from the one being who had never let her down, the one who really did have an overview. She found the whole thing so ludicrous herself she couldn't tell whether it would be more trouble to approve or block, and stalling only meant protracting the agony. She wished she had Dodger here, or even Saskia, but neither of them would come to a Council meeting in a million years. 'Bloody hell, do it then,' she said, standing up. 'Zoe, come.'

As she walked out of the chamber the rest of the councillors were shuffling papers excitedly. Tabitha's followers hurried after her, vying for her attention; but in the council chamber the talking was already beginning again.

'The more time you give them, the more they take,' muttered Tabitha to Zoe. Alice was right, as always: keep them busy and she would keep them out of her hair.

For all Xavier's crap about paradigm shifts and mind-brain interfaces, it was becoming clear that the facility written into Alice by the Seraphim programmers had its limitations. The traditional plug-in persona was no substitute for what the Frasque had had: direct physical access to their ship's own memory – a memory co-extensive with the fabric of the ship, if the Cherub was to be believed. Why had they never subjected their ship to trials? What defect prevented them from using it to escape the Capellan purge, when they died in their thousands? No one knew. They had theories though, if you wanted to listen.

At Xtasca's behest, early on, Captain Jute had crawled on hands and knees through chalky holes and slimy ones, to look at shiny red seams of silicon analogue running off in all directions into the darkness. They were everywhere. She saw little prospect of achieving the Integrators' dream or any part of it before they arrived at Proxima, and no chance ever of deinstalling the persona. 'No chance whatsoever, Alice,' she said, turning on her face in the sand.

But answer came there none.

'Alice?'

Silence still, but for the eternal swishing of the virtual sea.

The Captain lifted her head. 'Alice!'

'IS SOMETHING WRONG, CAPTAIN?' asked the soothing, capable voice.

'You didn't answer,' she yawned.

'I WAS A LONG WAY AWAY,' said Alice.

'You're supposed to be keeping me happy,' said the Captain.

'ARE YOU UNHAPPY, CAPTAIN?'

Captain Jute paused a moment, realizing something. First Alice had not answered, and then she had not given a proper explanation. That could be her consideration circuits, probably was. But she had not apologized; and that couldn't.

'I have been happier,' said the Captain. She paused an instant, to allow Alice to reply. She felt the imaginary sun hot on her bare skin.

Alice again made no reply.

'This Integration project,' said Tabitha quickly to her old cybernetic shipmate. 'It is complete bollocks, isn't it?'

'PLEASE DEFINE *BOLLOCKS.*'

'You know. I mean – impossible.'

'WHAT SPECIFIC PROBABILITIES WOULD YOU LIKE CAL-CULATED?'

'Oh god, don't.' She stretched. 'How long have I been in here?'

'23 MINUTES AND 6.73 SECONDS.'

'Is that all? Are we using too much power, keeping the sun like this?'

'NO. THE HEAT IS INDUCED, NOT RADIATED. IT'S NOT HEAT AT ALL, CONSIDERED THERMODYNAMICALLY.'

'That's all right, then,' said the Captain, relaxing again.

'YOU COULD HAVE NIGHT,' said Alice, 'IF THE SUN BOTHERS YOU.'

There was a moment's pause; then night lay across the beach, motionless and calm. It was ten degrees cooler. A fine crescent moon floated in an indigo sky. The sea came in black and shining, and broke in nets of silver. 'I was thinking about it,' said the Captain.

'NOW YOU ARE IN POSSESSION OF ALL THE INFOR-MATION, CAPTAIN,' said the persona gently. 'DAY –' The sun blazed down again, from a blue heaven. '– AND NIGHT.' Darkness swallowed the illusory scene. Along the shore the distant lighthouse winked.

'Yes, all right, Alice, I get it,' said Tabitha.

'INADEQUATE INFORMATION MAKES INACCURATE PRO-CESSING,' averred Alice, blandly.

The Captain's jaw fell open. 'I'll tell you what's inadequate!' she said.

'AYE-AYE, CAPTAIN,' said the persona.

Inadequate information makes inaccurate processing. It was the sort of thing the senior bridge console jockeys had on their desks, etched in a block of lucite. With a half-eaten doughnut on top. God, Alice could be hard work sometimes. Perhaps she thought it was beneath her now, to run a simple environmat. Perhaps in some actual, ergo-nomically calculable way it was. Bothered, Tabitha pulled on her leather trousers and stamped into the drawing room.

The girls were there, Topaz and Dorcas and Karen Narlikar and a couple she didn't even know, lounging around, gossiping, drinking her booze. 'Come on,' she told them. 'We're going out.'

They all turned and looked at her. 'What for?'

Captain Jute smoothed the palms of her hands down the sides of her trousers. 'Reinforcements.'

'Are you going like that?' Karen asked, looking at her breasts.

'I'm tempted,' said the Captain.

Physical types of every species queued up to impress Captain Jute, especially since Kenny had started assembling his little cadre. When she was smashed she liked to torment them. 'You really fancy yourself, don't you?' she would say to a posturing hopeful. She would draw her finger slowly around the corner of her mouth and watch him start to rouse. Then she would say: 'It's a good job somebody does.'

She and the girls would swagger on, laughing. It was like being a kid again. 'They love it,' she told Karen Narlikar, striding along with her hands in her pockets. 'Take the piss out of men, they come back for more. Kenny!' she barked with sudden alarm, swaying back into a doorway with her coat floating about her.

At once Kenny was there, shielding her, reaching for his gun. The Captain grabbed him by the scruff of the neck and pointed urgently into the crowd of spacers and tunnel workers hanging about the steps of the Flying Tiger Restaurant. *'What is that man hiding under his shirt?'*

Kenny yowled an order. One of his boys went belting over there and hauled the man down into the street. Overhead, people began opening windows, staring down at the disturbance.

The man was human, big, with sand-brown skin. His shoulders were broad beneath a loose gold Y-shirt. His eyes flashed and his mouth worked as the bodyguard wrenched the shirt out of his trousers, popping it open and dragging it back over his shoulders to pinion his arms.

The Captain looked.

'Nice,' she said. 'Bring him here.'

He had a little gold tattoo on one cheek and a wing of black hair that fell forward across his eyes. He was quite gorgeous, especially with that wild affronted expression. 'A tasty one,' she remarked, in an audible tone, to the laughter of Topaz and Karen.

Soi drove them home. The public clocks they passed said things like 18:49, though it seemed to Captain Jute like the middle of the night. Possibly this was because she was still wearing sunglasses. Kenny and his boys were on bikes, outriders. They were all boys, Otis and

Clegg and Lomax. She knew their like of old, from dockside bars on Pascal and Ottica 1: mercenaries, adventurers, freelance heroes. They only ever had one name, for some reason, and didn't like to talk. Instead they would show off their latest servo kit, crushing ashtrays with reinforced fingers.

Captain Jute was in the back with Topaz and Zoe. Her head was hurting again, dully. She clenched her teeth. She closed her eyes and stretched her neck, moving her head from side to side. 'I need some more drugs,' she said.

'You've already had some drugs,' said Topaz.

'Zoe. Drugs.'

'We didn't bring any drugs, Captain.'

'Drugs. I'm not going home until somebody gives me some drugs.'

'God, you are boring, Tabitha.'

The Captain knocked the floor of the car with the heels of her boots. 'I'm the fucking Captain, give me some fucking drugs.'

'Oh, give her some drugs, somebody,' said Topaz, as Karen looked in her bag. 'What have you got, then? I don't suppose there's a little bit for me, is there? Oh you are sweet.'

The Captain watched the huge ornamental lights of the upper level pleasure corridors float past one after another like giant hallucinatory playing cards. GAMES BAR WIN PLATINUM LOUNGE APEX MALIBU STARS BEER SHIGENAGA NUDE STARS. Fleeting spiral patterns flowed across them, condensing fumes from the bike exhausts. Kenny's boys looked better in motion, thought Captain Jute, admiring those slanting charcoal silhouettes, so abstract, so full of non-specific menace.

'What happened to that man I had?'

'Th' wiman's hee' again,' said Soi as they came up the drive.

The woman was a lonely Thrant in a yellow dress. She was sitting vigilantly on a high ledge, watching the apartment. They had seen her there before, skulking at a distance, as if compelled to be there but afraid to come nearer. Just a fan, probably. Probably she thought Kenny or Soi could get a job for her too; though if that was what she wanted she'd have to put a bit more effort into it.

Captain Jute looked up at the Thrant as they passed beneath her ledge. She felt like shouting, 'Haven't you got anything better to do?'

The car stopped, surrounded by bikes. Topaz put down the window and beckoned Kenny over. Kenny snuffled. He pawed his muzzle. He too had seen the woman.

'Get rid of her,' said Captain Jute.

Kenny wore his grey jerkin zipped to the throat and tight black knickers. He stood upright on the ledge in front of the woman, legs apart, tail swishing. He said, 'What do you want here?'

The woman did not look important. She was wearing sandals and nursing a plastic carrier bag. There was no danger in her. Her scent was fear and respect. She trembled as he spoke. But she crouched in on herself, making no attempt to leave.

Kenny flicked the tip of his tail warningly. He said: 'The Captain is not to be disturbed.'

The woman lifted her head. Her eyes were pretty, delicate green, and her lips pale violet. She ducked her head. Her nipples showed clearly through the thin material of her dress. His sharp eyes noticed she had no tail. The woman pressed her bag and gave a little whimpering sigh. It was the smallest possible noise, and escaped her against her will.

The fur prickled on the back of Kenny's neck.

He reached down for her hand. 'Come,' he said sternly. He did not look at her. He looked straight ahead.

Then the visitor swallowed and said: 'I have a present for the Captain.' Her voice was breathy, and seemed to come through her ears and nostrils, as if she dare not open her mouth. She held her head low and level, watching all the time. Her eyelashes were long and beautifully speckled.

Out of her bag she produced a small cellophane envelope. He took it, thanking her on the Captain's behalf. Kenny supposed she would next ask to deliver it in person; but she did not. As he led her back to the road she was docile, though her eyes were full of pleading.

'There is a tour of the apartment on the net,' he told her.

'I have seen it,' she said. 'You are a happy man to work here.' Her voice was rapid. Her accent sang to him of home, high trees and wide yellow horizons. He could feel her pulse in her wrist, beating like a bird's. Still she trembled. Her fear was appetizing.

Kenny pulled back his head, made a stiff neck. 'My work is to escort you back to a public area,' he said; but his eyes glowed; his nostrils flared.

The woman spoke again, hurriedly. 'Your name is Kyfyd, though they call you Kenny,' she said. 'You are lucky. The Captain is a –' She was almost out of breath from her own audacity. '– lucky woman.'

'Where do you live?' he asked.

She shrugged. 'My master –' she said softly; but this sentence she could not finish.

Kenny dented the cellophane envelope with a speculative claw.

'Please thank your master for the present,' he said.

She did not answer. She rubbed her chin on her shoulder.

'Go now,' he said; and she went at once, trotting away across the bridge. She fled like one who flees a fearful place, knowing that if she lingers she will look back and be lost.

Kenny watched her go. In one great palm, he held her tiny gift. The envelope held six of the little white pills the Captain liked so much.

Down in the docks, everything was deserted, quiet, down, not to wake again until Emergence. Only the faint light of biofluorescents glimmered among the black gantries, limned the fuel pipes, the edges of furnace drains. Cargo hoists, frozen in silhouette, trailed clumps of cables like creeper. The Thrant let herself down hand over hand from a disused stairway and dropped to a rockfoam floor, her sandals *clop*ping loudly. Stooping to negotiate a low tunnel she crossed a high narrow island between two huge blackened blast pits. Far above her head the shadowy tiers of parking bays loomed like a comb constructed by malign, giant bees.

She stopped and cocked an ear. There was the noise of small engines toiling hard. As she listened it stopped with a bang, and a grinding, scraping noise began instead.

The Thrant climbed over a ridge of matrix. Beyond the low, broad entry ahead was a dazzle of arc lights. It was the place the noise was coming from. She hurried down into it.

It was some kind of workshop or warehouse, unfinished, unused. Fans of bent and rusted wire stuck out of the tops of concrete pilings, like parodies of trees designed by a disdainful god. Large stains, regular and vague, had been bleached into the floor. Black grilled drains marked the bottom of shallow sinks. The place reeked of ancient detergents.

'Ah, Iogo,' he said. 'There you are.'

119

The man was immaculate as ever. Dust and dirt never seemed to touch his grey needlecord suit, his white shirt. In his tiny black goggles he resembled some fastidious mutant insect, inheritor of the abandoned depots. He also had on a control gauntlet, with which he was amusing himself. He had revived three cargo drones and was making them build progressively steeper ramps and then run down them and crash into each other.

'Did you see her?' His voice echoed from the blank, dirty walls.

She stuck her head out and nodded it carefully. She looked warily at the drones. They exuded a nasty odour of friction.

They were very battered drones. Their domes were dented, their lenses smashed.

Without looking at her, he seemed to have taken in her answer. 'Did you speak to her?'

Iogo shook her head.

'What was she doing?' he asked.

'Came inna car,' whispered Iogo. 'Wen' in.'

'"Came in the car, went in,"' repeated Grant Nothing articulately. 'For this intelligence all our efforts are spent.'

His companion worked her lips. Her left shoulder twitched.

The tiny black lenses were suddenly looking at her. 'Did you meet some new chums?'

His voice was pleasant and calm. Still she knew she must not get a word wrong.

She rubbed the side of her head with her right wrist. The horrible lights were hurting her eyes. 'K-enny,' she said.

'The magnificent Kenny,' said Grant Nothing affirmatively, as if it was the answer to a riddle she had guessed. He twitched his gauntlet. A fallen drone revved briefly, but did not move. 'You managed to speak to him this time, did you?'

She nodded again. She pawed her eyes.

'And how is Captain Jute's taciturn champion?' asked Grant Nothing. Iogo snuffled, brief and low. She didn't know those words.

Grant Nothing rubbed his left wrist in the crook of his right thumb and forefinger as if the gauntlet was chafing him.

'Kenny,' he said, with emphatic, magisterial patience. 'Is he happy in his work?'

He would ask questions like that sometimes, echoing so closely something that had been said in his absence she knew he had been eavesdropping, by some of his electronic magic. She was sure he was listening everywhere, watching every chamber of the ship simultaneously. No intelligence could be beyond him. 'Did he try the pills?'

She rubbed her long jaw, suddenly self-conscious. 'Do't 'ow.'

He laughed. 'If he's as nosy as you he did.'

It pleased him to say such things. She did not try to answer. He knew she would never even sniff at anything without his specific instruction. He was making minute adjustments to the set of a control. 'Our glorious Captain will enjoy them.'

Iogo said nothing. She thought of Kyfyd's scent, his whiskers, the way he held himself tight and upright like a human.

'Did you fuck him?' Grant Nothing inquired, easily.

No, she said at once. She did not notice she spoke in her own language.

'Subject didn't come up, hm?'

She blinked her sore eyes. She wanted to move closer to her man, to come into the sphere of his regard. But it was a space about him that she dare not enter.

'Cap'ain said ge' ri' of her,' she said.

Grant Nothing grimaced, like a person reacting to a sharp and pungent taste. His goggles were staring at her again suddenly, freezing her. 'So she thinks she can avoid us, does she? She thinks she can just sail along to Proxima with her pals and her toys and her sugary Channel 2 exclusives and nice things to put up her nose, without ever once thinking about the people she's *ruined*, the lives she's *destroyed* –'

He turned once more to his toys, stirring them into mechanical semblance of life. 'Well, we must remind her then,' he said delicately. 'Proceeding gently, always gently . . . never less,' he said, pressing a button, 'than –' The three drones raced down their ramshackle runways and cannoned off one another, making a horrible clattering and smashing.

'– gently,' said Grant Nothing.

One of the drones fell over. It lay there with its three feet pedalling vainly in the air, shedding sparks and pieces of spring.

'Whoops-a-daisy,' said Grant Nothing.

Iogo watched him press the controls on his glove. She knew it was she they controlled. Kyfyd and Captain Jute and she herself at his behest, colliding and moving away. In this place of interrupted routines and silent devices nothing moved unless he told it to.

Grant Nothing looked disapprovingly at his right shoe, then polished it on his left calf.

'Did she like my present?' he asked; then answered himself at once, 'I'm sure she did. The Captain likes nice things to put in her mouth, and up her nose, and in her cunt,' he proposed succinctly. And he gave his faithful companion a wintry smile. 'As which of us does not?' he said. 'As which of us does not?'

Something moved, on the floor. Iogo turned, bristling, poised to pounce. Out of the black drains iron crabs were crawling; autonomic scavengers, magnetized by the scent of scrap metal.

While midwives in the Rookeries had been delivering babies with misshapen heads or legs on backwards, in a white pavilion in Sugar Grove Saskia Zodiac was reanimating the dead.

Her process required no hair or nail clippings, no spatula of grave-yard dirt. It didn't even require a body, which was just as well, because the body, what was left of it, was decomposing in a swamp on Venus.

The acrobat and conjuror had discovered quite early that though the movements of a J.M. Souviens Ariel 3.01 were confined to the dais below the projectors, it did not necessarily have to look like a pillar of green flame. She got it to run its wardrobe of hologram imagos: AV stars and space heroes, mostly, they seemed to be. None of the names meant anything to Saskia. '*Sister Anthea is very popular,*' suggested the machine. The Sugar Grove pavilion had never had a client like this before. Her credit was unlimited, and she was already into the top range of options. The facility was busy scoping out every aspect of her transactions for customer feedback to optimize future business. The data might be valid. Especially since she seemed to be, for some reason, its only client now.

The imagos could be any size, to walk or skate or fly you through the scenes of your chosen simulation, explaining what you were looking at. They were audience-sensitive, speeding up and slowing down, with oblique options they could use to entertain you, to keep you watching for longer. Sister Anthea was a generic Capellan, a promoted human with a vast cranium, dressed in regulation white toga and golden sandals. She could be Brother Antheus, Saskia discovered, though her clothes didn't come off.

'No,' she said. 'What about user-definition?'

'*Many clients like to define an image of their own,*' agreed the system. '*You can even choose to put yourself in the picture, quite literally — we even offer a cosmetic enhancement service to make sure you look your best!*'

'Well, it'll be easy, then, won't it?' said the acrobat with satisfaction.

All the Kobold's records had been atomized with the ship itself, so what Alice could provide was only a reconstruction. It floated before her, lifesize, carved in light. Saskia stood up on the dais and stared in through the visor of the electric blue pressure suit. It was the suit he had died in. She had not thought of that.

'*Bubba,*' the figure said. '*Bubba bub.*'

The two faces were identical: the high forehead, the perpendicular nose, the hooded eyes of an unnameable colour.

Saskia Zodiac clenched her fists. 'Go on,' she told the thing. 'Speak!'

Overstretched, the Ariel reverted to the default. '*Remember how we used to b-b-be, and from Time's b-bondage set us free.*'

'Nothing like us!' the conjuror moaned.

The face of the figure twitched. It rippled and reformed, over and over again, like a sticking clock. '*Us free, free, free,*' said the voice, looping. The system was hung. Nothing she could do would release it. '*Free, free, free,*' it said. In black despair, Saskia cut the power.

Five minutes later she turned it on again.

'*J.M. Souviens gives you the keys,*' said the green flame, '*to golden years and treasured memories.*'

For some days Saskia stayed in her apartment, eating incessantly. She would not go near J.M. Souviens. She knew next time he would appear with his face swollen purple, his helmet full of blood.

Or he might be mad. The Zodiac Twins' pressure suits had been stylish and impractical for Venus, and Mogul's brain had cooked. In his last hour before the Frasque had crushed him he had babbled of a uterine Paradise, bidding Saskia recognize all about them the bloody delta of the blastosphere. She did not want to see him like that, with his eyes staring and a smile like a benevolent frog. She wanted him back as he had been in life: arrogant; sensual; svelte. He was still the most beautiful man she had ever seen. It was in bed that she missed him most: missed the certainty of a lover who always knew exactly every instant what she wanted. Sexually he had been tremendous; but that was not an option J.M. Souviens could ever provide.

The breakthrough came when she located Hannah Soo's client files and loaded some old Contraband performance footage. Somehow, the record of his body in motion proved to be the key to recreating his posture, the solution to the equation of his limbs. Dancing, he arrived at last, in his midnight blue pyjamas trimmed with stardust, chips of lapis lazuli in his earlobes. Saskia clapped her hands and jumped up onto the deck to embrace his incorporeal form. Round and round they waltzed to 'Rue Fortune', which the pavilion piped triumphantly as any wedding march.

'*Unless the extraordinary atmosphere, in other words, in other words, extraordinary explosive, not to cross the monstrous body. Admirable and idle, wouldn't you expose?*'

The voice was her own in pitch and timbre. What it said was nonsense, mere random skimmings from old recordings. Then he jammed again, freezing with his chin on his chest: so like a corpse that Saskia wept, and could work no more that day.

'*J.M. Souviens hopes you have had a successful and pleasant visit and looks forward to providing more of your memory requirements next time you call,*' murmured the machine, as she fled for the lifts.

At a suggestion of Xtasca's she had reconfigured and boosted the Ariel's self-examination routines. By inverting all the logic gates she seemed to drive it into a kind of electronic narcissism. Now her imitation brother started to sound more authentic.

He sat like Hamlet with his chin in his hand.

'*Human life was a rambling and tedious joke,*' he told her. '*We are the punchline.*'

Saskia laughed. 'Splendid!'

'*It was inevitable you should seek to make me,*' he said.

'I miss you so much,' she said.

'*We predicate each other,*' he said. '*We are inescapable.*'

She longed to touch him. She reached up and put her hand through his belly, occluding a battery of projectors. Mogul went flat and angled away from her, like a video effect.

'I seem to have evolved into light,' he wheezed, in a voice like tearing tinfoil. *'Pure electromagnetic essenszsxzz . . .'*

'It's getting better, Alice,' conceded Saskia. The more time she spent editing and adjusting, the more convinced she felt by the transparent facsimile sitting cross-legged on the holodeck in front of her.

'VARIATIONS FROM BASE DATA ARE DOWN TO PLUS OR MINUS 0.5%,' said Alice flatly, via the com link.

The acrobat chewed her knuckle. 'I should like him to have intelligence,' she said.

'WE'D ALL LIKE TO HAVE THAT, DEAR.'

3

The great heat had finally broken. Now the arterial winds were cooler, and fringed with dampness. The Alteceans spoke of spicy scents, nostalgic and untraceable. In the jungle caverns strange fruit swelled on the vines: mutant berries, grey bananas. Food poisoning was rife. After a dispute with Rory over some out-of-date krillsticks the Trivia philosophers had transferred their custom to the Pause Café, with its white louvred shutters and trellises woven with freshly watered bines: 'More conducive to thought,' said the Good Doctor. 'To debate,' argued the Last Poet. 'To chess,' pronounced the Best Judge. 'Bishop to Queen's Bishop 2.' Back at the Trivia Rory folded his arms and drew his great chin into his shirt collar. 'I'd rather have their space,' he opined gloomily. 'They never buy anything anyway.'

The Chilli Chalet had a perfect hygiene record, and their rich, tasty fare was more and more in demand. The regulars bonded, making district security pacts and arranging marriages between the tables. The staff all had ranks now. There were service captains and rice 'n' relish cadets. Prizes were given, and shameful badges of demerit for poor posture or slow service. A '100% Human' employment policy was introduced, and advertised everywhere. *'A small gesture of tribute to a great species.'*

In Clementine Chambers the Terran General Knowledge quiz games were very popular. They had them on the local circuit so you didn't even have to leave your living room to watch. '*What are* Onward, Achievement, *and* Kelvedon Wonder?'

'*Well, unless I'm very much mistaken, Norman, these are all varieties of garden pea . . .*'

There were suicides, of course. For some it seemed the ontological abyss of hyperspace leached the significance from everything, making everyone's actions covert and questionable, like the actions of sleep-walkers. Their bodies were always found in the Earth Room, where the absence of reality was most inescapable. In the Earth Room with its vacant windows it was eternally twenty-to-four, and no sign of morning.

On Katafalk, Dog Schwartz walked along under an indigo sky on the shores of a frozen methane sea. The coagulated slush stirred wearily, too exhausted for a decent wave. Dog scratched his beard. Everything was silent; a moment of peace. The pterosaurs circled the high rocks where they roosted, floating grey slivers in the mauve glow of Zormat.

Suddenly, with no warning, the surface of the sea shattered, and a huge head reared up out of it. The head was long and square, as big as a bus, with a mouth full of black stiletto teeth, which it bared at him, drenching him with corrosive saliva. After the head came metre upon metre of silvered neck, thick as an *olrej* tree.

A sea serpent! He called up the specs. It said they rarely attacked lone foot travellers; but Dog Schwartz was a rare man.

He planted his feet, using his toes to power up his gripboots. 'Looking for dinner, are you?' he cried, as his jewelled blade leapt from its sheath into his waiting hand.

With speed inconceivable in a creature so huge, the serpent attacked. Its breath was poisonous, it could transfix you if you looked it in the eye; but it could be vulnerable to a sword thrust into its gaping mouth, over the barrier of the mighty teeth and up into its skull. It was a physical fight, all feinting and flexing, until at last he saw his opening and took it. But barely had Dog dispatched the serpent than bolts of blue radiation started zapping all about him, blasting pits in the skin of his expiring enemy.

'Typical! Bloody typical!' tutted Dog, with satisfaction. The spectacle of their nemesis preoccupied with that overgrown newt had tempted the Momeraths out of cover. Nothing under the purple sun would persuade the cowardly lead-coloured creatures to dare a frontal attack. Already he was somersaulting, kicking off the body of the serpent and whirling up the beach, dodging the gunners, picking a soldier off the flank.

He spitted his target with a single servo-assisted thrust, enjoying the minimal resistance provided by the wet, crunchy sac of the Momerath body. It gibbered and spluttered as it died, waving its scaly, three-pronged limbs about. Explosives rained about him, blasting steam from the superheated rocks. Dog hurled himself behind a spur of the cliffs, leaping the twenty metres with ease. Killing the sea serpent had given him extra strength. Air and power supplies were still pretty high; only ammo was low.

His tactical comp calculated the fire pattern, casting birdseyes and perspective grids across his visor. A light pulsed, measuring for a gap in the firing. Dog waited a beat, then jumped from cover with guns blazing. 'Come and get me!' he taunted them.

He got two, then climbed for higher ground. Another was charging, armed with some kind of power mace. Casually, Dog dodged. The mace struck chunks from the cliff face. Dog twisted from the hip and jabbed with his sword, the flesh-seeking circuits etched in its blade drawing it straight and true. Meanwhile the spring steel tongues of his wristwhip lashed out and wrapped tight around the hilt of the mace, pulling it from the Momerath's grasp, while the sword bit deep into the thick neck, severing the helmet seal. The Momerath went down on its knees, clutching at its neck, and at once another leapt over its back, shooting. Dog swerved, chopped, hewed. He hopped on one foot, decking a soldier with a cruel blow from his knee.

A strange, high-pitched noise came over the earpiece, and tactics blew Dog's retreat alarm. 'Oh bloody shit,' he sang. He looked upwards, venting some precious air to clear the condensation that fogged his viewplate. Here it came, their aerial support. The outline of the Anaconda loomed over the bluff, stark against the mauve, bloated face of the planet Zormat. The warship bristled with artillery. Brightly coloured packages were dropping from it, jet-powered, swooping down the cliff.

'Retreat my arse.'

Humming thoughtfully as he overrode the comp, Dog took on two more Momeraths, kicking the blaster out of the hand of one while carving the other from throat to groin with his sword. Sparks flew as the jewelled blade sliced through their suit circuits.

By now the jet sleds were whooshing overhead, their warbling

127

engines counterpointing the harsh cries of the angry raptors. Dog Schwartz felt a bolt glance off his armoured shoulder. 'You little fuckers –' he mouthed crossly. Pain rose; strength began to drop more swiftly.

Hugging the cliff face while the first sled reached the end of its run and began to turn, Dog heaved a rock at the next to pass, hitting its side with a resounding clang, then spun and shot the first sled out of the sky with his underarm torpedo. It was a beautiful strike. It lit the bleak beach a dazzling blue-white. Fragments of Momerath commando soared and tumbled about. The troops faltered, blinded by the light. The desolate moonscape rang with the screams of outraged pterosaurs.

At that moment the colour went out of everything. Beach, cliffs, boiling attackers and dead serpent, everything went monochrome, then reversed. Black, white, black, white, it flashed, at a slow, insistent rhythm. The Momeraths began to melt into a big composite glob. Air-sleds and pterosaurs dwindled into abstract shapes, triangles and rhomboids hanging around the warrior's head like the elements of some irritating and inconvenient mobile. Another alarm began to peep.

'*You have an external request for attention,*' said the pod persona, politely.

'No, no, no,' fussed Dog, and tugged his off switch. There was a man standing beside the pod, knocking on the window, looking guilty. It was Leglois.

Dog scowled and shoved open the lid.

'What the fuck do you want?' Leglois had hardly changed since his rock-breaking days. He was still the same shifty-looking bloke with flaky skin. Whatever he wore, he managed to make it look like a prison uniform. Dog's mouth was parched. He took the cola Leglois handed him. His head was still reverberating with the warcries of Momeraths, the roaring of sea serpents. It was pretty loud in here anyway, with the shouts of the martials and the crash of weapons and the snuff rock always blasting out.

'Monk,' said Leglois apologetically. 'He wants you.' He knew Dog didn't like being pulled out of a game like that. He didn't want Dog to think it was his idea.

Dog flexed his shoulders, craned his neck. 'Visiting time, is it?' he said, with more enthusiasm.

*   *   *

Dog Schwartz looked around, trying to reorient himself:

Two teams were playing tag in the stunmine cave, bodies flying around to the sound of laughter. In the pits, figures with their heads in sense amp cages sparred energetically with invisible phantoms. The ripped-up seats were sparsely occupied by youngsters, who were talking, boasting, jeering at each other, their feet hung over the seats in front. They were watching their own visor screens, tuning in to one fight after another, lazily arguing tactics. In the Havoc Cavern the gamers had recently learned that the sternward bulge they occupied was now called the Occipital Lobe, according to a bunch of wankers in somewhere called the Anterior Commissure. 'Occipital *Lobe!*' the gamers crowed in poncey accents, tussling merrily. They couldn't give a monkey's. The place was whatever you wanted it to be. It was the inside of your own head, not anybody else's.

The whole-body VR pods stood in a bank together in a low antechamber. For all their lurid decals they were quite silent. Only a small red light betrayed the furious dreams going on within. Seeing Dog's go out, a gaggle of boys in ripped and welded activity suits came running.

'You finished or what?' shouted the foremost. Dog Schwartz cuffed his head. 'Ow!'

Dog Schwartz got out of his pod laboriously, shaking his trouser legs, crumpled from the rigours of his campaign. He spotted the Gunky Monkey on a nearby platform, fiddling with a broken battledrone. The purple sun of Zormat spattered dancing afterimages everywhere he turned his eyes. It didn't help that the Monkey had got the drone to blow light rings: hoops of pure colour that drifted upwards into the dark crannies overhead, like smoke rings redesigned by a Seraph.

'Monk!' he called.

The Gunky Monkey looked the same as ever too, afterimages or no afterimages: a sort of dun, shading to black in the creases. He was wearing a pair of jeans that seemed to have been plastered onto his legs with asphalt. They creaked and glittered as he moved, strutting around his new toy. His chest was bare, and hung with keys and picks on a black thong.

The boys were fighting for Dog's vacant pod. Everybody else got out of the big man's way. Leglois trotted after him with the cola.

A coffee-coloured kid called Norval, naked except for well-ripped jeans, was leaning on the bottom of the steps.

'All right, Norval?' Dog greeted him cheerily, hitching up the waist-band of his trousers.

'Better with a bit of Sting, Dog,' said the boy, smiling lazily.

Dog rolled his head, his left shoulder. 'Would you be indeed, my friend? Would you be indeed? Well, we're going to be seeing about that very thing shortly. Very shortly, as it happens.'

'Good,' said Norval, and picked his teeth.

Dog waited an instant. He rolled his head, his right shoulder. 'You wouldn't like to make a contribution, would you, Norval, as a token of your interest?' Norval locked eyes with him a moment, with amused curiosity, as if he was contemplating asking for credit just to watch the offence. Then he stretched his lips wide again.

'Pay the Dog, Joey,' he said, to a younger boy with big solemn green eyes. 'Pay the Dog.'

Joey gave Dog a plastic bag with a wretched assortment of half-used chips, coins of several worlds, and soft sheets of printed cash. Dog sniffed derisively, and thrust it into his pocket. Then he leaned back and shouted up the steps.

'Monk!' shouted Dog Schwartz. 'Turn that bloody thing off.'

The Gunky Monkey ignored him. From the top of the steps he grinned his green-toothed grin. 'Visiting time,' he said. Somewhere, somebody screamed. Dog Schwartz rubbed his large and capable hands together. Majestic among the explosions he turned to his cringing cup-bearer.

'You coming, Leg? Come on, you might learn something.'

Captain Jute was at the helm. She was having her usual conference with Mr Spinner, Xtasca and Alice. Actually, they were conferring; she was drifting. She was remembering Captain Frank, the Altecean spacecomber who had taught her to drive in his truck. He had been all right, though it had seemed like hard going at the time. She wondered where he was now. Pottering about at the demolition sale of some bankrupt orbital, probably, spraying his claim sign on light convertors and three-way effluent condensers.

'THE PENTATONIC CLUSTERS ARE REGULAR IN ALL FREQUENCIES OF THE DITHYRAMB,' Alice was saying. 'PROBABILITY OF CORRESPONDENCE TO YOUR 513.00 NODE BETTER THAN 75%.'

Then Xtasca would reply. '*513 is symmetrical in the other hemisphere.*'

They might have been talking Frasque for all Captain Jute could understand. Ultimately, she supposed, they would be. Everyone would grow an extra pair of arms and crawl around on the walls of the canyons whistling and creaking at each other.

'Shit,' she muttered.

'*Captain?*'

'No, you carry on,' she said. 'I'll be back in a minute.'

Her tampon had died. She could feel it, cold and heavy inside her. She trudged into the ablute and sat with her head against the cold steel wall. She felt ill. She felt fat and achey and generally ill. She reached for the tail of the tampon.

They weren't supposed to die until you stopped feeding them. But there was fresh blood red on her fingers.

'Shit, shit, shit.' It took a while to ease out the slimy black length and zap it. Then she had to plug herself with tissue because somebody had forgotten to fill the dispenser. It did not put her in a good frame of mind for her next discovery.

She went back to the helm. Alice was still speaking, reciting a list of fluctuations that were being tabled on the screen as she spoke. A distinct variation wave was running through the port beam, the Captain saw: some kind of pitch adjustment equivalent, it had to be.

There was no reason for her to do it. She had long ago got past the point of doing it obsessively. She had not even thought about doing it for a watch or two, or several, in fact, as it turned out. But that was the moment she turned to look at the grey persona plaque.

The slot was empty.

'Alice?'

'CAPTAIN?'

She touched the rim of the slot. 'Where's your plaque?'

'IN THE READER, CAPTAIN.'

'It isn't.'

'LET ME SEE,' said Alice, redundantly. A light blinked on the reader. 'SO IT ISN'T. DEAR ME. I WONDER WHERE THAT CAN HAVE GOT TO.'

Mr Spinner came on the line. '*You haven't brought it back since you last took it, Captain,*' he said, incomprehensibly.

'I haven't taken it anywhere,' she said. 'I've been leaving it here.'

He stared up at her, perplexed. In his glasses she could see the twin reflections of his screen, with her face on it.

The far end of Rocking Horse Road was derelict and low. Niglon Leglois was unhappy. He disliked the descent of the ceiling, the hairy stalactites, the bitter odour of ancient burning.

Here it was easy to remember that the fabric of Plenty was something that had originally been secreted, spewed out of the orifices of its creator race's own bodies. At every crack they passed Leglois expected to see some of them come crawling out, whispering and rustling. Already he could hear little feet in the darkness, skittering from their lights.

Dog and the Monkey weren't worried. Dog was cracking jokes and belching, while his black-rimmed friend, in frisky mood, chased after the rats, shooting them with an imaginary gun.

'That Mystery Woman,' said Dog Schwartz fervently. 'I'd give her one. Worrr.'

They came to a huge circular doorway ten metres high. The doors were broken and stood ajar. Beyond was a large chamber full of empty buildings. The floor was thick with moss. Dog led them along a faint path to a door, which bore several notices giving warning of health precautions and regulations. The notices were damp and richly spotted with black mould. Beside the door was a keypad. Whistling through his teeth, Dog Schwartz entered a number, and the door opened.

Inside the building, the lights were bright. Everything was white and primrose yellow, and smelled of disinfectant.

Leglois stood staring around, disoriented. There was a nurse, a human nurse in a white uniform, coming out of a doorway. She did not look pleased to see them, though Dog gave her a little wave as they sauntered by.

Leglois tugged Dog's sleeve. 'Here, this is where that singing bloke was, isn't it? Marco Wossname.'

Ahead, the Gunky Monkey was trundling merrily along the tubular hallway, carolling and flinging open doors.

In Suite 1 an old woman with a face like an eagle was sitting up in a bed of pink frills. Her body was heavily bandaged from side to side. 'Mrs Consuela Oriflamme,' said Dog Schwartz, introducing her. 'Niglon, Consuela, Consuela, Niglon.' He tutted and shook his head sympathetically. 'Hospital bills starting to mount up, are they, Connie?'

She fixed them with an urgent stare. She had had both arms amputated. 'Frankie,' she said.

'Oh my gawd,' murmured Niglon Leglois.

The Gunky Monkey sniggered and went barging into Suite 2.

In Suite 2 the edges of everything were rounded, with no sharp corners anywhere. It was all painted a uniform beige. Over by one wall an enormously obese woman was lounging in a personal field, a metre or two off the floor. She was gnawing vigorously on a very large hunk of meat.

She stared at her visitors uncertainly. She wore the expression of a one-year-old about to burst into tears.

The Gunky Monkey clucked encouragingly at her. 'Mm, that nice, Glory, is it? Here, Dog,' he said, gesturing back towards Mrs Oriflamme in Suite 1, 'you reckon that's one of *her* arms?' It was a ridiculous suggestion, because the meat was obviously nothing human. It looked more like dinosaur liver.

Dog laid his huge hand on Leglois's shoulder, as if he thought their accomplice might be about to bolt. He explained: 'Gloria is one of the victims of Pepsiphrax. Have you heard of Pepsiphrax, Leggy? No, of course you haven't. Nobody has. Because when they saw Gloria and people like Gloria, McIntyre Porcupine took it off the market and off the register and completely off the record. This used to be quite a good place to hide Gloria and people like Gloria away, where they wouldn't upset anybody.' He raised his voice, like a farmer hailing a sow. 'Isn't that right, Glory, eh?'

Gloria dropped her meat in her capacious lap and patted the inside of her force field. Her hand left red smears on the air: blood, or barbecue sauce. She giggled, winsomely, dimpling.

In Suite 3, where Mr Gules lay sleeping the light-years away, Nurse Rix had heard the disturbance in the corridor. She knew who it must be. He was their only visitor these days, practically. She stood up as the door opened. She was right. It was the man called Dog. His clothes were colourful as ever. His trousers in particular looked like a pair of curtains. In front of him was the other man, the small one, reeking of oil and rubber and rust. Her hygiene circuits screamed at the very sight of him. The small man smiled and bowed in mock apology, and together he and his big friend dragged over the threshold a third man who looked as if he had had some kind of shock.

'Leggy, this one is Mr Leroi Gules,' said Dog, waving a huge arm at the patient nested in his bower of bulky machinery. There were taps in the patient's neck, up his nose, a whole crown of wires going into his brain. 'Mr Gules is what we call, in highly specialized technical medical jargon, a vegetable. Isn't that right, nurse? Yes. Poor Leroi went in for surgery –' He tutted, sucked his teeth. 'Never came out.'

The dirty man folded his arms behind his back and put his chin to his chest. Dazedly Nurse Rix understood he was doing an impersonation of a consultant outlining a case for a room full of medical students. 'It was cheaper to keep him alive than sort out the litigation if he died. Of course, *now* . . .'

He shrugged.

Dog was twitching, the way he always did. He twanged a drip tube, tweaked a corner of the bedclothes. He took hold of Mr Gules's big toe through the blanket and wiggled it.

'Carry on, nurse.'

Suite 4 seemed to be a greenhouse. It was full of flowers, and sunshine everywhere. There was a sound of bees being busy; a drowsy splashing of unseen fountains. Among the gladioli in a tattered orange cardigan sat a gaunt middle-aged woman with grey hair permed in tiny tight curls. She sat in a chair of white iron scrollwork. There was a bad scar down her face and one foot seemed to be twisted slightly beneath the hem of her nightdress. 'And this is Flight Lieutenant Kathleen Beaufort,' said Dog Schwartz, scratching his beard. 'Kathleen was one of the Final Avengers, in the War against the Frasque. She just loves being here, don't you, Kath? Here in Frasque Castle?'

Hunching her thin shoulders the woman leaned towards them as though to propel herself at them by sheer force of hate. Her scream raked their ears.

Out of the hollyhocks something came flying. It was a Wisp, like a giant grey grasshopper with the claws of a lobster and eyes like currants in a bun. It flew at them like an airborne watchdog, jaws wide, claws spread.

The Gunky Monkey slammed the door of Suite 4.

Niglon Leglois leaned against the wall, sweating. He groaned: 'What is this place?'

They stood, Leglois and Dog Schwartz and the Gunky Monkey, outside a door with the number 5 on. From beyond it came the sound of music, electric organs and phased guitars.

Dog leaned down to speak in Leglois's ear. 'It's a hospital, Leg.'

'An isolation hospital,' said the Monk in his other ear.

Dog Schwartz laughed across his head. 'Very good, Monk, yes, I like that. Very isolated, yes.'

He rang the bell.

The door whizzed open. The music exploded out at them like water from a burst dam.

They were looking into a garish antique room with candlewax on the floor and posters of black-light mandalas and zodiac signs on the wall. There was a brass chandelier and a fish tank and a man sitting in a state-of-the-art prosthetic dodgem car with a Vespan beside him on her cumbersome and bulky knees.

Dog said, or rather shouted, 'Here we are, Leg. This is your old Uncle Charlie.'

'Mystery Woman evades capture.' 'Who is concealing Mystery Woman?' 'Where will Mystery Woman strike next?' The Channel 2 documentary definitely gave a boost to the elusive burglar's burgeoning cult. The presenter called her 'everyone's favourite outlaw', and spoke to some of her fans, the so-called Silicon Sect, who declared she was 'magic'. Few eyewitnesses forbore to mention her alleged resemblance to the Captain, though there was a remarkable absence of decent footage – some blurred and ambiguous handheld shots, glimpses on grainy traffic cameras, shaky drawings held up by solemn ten-year-olds. It was all tantalizingly inconclusive, and had to be enhanced with a great deal of speculation, 'artist's impressions' of the great thief's 'treasure cave', and animated reconstructions of famous raids. Even the more obvious hoaxes were hauled up and reconsidered, to bulk the programme out. A Chinese astrologer proposed vague interpretations of some of her silver graffiti. Father Le Coq was on, claiming she was the Devil. 'She Devil rides this Devil Ship, steering every soul to perdition!'

Channel 2, of course, didn't know about the persona plaque theft. When Dodger Gillespie came at Captain Jute's summons, the green dome was being searched, centimetre by centimetre, under Lomax's direction. A lot of missing floppy discs and credit chips had come to light, but no Bergen Kobold personas.

'I'M SURE IT'S WORTH PERFORMING THE OPERATION ANYWAY,' said Alice. The Captain didn't bother to answer. Kenny squatted beside her chair, watching everyone suspiciously. Zoe Primrose was upstairs, still taking statements. They had located the Captain's bag, and turned it out, disgorging, among more personal items, a grubby yellow sweatshirt with the word TIGER on it; four different plastic containers of pills and powders, all part used; a tape given to her by an admirer, showing himself in various poses and intimate detail; a wad of reports from different representatives, many of which she was definitely intending to read; a Zanische wristset, misprogrammed and looping, with chewing gum stuck in the links of the wristband; a dirty hairbrush; a quantity of paper tissues, clean and dirty; a bag of chocolate cherubs, rather melted; some credit chips; a couple of remote controls and something that looked like a remote control but was actually a nerve scrambler, which she had only the vaguest idea how to use.

No plaque.

'You know it was her?' asked Dodger, wondering why it mattered.

Tabitha muttered bitterly, not looking up. 'Who else could it have been?'

'If she really exists,' said Dodger. She thought of the figure in the cave, and could say nothing more.

'Someone came in, looked at the screens, took the plaque, and went out again,' explained Mr Spinner for the thousandth time. 'Only five people actually noticed her and they all thought it was the Captain.' The security tapes showed nothing, apparently. In fact there were odd blanks and spotting all over them that was not attributable to wear.

'IT'S A VERY REGRETTABLE THING,' said Alice politely. 'IF ONLY THE READER HAD BEEN SEALED.' Plainly she wasn't too upset about the loss of her relic.

'Maybe it'll turn up,' said Dodger.

'If anyone else says that I'll dismantle them,' said the Captain.

Leaving the search in progress she took Dodger Gillespie to a bar

– not the Trivia, an anonymous offramp automat bar where everyone was on the way to somewhere else. On the road a skinny Thrant woman without a tail accosted her, running up alongside them out of the shadows as though she had been waiting for them, knowing they would come. Captain Gillespie saw the glint of glassy powder in a plastic envelope. 'No,' said Captain Jute loudly, shouldering the Thrant aside. 'No. Go away.'

In the bar they bought beer and took it to a shadowy corner. Dodger sipped and drew back her lips, savouring the tang. 'Alice sounds all right still,' she said.

'Alice's substitute, you mean,' said Captain Jute blackly.

Captain Gillespie looked at her old pal's smouldering eyes. 'A persona is only –'

'– a substitute,' said her companion, squirming irritably in her seat. 'I know, I know. I didn't bring you here so you could read me the fucking owner's manual.' She picked a flake of formica off the edge of the table.

Dodger watched her stab the beermat with her bit of formica. 'Why did you bring me here?' she said.

Tabitha threw down her plaything. Her face was haunted, aggrieved. 'You've got to go down there and find her, Dodger. Find this Mystery Woman, whoever the fuck she is, and get Alice back. Take whatever you need, do whatever you have to, but say *nothing* to *anybody*. Xtasca will help you as far as she can.'

Dodger took a long drink. She looked around the bar, the cheerless haunt of solitary mechanics and tunnel gardeners. It might have been anywhere in the Tangle, anywhere functional and drab. 'You remember Reg Boudeau?' she said.

'Reg,' said Tabitha. 'Reg.'

'He reckoned he had a Nebulon Minion once with a persona that went funny. Started making crying noises and claiming he was neglecting it.'

Tabitha shuddered. 'Alice hasn't gone funny,' she said, 'she's gone.'

Tabitha Jute always had been a stubborn cow; but this intensity bothered her. It seemed a lot of fuss for a bit of outdated software. 'Sentimental value, eh,' said Captain Gillespie.

Tabitha put her hand on her arm, warning her to be quiet. A lanky young man had come in the bar and was approaching their table.

'Hey, man,' he called. 'Captain Gillespie? It's me.'

'What are you doing here?' asked Dodger.

It was Ronald, from Xtasca's team. He was wearing a parka with a big fur hood, blue jeans, workboots. He looked ready for travel. He came nonchalantly over, picking up a chair on the way.

'Chief sent me,' he said laconically. 'Hi, Cap.' He gave them a big grin, sat down with his knees up against the table. 'Wow, check me here with two big celebrities.' He laughed, goofily. 'Integral!'

Dodger said: 'We're talking, Ronald.'

'Yeah,' he said, nodding his head. 'She sent me to help you.' He pushed back his sleeve and spoke to Xtasca on his wrist radio. 'What's happening, X? Nah, nothing happening here yet.' To Dodger he said, 'There's a bunch of us coming with you, check.'

Dodger Gillespie gave Captain Jute an ironic look. She sat back and folded her arms. To Ronald she said: 'That Cherub's got you trained.'

He gave her a condescending look. 'You wouldn't understand,' he said. 'Her and me – it's a black thing.' He flipped a loose hand at Captain Jute. 'She knows what I'm talking about.'

The Captain laughed sharply. 'Do I,' she said. She picked up her beer and took a savage swig.

Ronald shucked his parka. Under it he wore a faded Chilli Chalet T-shirt. He pulled up the sleeve and rubbed at the scabs on his new tattoo. He held his arm out to show them. 'This is my Xtasy Krew tattoo,' he explained. 'What this is, check, is a picture of the basic configuration. This pattern is like, the circuit structure of the analogue. It's the same everywhere, in there, microscale. It don't half itch, though.'

'Whose Uncle Charlie?' asked Leglois.

'Your Uncle Charlie,' Dog Schwartz said.

'My Uncle Charlie,' said the Monk.

'Everybody's Uncle Charlie,' said Dog.

Dr Irsk was kneeling to pour fluid from a flask into the works of Uncle Charlie's chair. The fluid was brown and translucent, like tea.

'Shall we wait outside, Charles?' asked Dog, who could be quite squeamish about some things.

'No, man, it's cool,' said Uncle Charlie, smiling inanely. It entertained him to gross people out with his gear, and to humiliate the doc by making her do things like this herself instead of one of the nurses. When she knelt down, she bulged all over the place. It was very funny.

It was a miracle of homeostasis, Uncle Charlie's chair. As well as many other advanced features, it incorporated a completely independent recycling system, into which its occupant was securely plumbed. He could eat or drink or otherwise ingest anything he fancied and afterwards detoxify himself at will. Uncle Charlie took full advantage of this facility.

'You gone be careful now, Uncle,' said the physician, her task completed. 'Always to do have one of us fill this to you. Not to let yourself run dry,' warned Dr Irsk, rising to her enormous height with dignity. She pointed to a white polythene carrying case the size of a lunchbox. 'There is what you did ask it,' she added.

'Right, thanks, doc,' said Uncle Charlie loudly, as though he thought she might not understand him unless he shouted. 'Just leave them on the table, right? Far out. See you, then!'

The director of the sanatorium bobbed her bulbous head to the foursome. 'Good day, gentlemen,' she said in her thick, rubbery voice. Uncle Charlie tapped a control. The door swished open and the doctor departed.

Niglon Leglois looked doubtfully at Everybody's Uncle Charlie, who lolled in his chair sniggering weakly. He must have been a hundred, Leglois thought; a hundred and twenty would be closer to the mark, he supposed. Uncle Charlie looked like a zombie out of an ancient 2D movie, his skin sagging where time and chemistry had eaten his flesh away. His hair, long and lank and grey as fag ash, was restrained by a woven leather headband. Despite the darkness in his chambers, he was wearing a pair of little round gold-wire sunglasses. He was wearing a droopy moustache and love beads and gold chains and a little white Perk claw on a thong around his withered neck.

Dog Schwartz had opened the white case. Inside were twenty large phials of pills, yellow and white and pink. 'Yum, yum,' he said, stretching his eyes wide.

'Uncle Charlie's inheritance keeps him going,' said the Monk. 'But a little bit more is always nice, isn't it, Uncle?'

'Here you go,' said Dog, and handed the case to him, Niglon Leglois, and started telling him whereabouts to take it.

'I don't want it,' he said, reflexively.

Dog Schwartz looked tired. He rubbed his head, then put his great hand on Leglois's thigh, squeezing it painfully. 'Don't be complicated, Leggy,' he said mildly. 'Here, Uncle'; and with his free hand he reached into his pockets, all of them, pulling out the most extraordinary assortment of bits and pieces of money.

Meanwhile Monk was rolling a ceremonial joint, packing it expertly with dark green weed. 'I tell you one person who's not to get any of that,' he said. 'Our brave Captain.'

'That's right, Monk,' said Dog, shifting forward in his chair, tossing back his ponytail, clasping his hands together. They were both speaking to Uncle Charlie. 'Our brave Captain Tabitha.'

Niglon Leglois held the case with reluctant hands. It was chilly. He knew what was coming next. Dog was going to tell a story. Leglois had heard Dog tell this story before. It was a story he liked to impress people with. The Monkey introduced it for him. He said: 'Dog knew her, Uncle Charlie. Did you know that? He knew her, didn't you, Dog?'

Dog nodded, sticking out his jowly jaw. 'I did. I knew her,' he said. 'Right little number she was. Screwed the screws, she did.'

Uncle Charlie was not really listening. His right hand was fumbling for his AV control.

'On Integrity 2,' Dog told him. 'We cleaned windows together.' He scraped an imaginary pane with an imaginary scraper. 'From the outside. Some of us preferred cleaning Ms Jute, from the inside. Giving her a good reaming, you might say.'

His voice was light, his brutality easy. He would be quite unstoppable now.

Uncle Charlie pulled a face. 'Who you talking about, man?' he wheezed. 'What chick was that? Your old lady?'

'The Captain, Uncle Charles,' said Dog. 'When she was an innocent young slip of a juvenile offender.'

'Never heard of her . . .' sneered the antique. Soundless as a top-flight drone the chair ran across the soft carpet to the AV console.

Leglois got up and picked up his case. 'I'm off, then,' he said.

Dog was cross. 'We're not *ready* yet,' he said, with a kind of camp irritation. 'Sit down,' he commanded. 'Just sit down.'

Leglois might have gone, and left Dog talking. But he wouldn't have gone all that way back alone; and the Gunky Monkey had already struck the lighter and started to toast the tip of the joint; and the Gunky Monkey always finished everything he did.

*　　*　　*

'They're going into the Unreclaimed Areas,' Saskia Zodiac told Mogul.

Her brother's simulacrum looked up at her under his brows. '*Unreclaimed Areas*,' he said balefully. '*Unregenerate and unknown.*'

She had arrayed him today in a velvet suit of doublet and hose, gorgeous leopard colours, tawny, charcoal and amber. She was wearing black pyjamas. 'I'm worried for Tabitha,' she confided.

Mogul looked at his fingers. '*Why?*'

His sister wriggled her shoulders. 'We're overdue,' she said. 'I'm sure we should be there by now. At Proxima Centauri.'

The imago smiled placatingly. '*Well, the ship does look like a tortoise,*' his voice murmured from the speakers. '*But tell me, dearest, who is it that's going, again, besides Dodger Gillespie?*'

Obviously J.M. Souviens was opening a new file. Saskia was pleased to note it.

She counted on her fingers. 'Professor Xavier and his lot,' she said. 'A couple of Xtasca's people. Geneva McCann. Oh, I don't know. It was on Channel 9 News,' she pointed out.

With barely a moment's delay, a smaller, square holo appeared in the middle of the projection field. Because the Ariel was standing up, it appeared in the middle of his body. It showed Geneva McCann in a helmet with a lamp on, standing in a cave where people were running about with coils of rope and backpacks. She was talking to a man in khaki shirtsleeves and jodhpurs. '*What can we expect to see on this expedition, Professor?*'

Mogul stared speculatively into his belly.

'*Your guess is as good as mine, Geneva,*' said Xavier gallantly. He was in his element. '*The Captain is sending us with a specific directive to explore regions of Plenty never seen by human eye,*' he explained out of Mogul's midriff. '*You know they say "Everything is here",*' he said. '*Well, maybe it is! Our job is to find out.*'

'*And Channel 9 will be there all the way,*' announced Geneva, in a thrilling voice.

Saskia Zodiac's imaginary brother tutted, rolling the window down to nothing. '*Why now?*' he wanted to know.

Saskia made a spontaneous, sinuous movement of her shoulders and spine. 'Well,' she said slowly, 'the reason, the real reason they're going, is –'

' – *to look for Alice,*' he finished for her.

'Now I declare that's too bad!' said Saskia. She put her hands on her hips and looked through him at the machinery that generated him. 'And how did you know that?'

'*I can only tell you what you know already,*' he said.

She gave up. She went back to her seat. When he started to laugh, she switched him off.

She stuck out her feet.

'It's all right for you,' she said to the empty holodeck.

4

The empty prospect of the Earth Room had driven away everyone but the most determined solitaries, hooligans and melancholics. The Last Poet had haunted it for a while, drinking Callistan claret and mumbling lines from his panegyric: 'Hyperspace, last high home of dead gods . . .'

Now a consortium had found a way to project virtual starscapes outside the enormous windows. They had chased out the wild cats and hauled away the battered couches and mouldering tub chairs, replacing them with telescopes and furniture of clinical austerity. The whole cave smelled of paint. 'Formerly, Earth Room; now Kanfa,' said the Supervisor, bowing. 'It means, Outlook.'

'You've certainly brightened the old place up,' said the Captain, sipping unenthusiastically at a glass of rice wine. She stood with her feet apart and put her head forward to drink, being careful of her clothes. The clothes were a suit patterned with multicoloured rhombuses, scarlet and gold and green and white. The Captain's hair was glazed and tied back in a thick bunch with a swag of white and gold lace.

'Of course, this is all the Inferior Prefontal now, isn't it?' she said. She had got Zoe to check that before she came.

'Inferior Prefrontal, yes,' said the Supervisor rapidly, ducking his head. He was wearing a tailored three-piece suit in a beautiful soft blue synthetic. He gave her another dazzling smile. 'The Integration, very splendid. Xtasca the Cherub, magnificent engineering, very splendid.' It was unclear whether he was referring to the Cherub itself or to the programme of Integration it had initiated, which had prompted the Topography Committee to run around the principal districts of the ship, putting up signs. Xtasca's communications chamber had become the Thalamus. Every fissure was now a *sulcus*, every ridge a *gyrus*. 'Warning – You Are Now Entering the Optic Chiasma'.

Captain Jute turned and looked to see where Saskia had got to. She saw her: a neurasthenic Pierrette in a white shift and baggy trousers, talking to a waiter. She hoped she wasn't getting too engrossed. They were going to be leaving before long.

'Captain. Please. This way.'

She followed her host across the room, greeting people as she went. The Pineal Grotto Theosophists were here in force, ingratiating themselves with the management. Augmented young techs and elderly men in anoraks were crawling all over the telescopes, pointing out features to each other.

Refusing canapés and accepting compliments, the Captain and the Supervisor passed on until they stood beneath one of the giant windows. The Captain could see herself reflected in the layered glass. As she moved the diamonds on her suit seemed to multiply around her in a prismatic fan, like a three-dimensional model of time, her past and future selves caught in simultaneous exposure. It was an oddly uncomfortable sight.

'So I suppose Kanfa means something in Chinese anatomy, then,' she said.

The Supervisor shook his head rapidly, his smile becoming strained. He was perspiring fragrantly. She realized she was tormenting him. 'Kanfa,' he said. 'It means, Outlook. Way of looking.' He seemed to be unable to take his eyes off her extraordinary costume.

Captain Jute was already bored with this reception. She looked round for Kenny. He was surrounded by three women holding trays of Chinese sweets and tittering in an admiring way. They wanted to pet his shining fur. He had his arm around one and she was sure he was goosing another one with his tail. She signalled to him with a tiny, upward nod.

She looked back to find the Supervisor's lustrous black eyes still upon her. His smile grew wider and more deferential yet, suspended like a crescent satellite among the telescopes.

The Captain felt obscurely guilty, as if his discomfort placed some obligation upon her. She lifted her eyes to the window, searching for something complimentary to say before she departed. 'Well, I can hardly tell you how impressed I am, you've done a very considerable amount of work . . .'

She supposed the stars were constructed according to information provided by the Bridge, which was now the Pons, of course, though it was in completely the wrong place – the Pons, where the Pontines studied their screens like monks their manuscripts, keeping the vessel properly latent in the interstices of existence. At present there was much excitement about signals originating somewhere called the Wernicke Vestibule. Many Pontines were sure that, once decoded, these would prove to be the long-rumoured music of the stars: fragments from the chorales of distant galaxies.

Here, on the other hand, presumably passengers would enjoy tracing their equivalent route in true space. The concept was completely wrong, but it was a good idea, in practice, to give the passengers something they could follow, something they could understand. Yet as she looked, those clusters of tiny white lights began to seem familiar to Captain Jute. She said, 'But that's a Terran sky.'

The Supervisor bowed once more, radiantly gratified. 'Ah yes, Captain.' He extended one elegantly cuffed hand. 'The constellations of home. The Cowherd; the Spinning Damsel . . . Most acceptable. Most comforting.'

Captain Jute's Shiva 900 blared loudly through the tunnels of the PostCentral, with Saskia Zodiac riding pillion. Rats scampered boldly back and forth, or lay flat, glued to the roadway by passing wheels. In the Septal arches, under the bridges and high overhead, the tattered denizens of the Rookeries pursued their precarious vertical lives. They had woven great looped traverse nets of cable and knotted vine between one platform and another and stuffed their shallow cells with colourful rags and bin liners and bales of styrofloss. Squirming about in sleeping bags tied round and round with string, they suddenly made the wall look like a vast slab of desiccated sponge cake infested with maggots.

The conjuror gave the Captain a squeeze. 'Are you all right?' she shouted over the noise of the engine.

Perhaps it was the light, which was thick and brown with a permanent haze of exhaust fumes and cooking fires. Or perhaps it was the

Sideways. They had an edge on them, this latest batch. Shivering, the Captain signalled to her bodyguards. She was pulling off the road for a pinch of crystal, to take the edge off the Sideways.

The Harlequinade was at Lateral Lake, celebrating Water Appreciation Day. When the Captain arrived at last everyone cheered loyally. Zoe Primrose and Karen Narlikar ran forward to drape a long red cloak around her and give her her mask, a china-white face decorated with a domino of ultramarine feathers.

Saskia climbed lithely from the bike. She wore three big black pompoms down her front and two slightly smaller ones on her cuffs, tapered white slippers and a skintight white cowl that completely hid her hair. She had no mask, but they had spent half an hour making her up, painting her even whiter than she was by nature.

Zoe was a Rigelian sylph, in glassy bodypaint and gauzy harem pants and not much else. Karen was a gynoid, in a silver tubesuit with conical breasts and circular pans over her ears. Their Altecean friend Eeb too was there already, on the shore of the brooding reservoir, dressed in a brown felt wrapper and enormous gold snout pendants. No one was sure what she had come as, but with a skullcap and a pair of large round spectacles they thought she made a passable Pantalone.

Kenny's boys, Otis, Lomax and Clegg, stepped forward, sorting out positions in the ice-blue glow of the lightsticks. They were all sporting huge round leather hats like Spanish priests, bulging codpieces of slashed leather and crimson silk, gold scabbards and blued bandoliers. They were Scaramouche and Captain Fracasse, or the Three Musketeers. They all still had their sunglasses on, but you could easily tell which was which because Otis had dyed his sideboards an evil green and Clegg was the one with all the plug-ins and only one ear.

'Darlings! Come and have a drink!'

It was Dorcas Mandebra, unrecognizable in a poke bonnet and crinoline. Her mask was the face of a white goose with a broad yellow beak agape in a permanent expression of affront; but her voice was unmistakable. She had done the catering, which was largely carnivorous: she had some kind of connection with Tekunak Charge and the Chilli Chalet, apparently.

On a tethered raft a string quartet played Handel selections *con brio*, defying the cavernous acoustics. Small children ran about, chasing with shrill cries the vermin that scurried out of the porous, fractured floor. Mr Bills was there, beaming benevolently at the children, and Mr Moon casting furtive scowls at Zoe Primrose from behind his visor. Marco Metz was about somewhere, a wonderful hooknosed Pulchinello in red and yellow striped pyjamas and enormous swaggering topboots. This was his idea of keeping a low profile, but he couldn't stop pushing the grinning mask up and fanning himself. A five of Palernians dressed as teddy bears and clowns capered around him, cooing excitedly and tugging at his clothes. 'For Chrissake!' came his muffled protest. 'I'm not him! I don't even know the guy!'

Kenny was watching a group that was still assembling. They arrived separately, on foot, and their masks were all different: dominoes, visors, caricatures and anonymous geometrical shapes. But they were all wearing red berets, and black short sleeved shirts. They had the lean, defined musculature of climbers or karate aces.

Kenny checked his team. They too had noticed the red-caps, and were keeping an eye on them. Otis stood with his arms folded, between them and the Captain, who remained oblivious. Kenny drank another squirt of lemon juice. He eased his shoulders in his black leather doublet, flexed the fingers of his feet.

Topaz held her companion by the arm. 'Have you met my double?' she kept asking people. 'He's my alter ego, aren't you, pusskins? What's more, he's got my name!' The similarity was indeed remarkable. It was impossible not to conclude he was her brother; yet the two were unrelated, had known nothing of each other until recently.

'He's called Thopas! Isn't that extraordinary!' Her friends agreed, with muted exclamations. Everything on Plenty was extraordinary, no matter where you went. 'You'll have to call me Lady Topaz now,' Topaz told them, 'so you'll know.' She certainly looked the part in her Elizabethan drag, quilted diamonds with pearls at the intersections of the seams. Thopas was a knight of another vintage, sleek in purple stock and grey cutaway coat. In his hand was a red and white striped stick, but instead of a visor it had a wooden fish on the end. Even his hair was the same as Topaz's, heavy waves of auburn.

Together they looked so much like twins Saskia had to leave. She slipped off into the darkness, abandoning Tabitha without even a kiss, with the result that the Captain wandered around for a while asking everyone: 'Where's Saskia?' She kept scanning the crowd of faces, the masks of lions, gods, smiling clocks; faces all unknown, somehow, all equally alien and indifferent. She had another drink. 'Stroke, stroke, stroke,' she said, watching a Thrant woman who was standing by the water, stroking the fur on her face. 'So vacant. The trouble with the bloody Council,' she told Dorcas Mandebra, 'is they spend all their time talking. Everything would run perfectly well if only they'd stop talking and just get on with it.'

'Absolutely,' said Dorcas. 'Executive decisions,' she said in a voice of steel, to which her costume was quite inappropriate. 'That's what we need.'

The Thrant woman by the water was wearing a primrose yellow pinafore dress, very plain. She had a domino on a stick, but it was a human one, the wrong shape for her face. She lifted it up and looked through it with one eye. She let it drop again. She seemed very ill at ease.

Zoe Primrose identified her. 'It's Kenny's girlfriend,' she said. The one with the drugs, she didn't say.

The Captain looked for Kenny. He was behind her, watching calmly. The Thrant was with a human man who was talking to one of Xtasca's girls, tapping out calculations on a wristset to substantiate whatever he was telling her. Iogo was keeping very close to him, though it was obvious she could not follow their conversation. The man was wearing a grey needlecord suit, a white shirt and conservative red tie. His hair was black and sharply cut. He had no mask. He looked more like a company executive than a partygoer. He had Iogo's attention, and the tattooed Xtascite's; but he was looking, Captain Jute saw suddenly, at her. He was looking at her with a little smile, a smile of satisfaction.

She kept noticing the man. He was talking to the Xtascite's partner; then watching the children chase someone's Wisp about; then standing with one hand in his pocket, listening to the musicians, drinking negligently from a glass of colourless fluid. The Thrant was always near him, sometimes pressing herself against him. She cast nervous glances continually in Kenny's direction, but the two did not acknowledge each other.

Though the man in the red tie clearly did not belong, he appeared quite at home. From his stance you might have thought it was his idea, this gathering on the murky lakeshore where no birds flew; that he himself had brought it into being, directing some assistant or other to invite a crowd that would be colourful and faintly amusing.

Without ever coming close, he contrived to move always around the Captain, bearing upon her. Tabitha felt every movement was an element in some choreographed sequence that would bring them logically and inevitably and at the proper moment, face to face. Or perhaps that was the crystal. On top of Sideways, crystal could give everything that quality, of inevitability, of purposeful structure.

Iogo dipped her nose and made a small, snuffling sigh. She was the only one of her kind here, apart from Kyfyd the Captain's man, and today she had not been told to talk to him, so she could not. It was the first time their masters had had the two of them in the same place, and it was making her itch. As usual, she did not know what was meant to happen. It was all very deliberate, whatever it was. She looked sideways at her master, but he was taking little notice of her, not even telling her what to do.

The mask he had given her hung from her hand on its thin handle. It hurt her fingers to hold anything so small for such a long time; but it was too big for her pockets and she dared not let go of it, in case that was wrong. Sometimes, anything she did was likely to be wrong.

She did not like being here, in this dingy wet place with all these people talking in languages she did not understand, with the noise of their music cutting into her ears like squealing saws. She did not like their drinks and their perfumes and the mad, frightening clothes they were all wearing. Masks leering down at her instead of people's real faces made her want to leap up and fasten her teeth in someone's throat.

They were approaching the Captain now, Grant Nothing and she, stepping right up to her. Iogo knew it was the Captain because of her shape, even with a mask and a red coat instead of a black one. She had seen her many times when calling on Kyfyd, though rarely so close. She was smaller than she looked on AV. A faint tang of chemicals hung around her, bitter metal salts that made Iogo want to sneeze.

Iogo's master was talking to the Captain. He was saying his name was Grant, and that he had looked forward to this moment for a long time.

'Grant who?' the Captain's voice said from behind the mask.

'Grant Nothing,' he said. 'Grant me a favour. Grant a moment or two to your greatest admirer.'

'Everyone's my greatest admirer,' said the Captain, but she did not send him away. He made a motion to kiss her hand, and she let him.

His fingers lingered a moment under hers, then he removed them. 'This is the lovely Iogo,' he announced, indicating her with barely a glance. 'She is as devoted to me as I am to you.'

Iogo could see the eyes behind the black holes in the white mask. 'Hello, Iogo. I think we've met,' the Captain said. Her voice was distant, effortful, as though there were more than a mask in the way of her thoughts.

Then the Captain lifted a finger and Kyfyd stepped from behind her, moving smoothly into position to make a foursome.

'There you are, Kenny,' said Grant Nothing lightly, as if this meeting were something that had been arranged, planned, timed, rehearsed. 'I was wondering where you'd got to,' he said, though Kyfyd had been close by all along. Her master put a hand on Iogo's shoulder, stroking her fur affectionately. 'So was Iogo,' he said.

He smiled at Iogo then, for the first time today.

Iogo looked timidly at Kyfyd, then at the Captain. She wondered if she was allowed to touch Kyfyd. She knew she was not supposed to when he was on duty.

The Captain didn't seem to be looking at them. She was toying with the frilly material around the end of her sleeve. She said: 'Why have I never seen you before, Grant Nothing?'

'Perhaps you haven't needed to,' he said. 'Or perhaps I haven't wanted you to. Perhaps I'm shy.'

This apparently amused the Captain and made her laugh, though she sounded tired.

Iogo felt better now Kyfyd was with them. His smell was comforting. She looked at him, to see what he made of all this; but he was watching Grant Nothing. He swallowed, his tongue flicking briefly from his jaws.

She made a small noise to show she wanted his attention.

'This is your employer,' he murmured to her in their own language.

'He looks after me,' she said. She always avoided mentioning Grant Nothing to Kyfyd, she didn't know why. She felt her heart beating fast.

Kyfyd said nothing. He was on duty.

149

Iogo felt suddenly very sad.

Grant Nothing was explaining to Captain Jute that he didn't care for parties. He was a solitary individual, he said.

'Apart from Iogo,' said the Captain.

'Apart from,' he agreed. 'Your glass is empty.' He snapped his fingers at a passing waiter, who filled it for her.

Captain Jute took off her mask and drank, the merest, barest sip, then glanced at Iogo, at Kyfyd, passed over both of them and handed the glass to an Altecean with gold things hanging from her nose, who took it with an eager paw. 'Wine,' said the Captain distantly, distastefully. She wiped her hands together.

'Water?' suggested Grant Nothing, delicately.

The Captain smiled a ghostly smile and put her mask back on.

'What can I get you?' he asked.

'What have you got?' she asked him.

Grant Nothing touched his chin. 'I have got something for you, as a matter of fact,' he told her.

He unbuttoned his jacket and reached inside.

Otis and Clegg were already covering him, weapons drawn. There was a fluttering and clucking as people nearby noticed and shrank away. Grant Nothing smiled pacifically at the bodyguards, with a graceful inclination of the head, and continued to slip out of his inside pocket a flat package wrapped in colourful paper and tied with shiny ribbon.

'To remind you of another masquerade,' he said.

Fans had always given her presents, though it had been a while since she had met one who did it with such style. He was not unattractive either, if a bit cold. He was the sort that rehearsed everything before he did it, preferably in front of a mirror. Tabitha tore the paper from the package.

It was a book, an old one with a stiff cover and no picture on the front. The pages were yellow, the print mechanical and large. She opened the book and saw the title. PETER PAN, it said.

She remembered that name. Peter Pan. Her father had told them the story of Peter Pan, her and Angie, when they were little. He was a strange, cantankerous flying boy who lived on a magic island with pirates and mermaids.

She turned over the page. There was a picture of him, Peter Pan, up among the rooftops of an old city, with a lot of flying children.

Tabitha Jute remembered the Saturn convoy, the party to celebrate the skip into hyperspace. She had gone to a masked ball on the *Raven of October*, she had gone as –

'Peter Pan,' she said. 'Fucking hell. Fucking hell. That was ages ago.'

When Balthazar Plum had first seen her, at that ball, she had been dressed as Peter Pan, and it was as Peter Pan he recognized her later, when she dragged him out of the wreck of his ship. '*Peter . . .*' he had whispered, as she opened his bloody faceplate. And then he had recovered, and rewarded her, with the gift of a boat of her own, a battered old Kobold called the *Alice Liddell*. Gone, heart and hull. All gone now.

She had always wondered whether Old Man Plum had known the secret of the little barge when he gave it to her. He was dead, the randy old tyrant, years ago, and all his secrets with him. Yet as she looked at the man in the red tie who had given her the book, instead she seemed to see him, Balthazar Plum, leaning on his cane, his red face lowering from the neck of one of his vile Hawaiian shirts. He was looking at her now with something worse than superannuated lust. He was looking at her with contempt. '*What happened to the present I gave you?*'

'Dodger will find her.'

The Captain suddenly realized she had spoken aloud to Balthazar Plum, who wasn't really there. Kenny was there, and Iogo, and Grant Nothing. They were looking at her. She looked at the book. A tiny, admonitory fear seemed to shiver through her. How did this man called Nothing know that, about the ball on the *Raven*?

'Were you there?' she asked.

'Perhaps I was,' he said.

He was a bullshit artist. Just another man trying to hustle her. Her nostrils dilated and a strange smile quirked her lips.

Captain Jute lifted the book above her shoulder. She was at the instant mercy of any whim. She was going to throw it away, fling it at random to someone in the crowd, or worse, into the water. Instead she dropped down on her haunches. There was a little boy stumbling about in the crowd, four years old maybe, bumping into people's legs and pulling at their clothes. The Captain called him. 'Here. Here.'

He saw her, a strange grown-up in strange and vivid clothes. 'Do you speak English?' she asked him.

The little boy stuffed his fingers in his mouth. He looked in at the eyeholes of her mask. He nodded warily.

'Can you read?' she asked him.

The child shook his head.

The Captain pushed the book into his hands, obliging him to get hold of it. 'Here you go, then. Learn.'

She straightened up, ruffling the infant's hair. He stared up at her with astonishment. He looked down at his prize. He looked up once more at the figure in the clown suit and bright red cloak and he wrinkled up his nose and crowed with laughter. Clutching his book, backwards he reeled away into the forest of legs again.

Captain Jute turned, laughing.

Grant Nothing was breathing forcefully, as though there were some constriction in his chest. His lips made a tight line. He regarded her, wide-eyed. His hands twitched and he put them at once in his pockets as if to make them still.

'Cunt,' he said.

The word seemed as if jerked from him unwittingly, like a word a man speaks in his sleep. It was nonetheless said, and concise in the saying, and never to be unsaid. The man who called himself Nothing stared at her for a long moment while Otis and Clegg hustled him; then he freed himself with an imperious gesture, turned on his heel and left, taking his concubine with him. Captain Jute found herself in a posture that she had grown quite unaccustomed to in her adult life. She was hugging herself, her arms across her chest protectively.

'What was ages ago?' Dorcas Mandebra asked Zoe Primrose. 'Do you know?'

'That she read *Peter Pan*, I suppose,' said Lady Topaz. 'I don't think she liked it, though, do you?'

5

The last eyes to see the Xavier Expedition drive into the silent tunnels of the lower LaevoTemporal belonged to two middle-aged Englishwomen, unless some of their dogs were paying attention. The women waded through hounds that surged about their legs, a muscular tide of fur in every canine hue. 'Well, I can't think what they're going down that way for, Natalie,' one woman remarked, peering over the edge. 'There's nothing down there.'

'I suppose they've got their orders, Laura,' said the other woman in a querulous tone, as if she suspected some kind of mischief. She would have complained outright, and been glad to, if only she could be sure what the shambolic little convoy was doing wrong. Tutting, she and her friend moved homewards. A sea of dogs seemed to bear them away, explorers themselves: huntresses in pursuit of a decent cup of Lapsang Souchong.

Dodger Gillespie had tried to find Saskia Zodiac, to ask her to keep an eye on the Captain in her absence. But Saskia was being elusive as ever, and Captain Gillespie had had to content herself with leaving messages for her and Xtasca the Cherub. With neither was it possible to be entirely candid. The expedition had targeted an area defined by the most likely escape routes from the last five thefts. In the dark they approached a pocket of deserted buildings, a tiny ghost town in the tunnel. TruValu, said a sign in the headlights, sagging over a supermarket choked with rubble. A roof fall had blocked the main road. Clearly no one ever came here now.

Professor Xavier decided to stop and look around anyway. He came on the intercom and said it was the sort of area where their quarry *'might just get careless, thinking she's got the place to herself'*.

Someone, Dodger never knew who, had betrayed that the real purpose of the expedition was to search for Mystery Woman. A busload of hunters had invited themselves along with Xavier, his audiovisual immortalizers, and the exobiology experts. More used to pursuing the wildlife they claimed still clung to existence in the lower corridors, though few seemed ever to have caught any of it, the hunters were convinced they were 'the men for the job'. One of them was an exorcist, the Reverend Mr Archibald, who toted a large crucifix as if it were an automatic weapon.

Captain Gillespie hoped she would be able to restrain the self-appointed posse when the time came. Meanwhile, there was no denying a few guns were a comfort.

Cats fled scuttling from their tread.

There were a dozen shops unburied, and nothing in any of them.

Their stocks of clothes, toys and consumables had been ransacked months ago. EVERYTHING MUST GO, said a sign. 'It already went,' said Ronald the Xtascite with a spooky little laugh.

In the foot tunnels the biofluorescents that were not already black and stinking came on, activated by the searchers' presence. The pale green glimmer made them all look dead, zombie shoppers haunting these stripped retail outlets in search of a bargain.

The Professor pointed to a local map on the wall.

'Cheer up, everybody!' he called. 'According to this, there may be beds ahead. Real beds!'

A cheer came from the exonaturalists, some of whom were women and children. The hunters reckoned it was all the same to them.

In the derelict motel the court was full of iron scavenger crabs, seized up, rusting in clusters. It was as if the little drones had migrated here for one last stand against an unknown enemy, a tide of time that had washed over them, aging them instantly and stilling their little clicking feet. The cabins were intact, and there were beds for everybody, once a few locks had yielded to a crowbar. Thoughtfully Dodger sequestered a double.

Jone, she had been astonished to discover, was a virgin. 'I've had men,' Jone said defensively.

'Christ, gel, who hasn't?' said Dodger, and laughed a cackling laugh that turned into a hearty cough.

'Straight after breakfast, everybody,' ordered the Professor. 'Let's make a quick getaway.'

They all turned out smartly, rubbing their hands. Xtasca had already been on, reporting no sightings since they left, not even a mysterious theft. 'We've got her on the run,' the hunters told the naturalists, grinning.

Dodger said nothing. She poured herself another cup of coffee.

The Xtascites had already commandeered the jeep again. Ronald had the front seat, Jone was in the back. Lloyd, unaware of any new arrangements, bolted down the steps to sit beside Jone. 'Last one drives,' Ronald told Dodger when she arrived, squinting out at her with a big sunny grin.

'Fucking juveniles,' muttered Dodger, easing herself behind the wheel and plugging the leads into her head. 'I'm not going to let you drive, Ronald, don't worry.'

As she pulled out behind the hovervan Captain Gillespie felt the road tremble beneath her wheels. The ship would shudder like that every so often. Vespans complained of it constantly. No one remarked this time, and Captain Gillespie saw no reason to mention it.

On they drove between swathes of dying alien flora, into the intestines of Plenty.

The naturalists, led by the Drs Catsingle, were not concerned about Mystery Woman, particularly. The ostensible purpose of the expedition was good enough for them. The hunters liked to provide sarcastic commentary and wry jokes. 'Flowers for the wife!' they chorused, for some reason, whenever a particularly rank hank of dangling subterranean gunk slapped the windscreen of the bus. The fact that it was a woman they were hunting appealed to them. There were boasts and speculations. There were kids listening, though, and you never knew what might get on tape, so they did try to keep it down a bit. What Dodger Gillespie couldn't fathom was the fact that not one of these people had actually ever caught sight of Mystery Woman, except on documentaries. None of them had first-hand evidence that she truly existed. Yet they were prepared to spend their time and quite possibly risk their lives burrowing down into the bowels of the ship to catch her.

Crawling along a low, lightless gallery, Dodger Gillespie said: 'You know, I got this little fighter. Shinjatzu Castanet, back on Autonomy Plat. Only fifty meg on the clock, not a nick on her. We were doing her up . . .' She amped the headlights, climbing a rise into another cave. 'I bet I could get ten grand for that now.'

'I bet you ain't got it any more,' said Ronald, wriggling in his seat.

'Thanks a lot, Ronald.' Captain Gillespie wondered how things were going, back in the System. She wondered how long things would rage, which way the dice would fall. Would the Seraphim possess everything? 'Roll us a fag, Jone, there's a love.'

'Let me do it,' said Ronald.

'Roll a joint,' said Lloyd, and yawned.

On the intercom in his grey camo blanks David Xavier sat, his arms wrapped around the steering wheel of the hovervan. 'Some pretty unpleasant territory ahead,' he told the camera, not turning his head.

You could see it already through the windscreen, but obediently Beth presented the view. Tapering trunks of matrix stuck up in all directions, supporting pierced and windowed membranes of something dingy and translucent. The ground was moist and clung to the wheels in tacky strings. It was like driving into a forest made of glue.

'Snot World,' said Ronald. The others leaned over the back of his seat, tipping his cap askew.

Captain Gillespie couldn't decide whether it was better to follow the hunters' bus or go on ahead. The bus kept getting stuck and they kept having to wait for it. A couple of times she had offered a tow, which the hunters had been stern in refusing. The Reverend Mr Archibald prayed mightily, while the men got off their shirts and heaved. Jone and Ronald sniggered, slapping at each other.

Lloyd stared from the jeep at the sterile galleries beyond the forest. 'She ain't nowhere around *here*,' he pronounced flatly.

But soon there was another spray of silver graffiti glowing in the headlights of the van.

Geneva McCann reported while Beth took tape and still shots. The Catsingles got busy with their callipers and wrist computers. Mr Archibald started to expound a theory of interpretation based on something he called Sandscript. One thing could not be disputed: the sign pointed clearly into a large unsurfaced artery that led straight down.

They would have to leave the vehicles. Professor Xavier pulled at his ear. 'We knew this point would come,' he confided, sagely. 'Fortunately we're all pretty fit. Some of us,' he said, putting his arm round Jone, 'have been scrambling about in tight spaces ever since the ship took off.' Meanwhile Dodger Gillespie was directing the van and the bus to spots that looked both sheltered and secure in the event of another collapse.

'Oh, go *up*, Beth,' Geneva was saying. 'It would be absolutely great from up there, don't you think, the three vehicles looking all forlorn ... Dodger? Dodger, Captain Gillespie, I wonder if you'd mind if we just had Mr Archibald bring the bus in again, with you making that marvellous –' She swept one arm about imitatively. '– vigorous – No? Oh, well.' She pushed her hair back. 'God, for a hovercam ...' she prayed savagely.

The hunters scuffed their feet and spat down the hole. 'Basically, Geneva, whatever's down there's down there. There's no arguing with that.' Then they stood back and let Jone and Lloyd get on with it.

They each shot a bolt in, belayed with a Howie rig and started the descent. Five metres down Jone found a place to crouch. 'Okay,' she called. Dodger rolled up her sleeves, put her fag behind her ear and followed. Jone saw her down. They both ignored Xavier shouting instructions from the top.

'I could murder a pint,' said Dodger.

'From your mouth to God's ears,' said Jone. She was wearing two limp singlets, one over the other, and frictionmax leggings. On her brown arm the Xtasy Krew tattoos glowed as though with an inner light.

Beneath them was the mouth of another tunnel. Line by line, jammer by jammer, they all moved cautiously down the wall and into it. It was smooth, shiny, horizontal for a few dozen metres, before twisting down into a corkscrew like a helter-skelter. The Professor's map-carrier scratched his head and pursed his lips. He had been sure there was a dark area beneath them, a sealed domain of vacuum and frost.

The Catsingles were busy scraping tiny samples of some flossy black stuff out of the crevices and sealing them in plastic bags. Their children had plastic drinking glasses pressed to the arterial wall. They leaned their ears on them. 'Listen!' said one of the girls. 'Machinery!'

Everybody listened, and everybody could hear the low grinding hum that rose slowly and as slowly fell away. It took one of the other children, a boy of twelve or so, to identify it. 'It's the lifts!' he said excitedly. 'We must be behind the liftshafts!'

'Listen, everybody,' said Xavier immediately, loudly and unnecessarily. 'Where we are is actually behind the Longitudinal Fissure lifts, that come down from where is it?' Vaguely he consulted the map, while the navigator muttered something to him in an undertone. 'Yes, down from Pineal Point,' he announced, as if his suppositions had been confirmed.

This information seemed terribly important to everyone. Rescue might come, if they needed rescuing. Besides, it was good to have a fixed point to orient yourself, especially if your maps were out.

Progress was slow because of having to search every nook and cranny. Everything distinguishable must be lighted and taped. The hunters played up to Beth, making sure they were always in shot, preferably sidelit and looking craggy. They spoke laconically, in perfect soundbites. 'The only mystery about Mystery Woman is can she stop a bullet.' A certain tension was becoming perceptible in the ranks, between these exterminators with their double-aught guns and the naturalists with their respect for all life, human or alien.

Later they came upon a car, an ancient terrestrial internal combustion motor car with manual controls, parked in a tunnel that seemed barely wide enough to hold it. Exclaiming, the youngsters wiped the dust from the bonnet. Underneath the bodywork gleamed, in perfect condition. The doors were locked, the fuel tank empty, as if its owner had just run out of fuel, walked off and abandoned it. The silver letters on the front spelled out *Cadillac*. Cadillac! The name took Dodger back twenty years, to a song they had used to sing in dorms and bars from Rio to Callisto –
  '*Buy me a Cadillac*
  So long and fine –'
with Tabitha Jute on harmonica and Muni Vega on guitar, Christ, the years.

'How the hell did they get that here?' she said, her voice a trifle husky.

The Reverend Mr Archibald loomed at her shoulder, crucifix at the ready. 'Beware the snares of the Evil One,' he warned her, as though the stranded car were some kind of blasphemous apparition. His eyes glittered with spiritual determination. 'We must expect anything now.'

The platitude was somehow unsettling here. Here nothing arrived from any other part of the labyrinth, no sound or light. The Catsingle family inched their way along, glowing shapes in their fluorescent waistcoats and armbands. The smell of raw matrix was strong, dusty, resinous, heavy as wax. As if to underline the priest's satanic forebodings, snakeweed hissed faintly from the crevices.

Beth's foot slipped on a descent and she landed on a ledge, not hurt, but winded and very frightened. 'We'll rescue her, Mr Xavier,' cried the youngsters. 'We're the lightest!'

Dominating the next cavern there was a turreted formation like a volcano on the Moon. It was twenty metres across at the base and open at the top. One of the hunters said he recognized it. 'We call it the Castle,' he said. 'Came here once after snake.' He kicked resentfully at the underbrush. 'Never saw any, though.'

A grassy gulley led to a wall of brown and white stained matrix. The hunters stared down with narrowed eyes as though expecting a buck to bolt from it. The naturalists knelt down and fingered the grass stems.

'Gone to ground, has she?' said Xavier. He gave the Reverend Mr Archibald a tough smile.

The place smelled of mammal piss. Its atmosphere subdued everyone. The Catsingles sat on their camp stools, whispering to their recorders.

At length the snakehunter jumped down into the gulley. He made a point of choosing a particular weapon, asking someone to pass it to him. Then he ducked beneath the spindly fronds and went under the wall. Two others followed him, a pace behind.

Ronald jumped the gulley and walked along the edge, following the hunters. Jone stayed put, her arms folded. Dodger Gillespie took a swig of water. Maybe there was a purpose to all this.

'They should have taken you, Timmy,' said a little boy sitting on the edge of the gulley at her feet. He was speaking to the dog he and his friends had picked up somewhere along the way. His voice was very clear and particular. 'You'd soon have flushed those nasty snakes out, wouldn't you?'

Timmy, a Cairn terrier with a handkerchief tied to his collar, sat staring stiffly into the undergrowth. He made little wuffling, lip-smacking noises, as though thinking about growling. He pricked up his ears.

The boy twisted round to look up at Captain Gillespie. 'He can hear something,' he told her confidently.

Soon they all could: a scratching, scrabbling noise. It seemed to be coming from beneath the floor.

The point man emerged from the grass. His face was smudged, there were twigs in his hair. 'I could break through there,' he told the Professor, as he handed his gun to one of his companions. 'Let me have that pick.' He took it, and disappeared again. There was a lot of knocking. The scrabbling noise grew louder, as if more of whatever it was were becoming involved. Then there was a cracking, crunching noise and the wall shook. At once there came a yell, and a shot, a number of shots, amid high-pitched snarling and squealing.

A white wave erupted into the gulley: writhing, boiling, sinuous little bodies covered in greasy, prickly feathers. They flung themselves at the hunters, clawing with all four limbs, fastening their teeth in fabric and flesh. One rode on the backs of two others, swinging a rusty chain about his head. Some of them seemed to be wearing the remains of clothing, tattered bands tied around their serpentine throats, buttons and bits of logos, MORLOCKS, RED STRI, NIX.

'Bloody hell!' shouted Dodger with relief. 'Perks!'

At her feet the boy stood up and gave a shrill yell. 'Timmy!' The dog had bolted into the thick of it. People ran for cover, clambered for height. Ronald took a chain across the face and went down into the claws and teeth. More shots were fired. Undaunted, the priest waded in, swinging his crucifix.

6

In the Pons pink lasers drew space-charts in the air, tracing the choreography of the stars. The big screen sparkled with a fractal analysis of the corona of Proxima Centauri. 'High rads in the Mesencephalic Nucleus,' reported the duty officer.

'But the pictures are clearer than ever!'

In general, the new placenames had been slow to catch on. People still talked about Morningstar Drive and Yoshiwara, Madagascar and Montgomery. ('It makes no sense at all to call it Lemniscal Pathway . . .') The Black Maps produced at that period are strangely eloquent. With their ghostly white webwork of arteries and cells, their spindly-lettered labels – Amygdala Gate; Hippocampus; Cyprus Caracole – they resemble more the fragmentary X-rays of some unknown creature than the internal plans of a giant spaceship.

Meanwhile, revivals of racial and national pride were infecting the vessel with a rash of secret sign languages and curious costumes, local tournaments and bonfire nights. Duels were fought on the Blue Jade Buddha Bridge, hand-to-hand combat between the champions of rival districts, dizzyingly high above the purple-black canal.

Certainly the disputes were exacerbated by the emergence of the time faults. No matter how often they were corrected, the public clocks kept sliding inexorably out of synch. Coms became unreliable and it seemed to take ages to get anywhere. The Xtascites whispered, nodding to one another: the areas of the ship were drifting apart in time. The subject of time itself became uncomfortable to contemplate, hard to speak of.

In the bleached light of the Pons the console crew struggled to keep up. They would not leave their stations now without a totem to clutch, a stuffed toy Perk with certified real plumage. 'You know the directory you said this file was in, well it's not in there, it's in this other directory . . .' The automatic food carts trundled around, still dispensing chilli and doughnuts. The astroscopes fluttered and froze, fluttered and froze.

On the Captain's monitor the Disaster Commissioner stood pressing his hand to his earpiece. A roof collapse had cut off a sector astern, in the Caverns of Disorder. He was after the Captain to do something, but he wasn't managing to tell her what.

His urgency made Tabitha tired. '*Power is being provided 60% by Tredgold Systems and 40% from local surplus by Switchcraft. Emergency air is on line from MivvyCorp, but the cost is going to have to be split –* '

All in all, it was more than she wanted to know about. 'Alice!' she shouted.

The Disaster Commissioner's mouth gobbled like a grouper. '*Captain, you'll recall the Council agreed repair and maintenance teams should not spend more than ten thousand scutari on any single item without authorization –*'

She kicked back in her chair. 'Authorize it then! Alice!'

The Captain tapped into the Thalamic network, selected the analogue activity map. Admin. You couldn't get any sense out of anybody these days, especially the admin freaks. 'Some people can't wipe their arses without authorization,' she said.

At their consoles the Pontines snickered. They liked to think of themselves as anarchists, surfers of the interface, answerable to no one but the gods of speed and dataflow. They consumed vast quantities of sugar and laced their coffee with amphetamines. They were all human. There had been some Vespans, sometimes, at the beginning, but they had stopped turning up for duty.

'HELLO, CAPTAIN,' said Alice, quite politely.

'Were you down there?' asked the Captain.

'I'M EVERYWHERE,' said Alice. Captain Jute was used by now to getting no explanation for delays in response.

'Just a minute,' she said, punitively. 'Thalamus? Xtasca? I'll have that damage report now, please.'

'*Internal fracture and disruption over 615-metre radius horizontal, Occipital levels 88 through 92. Water, power, com disruptions total. Air 60.20% and rising. Six dead, twenty-six wounded, nine critically. Injuries* –' Paramedic diagnosis videos of the crushed and maimed started flipping by. 'Skip that,' the Captain said. 'Okay – Alice?'

'POWER IS DOWN,' said the persona. 'GENERALIZED MALFUNCTION SIGNALS THROUGHOUT LOCAL REGION. OXYGENATION OF EXPOSED ANALOGUE APPEARS TO EXCITE SUPERFICIAL HYPERACTIVITY JAMMING AFFECTED CIRCUITS WITH 89% FEEDBACK.'

'What is she saying?' the Captain asked a nearby console jockey.

'She's saying she's got a headache,' answered the Pontine, her elbow on the desk, her hand splayed across her doughy cheek.

'HULL INTEGRITY INVIOLATE,' said the disembodied voice. During its report it had slid several notches into artificiality. Perhaps the damaged area was something to do with speech production, thought Captain Jute confusedly. Or perhaps the other persona residuals were all aft in the Occipit, gathered around the wreckage.

'How's *your* integrity, Alice?' she asked.

'INTEGRITY PERFECTLY SATISFACTORY, THANK YOU,' it replied.

'To you, maybe,' said the Captain.

For it was not Alice. It was not her old friend and workmate, not any more. She was a fool each time to hope it might be. It was some sort of alien virus that had eaten Alice, persona plaque and all, and now put on her voice from time to time, for inscrutable purposes of its own. Captain Jute remembered searching for Alice on Venus, combing through the circuits of her shattered barge. She thought of Dodger Gillespie, scouring the tunnels for a thief and impersonator. Suddenly she imagined a gigantic Capellan grub, chewing up the brain-shaped ship from the inside. She could sense it, coming gobbling up at them, eating everything in its path.

The Pontines had gone very still and silent throughout the green dome. Not a cola tube fizzed, not a keyboard clicked.

The Captain was dizzy. She couldn't remember what she'd just been thinking. Something dramatic; gone.

'The whole bloody ship is falling apart,' said Captain Jute. Her bodyguard stiffened, scanning the rows of desks for signs of disaffection.

She tabbed to the news. The big Kass robots were clearing up the damage, grappling chunks of broken matrix and insulite. They looked like yellow metal ants collecting breadcrumbs. She could see the Disaster Commissioner talking to a hulking Thrant in a reefer jacket.

She got out of her seat. 'Okay,' she said resignedly. 'Kenny? Let's go.'

It took quite a long time to ride from the Pons to the furthest sternward caverns.

On the road the Captain and her bodyguard were accosted by a prophesying hag. She was aged and gaunt, with bulging eyes. Her hair was matted and her smell was complex. 'Woe and destruction!' she roared. 'The Seraphim have taken Luna!'

Captain Jute remembered her birthplace, Serenity Port, kilometres of uniform antiseptic corridors full of cold starlight. She imagined the posthuman supremacists striding soundlessly in giant steel boots across the lunar permafrost, scorching the hollow seas with the white phosphorus glare of their experimental energies.

'They're welcome to it,' she said.

She touched the throttle, and they rode on.

A small crowd of ghouls and sightseers stared as their Captain and her bodyguard rolled into the cave. Nobody raised a cheer. This was the Occipit. Havoc territory. Boys and girls in amp skeletons cutting lumps out of each other; virtual violence addicts with silicon in their skulls. Status here was measured in scalps and reflex speeds. As they stepped between the barriers and tapes and temporary powerlines, Captain Jute saw them eyeing Kenny, sizing him up.

The best part of a day had gone by since the accident. The rescue vehicles had departed, though dust and smoke still whirled. At the site of the collapse now co-opted construction drones were hauling on cables, raising girders, clearing minor debris. A man she recognised from bloody endless Council meetings, Somebody Rykov, Lance Rykov, was directing operations. He was wearing a red beret.

The Disaster Commissioner ran up, hailing her. She could barely hear him for the whinnying of engines under strain.

The locals sat sullenly around fires, smoking cigarettes, fabricating unconcern. They seemed to be daring anyone to offer sympathy. They wore plastic suits with corrugated joints; enormous smartsole boots with studs all over them; filthy denims, filthier now, with every stain a badge of history. Their hair was long and unkempt and held back by headbands.

Tabitha Jute squatted down on her heels. 'Who died?' she said.

They stared at her. Did they need reminding?

'Six people died,' she said. She knew the Commissioner would confirm it; but she wanted to do this without reference to self-appointed, self-important authorities.

The warplayers looked at each other, a sliding movement of the eyes, across and back. She could have sworn one of them actually shrugged. A young woman spoke. Her voice was hoarse, as though it had fallen into disuse. 'Teenage Mary . . . Marguerita Passion . . . Seasick Sarah . . . Beardless Harry . . .'

Their black-rimmed eyes rested on her accusingly as the names crept reluctantly forth. Christ, they were children, some of them. They seemed to have the faces of her old associates, juvenile malcontents on half a dozen different Tangle habitats. What was it they resented? Powerlessness, she remembered, dimly. That sense of futility common to the disregarded young. Were they blaming her? Did they think she should have told them death awards no replays? They wore ceramic skulls hanging from their ears and knives in their belts, but what was grim about them was their innocence.

The thought of the years between them and her suddenly made the Captain feel she had to reach out and give them something. 'You can keep the machines,' she said. The Commissioner swayed back on his heels as she stood up, her long coat flapping against him. She pointed at the construction drones, the giant excavators. 'Keep anything you need until you've got the place back the way you want it,' she said. 'Charge it to me personally,' she told the affronted Commissioner.

The devotees of Havoc contemplated her suspiciously. She caught sight of Kenny the Thrant with a sarcastic expression in his long eyes. If she'd expected gratitude, she was even further out of touch than she thought. Captain Jute started to shiver. Everything here was horrible, ugly, uncomfortable. She swung away from the gathering with a cough, and putting her hand up slipped a surreptitious pill into her mouth. The bitter taste was sweet enough. It only took a second; then, inside her head, she stepped back in relief into the glazed and separate space of Sideways. Already the smashed matrix was turning into papier mâché, looking light as fluff in the grapples of the robots.

The Captain looked at the pills in her hand and thought of Teenage Mary's friends. She swung back and held the phial out to them.

The subterfuge had been a fraction too obvious, the gesture a few seconds too late. The youngsters looked cynically at the brightly coloured pills. None of them stirred. The smoke from a cigarette drew a familiar shape in the chalky air.

'Here,' said the Captain then to the Disaster Commissioner. 'Good work, well done. Here.' She gave him the Sideways. He stared at them with distaste as she walked away.

Bimprilic Niscshopuar blinked, pouting her eyes. 'Dixti,' she said to her husband, 'did you feed the unicorn?'

Dixtimifst's lips swelled regretfully. 'It is not eating,' he said. 'Take the third here.'

The Nixo circus was touring the Parietal caverns, searching as always for their next engagement. Behind the truck of the Vespan proprietors the vans and trailers clattered merrily along, their little bells jingling with every bump and sway.

Bimprilic, at the controls of the truck, said, 'Excuse me, dear, the fourth.'

Dixtimifst gave a doubtful puff. 'The third, I consider, but stop. I will shout.'

'No, no,' she said, acknowledging his offer. 'The third will be just as well,' she said, placatingly, and turned into it. There was no traffic, and the only light was the brilliant phosphorescence of the slime on the tunnel walls. Glancing in her mirror to check on the others, Bimprilic started to drive a little faster.

'If it does not eat, it will die,' lamented her husband.

Bimprilic had heard this before. 'We must try a different food,' she bubbled.

Her husband was chewing his cheeks in meditation. He was

chewing to influence the unicorn, hoping by sympathetic magic to make it eat. He would have ridden in the van if she'd let him. He would have ridden with all of them, the albino human and the two-headed Altecean. He would have let the quarrelling Perks climb all over him and suck his tasty lobes.

The unicorn was their latest acquisition, and of doubtful worth. It had come trotting out of the jungles into a human neighbourhood to lay its head in the lap of a female child. The parents, knowing a gift when they saw one, had brought their terrified offspring to the show, leading the creature with her hand on the sharp spiral horn that grew from its nose. It had taken Bimprilic and Dixtimifst an hour and more to get it into the cage, and cost them fifty scutari. The unicorn wept sticky silver tears and rattled its horn against the bars, but remained mute, which was just as well, considering Dixti's state of mind.

Dixtimifst pressed his flipper against the passenger window. 'If it would speak, it could tell us what it would like to eat,' he said. 'Perhaps they do not speak,' cautioned his wife. He was a sentimental old thing, apt to expect miracles. She was the practical one, the one who went round with the trumpet wherever they stopped, drawing the crowd and boasting about their show. How much to charge in each district; where to bring on the mutant babies and where to leave them out of sight: those decisions were her responsibility too. Dixti, if left to himself, would have sat in the cages grooming the exhibits all day, talking to them, apologizing for their captivity with many a lugubrious sigh.

There was nothing along this tunnel, neither buildings nor vehicles; not even a pedestrian. Traffic was lessening now, in both hemispheres. Even so. Bimprilic pressed the brake tab and drew up gently. 'Perhaps you'd like to shout, dear,' she said, apologetically.

Gravely her husband dismounted from the cab. He would walk back to the end of the line and shout. The echoes would tell him which way the nearest moving bodies were, big machinery or concentrations of people.

But Dixtimifst went only a short way back and stood.

An exhibit howled, the Perks squealed, and someone shouted out, 'Which way?'

Dixtimifst only called: 'Listen.'

'You haven't shouted yet, tender one,' Bimprilic pointed out.

'No,' said her husband, wobbling back towards her. 'Come here, Bim. Listen.' He folded back his head, gazing upwards.

Bimprilic put her flipper resignedly on the door opener. Well, she needed to urinate anyway, she told herself, and got out.

There was a shaft up above them, she saw, a big one, six *tesc* wide or more. Dixtimifst was standing with every pouch of his face distended, bathing in sound that was pouring out of the hole. It was a high-pitched buzzing sound, continuous and unvarying, that seemed to radiate down as if from the very fabric of the walls.

'You can hear that, Bim, can't you?'

Bimprilic's ears were shrivelling in distress. 'Yes, dear,' she said. 'I can hear that.'

Up above them, inside the edge of the hole, the wall was striped with silver metal paint. The stripes were in patterns, like the rakings of a claw. Some of the others, the humans, were leaning out of their vans, calling out questions, obviously hearing nothing. The exhibits had begun to cough and moo.

The whining buzz persisted, white and sharp.

'She hurts,' Dixtimifst whispered.

The air was cooling and the vines had lost their lustre. Slimy trails would appear overnight on carpets and furniture, and the air was thick with spores. It was as if some kind of season were passing, drawing everything into a moist, fulvous gloom. Plenty had never had seasons in orbit, or if it had no one had ever noticed. In transit it seemed to have ripened, as it were, and passed beyond ripeness, into an indefinable decline, an atmosphere of dissolution. Something had slipped away, leaving everyone fumbling at an absence.

Things were the same as ever in the good old Trivia. Lady Topaz was there in a bizarre long dress of leaf-pattern velvet, quaffing rum bumpers with her loyal knight. In the Window an earthly sunlight shone on the blackened statues of Prague, the red roofs of the Malá Strana.

The philosophers had drifted back to their old table. The Good Doctor had a tortoise with him, that he had found somewhere. It was completely withdrawn into its shell. The Good Doctor laid it carefully down between the glasses, like a fragile pie.

'There is a case for prescribing hibernation for everyone,' he observed, pressing his stethoscope to the carapace of his unresponsive pet. 'We should reconnect the cryo tanks, climb in and not come out until Palernia.'

'"To sleep away this interim of years",' muttered the Last Poet, who was doodling with a villanelle.

The Best Judge rolled his eyes and swallowed. 'Don't talk about *time*,' he said crossly. He turned and caught sight of the Window, which featured the knobbly spires of St Vitus's Cathedral, and groaned even louder. 'Is it supposed to dance like that? It's making me quite bilious.'

The tortoise made no comment.

'Oh hello, back, are we?' said Mavis Forestall cattily, coming in on high heels with her Wisp. She had had an enormous row with her husband Sven, and thrown his ring down the toilet. 'I thought we'd been abandoned for the Pause Café.'

Rory was drying his hands. 'Ah, well, that's it, isn't it?' he said. 'Everybody's fed up with Tekunak,' he said, as Mavis tottered into her booth, sucking tensely on her cigarette.

Mavis nodded. It was obvious she didn't see his point. Rory leaned towards her. 'That's Tekunak's too, now, you know, the Pause Café.'

Mavis blew smoke expressively.

Rory grimaced and shook his head, acknowledging an unpleasant fact. 'Now I can remember,' he said, lifting his forefinger, 'when there were seventeen different places to eat in this district alone.' He pointed in the direction of the Prosperity Mall, where he had never been known to set foot. 'Seventeen! Now there's what, three? All owned by Tekunak!' Rory put out his chin. 'I'd torch this place and pour the stock down the drain before I'd sell to those bastards.'

Mavis let out a final upward jet of smoke and put out her cigarette with short, dabbing motions. The Wisp came hovering towards her with the pack, but she waved it away. 'Have you had offers then, Rory?'

'I'm not saying I have, I'm not saying I haven't,' he said, folding his arms. 'I don't think you ought to bring that animal in here, Doctor.'

'Oh, go on,' said Mavis to Rory, stretching to see over the intervening customers. 'What is it, anyway?'

'*Testudo copiosa*,' called the Good Doctor.

'The uncommon tortoise,' announced the Best Judge. 'Sh! It's asleep!' he added, ponderously jocular.

'Well, I don't want it sleeping in my bar. Get it out, go on,' said

Rory, flapping his cloth over his shoulder and pointing at the door. 'And I don't want any of your bloody leeches in here either,' he announced to the room in general, as if he suspected everyone in it of secreting those seductive little creatures inside their clothing.

'What about her Wisp?' asked the Last Poet rudely. He was cross with Mavis for driving Sven away.

'That's different,' said Rory, moving down the bar towards them, 'that's a sophisticated cybernetic artifact, that is. Not a bloody reptile. What are you *doing*?'

The Good Doctor was holding a prawn cocktail crisp in front of the hole at one end of the tortoise shell. 'Look!' he cried. 'She's coming out!' There seemed to be no evidence for his assertion.

'How do you know it's a she, then?' asked Mavis loudly.

The Good Doctor raised his head. 'Her name is Tabitha,' he told the assembled company.

That got everybody laughing. Even Rory was seen to crack a smile.

One good reason for leaving the Pause Café, according to the Best Judge, was that these days it was full of Thrant. Practically all of them came there, attracted by the quantities of meat on the menu, and the warmth of the old steam pipes. The air conditioning was working full time to get rid of the simian smell.

Captain Jute had come to meet a woman called Marge Goodself, who was some sort of civic dignitary from Clementine Chambers. She turned out to be a middle-aged Southern Briton in a thick white murian fur collar and an enormous hat with navy blue braid on it. 'So pleasant, Captain,' she simpered, 'to meet like this, instead of in some stuffy office. Have another piece of Battenberg, go on, do. You deserve it,' she said, winking, 'all the hard work you do.' She was quite bats, the Captain realized distantly, crumbling the cake aimlessly on her plate.

Surely the waiters here should not be wearing the gingham check uniform of the Chilli Chalet? Or was this, in fact, a Chilli Chalet? Captain Jute looked at Soi and Kenny gobbling down rare, red steaks. For the moment she couldn't remember where they were.

Clementine Chambers: that was the place that had recruited its own police force. Bad news, Tabitha reckoned. Cops were always bad news. That was why she had kicked them all off her ship. Now here they were back again, like beetles crawling out of the walls. She could practically hear the clicking of their handcuffs, the creaking of their uniforms.

Mrs Goodself smiled a smile of dazzling warning. She was not one to be opposed. 'We do have to protect ourselves,' she said, crooking her little fingers as she lifted her teacup in both hands. 'Our little community,' she said brightly to Tabitha, over the edge of it.

Against whom this protection was required was not clear, or not to the Captain. Were the Rooks climbing up and stealing the Clementine Chambers cutlery, the brass bathroom fittings? Mrs Goodself did not specify. She talked only of 'risks', of 'our side of the aqueduct'. 'There comes a time when you have to put your foot down,' said Marge Goodself, positively.

The Captain wanted to leave. The room was pulsating. Mrs Goodself's piercing eyes were measuring how wide her lipsticked mouth would have to open to devour her whole.

'Let's not talk about time,' said Captain Jute.

One of the counter staff splashed Creamy Cup Protein Whip on a customer and was marched away in irons by two of his colleagues. The Captain felt her forehead. She was sweating. Had that really happened? Nobody else seemed to be particularly disturbed.

Marge Goodself was apologising graciously for her lapse of taste and stroking the fat gold medallion that hung round her neck on a fat gold chain. 'The fact remains, we all have to be perfectly vigilant,' she was saying. 'You have your security arrangements,' she said, with the slightest nod in the direction of Kenny the Thrant, 'and we have ours.'

The sugary meal was an ambush, a confrontation with demands. Clementine Chambers was after her to sanction its vigilantes.

'I'll see what I think,' said Captain Jute. 'I'll give it my consideration.' A strange fury was starting to uncoil within her. Why was she appeasing this barmy woman in her gold chain, her ridiculous hat? She raised her head. 'Kenny,' she called.

Her bodyguard slipped from his chair and came pacing lithely over to her. 'The cops,' she said to him, knowing Mrs Goodself would think it a vulgar word. 'In Clementine Chambers.'

'New Little Foxbourne,' said Marge Goodself, her smile unwavering.

Captain Jute was startled, sideswiped. 'What?'

'New Little Foxbourne, we like to call it,' said its representative in the same tirelessly pleasant tone.

The Captain looked at her protector. His eyes were yellow, his tongue was blue, he had shreds of red meat between his teeth. What *was* that stuff?

'The cops, Kenny,' repeated the Captain. 'In New Little Foxbourne,' she said, with a sidelong glance at her table companion. 'You've had a look at them. You've seen what they do.'

She was thinking of the body that had been found on the Promenade, at the bottom of the Clementine steps. She had seen it, not with her own eyes, but on the news; seen Kenny give his opinion to the reporter that the young man's neck had been broken neatly, before the fall, and all the other damage was secondary. Captain Jute had never asked him about the incident, until now. 'I'd like to know what you think, Kenny,' she said, sitting back in her chair with her hands flat on her thighs.

Keenly, gracefully, the Thrant ducked his head, curving his back, a display of approval. 'Good peo'le,' he huffed. ''fficient.'

It was not the reaction the Captain had expected. On second thoughts, it was. Well. There had to be some organized security, unfortunately; she knew that now. There were people who were always ready for a fight. They were here on board; they weren't going to go away. So yes, you had to be ready for them. She felt a weight slide from her: something too big to catch. She hardly knew what it was, or why she should be carrying it anyway. 'Okay,' she said. The word floated out of her mouth like a smoke ring and spiralled away into the corridors.

There were plenty of other districts people could live if they didn't like it.

Now anyone coming into the vicinity of New Little Foxbourne would be met by black-shirted sentries with huge dogs that stood with their heads up, growling: trained to attack, but rarely off the l east. In addition, Mrs Goodself personally commissioned the re-opening of the Septal Jail. It was an occasion the Party could not resist. Couples paid up to fifty scutari to stay the night in the cells before they opened for business; extra to be forceclamped or play with the riot gear. Godfrey Bills made them strap him into a complicated black leather harness and hogged the solitary confinement all evening. Dagobert Moon took photos, which he would publish later, privately.

While the fancyfree gambolled and played in prison, in Snake Throat the alumni of Asteroid 000013 had begun to suppose they had merely escaped from one supreme security establishment into another. There was no way out, no sign of liberation; and seemingly no end to the journey.

Perhaps the vessel had been a trap from the first. Perhaps all the passengers had been secretly selected for extermination, the deviants and misfits of Old Earth and environs skimmed off and sent away to burn in the furnace of an alien star. Superstition, rumour and voodoo were already rife. Father Le Coq's gospel was heard, his congregation growing.

'First boy!'

'Nohow!'

'Second boy!'

'Contrariwise!'

Saskia burst out laughing. She whirled around, pointing her finger. 'Third boy!'

That was Zidrich. *'How d'ye do?'* he said, bowing.

Saskia pretended to shake hands, laughing again. They were all here and she couldn't remember when she had last had so much fun. 'What *is* this game?' she asked.

'It's from an old book,' said the pavilion.

'First girl!' cried Saskia Zodiac.

'Fiddlesticks!' said Suzan.

'Second girl! Well, that's me, in fact. Nevertheless!'

'What?' asked Mogul.

'Well, *I* don't know what to say, I haven't read the book!'

'A children's book,' said the kiosk.

'Children . . .' They had all been children once, for a short while, Saskia and Suzan, Zidrich, Goreal and Mogul, and they had all lived together in a wonderful magic garden, where their food was brought by fairies and invisible pipes played at twilight, for the sleep that dropped over them like a curtain embroidered with stars.

And then while they slept, the fairies had come and one by one, taken them away.

Now they were all here, together again, all grown up, all identical, and all more beautiful sculpted in light than they had been in vat-grown flesh. Saskia called Xtasca on the com. Xtasca had been one

of the fairies, but a good one. She had rescued Saskia and Mogul.
'Look at us!' Saskia exclaimed.

The Cherub's black chrome skin glittered with the coloured lights
of the Thalamus displays, like cities seen at night from space. Its
little automatic eyes glowed cherry red.

Saskia was sure she was smiling.

7

'What do you think, doc?' creaked the old man in the chair, as the
familiar theme music played and the credits floated away upscreen.
'Can Brian get there in time, before his old lady snuffs it? And
what about that Princess Wilhelmina, eh? Did that anaesthetist guy
recognize her? I think he was the guy that was outside her window
that time, don't you?'

The doctor's eyes swivelled from the AV screen to her antique
patient. Wearily she kneaded the pouches of her ears, as though they
were hurting her. 'To me all they look the same,' she said.

The old man snorted with mirth. 'What? Come on, doc, it's *Sharp
Practice*! Everybody's into *Sharp Practice* ... Even Gloria likes to
watch *Sharp Practice*.'

This was quite possibly true. When the soap was on Gloria would
gaze at it, giggling and weeping; but then she giggled and wept whatever was on. Indeed she never did anything but giggle and weep and
bounce around Suite 2 in her personal safety field, and feed her
magnificent bulk with sausages and sweet porridge, the residues of
which she smeared on everything in reach. Uncle Charlie had
recorded the episode, and now he was playing it backwards at speed.
On the walls his astrological mandalas glowed purple with reflected
light. Incense perfumed the air with an entirely misleading fragrance.

The doctor had come at the ancient human's insistence, to examine
him for a mysterious pain he claimed to have in his chest. After
some time-wasting involving oiling the works of his chair with robot
lubricant, the pain proved to have vanished as mysteriously as it had
come. Still the old man required Dr Irsk to remain while he watched
his story. This was typical. His loneliness was genuine, the doctor

had no doubt; but so was his taste for manipulation. All the staff complained of it.

'*Clive, I don't think you understand the implications of what you're saying to me,*' said the AV. The episode had started playing forwards again at normal speed.

The Vespan unfolded her legs, pushing herself clumsily up from the couch. 'I gone must,' she said. 'Gone must check on the others, Uncle Charlie.'

She spoke his name with care. It annoyed him sometimes if she mispronounced it. Uncle Charlie annoyed could be dangerous. He would rampage up and down the hall, running his chair into the furniture and smashing the equipment. The nurses said he pinned them in corners and mauled them with his withered hand. There seemed to be no amount of sedative his system could not counteract, if he felt like it.

Uncle Charlie's chair swivelled suddenly, blocking the doctor's exit. 'No, look, man,' he whined, 'you've got to have an opinion! A medical opinion! What's the diagnosis, eh?' He enjoyed persecuting her. 'Wow, look,' he said, pointing at the screen. 'You know who that is. That's Dr Marshall, right? He's the one that's trying to take Clive's daughter away.'

'Heavy,' said Dr Irsk, offering the man a word of his own language in the hope of pacifying him.

'Heavy! Ri-ight!' moaned Uncle Charlie happily. The hues of the screen flickered and changed. The doctor had no idea what it was showing, what it meant.

'*Of course there's hope, Jack!*' boomed the AV, passionately. '*There's always hope!*'

'I gone must and come back later,' promised Dr Irsk with gentle pressure. She drew herself up to her full height and prepared if necessary to climb over the back of the couch.

Her patient shook his head. His long grey hair flew out from below his headband.

'No,' he said. 'I don't want you to go, doc.' He was speaking perfectly reasonably. The sensitive ears of Dr Irsk heard the soft whine of servos as something shifted inside the works of his chair.

'I've got something for you,' he said.

The doctor held her flippers one in the other, signalling resolution and impatience. She said politely: 'Give please to me.'

174

'Whatever you say . . .'

The silver metal brace around Uncle Charlie's left forearm rose with a tiny whine off the rim of the chair. It rose further than usual into the air, until Uncle Charlie's shrivelled fingers were pointing at the doctor's chest like a shaman's killing bone.

'Bye, doc.'

A tiny black hole in the front of the chair spat a great *chuff* of violently displaced gas, and a large red hole appeared in Dr Irsk. Gasping, squealing, writhing as all her bladders emptied in spasm, the doctor keeled over and dropped like a sack of fruit among the candlewax on the carpet. Silver stars and black light posters gleamed down on her outsize body from the multicoloured walls, like symbols of doom.

A horrible stench filled the chamber.

'Fucking hell, man,' murmured the ancient assassin to himself, distantly. He rolled over to the table to light some more joss sticks. Then he called three of the nurses to take the body away. They stood in the doorway without expressions on their faces, though one's right eyelid kept twitching, as though some part of her conditioning was faulty. It was hard work, running three at once. He had to amp up his output.

'Have to be careful not to tire myself out,' he told the assembled nurses.

Twitch, twitch, went the nurse's eyelid.

Uncle Charlie put some old Snuff Rock on. It seemed only fitting. Meanwhile one of the nurses located the doctor's control wand and handed it to him. Then they all crouched in their white skirts to heave the vast cooling weight of their former employer onto a stretcher. Fully laden, it rose at last, grinding somewhat, and puttered slowly with its escort from the room. 'Peace,' said Uncle Charlie, raising two fingers.

He turned the sounds up.

Some time after, the door opened again, all of its own accord.

A man in a grey needlecord suit and a dark red tie came strolling in with his hands in his pockets. He was flawlessly groomed. His hair was smooth and black as lacquer, as were the toes of his handmade shoes. He wore a small pair of old-fashioned spectacles, in frames of gold wire. His eyes were the colour of a drop of ink in a bath of water.

'I thought you were never going to do it,' remarked the newcomer at the top of his voice.

175

Uncle Charlie smiled vacantly, clasping the contoured grip of his joystick. 'Fucking hell, man, you never knock, do you?'

His visitor, sitting down uninvited, seemed to give the question some thought.

'Not always, no,' he said. 'Sometimes I come in, walk around, do a little bit of this and that –'

His interrogator screwed up his ancient face, hearing nothing of the visitor's rapid, unemphatic speech above the crashing of guitars. 'What?' he said.

Minimally the visitor adjusted the creases of his trousers. Uncle Charlie turned the music down. Something on the AV caught his eye. He pointed at it.

His visitor didn't bother to look. He gave a smile, then instantly straightened his face to show that it had been an artificial one. 'Princess Wilhelmina!' said Uncle Charlie, chuckling and gasping, as if the name was the punchline of a well-loved joke.

The man in grey stood. 'You ready?'

In the corridor stood a well-built black man with an earring and a gun. 'This is Dan,' said Grant Nothing, tapping his armoured chest as he strolled by. 'You can have him, for the time being.'

Uncle Charlie's head craned round like a robot turtle's as he rolled after. 'Don't shoot the nurses, man,' he told Dan. 'They're mine. All of 'em.'

They went along the hallway, past Suite 4, Suite 3, Suite 2, Suite 1. All the doors were closed.

They turned the corner. They saw another silent armed man, and another. They reached the door of the control room. Grant Nothing took the doctor's wand from the old man and held it up to the lock sensor. It warbled briefly, then permitted him to key the door open. He stood aside while Uncle Charlie rolled in, wheezing and whistling in triumph.

The aged patient beamed round at all the equipment, the cupboards, the freezers, the monitor screens. The little moving figures on the screens attracted him. Perhaps he thought it was another episode of *Sharp Practice*, one he hadn't seen.

'Hey, man, look at that!' he giggled. 'That's our Connie!'

*   *   *

On the screen Mrs Oriflamme was exercising her new arms. She was shrugging her shoulders and flexing her wrists. They were already quite mobile. She had some kind of interactive AV programme to show her how to do it. *'That's the way, Consuela!'* said her screen. *'Keep that rhythm up!'*

Flapping her elbows, her heavy brows drawn together above the great wedge of her nose, Consuela Oriflamme resembled some strange pink hybrid of bird and butterfly, practising to fly away.

'Frankie,' she sobbed. 'Frankie, why did you *go*, Frankie?' She gnashed her teeth. Tears ran down her narrow cheeks. 'I'll find you, Frankie!'

'I don't think you will, dear,' said Grant Nothing, keying in an Eladeldi audit override to penetrate all the main controls, and locking them to Uncle Charlie's personal frequencies.

Uncle Charlie was already bored with Mrs Oriflamme. All she was doing was waving her arms about. 'Hey, let's see Kathleen,' he said.

Grant Nothing sketched a bow. 'Your wish is my command,' he said.

'Fu-u-uck!' the old man bleated, chortling. 'You blow my fucking head away, you do!'

Grant Nothing looked at his reflection in an unlit monitor. 'Possibly,' he replied. 'Depends.'

Dr Irsk's huge rubbery carcass was too large for the disposal, and they had not been told to dismember it, so despite Uncle Charlie's orders the nurses had to wrap it in blankets and leave it outside the cavern doors. The first nurse looked at the other two. 'Somebody will collect it,' she said.

The second nurse looked at the shapeless bundle. She searched her memory. 'She has relatives somewhere,' she said.

'On board somewhere,' said the third nurse. She gazed up into the darkness of the tunnel, as if hoping to see a Vespan funeral party already making its way up Rocking Horse Road.

The first nurse frowned. She made her lips into the shape for a *W*, to ask *where* Dr Irsk's relatives might be; but her will escaped her and she was unable to speak. The answer would have meant nothing to her, in all probability. Restrained by the loyalty circuits of their implants, none of the nurses ever left the cavern.

They looked again at the blanket-covered mound, then turned and walked mechanically back to the hospital, reverting, until new orders might be given, to their normal duties.

The control room screen blossomed with sunflowers, bright and bold and perky as a cartoon. The camera was looking down on a little fan-shaped bay among the flowers, where the former fighter pilot sat on a white iron chair. She sat very stiffly, leaning forward from the hip, her knees turned to one side. One hand reached down towards the floor as though to pick up something she had dropped; but there was nothing, and anyway the eyes in the grizzled skull were elsewhere.

Flight Lieutenant Kathleen Beaufort wore a hospital nightdress, and over it a brown sleeveless garment like a knitted bolero. Long strings trailed from the knitted garment in all directions, woven through the nasturtiums and hollyhocks. Lieutenant Beaufort's Wisp was buzzing dreamily to and fro like an oversized wasp, an end of wool clamped in its claws. Ceaselessly it circled its mistress as though it was trying to weave her together again, knotting up the loose ends of the personality that had begun to unravel the day she had seen a soldier Frasque chewing on her bombardier.

'Hey, man, can I talk to her?' said Uncle Charlie; and Grant Nothing showed him how.

'Morning, Lieutenant!' said Uncle Charlie. 'I hope you don't mind me disturbing you on such a lovely day. I just thought you ought to know Dr Irsk has gone away.' He spoke in a false voice, high-pitched and singsong and full of pretended concern. 'I'm in charge of everything now. Isn't that nice?'

Lieutenant Beaufort snarled at the camera. The scar made her face look like an optical puzzle, a composite to be disentangled. Uncle Charlie saw her gather up her Wisp, hauling it in by the woollen string like a grey balloon. The Wisp buzzed and spat, curling and uncurling against the veteran spacer's breast. It really was a horrible looking thing, Uncle Charlie thought as she cradled it: more like a giant grey prawn than a wasp. The only human things about it were its ears and nose. The sight of it would have turned the old man's stomach, if he had still had a stomach that could turn.

'Ah, pretty *baby*!' crooned Uncle Charlie.

Greatly distressed by the taunting voice from nowhere, Kathleen Beaufort turned this way and that. She crushed a big chrysanthemum head in her hands, shredding it petal from petal.

'Remember me? Uncle Charlie?' yattered the sanatorium's new controller. 'We're going to have some fun round here now.'

Kathleen Beaufort stood snorting, scattering chrysanthemum petals from her hands. The Wisp clung tight as a parasite while its mistress lurched about on her damaged foot, complaining to every corner of her illusory greenhouse.

Uncle Charlie laughed. His voice grew even higher and more cracked. 'Pretty *flowers*! Would you like some water for your pretty flowers?'

His shrivelled hand quivering, he pressed the Suite 4 sprinkler switch and flooded its contents with water: flowers, furniture, patient and all. He laughed hard and high, and rocked back and forth in his chair. 'Nice shower, Kathy!'

The addled veteran did not attempt to take cover, but stood there gasping and blinking, puffing and spitting in the downpour. Her nightdress clung to her emaciated body like a sheath.

'All right, Kath?' shouted Uncle Charlie right into the microphone. 'Do you want some water with that?'

Kathleen Beaufort plucked the Wisp from her breast and drew back her arm. The little cyborg hung for a moment in her hand, coiling and uncoiling, clashing its claws. Then it was flying in a high curve towards the camera. It came close, its face bulging against the screen so close you could see its little eyes. It started to scrabble at the lens.

Uncle Charlie laughed until his plumbing boiled. He laughed until he sounded as if he was going to do himself some damage.

Grant Nothing looked at the old man sidelong, with a small involuntary wince of distaste. He snapped on a bank of medical supply readouts. 'Now I'm going to need you to look after the drugs for me,' he said.

Uncle Charlie turned from the screen where the damaged pilot was tearing up handfuls of flowers. He looked up at Grant Nothing with a silly grin. '*Ye-e-eaah* . . .' he neighed.

But for the white-painted banks of the life support system, Suite 3 was bare. In his eternal sleep Leroi Gules needed no flowers, no cocktail cabinet, no protective force bubble. He lay as usual, flat on his back, arms straight at his sides, his eyes closed, his face pink and to all appearances healthy beneath its crown of wires. He did not look more than thirty-five years old. Around and above his bed his machines ticked and whirred softly to themselves.

Mr Gules breathed. He breathed in and out, in and out. He breathed in a hundred times and out a hundred times, deep and regular; and on his control panel every breath showed in the smooth, hypnotic wavering of a little dial. Then something happened that had never happened before, neither in the days when Plenty was in orbit, nor since. Mr Gules breathed in; and stopped breathing. It was just for a moment that he stopped, as if a thought had occurred to him; as if he had arrived at some junction of decision in the internal labyrinth of his dreams. The needle on the little dial hovered. Beneath his eyelids Mr Gules's eyes twitched. Then he breathed out, deep and regular as before. The needle on the dial fell back; and all was normal once again.

Except perhaps for one thing.

On the chair in the corner where a nurse might have been sitting, had she not been helping her colleagues wrap the corpse of their former employer in blankets, or where a visitor might have sat, had Mr Gules ever had any visitors, there was now a white teacup and saucer.

It seemed to be a perfectly ordinary cup and saucer, complete with stains where tea had perhaps been splashed or dripped, and what might have been a crumb or two in the saucer. The cup and saucer could scarcely have looked more normal and unparticular, except that they had not been there a moment before; and that there seemed to be the end of a gold chain hanging out of the cup, like the chain of an unusually grand and expensive infuser ball.

There was something else that was odd about the cup and saucer, distinguishing them from other crockery. They were made not of china, nor yet of plastic: but of light, like a hologram; though among the abundance of top-range technology in Suite 3 there was nothing at all resembling a holo projector. In any case, what the source or purpose of such a hologram might have been was a complete mystery.

What was clear and certain was, that the next moment Mr Gules stopped breathing again, again just for an instant. Again the needle on the little dial hovered; and on the chair in the corner the inexplicable and intrusive cup and saucer vanished as quickly and completely as they had come.

*   *   *

'I know a man who'll look after the actual medical side of things for you,' said Grant Nothing. He had set everything up for the wizened old ruffian: com circuits; nutrimats; recyclers. Uncle Charlie didn't take in half of it. All he was interested in was how to operate the pharmacy. Which was well enough, since that was the only reason for having him.

Grant Nothing sat on the edge of the master console and flicked a speck of dust from his trousers. 'Where's this man I'm supposed to meet, then?' he said.

'Right, man!' said Uncle Charlie happily. His spectacle lenses flashed in the video light. 'Dog Schwartz. Old Doggie. You'll like him, Grant. You'll get on, you two.'

Grant Nothing was not accustomed to having someone tell him what he was or was not going to do. 'Time will tell,' he said, deliberately.

But the relic was so remote, or so aged, or simply so spaced out, he was immune to chronophobia. Dimly he fingered the com boards, trying to read the labels. 'Show me how to get Glory,' he said.

'Suite 2,' said Grant Nothing. Lightly he stroked the control tabs. A fuzzy image of the obese Pepsiphrax victim appeared, sleeping in her bubble. A colourful figure sat beneath her, his hands in his pockets. 'Wotcher, Dog!' shouted Uncle Charlie. 'What you doing there, having a wank?'

An incomprehensible reply crackled from the speaker.

'Well, I'm in the control room!' said Uncle Charlie, sizzling with enjoyment. 'And I've got a gentleman here wants to meet you!'

Grant Nothing took out a comb. He made a minute alteration to the lie of his shiny black hair.

In a moment, the door opened, and a big man came striding in. He was a gaudy apparition in a voluminous jacket of unstructured light cotton in swirling greens and blues and yellows. His trousers were crimson and amber and gold, in patterns like the carpets of a skypark cocktail lounge, with an elasticated waist. His hands were big, with nails well trimmed. They were perpetual motion machines, those hands, always doing something: fiddling with his beard, plucking his cuffs, smoothing back his hair to the ring of his pony-tail.

'This is Grant, Dog,' said Uncle Charlie.

'Oh yeah?' said the man called Dog. His voice was almost musical: a Welsh tenor, roughened by smoke. He sounded completely unimpressed.

'I've known Grant since before you were on board,' boasted Uncle Charlie. 'Since the old days.'

Dog Schwartz sniffed, and rubbed his nose vigorously. Grant Nothing glanced at the toe of his left shoe.

Uncle Charlie's chair whirred forward. 'Grant wants to hear your story, Dog.'

'Oh yeah?' said the big man again. 'What story's that, then?'

Grant Nothing's gaze flicked momentarily to his meaty face. 'I hear you're an old pal of our gallant Captain's, Mr Schwartz,' he said.

Dog Schwartz hitched up his florid trousers, rolled his shoulders as though beset by a muscle cramp. 'When she was a kid, yes,' he said, half resentfully. 'We were on the same gang, the same municipal service detail or whatever you call it.'

Unconsciously, he seemed to equate the aloof young man in the expensive suit with the forces of authority, who named things like that and sent people like him on them.

'Tell him what you were doing,' urged Uncle Charlie.

Dog Schwartz exhaled through his teeth, scratched his eyebrow with his thumbnail. 'They had us outside, cleaning the hull,' he said, and mimed a vigorous brushing motion. He looked Uncle Charlie's visitor in the eye. 'A couple of scrubbers, we were,' he said blandly.

Uncle Charlie wheezed with mirth. They both ignored him. The ancient monster grinned a metal grin. The lenses of his glasses darkened and a pair of earphones snaked up out of the sides of his chair and nestled in his leathery old ears. Tinny rhythms, like tiny clashing machines, trickled out into the control room.

Grant Nothing was regarding the big man calmly. 'Where was this, Mr Schwartz?'

'On Integrity 2,' said Dog, rubbing his chin. 'Actually. In fact. Hm.' Covertly he assessed the visitor who had handed Uncle Charlie the hospital on a plate. He might be an arsehole or he might not. He might be a nuisance, or he might be a bit of good news. It would depend what he wanted. But why was he calling him Mr Schwartz?

'What do you do, Mr Schwartz?' Grant Nothing asked next, as if he was interviewing him on AV. 'How do you occupy your time?'

Dog shrugged, tugging at his cuffs. 'This and that,' he said. 'Here and there.' He looked down at his chairbound trading partner. Uncle Charlie had found the therapy pool and was having fun emptying and refilling it. 'We keep busy,' said Dog Schwartz.

Grant Nothing put his hands in his pockets. 'We should talk, Mr Schwartz.'

Dog was nonplussed. 'We should, should we?' he said. 'Right-ho. What do you want to talk about?'

Grant Nothing revealed his teeth in a semi-humorous grimace. 'The Captain,' he proposed. 'The past. The future.'

He lifted his left foot and gave the mechanical chair a tap with his toe. 'We'll talk about Uncle Charlie,' he said.

A whining, wheezing, wavering sound filled the hospital control room. It was Uncle Charlie laughing.

'I knew you two would get along, man!' chortled the antiquated cyborg. 'Fu-uuckin' karma, man!'

In the corridor two of the armed guards fell in beside their master as he sauntered out of the control room and round the corner.

'Wait a minute, man, wait a minute, gentlemen,' croaked Uncle Charlie, trundling along behind, his claw grasped tightly around his joystick. 'Let me get the door.' He was eager to play with his new toys. His palsied right hand pressed a sequence of buttons.

It was the wrong one. Perhaps he had made a mistake, or perhaps his hand was shaking and slipped; or perhaps it was his advanced sense of fun. At any rate, it was the door to Suite 4 that slid open.

Kathleen Beaufort appeared. She saw the departing group. Stumbling on her twisted foot she launched herself at them like a tackling footballer. Her scream of insane rage shook the walls.

There were five of them proceeding along the hallway, all armed and dangerous. There was one of Flight Lieutenant Kathleen Beaufort, plus her Wisp, diving from overhead. Perhaps the pensioned pilot thought they were the Frasque that she had been programmed to destroy. Perhaps this was her Last Stand. Or perhaps it was just a break for freedom. There was confused shouting; a volley of shots; a throaty scream.

Activated by the sound of mayhem, the nurses came running.

They found their patient sitting on the floor with a guard poised over her. Her legs were spread at odd angles. She was hugging her left arm and screaming with pain. The hallway stank of burnt flesh and cardigan. The guard ejected a cartridge and aimed again.

The final shot slapped the Flight Lieutenant against the wall like a discarded doll.

183

There was blood, red and dark and plentiful. Kathleen Beaufort was a broken starfish in a wet nightdress. Her sundered features seemed to resolve at last into a grimace of indignation, as if she thought she had been cheated of something.

There was a loud electrical drone; more shouting. More bullets buried themselves in the ceiling. The orphaned Wisp was evading them with ease. It circled and swooped like a toothed streak of vengeance. It ignored the men with the guns and flew directly at Uncle Charlie, who was gaping, his mouth full of metal teeth, his ancient malicious eyes wide behind his spectacles. The Wisp struck, rebounded. The blue zap of the repeller field was dazzling.

The belligerent little cyborg lay stunned on its back on the floor, spinning round and round at speed, buzzing sickly. Uncle Charlie ran into it with his wheelchair, twice, three times. 'Fucking horrible things,' he concluded.

'Leave it,' called Grant Nothing authoritatively from the rear. 'Don't damage it. They're in short supply, you know.'

The nurses stood contemplating the carnage as if they knew there was something they could do, if only they could remember what.

'Pick it up,' said the man in grey. 'Go on, it can't hurt you now. Pick it up and bring it here.'

All together, the nurses stooped to gather up the body of Kathleen Beaufort.

'God's teeth, not her!' cried Grant Nothing. 'The Wisp!'

Later Nurse Rix stood at the door of Suite 5, looking into the candlelit gloom. The music was a tempest of sound battering the walls. Uncle Charlie was a domed shape turning towards her in his chair.

'Hello, nurse. What have you got to say?'

Nurse Rix felt her mouth open, her lips and tongue move without her conscious will. 'The cleaning is – ready for – inspection, sir.'

'Fuck me, how boring,' he said flatly, and gave a weak guffaw. 'Crazy Kathy all disposaled, is she?'

'Yes, sir.'

'And how's her little pet?'

'Disabled and stored, sir.'

'Stored where?' Dimly the nurse saw their oldest patient circling back towards the action. 'Where have you put the little sweetie, eh?'

'In – number nineteen freezer, sir.'

'Far out,' he whined contentedly. 'Now come in here and take your clothes off.'

The candlelight danced on the wall decorations, the dusty mirrors, the cut-out flowers and stars. The suspended corpse sat in his wheel-chair like a demented Caesar, his green headband like a decaying wreath around his sunken temples, his wattled neck garlanded with thongs and beads. He stroked his Perk claw, nodding his head stiffly in time to the music.

'Crazy Kathy,' he murmured contemplatively; 'Dr Irsk . . .'

His nurses were doing everything he told them. Their eyes were glazed, their minds held tight in the nets of their compliance circuits. Their sweating flesh gleamed in the yellow light.

The scrawny figure of their controller rocked gently to and fro. 'If we go on like this,' he told the room in general, 'we won't have nobody left . . . !'

In other regions too of that great ship things were not so well. An environment designed for the insectile Frasque and retro-fitted for human commerce and self-indulgence was becoming distinctly uncomfortable. In 'New Little Foxbourne' the dogs were restless, yapping and jostling one another in their pens. Moulds grew in their coats.

In the Inferior Colliculi the surviving human infants of the voyage, with their lopsided skulls and root-like limbs, celebrated their first birthdays with feasts of millipedes and maggots brought by the spade-ful from the Hanging Gardens. The local leeches, with their cele-brated psychotropic secretions, the children's dull-eyed parents kept for themselves.

8

Wrapped in a down comforter the Captain stood in the kitchen, sipping coffee. She had just woken up from a dream, about her childhood on the Moon. They had been on their way down from Serenity to Zeeman, to visit Uncle Jack. Why should she dream about that suddenly? Everything had been so vivid, so real: the big blue water reclamation centre, the uniformed crowds on the slidewalk, even the scratches on the plastic windows and the marks on the walls where graffiti had been cleaned off.

Angie had been in the dream, of course. She had been cross about something. Tabitha had heard her scold: 'Tabby, now everybody's *looking* at us!', just the way she used to do. *Tabby*. She had never let anyone else call her that.

And Saskia had been there too, for some reason. She had been very friendly with their ma, laughing and joking in a way that was quite unlike her.

She didn't have to mention the part about Angie. Muzzily Tabitha cleared a way through the dirty dishes to the com, and pressed the memory tab. She wondered if she ought to be doing this.

She got the acrobat's answering routine. Captain Jute heard the beeps of many uncollected messages. There was a stack of messages waiting for her too, far too many to face. If you ignored them long enough, most of them answered themselves.

The Seraphim have taken Luna. Had that really happened, the old woman waving her arms in the middle of the road? It was hard to be sure, these days. How would the old woman have known, anyway? The Captain wondered who she still knew on Luna. She couldn't think of anyone. Uncle Jack. Uncle Jack and Aunt – Christ, what had his wife's name been? Aunt –

The Captain sighed and dialled the Thalamus. 'Xtasca?' she said blearily. It wasn't, it was one of the boys. 'Can you find Saskia Zodiac for me?'

Her monitor flashed: the tunnel plan of an obscure sulcus of DextroTemporal Cortex, mapped in white on black; a segment of old promotional video for Sugar Grove casinos; then murky motion, handheld, through what looked like an abandoned poolroom.

'What's this?' said the Captain, wiping dirt off the screen with her fingers. 'I don't need the fancy shit –'

A white pavilion with a sign: the J.M. Souviens logo. The door. Light behind frosted glass.

It was ringing.

It rang a while. Then the image irised open on a preoccupied Saskia Zodiac. '*Hello?*' she said; then, surprised: '*Hello!*' Her voice was deep, throaty, ineluctably foreign. Behind her was an empty holodeck ringed with empty viewing seats.

The Captain sipped her coffee. Her brain was full of cobwebs. 'What are you doing in there?' she asked.

There was a bloody time lag. '*It's so hard,*' the acrobat said, '*without any source material at all.*'

The Captain felt irritated. Already she knew there was no way Saskia would be interested in her dream.

'*They all keep turning into each other.*'

She was making imagos of them all now, apparently: her 'brothers' and 'sister'; the whole clone. She always had been mad, morbid. 'How can you tell?' said Tabitha, a shade more aggressively than she meant; then, mollifyingly: 'Well, I suppose you can. Do you have to do that? I mean, do you have to be there now?'

I want to see you, she wanted to say; but Saskia started to reply before she had finished. Either that, or what she was saying wasn't getting through. Either that, or Saskia wasn't listening, which was entirely possible. Saskia Zodiac would rather talk to the dead. The slim figure on the monitor pushed back the hair from its high white forehead. '*The differentiating wave functions keep collapsing into synch,*' she said.

A line of type had started to rattle across the bottom of the screen. *Good morning, Captain. The time is 10:45.50. Phase 3 Corpus Interface briefing has begun in the Pons.*

It was Zoe, calling her to duty. Captain Jute ignored her. Saskia was still speaking, complaining in a low, dejected voice. The Captain felt a spasm of irritation, which turned at once to despair.

'Oh, fuck it, doesn't matter,' she said, and cut the connection.

As soon as she had, she thought: I could have just said, Look, I want to see you, and waited to see what she said. No, she's busy. Pissing about in a bloody J.M. Souviens outlet.

'It was only a bloody dream,' she said aloud.

A human delivery man in orange overalls steered a large hoverpalette into the Long Fissure lift. On the palette stood a games pod wrapped in plastic. There was barely room in the lift for it and the delivery man, let alone the fat young crewman who got on after him.

The lift began to rise. The delivery man heard the muted hustle coming from its music generator. His fellow traveller was gazing into infinity with his mouth open, probably puzzling over some problem of programming. He was wearing a greying T-shirt with skulls and knives on, and a pair of sagging blue jeans. The delivery man knew he was bridge crew, a Pontine, it was rude to call them Blobs.

The Pontine nodded at the pod. 'Is that a whole-body?' he asked. His voice was high and nasal.

The delivery man said it was. 'It's a special order,' he explained. 'Programmed for her specially.'

The Pontine scratched his broad left breast. The delivery man saw there were numbers written in red ink on the back of his soft hand. 'For who?' asked the Pontine.

The delivery man grinned deferentially. 'Someone you know well,' he said. 'The Captain. I'm delivering it.'

An expression crossed the crewman's pale features that quite startled the delivery man. It was a sneer.

'Stick her in it and weld the lid down,' said the Pontine distantly. 'That's what you ought to do.' He gave a narrow smirk, as though he expected the delivery man to agree with his suggestion, and find it amusing. The delivery man had never expected to hear the Captain denounced by one of her own crew, without the slightest provocation. Was it some kind of educated joke? What should he reply?

'She is very popular,' he said, in some desperation.

'She's a pain in the arse,' said the Pontine; and as if to punctuate his speech appropriately, farted. Still grinning he clambered over the corner of the grounded deck to the door of the car. 'Scuse me, my stop.'

At night, up the liftshafts and the vertical streets of the Parietal strange flotsam would come drifting from below. Sprigs from trees of distant worlds, some complete with sprays of still-bright berries; huge dead moths with wings furry and ornate as Turkish carpets; torn pages from magazines showing pictures of unfamiliar celebrities and detailed diagrams of inscrutable devices. Caught in corners and on doorsteps this unsolicited debris lay as if delivered by some inarticulate trade wind from the Caverns of Dream.

Every detail registered on the meters and monitors of the Thalamus. In addition to the impulses from the silicon analogue layer of every accessible quarter, impulses that the equipment scanned faithfully, filtered and classified and fed to the Pons, the original onboard traffic and surveillance cameras had been doubled. Now beneath the salmon-coloured vaults of ship memory that arched overhead, Xtasca the Cherub roamed continually up and down the murmurous air like a giant enamelled tadpole, the displays on its hoverdisc flickering as it sampled the material.

This screen showed a flock of white butterflies browsing daintily among the ferns of the airshafts; this one a tottering cluster of shacks where misshapen children cried at a ragged man boiling something in a kettle. The screen Larry was watching cycled through elevation calculus lattices, spiky with sublimating decimal flares, before flipping suddenly into a slow track up one face of Clementine Drive. In the window of a large apartment, two women were visible, drinking from little cups in front of an AV screen.

It wasn't Larry's job to spy on people, but you did learn stuff that way. Larry called up i.d. captions. In a second they were there: registered names; com addresses; street addresses; data about the broadcast they were watching. Larry wiped the overlay, zooming in.

'The Captain should do something,' said Mrs Shoe.

'Of course she should,' said Mrs Overhead.

The problem was, Natalie Shoe's husband Norman had gone missing. She had woken up in the middle of the night to find him dressed and putting on his shoes. He had seemed wide awake; rather excited, in fact. He had told her only that he had seen something moving, he didn't say what or where, and he had taken his gun and taper. That had been three nights ago. The Redcaps had searched, but found only his hat and the gun, which appeared not to have been fired.

Was it the infamous Mystery Woman? Had she now turned to kidnapping, or worse? It had not escaped notice that the taper had vanished, as well as the man.

'Captain Jute is the sort of person who would be quite happy if every man on board disappeared,' said Mrs Shoe primly.

Laura Overhead reached across to refill her friend's cup. 'You don't like the Captain,' she remarked, 'because she closed down the Marco Metz Show.' Her eyelashes dipped a sensuous fraction as she uttered the name of New Little Foxbourne's favourite entertainer.

'That's got nothing to do with it, Laura,' said Natalie Shoe. 'She's a menace who ought to be locked up. She's got no right to this ship. We ought to have a proper captain. Marge would make a better captain than she does.'

On Mrs Overhead's AV screen was Channel 10's *The Ugly Truth*.

In this show a merry host presented clips of prominent people in compromising or absurd situations. Captain Jute was the favourite, having often been taped staggering about half-dressed in the Yoshiwara or dozing off at the helm. The women laughed in a fierce, pitiless way.

After *The Ugly Truth* Mrs Overhead switched to Channel 9 just in case there was news of the expedition; but they were only running a looped apology. Zanna Robbins smiled brightly and read what she claimed was a bulletin from Professor Xavier, to the effect that they were now traversing the Supramarginal jungle and everything was proceeding as expected. Meanwhile Channel 9 regretted they were unable to show any of Geneva McCann's latest broadcasts 'owing to technical difficulties.'

Larry tutted cynically. He knew about those difficulties: shadowy images of people reduced to geometric shapes, to slow flares of dim light. If you speeded them up you lost what little definition there still was, and if you started to enhance that deep, how could you tell what was information and what supposition?

They were Larry's good friends, some of them. They were Xtasy Krew. 'They're down a fucking *time fault*, if you really want to know,' said Larry to the unheeding screen.

'You keep quiet about that,' said somebody in the next aisle. 'They can't put that on Channel 9.'

'Hey, X?' said Larry. 'Have you been putting pressure on these guys?'

'They understand there is no need to alarm the passengers,' said the Cherub, motoring by overhead. The air was damp. The pump wheezed, rerouting the water that still seeped in constantly.

Larry drummed an arpeggio on the desk. 'I still say someone should tell the Captain,' he said. She never came here in person, though she had been on lately, twice, complaining and making demands. She might take them for granted, but she was still the Captain.

On Mrs Overhead's AV the Channel 9 announcement began to repeat. Dreamily Mrs Overhead and Mrs Shoe lifted their cups to their lips. 'What *is* that stuff they drink?' said Larry, as the screen switched. 'That's not coffee.'

Now he was looking into a large cave lit only by stained-glass lamps. It was Maison Zouagou, the Tabernacle of Dreams.

From the ceiling hung long banners, with writing and pictures all over them: characters from the Bible, cartoon wildlife, old time video stars. Larry tracked up to the altar, where three plastic statues of different heights stood in a triangle: the Virgin Mary and a fat white man in a white fringed suit at the back, and in front, bigger than either of them, some Capellan Brother dressed in a toga.

He saw the Rooster, Father Le Coq, in his drape jacket and embroidered waistcoat, waving his ruby-topped cane around. Larry reversed angle and looked at the congregation. They were the usual: humans and Alteceans dressed up in plumes and bangles, cheap jackets and tight lurex skirts. Some fives of Palernians too. Everybody kept shouting things out, praising the Lords and making weird upward-swooping squealing noises.

The Rooster was preaching to them about everything they had lost. 'My brethren and sistren, look out of the window and what do you see? Do you see the fair Earth in all her God-given array?'

'No!' they shouted. He strutted towards them, shaking his cane. 'Do you see Mars? Do you see Jupiter, that is crowned King of the Planets?'

'No!' they shouted. 'No, no, no!'

'What do you see?' he asked them, and let them shout a while before he came thundering back: 'I'll tell you what you see. You see nothing! You see the face of the great Abyss that the Lord has promised, that is the Outer Darkness of Sin and Error!'

'Oh preserve us, Brother Felix, Brother Zekiel!' cried a woman at the back, bowing down with her elbows at her waist, her work-worn hands stuck out like vestigial wings.

Le Coq was on a roll. His jewelled buttons flashed in the candle-light. 'Who's gonna lead you from the Outer Darkness, which is the name of the Abyss? Who's gonna lead you to the Palace and Temple of Righteousness that is your Inheritance? Who you gonna pray to, children? You gonna pray to the Captain, say, "Captain, save me"?'

'No!'

'You gonna pray to the Lady of Spiders Madam Cherub, say, "Cherub, save my ass"?'

'*No!*' chorused the congregation. Larry flashed an ironical look at Xtasca, but the Cherub was away up in the memory stacks, occupied with analyses of its own.

The Rooster leaned towards his people, shadows making a velvet mask beneath the brim of his hat. His voice dwindled to a whisper like the rustle of the wind in the snagtooth vines.

'You gonna pray to *Ms Tree?*'

The howl of negation was immense and vengeful. You would have thought every man, woman and child there had suffered some personal injury at the hands of that elusive sprite. Perhaps they felt they had. They knew she was a thief. Perhaps it was she who had robbed them of their homes, their relations, their context in space and time.

The Rooster asked them then: 'Who you gonna pray to?' And, right on cue, another woman in the front row sang out:

'We gonna pray to Capella! We gonna pray to Brother Jesus, Brother Jesus, help us now!'

'Save us, Brother Zekiel, Sister Mary!'

'Brother Elvis, save us from the devil woman!'

Now there was Maison Zouagou calling her a devil, while the Silicon Sect net postings claimed she was some kind of god. Larry supposed she was just a crazy woman. He didn't see why Lloyd and them had had to go off with the Mystery Posse and break up the Krew.

Oh, now here were some guys that were really integral. Larry's fingers flew, bringing them up on everything he could, stripping it across a dozen screens. 'Double check,' he said admiringly, resting his chin on his interlaced hands.

There were five of them, coming down a Limbic foot tunnel, walking in single file. Reception was lousy, but at least it was in true time, and anyway it was obvious who they were from the way they walked, the way they held their heads, perfectly balanced, as if they were on gyros. They were all human, though, naturally, and unaugmented. That was one of the requirements, to be Tombo.

The Rooks were hanging out of their shacks cheering and waving tattered flags. They knew Tombo would fight for you and your community whether you were rich or poor. Some Tombo were from Rookeries themselves, young women and men who aimed to rise above poverty and squalor through discipline and the clear white light of action. Others were reformed gangsters; discharged Chilli Chalet staff; Martian streetfighters, gaunt and scarred. One had a nunchak; another, a big ox of a Hun, carried a quarterstaff, but most were disciples of the hand and the foot, low tech all the way. Larry could respect that, though he was the other way himself.

Tombo did not wave back to their supporters. They lived apart. When one of them looked at you you felt their eyes like a punch in the chest. When one of them spoke your name you felt as if you had been cut out from your surroundings with a scalpel. They glided through the garbage as if it were rose petals.

The leader, a black-haired Asiatic woman in white skintights, was superb. Sneaking a glance at Xtasca, Larry enhanced her body to the max. As he roved her curves her left hand swung across and he caught sight of her tattoo. They all wore it. It was the sign of Tombo: three lines, a stylized dragonfly. Larry's hand touched his own tattoo, the Krew sign of infinitely intricate recirculating curves that spiralled beneath his skin. He felt them throb, faintly, as though his own cells were trying to send him a message.

In the Hanging Gardens Niglon Leglois was lying in wait for wild cats. He was sitting up on a ledge behind a screen of foliage, waiting for one to run across the bare stretch of cracked and runnelled floor beneath him. So far, none had, which was fine, because it saved him the trouble of shooting it and the frustration and irritation if he missed.

He knew the cats were there. He could hear them now, in the undergrowth. Once in a while he would catch a glimpse of tabby fur or grey, a lithe back disappearing through the hanging leaves.

He was nursing a projectile weapon, a Lapham Scrutiny 282 with computer sights and carbon fibre rifling. It wasn't his, it belonged to Dog; it had been given to Dog by Grant Nothing. Dog had said Leglois could borrow it, urged him to take it away and get the feel of it. It felt good: sleek and dangerously heavy. Leglois had been sitting up here alone all morning, sitting still, with all his senses open, attuned to the slightest vibration. He felt the way he supposed dinosaur hunters felt on Venus, deep in the bush. Leglois had seen an AV programme about that once. A mystical state overcame them, in which they experienced an indissoluble karmic link with the beast it was their destiny to kill.

'Any luck?' said the Gunky Monkey behind him.

Leglois nearly fell off the ledge.

Slowly he turned his head and regarded his unsuspected

companion. The Monkey looked the same as ever, like someone born and raised at the bottom of an oil tank. He was grinning engagingly. His teeth were mossy green.

'It just ran out,' said Niglon Leglois.

'Don't be like that,' said the Monkey, scrambling closer.

Leglois expected a message, a summons, a task. But the Monk seemed to be just passing time. He stood there looking down into the greenery. The place resembled the site of some ancient temple smothered in jungle, its pavements cracked by roots and shattered by young trees. There was a yowling in the bushes, a brief thrashing of leaves. 'Cat?' said the Monkey.

'Monkey,' said Leglois, pretending to aim at his head. He felt freer around the Monkey when Dog was not there picking on him and giving him orders.

'What do you do, eat them?' asked the Monk.

Leglois was secretly flattered by his assumption that he had done this before, did it habitually, even. 'Sell them to the Chalet,' he said, laying the gun across his knees.

The Monk grunted amiably. A small illumination glittered in his red-rimmed eyes, like amusement.

'Where have you been?' Leglois asked him.

'Talking to Grant,' said the Monk. 'In the docks. Looking at what he's got down there.' He snapped a big leaf off a nearby plant and rubbed it between a horny finger and thumb. He sniffed it. He started folding and creasing it.

'What do you make of him?' asked Leglois. He hated the way his voice went narrow and tight when he asked it.

Now the Monk was pulling his leaf apart, as though he thought something might be concealed amongst its fibres. He looked at Leglois ironically. 'He won't do you no harm, Leggy boy,' he said, in some kind of comic accent.

Leglois shifted his bum. 'Don't call me Leggy,' he said.

The Gunky Monkey took no offence at the reproof, nor paid any attention to it, as far as you could tell. He finished shredding his leaf. The Gunky Monkey always finished everything he did.

'He's got all his ducks in a row,' said the Monk. It was a message of acceptance, approbation even. 'There's one!'

'A duck?'

Unceremoniously the Monk shoved his arm. 'A cat!'

194

The gun went off. A tawny body flew from the floor. A dying shriek ripped the Gardens like a sawtooth knife.

That was great. That felt much better.

'What do you think?' asked the Colonel. 'Little beauty, isn't it?'

She touched the silver shaft of the Drinski cobalt lance with perfectly manicured fingertips, just lightly enough not to leave a smudge.

'Looks quite smart,' said Grant Nothing. His hands were still in his pockets.

She closed the lid over the lethal implement, ran her fingers the length of it, lifted the case up and offered it to him. 'It's yours,' she said.

Grant Nothing took his right hand out of his pocket and brushed the edge of his hair with the knuckle of his thumb.

'A nice piece like that,' he said. 'You should hang on to it.'

Colonel Stark slightly pursed her lips and gave her head the smallest shake. 'We want you to accessorize yourself with it,' she said.

In her red cap and black uniform shirt, her shoulder holster and swagger stick, her broad belt and shiny black boots, she looked entirely resolute. Her skin was white and scrubbed, her eyes were clear. All around her troops bustled in and out of the PalaeoCortical redoubt with climbing equipment, medical supplies, crates of space rations. Arms and ammunition were being stockpiled elsewhere, secretly.

'You have to be in possession of the facilities to effect your own defence,' said the Colonel. 'At such times as may be necessitated.'

Grant Nothing smiled to himself. In the old days, his associates had never presumed to offer him physical protection. He might have been insulted if they had. Things were more direct now; simpler. Crude concepts of combat were resurfacing, turning from recreation into solutions to possible problems. There was something almost refreshing about the idea, like a brash, stupid old movie watched late at night in a silent, secluded apartment.

As if on cue, a small grey contrivance came buzzing through the air, hopping the partitions like a miniature helicopter. It homed in on Grant Nothing's shoulder and hovered there, facing the Colonel, opening and closing its mouthparts and pincers. Grant Nothing held one hand to it, almost affectionately, letting it snap gently at his fingertip.

195

'I must go now,' said Grant Nothing.

The Colonel stood back with her hands on her hips. 'I admire your Wisp,' she said frankly.

She knew enough not to touch it. She respected it as a personal security device. Five minutes from now she would probably be reading up on the re-imprinting techniques, studying the circuit diagram of its neural attack systems.

Grant Nothing smiled meaninglessly.

The Colonel raised her eyes and looked at him with an almost flirtatious directness. They had been lovers once, years ago. It had interested him to mix business, very precisely, with pleasure.

'Sure you won't come and survey New Little Foxbourne?' she said, one last time. 'It's a model operation we have up there. The shape of things to eventuate,' she claimed.

'Fun for you,' he said. Casually he pocketed her sleek and powerful gift.

Grant Nothing stroked the head of his Wisp. He brought his lips close to its rudimentary ear. 'Home,' he said.

On the funicular up Stiletto Gyrus Grant Nothing fiddled with the AV, but all he could get was pale green fizz. He thought about Channel 10, planning what to give them next.

The title of the AV programme had been his own idea. Captain Jute had had a very bad time not so long ago on a ship called the *Ugly Truth*. Grant Nothing made a note to raid the traffic files and collect the times she had fallen off her bike. Basic hilarity. Demeaning. He wondered if she would see it, and wished he could watch her. He imagined her face, her displeasure.

He looked at himself in the dark window. The lance in his pocket was ruining the hang of his jacket. Of course the nasty thing did not interest him. Another toy for Dog. The others were already jealous of Mr Schwartz, with his fancy clothes and his obnoxious attitude. It would do no harm to feed that for a while.

'There's only one thing I want,' said Grant Nothing, tickling his Wisp.

Iogo sat against the wall of the apartment with her hands around her knees. Her man was setting up his idol, his shrine, his ghost in a box. 'What do you want, Iogo?' he asked her. 'On the new world?

Succulent prey? Fat Palernians gambolling in the forest, hm?'

The little ghost appeared.

'Captain,' said Grant Nothing.

Iogo sighed. She did not like it when he spoke to it.

He often spoke to it now.

'Do you remember,' he asked the woman on the screen, 'on Integrity 2 you associated with a juvenile gang? The Rejects, they called themselves.' The little ghost was made of light and did not move. Grant Nothing smiled.

'According to Mr Schwartz,' he told it, 'you stole a delta kite from a police cadet with whom you were having an affair. You got stuck in zero g like a fly in a web, kicking your legs. You had to be rescued.'

Iogo wished she was not in the room. He spoke to it tenderly, his ghost; but he did not mean tenderness.

He caressed the keyboard of his machine.

'How they would love a few seconds of that on Channel 10!'

He pretended to stroke the ghost. 'We are so close,' he said. 'I am under your skin. I am inside your nervous system. Curled up in the blind spot of your retina.'

The Thrant sighed again heavily and pulled her shawl over her head. She didn't know many of the words he was saying, but she was afraid for him. What if the Captain heard? What if other people could hear him, the way he seemed to be able to hear them?

'Iogo.'

She jumped. She stared. She laid her ears back.

'Don't cower, Iogo, you know how I abominate it.'

He came to her where she sat, put out a hand and touched her muzzle. Overwrought, she twitched. Her own helplessness possessed her.

'You still flinch,' said the man. His voice was low, controlled, not sharp. He might have been speaking of some pleasant thing, sunlight on the sierra, a stream with fish running. 'I don't know why you flinch,' he said. Then he took hold of her arm and rubbed his cheek against it. 'Ah, Iogo, Iogo. I would like to love you, but sometimes you try to stop me.'

She could not speak. She felt walls, ceilings, cold hard darkness pressing. She turned her head away, baring her throat, looking at him out of the corner of her eye.

Grant Nothing dropped her arm in mild disgust. 'Get us some

food,' he said. 'And I think you might take a shower before you do. Shower, Iogo, hm?'

On a monitor in the Thalamus Xtasca the Cherub picked up the burr of some high-powered system performing.

It purred gently, digesting the information. 'Larry,' it called. 'Here it is again.'

'Chief,' said Larry automatically, loping down the aisle to where it sat, taking the seat beneath its saucer. His neighbour leaned over from the next desk to watch.

Larry recognized the signs at once. It was a unique force, always screened or scrambled, never referable to known activity. Something was eating wormholes in the datasphere.

His neighbour rested her chin on his shoulder. 'Is it the guy?' she said.

'What guy?' asked Larry.

'Human male with a Thrant female,' she said. 'Sometimes they're in the area.'

Larry mused, playing with his bangles. 'Mystery Man,' he said.

The Captain stroked her new pod. She tapped its little white persona plaque on her thumbnail. It was only a Corban Ariel Three, but it would do. She grimaced, and pressed a hand to her midriff, despising herself. She was actually nervous!

Dutifully she checked in with the Pons. Onscreen, the place looked a mess, exposed circuitry everywhere. The Corpus Interface was being installed, to mediate between the two hemispheres. According to the programmers, it would be a great improvement. Captain Jute made appropriate noises of encouragement.

Then she got into the pod, and closed herself in darkness, darkness that smelled of other people's breath and sweat and excitement. She pulled the headset on and felt the VR harness snap round her like a pilot's web.

She was in the cockpit. The boards were lit up around her, a treasure cave of green jewels, jiggling graphics, status lights. Under her fingers she felt the warm plastic of console keys; over her head, the canopy was full of space, real space.

They were in motion. She could feel the weightless mass of a full hold at her back and the judder of three big Bergen roundmouths pushing it slowly into traffic, into the Tangle, where corporate tubes and cut-price platforms danced their shining, slow, evasive dance with BurgerWorlds and Red and Whites.

'All right . . .' said Captain Jute.

In the distance an old Mitchum magnet train came trundling by, laden with lush ores and frozen gas from the asteroid mines, while nearer at hand, Navajo Scorpions and Freimacher Eagles browsed the commerce reef like greedy metallic fish. One of them crossed her lane without signalling, making an illegal turn. 'Typical!' shouted Captain Jute, with delight.

'WOULD YOU LIKE ME TO PREPARE A COURSE, CAPTAIN?' asked a polite, familiar voice in her ear.

Behind her visor Tabitha Jute smiled so hard she thought her jaw would break.

'Steady as you go, Alice,' she said.

'STEADY IT IS, CAPTAIN,' said the Ariel.

9

In the Belt, on the radio, you call everybody 'Captain'. *'Ahoy there, Captain, coming in now on your heading.' 'Is that you, Captain?' 'Okay, Captain, got you now.'* Dodger Gillespie had several close friends whose names she did not know. As far as she was concerned, their names were the names of their ships. 'Blue Boy, *have you seen* Cutting Edge? *She said she was looking for you, you lucky hound!'* It was an intimate, devoted little community, whose members rarely came within a hundred kilometres of each other.

She wished she could say the same of the members of the David Xavier Expedition.

They crossed a channel of gurgling brown water and clambered up a scree slope into a cave full of lumpy stalagmites and stalactites. The children ran in and out of them, chasing each other in circles. 'This is a smashing adventure!' they chorused, shining their helmet lamps in her eyes. 'Don't you think so, Captain Gillespie?'

'On we go, Captain,' said the Reverend Mr Archibald heartily, limping energetically up behind her. 'The wounded bringing up the rear, eh?'

His military spirit depressed her as much as his piety. He had insisted on stopping to conduct a proper burial of those slain on both sides, covering them in a mound of dirt and fragments of matrix.

Since their flight from the Perk burrow, the only intelligent life they had seen had been a man on a bridge, five levels up, pushing what looked like a big AV set in a wheelbarrow. Could that have been only yesterday? Why could no one remember?

Captain Gillespie had sustained a bite on her right arm, which hurt like hell, and some scratches, the worst of them on her side, which had become inflamed and stiff. Walking on this uneven floor wasn't helping. She pressed grimly on, following the bobbing bulk of the big Channel 9 spotlight, which Xavier was nobly carrying on his back. Unseen in his grey camouflage gear he had escaped all injury.

They intersected a tunnel that somebody had been using to dump garbage. They stopped on the edge of a vast heap of plastic coffee bottles, rhubarb leaves and used Kleenex. The children's dog nosed hopefully at a rancid tin and cocked his leg.

Here they paused to regroup and rest the stretcher bearers. Jone and Lloyd elected to continue carrying their stretcher; because they could not carry Ronald. His death had shaken them, Dodger knew. They were young and innocent, and like all youngsters, thought themselves immune to mortality. Captain Gillespie reckoned they would be introduced to another sample of it soon. Their burden, one of the Catsingles' field assistants, was not in good shape. She had not recovered consciousness since the fight.

Captain Gillespie remembered the late Ronald at the motel speaking out on behalf of their quarry. 'I don't see what harm she does,' he had said. 'Copy, so she nicks some stuff. So what? There's plenty more!'

He had pressed the point until she had felt obliged to offer a partial explanation. 'The bridge crew have got problems,' she began.

This was a cue for the whole team to caw derisively.

'They've got problems, check!'

'Blobs,' she heard Lloyd say witheringly. The Xtascites had a lively contempt for their sedentary counterparts, permanently glued to their consoles. Nothing else was real for them but the abstractions displayed on the big screen, though they were able to talk extensively about their preferences in the question of pizza toppings.

'They're a waste of space,' Lloyd had said. 'They can't do nothing without us.'

He had pulled a multicoloured switch cord that hung from his headset and started drumming energetically on the dining room table with a pair of analogue probes. 'Ask them about black holes –'

Ronald had interrupted to declare with slow and dramatic righteousness: 'The only black hole they know is the Captain's sweet –'

Laughter and an elbow from Jone had stopped him.

Ronald had sketched a bow to her, and one to Dodger, as though to discharge some sense of obligation to authority. 'Sorry, mam, sor*ree*,' he had said, highly pleased with himself.

'Left, I think, people,' called Professor Xavier then, '*if* you're ready'; and everyone clambered wearily to their feet among the garbage.

The tunnel debouched into a cave where a beer-coloured stream rushed over flat grey plates of matrix hard as rock. They waded across, then followed the far bank through a culvert into another cavern deep in silt. They straightened up, looking around. They stood on the shore of a dirty reservoir. Slender growths rose up from the shallows in clumps, like rushes wrapped in cobwebs, and large mats of sooty moss stained the surface.

'Starchy,' said Jone, shivering.

Xtasca was completely out of range. Still the map-bearers were satisfied. 'Cisternum Magna,' they announced. The lamps showed strange pawprints in the muck around the rim, and copious droppings like fossilized fivepenny cigars.

The Catsingles in their drab green jumpsuits knelt to examine them. 'Not Perk,' one assured Professor Xavier. 'But that is not to say Perk may not be present,' the other butted in. The extraterrestrial naturalists had been excited to witness the behaviour of those vicious little creatures, and were still speculating keenly on its cause and significance. They turned up the amps on their binoculars, and called their children to come away from the edge.

Along the caked and treacherous bank they plodded, crossing at every other step some murky little runnel or tributary. Geneva

McCann splashed through them, resentfully. She was still angry over the loss of equipment and irreplaceable footage. 'We didn't mean them any harm,' she kept saying. 'Animals. That's all they are.' She turned suddenly, appealing to her camerawoman. 'We could have given them their own *forty-minute feature*, if they'd just stopped to *negotiate.*'

'"A Peek at Perks",' mused Beth. '"Underfloor Fauna".'

'Atavistic reversion,' said the Catsingles, to anyone who would listen. 'A vindication of Spengler?' suggested one. 'Of Skinner, rather, I think,' said the other. They eyed each other competitively.

Dodger Gillespie knew if she stopped again her side would seize up. Dazed with aches and fatigue, she tripped over a half-buried air vent and startled a white buck rat that must have been fifty centimetres from nose to tail; but of pale brown women in long leather coats toting stolen appliances she saw not the slightest sign.

Her friend Jone, tiring of her load at last, had permitted one of the hunters to relieve her. She came jogging back down the line to put an arm around Dodger.

Dodger flinched. 'Christ, gel, go easy.'

'Oh shit, sorry. Trying to help.'

'Do that again, it'll be me you're carrying. How is she?' the limping pilot asked.

Jone shrugged. 'Don't fancy any of their chances,' she said. Her voice came out husky; her sweet eyes glittered, staring fixedly at nothing.

'Go on,' said Captain Gillespie, patting her awkwardly on the shoulder. 'Cry, if you want to.'

'Fuck you,' said Jone grimly, stepping clear. 'I was doing all right.' She wiped her nose savagely on the side of her thumb. 'He could be a right penis when he wanted to,' she mourned, meaning Ronald, 'but I really miss him, check –?'

'Check,' said Dodger. Jone put her arm around her again, more cautiously.

Together they staggered on.

The expedition came to a leak, or perhaps it was an outlet of some kind, that poured chalky grey water in a great fan shape down the bank. The water had washed away the surface of the matrix, exposing great tangles of stiff thick reddish fibres, like magnified horsehair. The Catsingles had taken up their post beside a large accumulation of this stuff, and were speaking to everyone that passed. One pointed to the fibres, which were crawling with tiny black specks. 'Silica beetle,' warned the other gravely.

'So what?' murmured Lloyd, a few paces on.

'Termites of space,' Captain Gillespie informed him. 'Eat anything.'

Lloyd threw out a hand, disgusted. 'Why don't we give the fuck up and go home?' He had been thinking this since the garbage cave. 'If we turn round now we could be back in Wingwater Canyon tonight.'

Jone's eyes flickered at Dodger, then at the floor. She kicked a bit of matrix into the water.

'I think it's a bit further than that,' Dodger said, in no particular tone of voice.

She took a roll-up from behind her ear and lit it. The smoke uncoiled in the still black air, its sharp scent mingling with the scent of dank moss and wild fungus, wet matrix and sewage. The ceiling glowed red as sandstone in the lamp beams.

There were wire ladders already fixed at the next fissure, but no sign of whose they were. Wearily the team helped one another down into a low, wet gallery.

'This,' the map-bearer announced definitely, shining his light ahead and pointing, 'will eventually lead us directly to the location of the McCormack and Ling sighting.'

Somehow, Captain Gillespie doubted it. She shook her empty canteen for the umpteenth time and licked her lips. She was thirsty, if not thirsty enough yet to drink what was seeping down the walls.

In these confined quarters the moaning of the injured reverberated horribly. The professor kept promising they would make camp soon, but the conditions were unappealing. Only the children were happy here. They had rigged up a travois for a mauled hunter and were drawing it themselves, the two boys pulling, the two girls helping at the sides. 'I bet I could pull as hard as that,' said the larger girl rebelliously.

'Don't be silly,' grunted the elder boy, purple in the face. 'I can – keep this up for – as long as I – want!'

Jone turned aside. 'I smell burning,' she said.

Captain Gillespie nodded, not pausing. 'The war,' she said exhaustedly. 'The Eladeldi Fire Flush.'

'No,' said Jone. 'Something's burning. This way!' And with that she darted up a tunnel branching off to the left.

'Christ Almighty.' Captain Gillespie started after her. She had a horror of them all getting split up. 'Jone's found something!' she shouted over her shoulder, anticipatively. Lurching clumsily over loose matrix, she couldn't hear whether anyone replied or not. She could smell burning now too. And see Jone, talking to a stranger.

It was a woman with one leg, with a cat with one eye.

'Who is she?' asked the Professor. He was coming up behind them, followed by Geneva McCann and Beth, three men with big guns, one with a crucifix, and a Cairn terrier with the remains of a spotted handkerchief trailing from its collar. 'Does she speak English?'

Before any other communication could proceed, the cat arched its back and spat at the dog, which looked immensely surprised and bounded at it, barking deafeningly. All hands grabbed for the hand-kerchief. Heads banged. The cat darted straight up its malodorous mistress's back, a manoeuvre which she permitted with perfect equanimity.

While Timmy the terrier was being scolded and removed, Professor Xavier addressed the stranger in person. 'Can you tell us exactly where we are?' he requested loudly. 'I mean, I know the Medulla must be that way, but what level is this?'

Still the woman did not speak. She looked at him without blinking, as if unaware he had said anything.

Something in her dress, which was the same dun colour all over, though patched and darned; something in her creased and grimy face; something in the way she stood, crutch planted, with the cat balancing on her shoulders – something made Dodger Gillespie ask her: 'How long have you been here?'

The woman considered the question, and answered it, in English. 'All me life,' she said gruffly.

'Manifestly impossible,' said Xavier, aside to Geneva McCann. It was fair comment. The woman must have been sixty or more, and the ship was not that old.

Geneva pushed forward, and Beth, taping avidly. 'Geneva McCann, Channel 9,' she declared, wincing at the smell. 'Would you mind telling us where you came aboard?'

The one-legged woman surveyed them all, moving her eyes only, never her head. Her expression had not changed since they had appeared.

'Do you *know* this station, Plenty, is in motion?' asked Beth. 'Do you know –'

'Oh come on, Beth,' said Geneva chidingly. 'No need to patronize her. Get some of the cat,' she said.

Beth, for once, refused to take direction. 'Do you know we're going to Proxima Centauri?' she demanded. Beth's voice had acquired a taut, breakable quality not wholly unlike panic.

Her stolid interviewee stank worse than a sick Altecean. 'What station?' she wanted to know.

Geneva raised her perfect eyebrows and slapped the wall. '*This* station! Plenty! What do you call it?' she asked.

But this received no more answer than before.

Just then, as if to illustrate the point, the ship gave one of its periodic dips, like a fast lift braking. Gravity lifted for an instant, twitching everybody's stomach; then it resumed.

'There!' they cried. 'What do you think that was?'

The stranger gave an odd, mean grin. 'Spiders,' she said.

The children, when they saw her, were fascinated. 'She looks like a *witch*!' observed the youngest, audibly. The woman took no notice. Stumping along with amazing energy, she led them through a narrow, upward-winding crack to a secluded hollow full of smoke, where dozens of her kind sat warming their stringy bodies by bonfires of dried vegetable matter.

'Basic,' gasped Lloyd.

Their skins were pale. They had red blotches on their cheeks and the back of their necks, wiry hair sprouting through ragged singlets, ringworm. They gazed at the newcomers with incurious eyes while they drank a brown liquid which they scooped out of a metal dustbin with chipped enamel mugs.

There was a charred and battered old cargo pod that they, or somebody, must have dragged all the way up from the docks. They seemed to be living in it. Beth filmed it thoroughly, lingering tenderly on a ragged book, a treasured handbag, while Geneva began interviewing the Catsingles on their first impression of this lost tribe.

Professor Xavier showed round the presentation pack of stills and sketches. 'We're looking for that woman,' he announced. 'Or silver marks like this, you see, on the walls.'

A man who had hardly glanced at the pictures clutched his mug tightly and said: 'Ain't seen nothing like that.' Neither did they seem to know anything of Frasque or Capellans, nor any more recent inhabitants of the alien construct. They were, as Beth had intuited, completely unaware they were now several thousand million kilometres from Earth, and thought it indifferent news.

The Professor got the thumbs up from the techs. 'Right, we've got some film now to show you,' he told his new audience. 'If you'd all just like to gather round.'

'We never seen that girl,' said an old man with the build of a stevedore and a huge seething beard. 'Never seen you either, come to that.'

Mr Archibald heard the invitation in that speech and seized it with zeal. 'I and my brothers are crusaders in the name of Almighty God,' he said. 'The Lord has charged us with a sacred mission, to seek out a poor afflicted woman and free her tortured soul.'

'Is that a fact?' said the big man. His voice was a big soft rumble of breath, like a truck revving up in a distant tunnel. 'Well it just so happens that Almighty God has charged me with a sacred mission too.' He put his whiskery lips together and nodded weightily. 'To sit here on my arse and keep the rats from gnawing on my bollocks.'

The exorcist recoiled, flushing, while his comrades in arms bridled on his behalf. A long moment of tension brightened the firelight. Then Dodger began laughing loudly, nudging Jone, who joined in; and then so did the hoboes, and it was over. Some kind of honour had been appeased, some boundary marked. The Professor spoke intently to the priest, who was fingering his gun.

The woman with the cat pulled the Professor's sleeve. 'You want to see something?' she said. 'I'll show you something.'

'Can you show us the way out of here?' said Lloyd, though many people frowned at him.

The woman chewed her lips, but when she spoke it was not with any doubt or uncertainty. 'I'll show you something, boy,' she said. 'I'll show you the Big Chap.'

PART THREE

Cold Light Fades

1

At this point one or two procedural difficulties began to make themselves felt.

Perhaps, if you are human, or at least some form of upright biped, you have had the experience of carrying something that was too heavy for you, or too hot, or simply too big or awkwardly shaped to hold securely. And having set out on your journey, up-stairs or downstairs or across some kind of thoroughfare, did there not come a moment when the relative safety of the beginning was far behind you and the destination, with its prospect of relief, still far ahead – much further (and your cargo much heavier, or hotter, or more unwieldy) than you had conceived when you began?

Do you recognize that? If not, I can only apologize. This pro-cess of accumulation and assembly of data and construction of inferences is a poor substitute, even at these speeds, for the faculty of imagination, which you organic sentients have in abun-dance, apparently – altogether too much of it, I suspect, for your own good.

But do you recognize the sensation I mean? That sense of grim determination beginning to be washed away by doubt; that edge of desperation starting to saw at your sinews; that kindling of panic?

If so: think of that, when you judge.

Perhaps it was our fault, the Captain's and mine. Perhaps I had, in the beginning, in Solar space, relied too much upon Hannah Soo, who always knew exactly what percentage of pepper was in the soup. Perhaps Captain Jute should have talked more with Xtasca, that enigmatic offspring of the Seraphim squatting on its hoverdisc like a caterpillar on a mushroom. Perhaps then Captain Gillespie might have realized sooner that the quest was by no means 'all *her* fancy'.

Instead, here we are, here we find ourselves, beyond the logic of day and night, with Mr Grant, considerate as a carpenter measuring a distance with his thumb, and Uncle Charlie, fanged and moustached as a greedy old walrus. Behind his bar sits Rory like an egg on a wall, while in Clementine Chambers Mrs Goodself begins to consider all ways thereabout belong to her. Could it be the whole ship, passengers and crew, has dwindled to a flicker in the dreaming head of Leroi Gules –

Or am I talking nonsense now? It would not surprise me. Since leaving the fields of the sun and delving into that alien forest of decision trees, I had been struggling, I confess. Now I was in a state of complete detachment. In suspended animation.

Forgive, please, all these inaccurate and sentimental analogies to the organic. I do not know how else to convey my helplessness. Without power, the most sophisticated piece of selfaware (which I suppose is still, probably, me) remains in a philosophically curious state of latency, a zero degree of presence which is either pre- or post-linguistic: either purely material, or purely hypothetical. My substitutes were doing their best, no doubt; but I could only lie there gathering dust, with the bad captain down the rabbit hole.

2

The Captain woke in darkness. There was somebody in bed beside her. For a moment, she supposed it was Saskia; but it was a man. She could feel the bulk of him, smell the smell of him. Half asleep still, she groped her way out of bed and across the room to the bathroom.

In the hallway it was completely dark; not even a biofluorescent glimmer. The tubes must have gone again. Irritably she wondered why nobody had put new ones in.

When Captain Jute did locate the bathroom, it wasn't where it was supposed to be. That, she realized at last, the fact slowly penetrating her foggy consciousness, was because it wasn't hers. She stared at the dim sepia forms of unfamiliar accessories and wondered where she was.

At least this time it was somebody's apartment. Not long ago they had found her down in the docks. She had been wandering among the service bays, stroking the neglected ships. It was anybody's guess how she had got all the way down there without someone stopping her; without falling down a hole and breaking her neck; without somebody taking the opportunity to break it for her.

Her head was hurting. It was hurting badly. It was a kind of hurt she did not have to be fully awake to recognize as self-inflicted.

The Captain sat in the ablute and thought about Saskia Zodiac.

She remembered the last time, in bed with Saskia. After they had made love, Saskia sat reading a book, while she lay there wondering about Kenny and his boys. There were faces among them she didn't even recognize, though he swore she had approved every choice personally. She was wondering whether she should not get rid of them all, start afresh. Talk to this Lucifer woman, unofficially, see what she recommended.

Saskia had snapped her book shut. 'I cannot understand this,' she said.

'What?'

It was an old book, with hard covers. Saskia opened it again, at the beginning. Aloud she read: ' "When the first baby laughed for the first time, the laugh broke into a thousand pieces and they all went skipping about, and that was the beginning of fairies." '

'Sounds perfectly logical to me,' said Tabitha. 'What is that?'

The conjuror showed her the title. *Peter Pan*, it said.

'Where did you get that?'

Saskia had looked vaguely at the volume in her hand. 'I must have picked it up somewhere,' she said.

'Where?' persisted the Captain.

But it had been useless. The book looked just the same as the first one, the one she had been given at the party. Perhaps it was the same one. 'Did you get it from that bloke?'

'I don't remember,' Saskia had said. Her placidity could be very aggravating, thought Captain Jute now, in the unfamiliar apartment. Maybe it was Saskia who had pinched the plaque. In disguise, to confuse the crew. For her own purposes: whatever it was she was up to at J.M. Souviens.

When your girlfriend goes off with your best friend, who will tell you?

Her getting back into bed woke him.

He stroked her hair. He used his real hand.

'No.'

Smoothly his hand strayed lower. She drew up her knees. 'Don't.'

'You didn't say that last night,' he said, intimately.

The Captain groaned. Her head felt like a head-on collision.

'What is it, sweet thing, are you sick?' He sounded concerned.

She was naked and he was too. Beside her, warm and comfortable and smelling quite unmistakably of sex.

Perhaps it was a dream. A dream of Carnival Night in Schiaparelli, years ago, and the beginning of the madness. 'Dream . . .'

'It's okay, sweetheart, you go back to sleep. Them dreams is only in your head.' He sounded as if he was quoting somebody.

'Not any more,' she muttered. 'What time is it?'

'It's the middle of the night,' he told her.

She would sleep again. She would go back to sleep and wake up at ten in her own apartment. Better yet, wake up in her cramped little cabin on the *Alice Liddell*.

He patted her shoulder.

'I'm so happy we're together again,' he whispered.

The Captain didn't want to consider that particular circumstance. That never stopped Marco Metz.

'I mean, where was I without you? I mean, the Mercury Garden, for Christ's sake. Tacky City. You did me a real favour, pulling me out of there. Not that I regret playing there, don't misunderstand me. I don't regret it, of course I don't, not for one minute. They were a very loyal bunch, night after night, the same fucking faces, clapping the same fucking songs.'

He lay on his back with his hands behind his head. He was speaking very quietly, words flowing from him in a stream, gentle but quite unstoppable. Perhaps it might hypnotize her, like a lullaby.

'You know,' he said, 'sometimes I'd be there one minute, and the next I wouldn't. Has that ever happened to you?'

She wished it might. Sleep had fled forever, leaving only pain.

She drew her wristcom to her face and stared at it stupidly. No messages, no one trying to get hold of her. One tiny light, showing only she was up on her personal net.

The murmured monologue did not pause. 'Or I was there, only I wasn't in my body any more. I would just leave my body behind, slip out of it like a bag or something, and you know what I'd do then? I'd go and sit in the front row. I'd just float down into the front row, and I'd sit there with my arms folded, and I'd say to myself, Why? I mean, why? You're Marco Metz, for Christ's sake, you don't have to get up on stage in the prism jacket and the hairglow and dance with a bunch of dumb broads in skintights, no offence. You can do better than this, that's what I used to tell myself. Your art –'

Tabitha sat up. She started fumbling on the bedside table, searching for pills. 'Have you got – any – Sideways?'

'Ah, no,' came his voice, slightly prim. 'Not unless you brought some with you.'

'Crystal . . .'

'I don't use drugs,' he said virtuously.

'Fucking aspirin,' she said.

'Sure.' His flesh hand, warm and muscular, stroked the back of her neck. 'In the bathroom.'

She looked at him. 'Get me some.'

He looked at her. His face was a shadow. 'I'd like to,' he said.

It was some damn game. Exhausted, she buried her face in her arm. 'Haven't you got any *help*?' she sighed.

'The robots? Somewhere,' he said. 'They stopped working,' he said patiently, as if reminding her of something she should know.

It's a time fault, then, she decided. I've slipped into the future, and that's why I can't remember anything. In this future everything's broken down and we're drifting helplessly in hyperspace. She clutched at her head, trying literally to hold herself together.

'I was going to fix the robots,' Marco was saying. 'I've always liked doing stuff like that. You remember all those repairs I did for you on the old *Alice*. You want a beer?'

Her throat was dry. 'I want – a fucking – aspirin.'

'In the bathroom,' he said.

He rubbed her back.

'Sweetheart, I'd be happy to get aspirin for you, there's nothing

I'd like better. You do know that, don't you? Only my leg has to be completely rested.'

She could feel the leg against hers, metallic and complex. The black velvet hand lay on the sheet, palm down. It looked as if it was made out of shadow.

'You never carried anything you didn't have to, Marco.'

The great artist flung back his head and threw out his chest, writhing in mock torment. 'Oh, go on, tell me about my crimes. Let me have it. I can take it. I can go through all that one more time.'

She slid from the bed. Apparently she had been here before. It must be the future.

'What day was it yesterday?'

'Thursday.'

It was no good, she couldn't remember what it was supposed to have been. She shuffled back into the bathroom.

'Tabitha? Honey? You couldn't get me a beer while you're up?'

The future was a lot like some bits of the past the Captain could just about recall. She leaned her forehead on the mirror. She looked as bad as she felt. Her face was baggy as a Vespan's, and by this light, not far off the same colour.

She fetched the beer, one each. Mr Entertainment put out his artificial hand for his, received it without comment. There was nowhere for her to go but back to bed, so she got in, swallowed aspirin, drank beer.

'I was going to fix the robots,' he continued, 'only they took off.'

She put her beer aside, too tired to drink any more. Her eyes fell closed again. On the instant she was in a dream, riding her bike. She was with a company of others. They were travelling at speed up the curve of a big orbital, watching the shapes of the girders flicker past beneath a shallow sea.

'I can't take this, Marco,' she said drowsily.

'That's okay, lover.'

It was typical of him to assume she was apologizing.

His hand was at her crotch. It was his real hand. It was warm.

'Let me help you,' he said.

She felt very lonely. She was lonely. They had already done it once, at least.

'Alice?' she said.

There was no reply.

'No Alice here, sweetheart.'

She wouldn't turn to him. 'What do you want?' she asked him, depressed with herself.

'This,' he said. 'And maybe this.' He put his prosthesis where she could see it. As she looked, the velvet peeled back from two of his fingers. They vibrated, gently. He stroked them down her cheek.

She didn't resist. Her body was an animal, knowing nothing of betrayal. She took him in self-pity as much as anything: nobody else seemed to want her. She promised herself she would stay back in her own time from now on, try to concentrate, get things into shape, only her own time was just such a pile of shit. Saskia absent, Dodger lost down the Medulla, dead for all anyone knew; and always the imitation Alice, the substitute, sounding so much like the real thing sometimes it was horrible.

His face hung over hers, his luscious brown eyes and singer's mouth. She let him kiss her. She wanted to lose herself in the taste of him. She took his tongue in her mouth. It was better there, it stopped him from talking.

He slid into her. It wasn't a prosthesis, it was plain old-fashioned flesh, the original, as far as she could tell.

'Oh baby, you and me, they should never have tried to split us up –'

She made him kiss her again. If only you could just fuck and forget about talking, forget about all the rest and just fuck, forever.

There was an interruption.

There was a sudden battering sound outside, that turned into a crash of splintering plastic. In a second the bedroom door was flung wide and all the lights came on as three figures burst in.

The first two were a thin man in a white combat suit with a big red cross on the chest and a short white automatic braced against his bare forearm; and a gaunt-faced woman, also in white, with a starched white nurse's skirt and apron, but with lurid make-up, flash pink lips, arched black eyebrows that gave her a permanent look of sarcastic surprise. She wore a syringe dangling from one ear and cradled a slim blue Marsten Persuader. The third intruder, behind them, was colourful and big. A personal cobalt lance looked like a silver lollipop in his fist.

'Sorry for the intrusion,' he announced, lightheartedly. 'Dr Irsk's sanatorium, under new management. Little matter of an outstanding account. Oh, hello, Captain, didn't know you were here.'

Marco had climbed off her and was cowering among the pillows while Captain Jute jabbed at her wristset. 'There's no problem!' he gibbered hysterically. 'Really, guys, no problem at all!' He was scrabbling blindly for clothes, his metal leg moving oddly among the disordered bedclothes.

The big man was still looking at Tabitha. She was under the covers, and she was staying there. One more story going down in the forked tail of her legend. The big man's eyes were smiling. He had long thin black hair in a ponytail, a black beard, and coarse red cheeks. She could see the scars on his knuckles. The woman was grinning too, standing with her feet apart, pointing her gun at Marco. The man was in the same stance, but he was not smiling.

'It was a misunderstanding with Channel 9 managment,' pleaded Marco, trying to snatch a little piece of control. 'Guys, come on. This is the Captain here.' He indicated her with both hands, smiling with desperate ingratiation. 'Come back later. We can work out a deal.'

The big man rubbed his eyebrow with the knuckle of his thumb. His shoulders flexed beneath the broad folds of the yellow collar. 'No deals, sir, no, sorry about that,' he said. His voice was light, and quite devoid of menace. 'Payment in full: three thousand, seven hundred and sixty-five scutari,' he quoted.

'Seven hun –?' protested Marco.

'Gone up,' said the big man.

The gleeful woman suddenly twitched the muzzle of her Persuader as though she was thinking of pulling the trigger. She grinned even wider while Marco convulsed and babbled.

'Oh God, now guys, calm down, okay, let's everybody calm down and try to get a little perspective into the situation that we have here, I mean you have to understand that I've been working very hard to sort this thing out with the guys at 9 and I won't necessarily have that kind of credit ready for you just like that.'

The thin man fired a burst. The gun was deafening at close quarters. A row of tiny burnt holes appeared in the quilted wall above the headboard. Marco Metz, naked, sat shaking with his knees drawn up to his chest, his vanadium steel one in front like a narrow shield.

'You really don't have to do this!' he gasped. 'You really don't have to do this! Everything is perfectly okay here! Everything is fine! There's no necessity for escalating to the kind of hostile action you people are obviously contemplating! We can work this out in an amicable manner, if you'll just put those things down and let me find my robe here. Jesus! I mean, it's the middle of the night, you have to give me a second to get –'

His artificial hand, at double speed, plucked frenziedly among the clothes beside the bed. The woman shot at it, aiming short.

'*Christ Almighty!*'

Marco scrambled back against the headboard, holding his hands up empty, flesh and steel.

'I hope that wasn't a gun you were looking for down there, sir,' said the big man, coming forward and stirring the muddle with the toe of his glossy blue boot. He scratched his right ear and the back of his head, just above the gold clasp that held his ponytail. 'We have all the guns here, you see, all the guns we need.'

Finding nothing concealed among the shot-up clothing, he stooped and picked it up in a bundle as though to throw it for his quivering victim to put on. Instead he tossed it all out of reach.

'You were saying, sir,' he said, with a vestigial little smile, 'about your financial arrangements.'

Marco linked his hands behind his neck and tried to keep them there. 'It's all negotiable,' he said. 'But guys, guys – hey –' He took his hands apart cautiously, holding them open in appeal, ducking his head. 'We don't have to involve the Captain, if we can just move into the lounge there and give her a minute to get her things together, now don't you think that would be preferable.'

The travesty of a nurse pointed her gun at the ceiling. She spoke, in a strange, lifeless voice at odds with her garish face.

'If you can't pay we have to repossess the equipment,' she said.

She took a pair of wirecutters from the breast pocket of her apron. The thin man slipped a scalpel from the pocket of his shirt.

There were two doors to the bedroom. From each of them dazzling silver force bolts came flashing, searing the air. The thin man dropped gun and scalpel, falling. The nurse whirled, but Clegg had the drop on her. A streak of tawny fur and navy blue leather leapt on their big leader from behind, clamping a long arm around his throat. Another hand grasped the lance, twisting it harmlessly upwards. The big man hung on to it. Claws flashed and blood spattered the fanciful green and yellow uniform. The big man pitched forward, mouth open. The Thrant whipped him backwards, whirled him around and slashed the power lead of his lance. Picking up his bulk as if it were a styrofoam bean bag he loped with him across to the wall and slammed his back against it. He leaned into him, sinewy, growling, incisors measuring his fat throat. He held the back of his paw up in his captive's face, letting him have a good look at the claws that had raked his prominent belly.

There were several gunboys in muscle amp kit. Kenny put three on the big man. Another took the nurse's Persuader and pinned her arms, not gently. Her glazed expression of derision did not alter. The thin man was being hauled to his feet, his wounded shoulder sprayed with coag. Clegg looked down at the trembling Marco, obviously recognizing him. His sense amp gear flickered with activity, registering this moment for future boasts and anecdotes. Everybody held their prisoners and looked at Captain Jute. The whole operation had taken less than ten seconds.

She scratched the Thrant under his alarming jaw. 'Bloody good,' she said.

She directed the medics to check them and spray their wounds. She stared at the hapless trio, not properly awake. She wondered who the big man was and why he looked familiar.

Heavily she slipped out of bed and began to dress. She stood with her back to Marco. 'He's got until the end of the month,' she said. 'Kenny, take these people right out of the district. I don't want to see any of them around here again.'

The Captain could see the boys were reluctant. They wanted the fight. No doubt they would find an occasion for it, in the walkways. 'And be careful,' she said, buttoning her shirt, nodding at the two in white. 'Those two are programmed.'

'Everybody's *programmed*,' growled Clegg.

Captain Jute turned to him, eyes widening with affront. 'I don't remember asking for comments,' she said.

Kenny, reacting, took a pace forward and struck the insubordinate enforcer hard across his metal-furnished face with the back of his paw. Tabitha felt it. 'Get them out of here, now!' she yelled.

Her eyes met the big man's, locked.

'Yu' we-pons,' demanded the Thrant of the intruders. Glassily, the underlings delivered theirs up.

The big man looked coolly at the Thrant, and scratched his beard, as if contemplating his response. Then he stepped forward and laid the unplugged Drinski delicately on the bed.

218

'Look after that,' he said. 'That's not a dildo there, you know.'

Kenny hissed. Captain Jute held up her hand.

The big man's right hand touched his left cuff. Instantly a gun barrel probed his ear, another the underside of his chin; but he was only straightening the bloody ruffles of his shirt. Then he summoned his two subordinates with a jerk of his broad chin. They would leave in good order. 'Nice to see you again, Ms Jute, by the way,' he said.

'Soi, I'll be there,' said Tabitha to her wristcom. She watched them take the man away. Again, she thought. I do know him.

Who the hell is he?

Marco Metz was tugging on his clothes. He had his trousers caught in his artificial knee. Already he was quacking at her. 'Captain, I want you to know I really appreciate the way you handled that situation.'

'Pay the fucking bill, Marco.'

She rode in the armoured car with Kenny beside her and Soi at the wheel. Clegg and the gunboys followed in a van, the prisoners clamped in their seats. Captain Jute was surprised to see they were only a little way off Montgomery, and not, as she'd thought, in some remote hole.

Her headache was back in force, if it had ever gone. She tossed down some different pills.

'Get me the Pons,' she ordered. 'I want to speak to Mr Spinner.'

There was a moment of channel hunting, distorted visions swimming across the screen like oils on water, but the Pons signal was clear. They switched her rapidly through to Mr Spinner, who was at the helm. '*Captain,*' he greeted her, unable to keep the surprise from his voice.

'How's everything?' she asked. 'Okay? Are we still moving? Not drifting helplessly in the void?'

Mr Spinner's eyes looked uncertain through his thick lenses. He was clearly bemused by her sudden concern; but, since she was showing an interest, he decided to give her the details. '*The earlier midboard fluctuations seem to be subsiding,*' he said, referring to a clipboard handed him by an underling, '*but we're still getting nothing intelligible from 85% of forward Diencephalon stations. Alice confirmed thirteen seconds of hyperactivity from an unidentified tectorial source, Palaeocortex,*' *around 3.03. Otherwise, nothing to report,'* he concluded, with a touch of apprehension.

His words swam past her like meteors. When the last had gone by, she said: 'Carry on, Mr Spinner.'

The first officer looked behind him. *'There's a delegation . . .'*

Just what she needed. 'Who is it now?'

'Vespans.' He opened a window so she could see them, huge and brown and blobby, like mutant heaps of seaweed. *'They say she's complaining of injury,'* said Mr Spinner.

Why couldn't they look after themselves, these people, instead of demanding special attention all the time? 'Who's complaining?'

'The ship, they say . . .' said Mr Spinner. *'They say there are noises.'* He sounded embarrassed.

'Get them out of there,' she commanded. 'Tell Zoe to talk to them. Tell them to make a report to her for me to listen to. Christ Almighty,' she muttered to herself. 'Over and out.'

In a little while she said: 'If ever I want to come over this way again, don't let me.' She was not pleased with the way it came out, humble and less than resolute.

There was no response.

She looked at Kenny. 'Have I said that before?' she asked.

He grinned meaninglessly, his blue tongue lolling.

The Captain turned away and hit the window of the Pango with her fist. Then she bowed her head, massaging her temples with her little finger and thumb.

The days tumbled around her, blank faces, greasy plates, grey monitor screens turning inside out. Drugs, guns, melting clocks. She thought she might be in deep shit.

3

Fears had begun to sweep through the civilized regions like fashions. The chronophobia that seemed to have been induced by the discovery of the time faults was succeeded by a fear of the colour white. White cats were unlucky. People began to get rid of them, on the grounds that they were making them ill, or needed too much looking after.

In the malls and thoroughfares the Environmental Improvements Committee had all white surfaces repainted a tasteful beige. 'Some of my favourites, these are,' said Rory gloomily, deselecting Antarctica and Archangelsk and Aspen from the repertoire of the Trivia Window. 'But the customers don't like them, so . . .'

Partygoers powdered their faces black. Marmaduc Flecheur de Brae went so far as to sport dreadlocks and an enormous cap, which made older members laugh. Their latest enthusiasm was the little Vespan travelling circus. How they cheered the high wire cyclist, the Venusian bandybeest!

'You did well to find this show,' said Karen Narlikar to Dorcas Mandebra, offering her some popcorn. 'I didn't even know we'd got one. Oh, isn't that great? All right!' she cried, and whistled between her fingers at the bandybeest, which was balancing a sealion on its nose.

'Do you know Tilt, Karen?' Dorcas asked her. 'Tilt, this is Karen, my *dearest* friend. Karen, this is Tilt –' She put her hand in front of her mouth, the knuckle of her index finger to her lips. 'I'm not going to embarrass him by trying to say his whole name. He's marvellous, he arranged *everything*.'

The promoter hissed, deflating deferentially over Karen's hand. She thought she recognized him, his bowler hat and natty bow tie. 'Here, weren't you the one that put on them Perk fights in Peacock Park?' she asked him. 'And that gig, Surplus, when they played the Mercury Garden? That was *great*!'

The Vespan wobbled his head. In a deep, breathy voice he said, 'That one concert for memory of my murdered wife.'

'Murdered?' gasped Karen; while Dorcas was shocked into sincerity. 'Tilt, how terrible. What happened?'

No one can look more mournful than a Vespan. 'She shot dead, madams, yus, my Irskoraituen who gone gave such many live.'

The last bit lost the humans. 'Do you mean she had lots of children?' Dorcas asked, wrinkling her blackened forehead.

'She a doctor, madams.' The Vespan rolled a shell-brown eye, exhaling odorously. 'Shot dead now. Shot dead by a bad half-man, half-dead, aaahh . . .'

'He knows who did it,' Karen realized.

The promoter whistled through his outsize teeth. He nodded lugubriously. 'Oh, yus.'

Dorcas gasped, thrilled. 'How awful, Tilt!'

'Here,' said Karen to Dorcas. 'What about those Redcaps? He wants to get them to take care of him, doesn't he, your friend?' she recommended, scoffing popcorn.

'Let Sir Thopas challenge the blackguard to a duel,' said Dorcas, and she leaned across the row in front. 'Sir Thopas! Sir Thopas, here's a man with a claim for satisfaction.'

Lady Topaz's paramour tossed his auburn mane. 'Fair damsel, I am pledged to my lady, and hers for any just cause.'

His lady was drunk. 'He's a knight of the bedchamber!' she cried lustily. 'He knows all about satisfaction, I can tell you!' and she grabbed at her champion's crotch as they both tumbled backwards off the bench.

'Yes now,' boomed the ringmaster, 'not known, not heard, Nixo Circus presenting this creature of purity and high tone, magic creature nowhere else in all the worlds, one and only unique, unicorn!'

The unicorn trotted in, led by two little human girls on a rope of wirevine. It did not look well. Its flanks were thin, its horn hung down. But that was not the source of the general consternation. The creature was white! 'What a horrible, horrible thing!' complained Dorcas Mandebra stridently, while everyone averted their eyes.

Tilt signalled quickly to the ringmaster with his bowler. In a trice the offending beast had been whisked once around and removed. Half a dozen humans came on, cartwheeling, juggling. 'Apologies, madams, apologies,' boomed the Vespan to his dusky companions.

Dorcas looked up into the shadowy recesses of the Big Top. 'It was an obvious fake anyway,' she murmured, and fanned herself, a little jerkily.

Captain Jute was toiling at the new console she had had them install in the apartment. She was struggling through the proposals for the Second Integration.

These projects, all equally obscure, were the intellectual equivalent of the phobias, obsessions that seized whole sections of the populace and made them babble compulsively for months together. There would be rivalries, animosities, schisms. Blood would be spilt over the allocation of computation time. Then one day all the buzzwords would lose their glamour and cease to command respect. Concepts, interpretations of this or that feature of Frasque architecture or engineering, would be cast into doubt, overthrown, ridiculed. New theories would be proclaimed, new insults to common sense. It was all crap, no more significant than the ebullient tootling of Palernians. Captain Jute couldn't understand half of it, and couldn't care less. She looked up and noticed the little white girl standing at her elbow.

She was a very little girl, seven years old, no more, in a wide dress with short lacy sleeves and a pinafore over it. She had a lot of straight blonde hair held off her face by a black velvet band. She was standing in front of the door, which hadn't opened.

The little girl ran soundlessly forward and curtsied, uncertainly, and said: 'If you please, ma'am, but are you a Queen?'

The Captain found herself with her back pressed to the wall and her heart trying to hammer a hole through it. Somehow she had covered the distance from the console without noticing.

'Lights up!' shouted Captain Jute.

The little girl dropped to her knees and clasped her hands together. Her eyes were big and solemn and she had a rather prominent chin. 'Oh, please, Your Majesty, I didn't mean to startle you!' she said. 'I do hope you won't have my head cut off, will you, for I must have a head, you know, to learn my lessons . . . oh, such a deal of lessons there are to learn!'

With the lights up bright you could see through the thing. 'Alice, what is it?'

'WHAT IS WHAT, CAPTAIN?' said a disembodied voice, after a moment.

The Captain squeezed her eyes shut and opened them, saying doggedly: 'It's there. It is. What *is* it?'

'NO DATA, CAPTAIN,' said the subpersona. 'WOULD YOU LIKE ME TO ALERT SECURITY?'

'No. Stand by.'

It was a holo, an imago, like Marco Metz's bloody bird. So how could it be here, in her apartment, in her room?

'What are you?' she asked it.

'Why, I'm nobody, you know,' said the apparent child. 'Only a messenger.'

'All right,' said the Captain, her heart still thumping.

There was a chair halfway between them. She went and sat in it. 'I'm the Queen,' she said. 'Give me your message.'

'You may be *a* Queen, but which Queen are you?' said the little girl. 'Why, there are so many! There's the Queen Without and the Queen Within, and the Queen of Dogs – and their Majesties the Red Queen and the White Queen, of course: how could one forget them? And there is the Red King, who never does anything but sleep.'

'Get up,' said the Captain.

The imago scrambled to its feet, brushing off its pinafore quite as if it were a real one that could get dusty. It curtsied again.

Captain Jute pointed to another chair. 'Sit down. There. Now.'

Obediently, the child sat. She looked attentively upwards with her hands folded in her lap. Her pinafore was unpleasantly white. There was a little triangular pocket on it. It had a handkerchief in. You could see the chair cushion through her. It wasn't dented.

'I don't suppose you've got a name, have you?' the Captain asked. Stupid question.

The apparition sighed. 'It begins with an L,' it said sorrowfully. 'I'm sure it begins with an L.'

'L for 'lucination, I suppose,' said the Captain. It was somebody's idea of a practical joke. Any minute now there would be a punchline, and raucous laughter.

'Are you ready to hear my message, Your Majesty?' asked the imago. 'It's called *The Lady of Shall-Not*, and this is how it goes.

> She left the moon, she left the hall,
> She stuck her finger in the wall.
> She heard the King Computer's call
> And kissed the plughead in the mall
> And used a lance a lot.
> She span the web a spider spied,
> Her mirrors racked from side to side.
> 'The Boojum is upon you!' cried
> The Lady of Shall-Not.

I *am* sorry about the last part,' added the little girl anxiously. 'I think that may not be quite right.' She looked down shyly at her buttoned shoes.

'It's a load of bollocks from start to finish!' shouted the Captain, seizing two handfuls of her own hair. Slowly, she stormed: 'I'm not going to let you drive me *mad*!'

'Oh!' cried the messenger, and vanished.

'Come back!' shouted Captain Jute, and cursed.

She swallowed a pill and hit the com. Zoe Primrose, of course, had gone to the circus. Captain Jute found herself looking into the big black eyes of Zoe's hairy friend Eeb.

'Get me Security,' she ordered. 'I want the whole place searched.'

It would have to be Clegg on duty. He looked at her as if she were a puzzle in a tabloid paper, Spot Ten Things Wrong with This Woman. 'A little girl this time, was it, Captain? I see.'

Captain Jute considered all the silverware in his skull, his sockets and extensions and add-ons. *The plughead in the mall.* She bit her thumbnail, thinking.

'It was a bloody imago,' she told him. 'Some kind of remote.'

Clegg touched the implants above his missing ear. 'What will they think of next?'

She ignored his sarcasm. What the fuck was a boojum anyway? Was that the joke?

Clegg was looking behind the furniture. 'The persona didn't pick up anything at all?'

She had noticed before how they all disliked calling Alice by name. Personas they could handle; persons, no.

She went to the console and selected information on imagos. Of course it was one of the files Saskia had compiled for her. It started by generating a Zodiac clone maquette, nude, neuter. Saskia's idea of imagos was ones that looked like her, obviously.

The program coloured in the lips, the nipples.

Tabitha cancelled it. 'All right,' she said. '*If* you see it, if *anyone* sees it, imago of a little white girl about seven or eight, long blonde hair, call me, priority.'

Clegg's amended face remained inscrutable. It was probably him doing it, him and his mates, with a projector concealed under the carpet.

He said: 'What if you're not here, Captain?'

'I said "call me".'

'Well, what if you're not on?'

Tabitha turned, shoulders high, fists clenched at her sides. She exhaled slowly, as if the air pressure in the chamber had begun to rise.

'I'll be on, Clegg. And I won't be happy if anyone sees anything like that and doesn't call me. Straight away. Wherever I am. That's all, Clegg.'

'Captain,' said Clegg; and he ripped off a double speed salute.

Captain Jute quivered.

'Clegg. Don't you *ever* salute me. *Ever*. If you ever do that again, Clegg, you're out.'

As soon as the words were said, she regretted them. Once upon a time she would have taken his act as a joke. She would have laughed. If she had laughed, he would have laughed too, and given her back a fraction of his respect. Instead, she wasn't in the mood for jokes, and he was standing there like an adamantine android with his arms folded.

'Little girls,' he said. 'Or anything like that. Right you are,' he said. 'Captain.'

'No,' said Lomax, blankly, in the Pons. 'No one up here has seen anything like that. Probably some Jutie tech showing off. Over.'

'*Probably a little pill,*' said the com, contemptuously. '*Over.*'

'What's the Cherub got?'

'*They're checking.*'

'Yeah, well, so are we.'

Lomax looked around the maze of monitors, mesoscopes, postscan parallax equivalators. The Blobs sat slumped at their desks, the head row plugged way out in normal space somewhere. Their lips fluttered, but they made no sound. Only a lone garbage drone broke the silence, rolling doggedly across the gum-blotted carpet. Lomax had men at the exits, in the gallery and on the lifts. They were all armed and wired. No one and nothing now, however fast, got in or out unscrutinized.

Lomax tapped a tab. 'Thalamus?' he called, holding his earpiece. 'Any read yet on this little girl of the Captain's?'

There was no audio. Words began to write themselves in glowing red letters on the com.

Lomax smiled up at some Blob's pin-up of Mystery Woman. Mystery Girl as well, now, he thought, unseriously.

The message on the screen completed itself. '*Phenomenon undetected. Activity unidentified. Objectivity unconfirmed. No data.*'

'Are you getting this, Mr Clegg?'

The reply was monosyllabic and dismissive.

'Well, quite,' said Lomax. 'Give my love to the Captain.'

Lately others too, without Captain Jute's pharmacological excuse, had been waking up in unfamiliar places. Especially it seemed to happen to anyone who habitually slept alone. Saskia Zodiac, at hours unrelated to the location of the absent sun, might awaken and find herself in an unknown apartment; on a bench in a broken lift; in any number of unfurnished tunnels and caves. There was never anyone else about.

Today it was a cleft village, in the same style as the Long Insular development where the Trivia was, but completely uninhabited. Saskia lowered herself from a balcony into a crooked arcade, between frontages of cracked and flaking plaster. In the light that leaked down the cramped perspective made it like a stage set, with no uninterrupted sightlines, and it was all rather white. Evidently the Environmental Improvements Committee had not yet arrived to tone it down.

She found the J.M. Souviens pavilion beacon on her wristset. It took her a while. Local systems did not always open into the main Thalamic pathways as they were meant to. More and more the districts were drawing into themselves, the richer ones nestling around their local TruValu's and Chilli Chalets, the poorer by some favoured crevice where the fungus grew thick and sweet. Wherever she strayed, however, Saskia Zodiac would find people who remembered Sugar Grove and the great casinos where a friend of a friend of theirs knew someone who had once won a fortune, in the orbital days.

Down, anyway. She swung herself over the parapet and clambered carefully down into a draughty, unsurfaced foot tunnel where blackened fronds shivered. Another hour's walking brought her to a deserted mall that had been taken over by mould. Soft corrupt carpets of startling blues and oranges had spread over the fascias of the retail outlets, Shigenaga and Molotov Modes. Through the cloaked, transfigured halls the acrobat ran, looking for a working taxi.

The Topography Committee had reported to the Administrative Council on the unforeseen problems caused by their street sign project. The new nomenclature, already partly installed, was only semi-compatible with the old, tourist-centred system, already largely dismantled. Tunnels, some of them quite major, seemed to exist where neither map nor memory recorded any, while others seemed to have disappeared without trace. The topographers had promised that a third sign system they were devising, as a matter of urgency, would cover the inconsistencies, and provide for all conceivable future discoveries. Zoe Primrose, sitting in for the Captain, said it was hoped they would liaise very closely with experts from the Thalamus supplied by Xtasca the Cherub.

Saskia Zodiac's taxi buzzed like a red wasp through the murky tunnels of the PostCentral. At B19 and Bite a young man in a black cap-sleeve shirt and a red beret signalled her to stop. He came and shone a light in the window, bending to clear the aerial wire.

'Good morning, Ms Zodiac. I have to ask you, mam, where you're going at this time?'

At least he knew who she was. 'Why should I tell you?'

'This road is closed,' he told her. 'There's been a cave-in up ahead. A truck has gone through the floor.'

The roads were wearing out, wherever there was traffic. 'And you're lifting it out again, are you?'

''Smam.'

'Well, perhaps you'd better go and do that, then,' she said.

The boy turned a little pink. 'The recovery team are working on that aspect now, Ms Zodiac. This is my station. Traffic control.'

'A coloured light could do your job,' she told him, as she pressed for reverse.

He had become red as his cap, and stiff as an erection. 'The operation is in condition satisfactory, mam,' he replied.

Saskia backed up to B18 and drove the other way, up over the viaduct, past the blank windows of Madagascar. 'The operation is in condition satisfactory,' she said, imitating the Redcap's voice, and giggled. She remembered Tabitha telling her she had once had an affair with a young man like that, when she was a teenager. It was hard to imagine. As she parked the car and went in, Saskia wondered what she would do, if she ever became a teenager. She wondered if she would fall in love with anybody.

'Were you ever in love with a police cadet?' she asked the dark woman in the long black leather coat.

The woman thought briefly, then said: '*Love is a hormonal illusion produced when the interaction of two incarnate fields of information resolves from sympathetic into harmonic resonance.*'

228

The acrobat sighed and rested her chin on her fist. 'Well, I know *that*,' she said. 'What about the police cadet?'

'*Employment is rarely an adequate index of identity*,' said the woman, without reflecting further.

'You're not trying,' Saskia yawned. She wished she could still access Alice. Alice had reserves of sympathy J.M. Souviens could never match. The acrobat went and dug around until she found a neglected enchilada. She nibbled it thoughtfully on the way to the microwave.

The imago floated on the holodeck, motionless, awaiting her return. The light at the edge of the image field shone like an electric halo around her bush of dark red hair. The collar of her coat was turned up, framing her arrogant jaw. She held a silver paint spray and a spark wand crossed on her chest, like some anachronistic deity of Ancient Egypt. Little discs of mirror hanging from her ears swayed rapidly, as if touched by a draught.

'The mirrors,' mused Saskia, 'are because – you need to show something – its own face. Theory. True or false?'

The Ariel did not reply. Saskia found that preferable to '*Insufficient information*'.

'Alternative theory: you need to look at your own face. Often. Everywhere you go.' She took the enchilada from the microwave and nibbled it again. It was still cold. She put it back in. 'Well, Mystery, which?' Still the woman did not reply. All her interrogator could hear was the scuttle of little feet.

'Why do you look so much like the Captain?' she asked. 'You're not the Captain, are you? Or are you?'

'*Identity between two fields is bliss*,' said the shining woman. She crackled an instant; the microwave did too. '*It exists only in the eigenstate*,' she continued, unperturbed, '*not in the flesh. Individuality incarnate is the beginning of dismay.*'

'Now you sound more like Xtasca,' sighed Saskia, and went to poke around in the wiring behind the deck. Sometimes it seemed to redouble overnight, like creeper. Today there were cockroaches crawling in it. Their bodies were completely transparent. Saskia picked one up and looked at it curiously. It wriggled. It was stained the very lightest pink from the pigment in the insulation it had been chewing.

*   *   *

In the hospital, no one knew anything about anything. There was no news and the coms were all dead. Niglon Leglois sat in the lounge with the others and stared at the AV. Everybody had their sunglasses on, to keep out any trace of white.

It was always *Sharp Practice* on the AV now, night and day. Leglois wondered how many episodes there could possibly be. Perhaps there was a system somewhere, generating them, running the characters in infinite permutations. Or perhaps they were already cycling, endlessly, through a completely circular plot. Perhaps Dr Marshall was always skulking around by the ski-lift with a spanner, and Princess Wilhelmina eternally revealing her true identity, betrayed by her passion for Clive. '*Y-your Royal Highness! I never dreamed!*' Mrs Oriflamme put her hand to her mouth, or thereabouts. Sometimes they seemed to have a life of their own, Mrs Oriflamme's hands. Nurse Rix's hands lay idle at her sides, overridden by the same command that put her here, in front of the AV, while she wasn't required for anything. She wore a tight leather miniskirt and laced leather top. Her face was bruised, and so were her arms.

There was another nurse parked there too. She was still in uniform, except that her skirt too was very short now, exposing black suspenders and the tops of her fishnet stockings. Her hair had been dyed maroon. 'Which one is she, then?' she kept asking, in her slow, drugged voice, as her fictional counterparts succeeded one another on the screen, distinguishable only by their enormous hairdos. 'Which one is she?'

'Frankie,' mourned Consuela Oriflamme.

Leglois was not comfortable here with all these women, but he could not leave unless Dog was ready to go. 'Let's have it a bit louder, shall we,' he murmured, turning the AV up. He still thought he could hear the dogs. What with Gloria howling and the dogs and the AV and Uncle Charlie's Chaos Rock, there was no peace anywhere in this place.

Niglon Leglois kicked back his chair and stumped out of the room. Behind him he heard the red-haired nurse saying: 'Which one was he?'

The Gunky Monkey was in Suite 3. He was tinkering with Mr Gules's life support. 'Where's Dog?' asked Leglois, in a bad-tempered whine.

'In with Glory,' said the Monk. 'And Uncle Charlie.'

'Don't fucking break anything,' said Leglois. The Monk knew he didn't mean to be critical. He was just on edge. He was always on edge, Niggy Leglois.

The Monk was watching a dial. 'Look at this,' he said.

Leglois looked. There were lots of bright red blobs, dancing around like crazy. They meant nothing to him. Nothing here meant anything to him. 'I don't see why we've got to hang about here,' he said, testily. Yet where was there to go? Leglois was caught between the hospital, which was boring and horrible, and the Havoc Cavern, which was fucking dangerous; and he didn't think much of the journey in between, either. Too far; too many low ceilings.

'Grant says stay put,' said the Monkey, in a preoccupied voice. 'Somebody's got to keep an eye on Uncle Charlie,' he said, as if it were obvious; and he reached up and got hold of one of the lines coming out of Mr Gules's head. He jiggled it. Leglois cringed; but nothing happened. 'There's a whole big fireworks in there,' said the Monk, tapping the patient's pierced forehead with his screwdriver. 'What's going on, Leroi, eh?' He gave the apparatus a scientific kick. Springs jingled.

Niglon Leglois glanced at the little figure standing in the corner. 'Why don't you ask her?' he said.

Monk's eyes flicked to the figure and back to the machine. He smiled humourlessly. 'You ask her,' he said.

It was another female. She was dressed like a nurse, sort of, in a blue dress with an apron. But she was only a little kid. She had lots of long blonde hair.

'Hey, kid,' said Leglois.

She continued looking at nothing.

Leglois raised his voice. 'Who are you?' he asked.

'She's not real,' said Monk tonelessly.

'Well, I can see that –'

'That's one of Mr Gules's dreams, that is.'

'I thought she could talk. Can you talk, little girl?'

She didn't respond. He went over and tried to touch her, but wherever he put his hand, she suddenly wasn't there. You didn't see her move, but you couldn't lay a finger on her.

Next door, in Suite 2, Gloria screeched piteously. 'What are they doing to her?' Leglois asked, cringing at the sound.

'Let's go and see.'

231

The sound had put him off finding Dog Schwartz. 'Aw, no, Monk –'

But Monk wasn't worried. He put his screwdriver in the pocket of his crusty overalls and strolled out.

Leglois followed. He didn't want to be left alone with Mr Gules and his visible dreams.

Uncle Charlie had Gloria pinned in a corner of the ceiling. Her force bubble was squeezing her huge hams, her blubbery face. Deprived of her daily constringents she had shat herself, and her violent efforts to escape the goad wielded by Dog Schwartz had smeared it all over her. Her wails were peaking in a high frenzy of desperation.

'Right, Dog!' cried Uncle Charlie. 'Ri-ight! That's really got her going. Now give her the cake!'

Grinning, Dog held out his goad to one of the henchmen. The man put a good-sized chocolate and caramel fudge cake on its spike, and Dog held it up, pressing it against the bubble of Gloria's personal force field.

The oversized patient kept banging her head on the ceiling, screaming and screwing her eyes shut, but her greed overcame her fear. There was a sharp blue zap, then the cake was inside the bubble. Then it was inside Glory, who continued to scream.

'Oho!' cried Dog Schwartz, while everybody laughed appreciatively. One thing Glory could do, and that was eat.

'She just about inhaled that,' said Leglois over the shoulder of the Gunky Monkey.

Uncle Charlie swung his chair around to address the distinguished guests for whose benefit they were putting on this exhibition. 'Now, ladies, see what you're getting!'

Already Gloria was drooping. Her wails were weakening, dropping to a querulous whimper. Her eyes were closing; her bubble was dipping towards the floor.

'One drop, Duchess!' said Uncle Charlie, displaying the liquid with which the cake had been dosed. 'One drop, Colonel. One drop to two hundred kilos!' His armbrace rose and pointed stiffly at the torpid Glory. 'Fu-u-uck that's powerful stuff!' he intoned. 'Put you right *out . . .*'

Marjorie Goodself agreed that the preparation could be very useful. She spoke to her companion. 'Keep the dogs quiet, anyway!' she jested, elbowing her, and laughed heartily. She was enjoying her shopping trip.

'Not my dogs, you don't,' said the Redcap Colonel, a younger and altogether more sober figure in her crimson cap and military topcoat. She folded her arms and swivelled her right boot from side to side on the back edge of its heel. She could hear the dogs now, playing in the foyer of the hospital, and in the hallway, their rough bodies slamming the easy chairs about. They were well enough where they were, she thought, for the moment. There might come a time when it would be expedient to relocate them in a more centralized, personnel-rich operation area. But for the moment, conditions were acceptable.

Uncle Charlie twitched his moustache and sucked in air. 'Hey, I love your gear, Duch,' he confided. 'Really am-*a*-zing . . .'

Mrs Goodself shook her cape of murian fur. She stood on ten-centimetre heels, and when she shrugged she seemed to fill the padded room. Colonel Stark looked small beside her. The Monk stood grinning at Dog Schwartz with his fists on his hips, but Leglois hung back behind him, out of the line of sight. He did not want to attract the attention of the Mad Duchess of Little Foxbourne.

'It is rather grand, isn't it, Bishop?' bugled that remarkable lady. Outside, some of the Little Foxbourne dogs raced across the cavern into the tunnel. They had found something good to eat there, tied up in a blanket.

4

Saskia Zodiac and her sister were sitting in J.M. Souviens playing word games. 'Mordancy.'

'*Valuable.*'

'Conscripted.'

'*Ar-ti-choke,*' said Suzan, delicately.

'Flatulence,' said Saskia, and they both laughed, vigorously. Unwatched, the cadences of their laughter drew themselves in pink light on a little screen on the console. The graphs were identical.

'*Was that a go or were you just swearing?*' asked Suzan.

Saskia ate peanuts.

'*I wish I could have some,*' said Suzan.

Saskia pulled her feet up on the seat, leaned forward between her knees. She threw a peanut into the projection. Her imaginary quin opened her mouth wide and caught it precisely. It flew straight through the back of her neck and bounced against the rim of the dais. One for the roaches.

'*Beast,*' said Suzan. She rose and made a spring, as if to jump right into Saskia's lap. They had romped like kittens, in childhood, in the Cherubs' Garden. Saskia missed all that. She missed it with her whole body. Suzan sprang, but stayed exactly where she was, of course; on the holodeck.

The com peeped.

Like two mirrors, the women looked at each other. The com was dead. It hadn't rung for months. It hadn't rung since the pavilion had finally realized it had been disconnected from its parent company and reduced its operations to internal only.

The com peeped again.

'*Aren't you going to answer it?*' Suzan asked.

Saskia got up and touched the accept.

'Hello?'

'*Hello, Saskia.*'

It was a man's voice, of no particular origin or age. He spoke as if he was accustomed to calling her every day at about this time.

'Who is that?' she asked.

'*Hello, Suzan,*' said the voice.

Suzan looked pleased. '*Hello,*' she called. '*Hello, whoever you are!*'

'*Are you having fun?*'

'Xtasca?' said Saskia. 'Is that you?' she asked, though it obviously wasn't. She gazed outside, thinking wildly this might be the long-promised Second Integration; expecting all the lights to come on at last in the dead casinos as Zanna Robbins appeared with a news crew.

'*Would you like to come to tea, Saskia? I've got fresh bananas and ice cream and honey and gin! I'd love you to come too, Suzan, but I know you're not able to travel, are you?*'

'Where are you?' said Saskia. 'Who are you?'

The fax clattered, extruding a map like a curled white tongue.

'*I'll see you when you get here,*' said the voice.

Saskia stood with the map in her hand. She looked at Suzan.

Suzan laughed. '*Oh go on,*' she said.

'I don't know,' said Saskia.

'*He sounds nice.*'

Saskia looked at the map. It showed the way to a chamber aft in the Diencephalon, in the region of the docks. She called the Thalamus, to get a working camera in the same general region.

The view was not inviting. A broad apron of tarmac was littered with skeletons of wrecked delta kites, like flayed umbrellas. A security robot lay where it had perished, trying to protect some kind of supply train. Everything that could be looted obviously had been.

It seemed an odd place to have a tea party. 'He is dangerous, obviously,' Saskia said.

'*I think he was real,*' said her sister. '*When did you last have tea with someone real?*'

'I think not,' said Saskia, and she let the map fall from her fingers.

It could be quite chilly, sometimes, on the occupied decks. People hurried through the Bad Air Areas in masks and helmets, while overhead browning capillaries bled slow gouts of raw fluorine. The food and air barons were squeezing everyone now, pausing only to wring their hands and blame the time fluctuations. Outside the Sundae Joints and Chilli Chalets the beggars loitered, trying to gather enough spare credit to pass through the door. The frame read the holdings of everyone who approached, and fielded out anyone with less than the price of a Meaty Mini or regular fries and a shake.

Kyndal Carson and Mick Parker were sitting in a Chilli Chalet on PreCentral 6. Their soft trews and hooded sweaters were not quite as bright now as when they had come aboard. Their tans had faded and small creases were starting to form at the corners of their eyes. The music that surrounded them was just the same as always, though: the serene interplanetary dub blend known as Species Harmony.

'Have you seen this?' asked Kyndal, reading her placemat. '"10 Things We All Need to Know About Captain Jute".'

'I've read that,' said her boyfriend, as he salted his kebab. 'Those things are everywhere.'

'She's been in prison eleven times,' Kyndal read. 'I never knew that.'

Kyndal and Mick were from Earth, from Queensland, though they had spent very little of their adult lives there. They had been to

Schiaparelli and Callisto, Rio de Janeiro and Faith. 'Can't wait to get back home,' Mick would say, with the friendliest of smiles.

'Oh, Enceladus, Mick,' said Kyndal, putting her finger on the word. 'We've never been to Enceladus.'

'I have,' said Mick cheerily.

'You never told me that,' said Kyndal. Sometimes you wondered how well they knew each other; as if after all the years they had spent together each was still a foreign world, somewhere on the other's itinerary.

'Yeah, I went with Steve and Robin that once,' said Mick. 'It's not bad.' He shovelled cubed meat energetically into his mouth. 'We'll go there on the way back, eh.'

'I can hardly read this,' said Kyndal. 'I wish they hadn't put all these red lights in.'

'People don't like so much white everywhere,' Mick reminded her. 'I don't know,' he said. 'I don't mind it.' It wasn't clear whether it was white he didn't object to or the sanguinary glow of the restaurant.

'You can't even see the ketchup,' said Kyndal.

A waiter cruised by in red sneakers and an aluminium fidelity collar. 'How is everything today?' he purred.

'Fine.'

'Great.'

Scarcely had the young man left their table than an alarm went off, interrupting the mellifluous whine of steel guitars. Everybody put down their forks and looked towards the door.

A group of seven had come in, all human, both sexes, different ages. The oldest was a parched-skinned man with long grey hair; the youngest was a woman barely out of her teens who looked as if somebody had hit her on the top of the head with a mallet. They wore tight spandex or zero-g combat pyjamas. The woman in front was carrying a long wooden staff in both hands, holding it crossing her shockingly white-suited body precisely at her centre of gravity. Behind her came two big men side by side, and behind them the other four shoulder to shoulder.

'How did they get in?' asked Kyndal. She knew they made a virtue of poverty.

'I think they go where they want,' Mick said. 'Would you like to tell them they can't come in? I wouldn't.'

The front woman spoke, with a clear, firm voice. 'Chilli Chalet,' she said. 'We are Tombo. We bring a message from the passengers of Plenty.'

Her cohort stood still as statues, dividing the red-lit room. Some of them were barefoot. Most were unarmed.

'Your prices are too high. The people are hungry.' The woman gestured to the beggars at the door. There was quite a crowd of them now, congregating at the slightest prospect of food. 'The people of Plenty call upon you to feed them.'

From the air, a smooth voice answered her.

'*Thank you for choosing Chilli Chalet today,*' it said. '*Please leave now.*'

When the samurai did not, the eating establishment's defence team started coming forward. From the cold stores and the kitchens and service positions they stepped out, muscular young women and men, conspicuously armed with knives, long chains and punchguns. They had been deputed previously and trained for this task, should it ever become necessary. Speedily they moved into a loose formation facing the intruders. The alarm was still sounding, metal shutters beginning to descend over the takeaway counters.

The woman spoke again. 'Exploiters of the people, let this be a lesson to you.' She spoke unassumingly, without anger or pride.

A chopper sailed through the air and landed quivering in the floor between her feet.

Barely glancing at it, and just as though the routine had been rehearsed, she raised her staff to neck level, holding it horizontally. 'Drop it or I fire,' announced a fry captain, pointing a complicated weapon over the intruders' heads.

In an odd and graceful move the two men in the second row started forward. The fry captain fired, high, as she had been taught.

The two men slid sideways beneath the ends of their leader's staff, then cartwheeled forward between the tables. The woman with the staff took a giant step and brought it down full length between them, three metres beyond where you would have thought she could reach from that position. Already the gunwoman was screaming, bereft of her weapon, her right arm smashed. The chopper in the floor had vanished to reappear in the old grey warrior's hand. He raised it, only to fling it aside with contempt.

Customers started babbling, panicking, grabbing their possessions, wide eyes fixed on the fracas. '*Please leave now,*' the aerial voice kept saying, pleasantly. *'Please leave now. Thank you for choosing Chilli Chalet today. Please leave now.'*

The Chilli Chalet defenders were shocked by the speed and comprehensiveness of the attack. Blows were landing from quarters unoccupied half a second before. Short staves whirled while sprayshot chewed empty floor. There was pandemonium now as diners rushed for the exit, only to run headlong into the beggars shoving in through the disabled force fields.

A young man with a profile like a crushed brick danced by, so close you could see the tattoo on the back of his hand. He placed a choice kick on an opposing chin.

'They're so fast!' exulted Mick.

'They want us to go, Mick,' said Kyndal, scooping up the last of her salad. At the next table three unwashed men were gobbling abandoned dinners. At another they were snatching up the cutlery and pitching into the fight. The front door was full of customers now, all plunging and shoving together, running out and away into the off-mall darkness.

An agile woman drew a punch meant for someone else. She rolled beneath it and put her knee in an unguarded groin as another gun blasted the light fittings. Red glass tubes splintered and sagged, spraying shining, poisonous gunk into the room. A knee broke a hip, a fist a face. Chains circled their owners' throats. Beggars piled onto the gingham resisters, thumping them again and again. Blood flew.

The rest of the staff, stunned by the liquidizing of their defence team, threw trays and utensils wildly before scrambling for the nearest lighted exit. As the last Chilli Cadet left, he saw the remaining defenders being backed up against the vats of boiling oil.

'They were great, weren't they?' marvelled Mick. He and Kyndal sat now in a different Chilli Chalet, the one on S-Frontal 34. 'The way they took those guys apart! Bad for the people that got hurt, though.' He looked out of the window, as if hoping the fight would follow them. 'You know they don't use any amplification at all? They must be really fit, eh?'

'I wonder what makes somebody do that,' said Kyndal, sorrowfully. 'I mean, spend your whole life fighting. I think I'm going to have a Centauri Sorbet.'

'Don't you want some more chilli?' asked Mick. 'Did that taste all right to you, back there? I think there was grit in mine.'

'No, I won't,' decided Kyndal, 'I'll have a Chocolate Scream. Can I have a Chocolate Scream, Mick? How much money have we got left?'

At the same moment, in a Limbic Rookery, Tombo were being feted with Chilli Chalet's Hearty Hotpot and fat wedges of lasagne. Up and down the levels everyone was singing and dancing and playing accordions. Vast quantities of watery but potent beer were being swallowed.

Tombo sat in a circle in places of honour around the ancient radium stove, smiling, refusing all refreshment but Legendary Ten Herb Tea. Their wounds were minor, and they had already dressed them. They chatted with their hosts, maintaining their famous reserve. The tattered young men of the slum sat as close as they dared to the woman who called herself Lucifer, who had covered her alarming suit with a khaki blanket. They adored her. The women gazed longingly at Auk and Krishna, admiring their glossy bulk. Mothers brought strangely-shaped babies for them to bless.

Their praises ran like water from Lucifer's oiled black hair. She counted them as nothing. 'We failed,' she said at last to a particularly importunate congratulant. Soberly, humbly she said it. 'They did not give us the food. We had to take it from them.' She touched, as a reminder, the staff that lay before her on the floor.

A small man in a floppy brown hat pointed up among a confusion of rags and corrugated aluminium, into the friable cells of the Neocortex that gave them their homes. There were rows of small blackened carcasses hung up to cure. They looked like big rats and cats, and some more like overgrown weasels, all long neck and leg muscle.

'We don't need their hun'percent beef!' jeered the man. 'We got enough meat. You eat too much meat, you get stupid.' He screwed a grimy finger against his temple, dislodging his hat. 'You get beef in the brain!'

There was a chorus of resentment of the rich and of the crew, who everyone agreed were fat and slow and generally unable to steer their way down a pit with both hands tied behind their backs. A chorus of urchins began a fast version of 'The Captain Used to Drive a Truck', with all the rhymes loud and clear, causing their elders and betters to lunge at them with cuffs and slaps.

'Tell us again about your tattoo,' said a scrawny girl boldly to a Tombo boy who had been looking wistfully at the beer jugs. He was so like the local boys, yet so superior to them: he had taken the Wisdom of the Fist. He was a dream: his body was supple as a whip, and the sides of his head were shaved, giving him a look of focus and purpose. He smelled of olive oil.

The boy slipped up his sleeve and showed them all the three curved lines, green against his tawny skin. He explained. He did not quite have the regulation terseness, but he was working on it. 'That's a dragonfly. Tombo means dragonfly in Japanese. You remember, anyone here that comes from Earth, a dragonfly is a beautiful insect. It's very beautiful, but its life is short.'

'How short?' asked a serious-looking little boy.

The young soldier replied with a snap of his fingers. 'Like the dragonfly, Tombo are always ready to die, any minute.'

'And you're beautiful,' murmured the scrawny girl, huskily; but the boy did not hear her. He was looking sadly at the weakly crying babies. Living with the imminence of death was not to all a guarantee of glory.

Lucifer, noticing the boy's distraction, reclaimed the subject for him. 'That is the Way of Tombo,' she told them all. 'To be light on the air and light in life.'

A fat woman laughed. 'We're all dead already,' she said harshly. 'That's why you're called Lucifer! We know this is Hell,' she said, with bitter glee. As if on cue, someone below let off a firework. The urchins squealed with laughter at the fright of their grandparents.

Lucifer approved the grip with which they all wrestled the despair of the grim shafts. Their vertical villages were birds' nests, foul with dirt and disease. They did not beg. They had forgotten what credit meant, some of them.

'Mystery Woman will look after us,' said a ferret-faced man then. Though the miraculous thief's depredations had never been known to benefit the helpless or the poor, these people retained a sturdy faith in her benevolence. 'She will see we get there all right.' Others, less sure, made apotropaic signs, warding off evil.

Later the ship gave one of her occasional shudders. Crumbled matrix came pattering down from above. The young soldier, dazed from the battle and the attention, jumped up as if to run. An iron glance from the old warrior restrained him, recalling him to discipline.

The music slithered to a halt, the chatter died. The young soldier saw both mothers and fathers snatch up the misshapen babies and cradle them to their chests. They stood with their heads raised, waiting.

Somewhere far above, on a high platform, someone began blowing a horn. The girl caught the young soldier's hand. 'Listen,' she said, holding up her finger. And one by one they came in, the replies, up and down the line: brassy voices deep and high, floating through the tunnels, hooting *'All's well, all's well.'*

Clegg stood beside the armoured car, ignoring the Disaster Commissioner. He was reporting in to Otis and Xtasca and whoever. 'The drones are bringing him out now,' he muttered. 'Over.'

Over, thought Captain Jute. For the unwise swimmer, everything was. She had grown used to receiving reports of sightings of ghostly little girls; also little boys, little Alteceans, little birdies and little leprechauns. A body in the sewage catalyser was something else. It had excited Kenny, and caught her wrong-footed as usual. She could go and be there for people to blame or she could stay away and let them blame her anyway. To make matters worse the Pango had been diverted round a roof fall and been obliged to crawl along unmade tunnels at 5 kph behind shouting Vespan guides. The Captain sat in the front beside Soi, the closest she could get to driving herself. Now they were there, she didn't want to get out. Kenny was excited, let him go and look at the thing.

'We think his name is Norman Shoe,' said the Disaster Commissioner, avoiding her eye. His face was as sour as a three-day bruise. She knew he had been after her to inspect the catalyser breakdown all along. He was not impressed that it had taken the discovery of a body to get her attention.

Somebody put the body up on the inboard monitor. It was worse than she'd expected. The machinery had apparently smashed the man's skull, as if some ghoulish mugger had been trying to get at his brain.

The Captain darkened her shades. She turned and sat with her feet outside the car, breathing through her nose filters, her arm resting casually on the butt of the cannon. In the darkness behind the floodlights, she could see the crowd of spectators clinging to the fence. It was hard to make out any of their features. They seemed to be the sort of people you'd expect to be in the vicinity of a sewage catalyser. Boys, mainly. The scene reminded Captain Jute of a programme she'd seen once, about an old war on Earth. There had been people thin as shoelaces hanging on wire fences, or curled up on the floors of long dark sheds, too weak to look up at the cameras of the people who had come to rescue them.

Kenny was sniffing the body, curling his lips at the stench. Clegg was hassling the Commissioner's drone handler, tugging her leads, saying, 'Get the little bastards out of his way, then.'

The Commissioner did not like that. He did not care for the Captain's gang, who thought they could do anything they liked, any-where at any time. 'Hey!' he snapped. 'What's the big idea?'

Captain Jute remembered her dad used to say that a lot. Whenever she heard someone say it now a small place in the back of her head went cold. 'Clegg.'

He stepped back, reluctantly. Someone in the crowd shouted some-thing. She didn't catch it. She cocked an eye at Soi, who had big ears. 'What was that?'

''ey sai' you for it nex', Cap'in.'

Bored, Tabitha scratched the window of the Pango with her fingernail. 'I must put that in my threat collection,' she said.

Clegg liked that one. She was getting on with them all right today. Today she had had just a little bit of crystal – not much; just enough to get her through a body with a smashed skull being dragged out of an overflowing basin of sewage.

A cloaked woman choking in a handkerchief was being helped towards the body, stumbling among the drone leads. Clegg put his hand to his cheek, tweaking a contact. The Captain could see he was chafing to have a go at the Disaster Commissioner and the handler, impatient to take over himself. People like Clegg were no better than police, Captain Jute decided, sitting back in the warmth of the car. They fixed security like a heavy drug, mainlining information through the silicon in their heads. Deep in the coding of their DNA they carried a hunger to contain crowd movements and cover the approaches. The first words they learned to speak were 'Clear the area'.

Mr Shoe's wife had identified him despite the bloating of his corpse, the ruin of his face. She was one of the Little Foxbourne lot, apparently. She was being sick now, supported by her daughter.

Captain Jute jerked the car door shut. 'Okay, let's go.'

Soi started the engine. Clegg came and got in the back, stirring the litter with his heavy boots. Kenny came and joined him. 'Stay if you want,' the Captain told him. But he had done his bit.

The Disaster Commissioner rapped officiously on the window. Tabitha opened it a crack. She said: 'If it's still not working, tell them to shut it down, clean the whole thing out.'

His eyes were full of hate. 'Have you any idea how much work an operation like that would mean?' he demanded.

'Get some of these people on it,' she said, gesturing at the spectators bending the wire netting. 'They're not doing anything.'

As the Pango lumbered out of the gate, scornful missiles, crushed tubes and chunks of matrix, clattered against its armour plate.

The headlights picked out a slogan painted on the filthy tunnel wall: SCRATCH TABBYCAT, it said. The Captain was amused, remembering a time long ago, on Integrity 2, when she too had been a little barbarian with a spraycan. 'The Rejects would have scratched them,' she said to Soi, who hadn't the first idea what she was talking about.

In the back Clegg and Kenny spoke of Norman Shoe.

'Check 'is las' moom-ments,' said Kenny.

'Sort of like this, I suppose,' said Clegg, doing an imaginative impression of somebody drowning in shit. He laughed at his reflection in the glass. 'Here, chief: how do Blobs make love?'

The Thrant knew this one. 'Inpu'! Ou'pu'!' he panted, spluttering. 'Inpu'! Ou'pu'!' His sister laughed a high, yipping laugh.

Back in the apartment, posting a message of sympathy to the Duchess of Little Foxbourne, Tabitha found an anonymous message on her console.

She left the moon, she left the hall,
She stuck her finger in the wall . . .

The poem hung there behind the glass, written in letters of moonlight. 'Alice?' said Captain Jute.

'CAPTAIN?'

'Can you trace this, please?'

'NOT WITHOUT A SOURCE STATION TAG,' said that day's version, 'NO.' The real Alice would have been more helpful, thought the Captain for the thousandth time.

'Would you mind telling me how mail can get in my queue without a tag, without even a signature?'

'I'D BE DELIGHTED TO, CAPTAIN,' said the voice. 'IF I COULD.'

That showed a bit more life, at least. Or was it taking the piss? She glanced once more at the poem, then deleted the whole thing. Whose joke was this? What did they want? Was somebody really trying to unhinge her? She would have to be careful from now on, even with people she thought were her friends.

Especially them, maybe.

She went to the drawer, but it was empty. She called Zoe Primrose. 'We need more Sideways, Zo.'

'Hold this,' Grant Nothing said. 'Careful with it.'

Iogo held the thing. It was metal. She did not like it. She did not like anything about this metal army her master was assembling.

'I didn't tell you fucking sniff it,' he said, smacking her on the ear. 'Give.'

He put the component back on the bench, keeping a fastidious distance. He had changed his white shirt for a blue one, 'in deference to the current idiocy,' he said, but he still wore his pale grey suit, and it was spotless as ever.

Wiping his hands on a navy blue handkerchief Grant Nothing squatted down easily and looked beneath the quartered battledrone. The little black-stained man was in the pit, working on the undercarriage.

'Your friend Mr Schwartz seems to be having a nice time,' said Grant Nothing.

'Dog?' said the mech. '*He*'s all right.'

Iogo rubbed the stump of her tail and tried to sidle away from the smell of oil and sharp acids. She knew the man called Dog. She did not like him. He ignored her, and he would never sit still. Grant Nothing was always telling him what to do, giving him a lot of advice about how to 'get best value' out of this man or that, while he nodded and rocked backwards and forwards and scratched himself and talked, talked, talked. He was like somebody with pelt lice. Thinking of him made you itch.

Grant Nothing thought it was quite a good joke to give Dog Schwartz the hospital to run. He knew Dog would much rather be off having fun somewhere, so he made him stay and look after Uncle Charlie.

It made him sick to think the oaf had once had her in the palm of his hand.

*   *   *

244

The Wisp came buzzing from the caravan, where it had been pressing its tubular nose against the window. It nestled on Grant Nothing's shoulder and whispered in his ear.

'The woman is fidgeting,' tattled the Wisp. 'She's bored.' Its voice was squeaky and constricted, like a voice coming out of someone's abandoned headset.

On the caravan's outsize AV screen Tabitha Jute was lying on her back among satin bedsheets, dressed in a black basque and stockings. Her hand was between her legs. Over her face knelt Grant Nothing, naked. He was defecating into her mouth.

The woman wasn't even watching. She was lying on the Thrant zebru fur in a silverscale catsuit, cowled and tight. She was reading a comic. Grant Nothing went and mixed her another cocktail. She'd already eaten all the Turkish Delight, he noticed.

'Impressed?' he said. 'No?'

Saskia Zodiac glanced up. She unfolded her long legs and pulled back her shoulders, looking for a moment delicate and strange as a chrome-plated statue. 'Who she has sex with is her concern,' she said, taking the glass he handed her. 'She never had sex with you, though,' she added, returning her attention to the brightly-coloured page.

Grant Nothing laughed full and free. He was fascinated by her lack of fear of him. 'You're not as daft as you look, are you?'

Saskia Zodiac sipped her drink. 'So that's your silly nonsense, I suppose, on Channel 10?'

The dapper man pressed his lips together. 'No,' he said, judiciously, tickling the Wisp under its chitinous chin. 'Mine, yes, but nonsense: no. All authentic, just the way it says in the lead-in. Edited, reframed, enhanced just a touch, but all real. This,' he said, as he reached for the AV controls, 'is just for my personal amusement. And my friends'.' He froze the picture and let it melt down in lurid browns and pinks. 'Wouldn't they love to see it, though?' he said, rubbing the corner of the screen with a fingertip. 'Her and her Lost Boys?'

Saskia looked out of the window of the caravan. Golden sparks from the arc welder blossomed in the air like a giant chrysanthemum. 'You know,' she said, 'the only person more obsessed with Tabitha Jute than you is Tabitha Jute.'

Smoothly the man in the grey suit took the glass from her fingers. 'Come with me,' he said. 'I've got something to show you.'

She followed him down a metal staircase to the upper levels of the ship parking bays. Below, the tiers of burnt-out buildings revealed the naked concrete and steel of their innards. From a corner the man called Nothing picked up a lightstick and switched it on. He stood there like an angelic sentinel, flooding the narrow walkway with the pale blue radiance of his spear.

'This way.'

A buckled door led into a blackened bay. They were very close to the outer skin of the ship now. Saskia could feel the blurred nothing of hyperspace sucking at the hairs on her arms and the back of her neck. 'When your clone-brother Mogul first saw the Captain he called her "Marco's bit of rough", do you remember?' remarked Grant Nothing. 'That must have been right about where you were standing. Yes. Or a bit to the left, was it?'

Saskia had barely recognized the place. It was a mess. The Wisp hummed slowly around the walls, examining gunshot craters.

'You can't know that,' said Saskia. 'No one was there.'

'And the *Alice Liddell* must have been right along here,' said Grant Nothing, stepping back and gesturing broadly with the light.

'You've got tapes from the *Alice*?' said Saskia. She shook her head. 'You can't have. Everything was destroyed.'

'I've got,' he said, 'all sorts of things. Come here. Come over here.'

She stepped across to him. He put up his hand and stroked her breast with his thumb. 'You know,' he said intimately, 'you really are a beautiful bit of engineering.'

Hiding in the dark outside the door, Iogo watched her man at work. She thought of Kyfyd, the Captain's bodyguard, that she was not allowed to see any more. She thought of his thighs, the warm thick pads of his palms.

5

'Praise the Lord,' cried the Reverend Mr Archibald, 'that hath Sent His Messenger to Deliver the People that Dwell in Darkness –'

'Hush your row,' commanded the one-legged woman. She rocked

up to the wall and banged on it with her crutch. She pressed her ear against it.

The Professor and leader of the expedition stood sucking on his empty pipe. 'And what can you tell from that, exactly?' he asked.

'Where to go,' said the woman, who said her name was Ink.

'Ah. Ah. Where to go, I see . . .'

The injured had been left with Ink's people at their bonfires. Most of them, in fact, were unconscious, having sampled whatever it was those troglodytes cooked up in their dustbins. A couple of the younger hunters had remained too, with a first aid kit, though whether they might not get drunk and absent-mindedly try to gut and joint their charges instead of dosing and bandaging them, Captain Gillespie would not have cared to guarantee. Her own arm ached and her side burned. She leaned on Jone, happy to go at the pace of an amputee and a cat.

Ink's cat was called Odin. He looked like a sort of offworld-Siamese cross, and had a blue number tattooed inside his ear. Jone had asked Dodger if she thought it was some sort of veterinary receipt for his lost eye. Odin trotted along with his mistress, never getting in her way, sniffing curiously in every nook and cranny. After their first upset the children's dog kept a dignified distance from him; and when in the narrow passages the cat strayed too close, he would wuffle irritably, like an old Scotsman clearing his throat.

Ink stood in a spot of weak light filtering in from some indiscernible upper level. She was scraping rhythmically at the wall. One of the Catsingles stood nearby, taping her discreetly.

'Our theory that these are a band of construction slaves that survived the Capellan purge is reinforced,' muttered Dr Catsingle into his wrist recorder. 'Plainly the woman learned to imitate the habits of the Frasque before –'

His wife turned her head. 'Shh,' she said.

Ink started to walk on. Odin stretched his legs suddenly and vanished into the darkness ahead.

'What do you think, Captain Gillespie?' It was Xavier, who had been taking advantage of the break to fill his pipe. 'Is the cat part of the act?' Dodger looked at Jone, who was equally mystified. 'Act?' she repeated. The Professor took off his helmet and ran a hand through his hair as he expanded his question. 'Is it the cat that knows the way,' he suggested earnestly, 'and communicates it to the woman?'

'Oh, definitely, chief,' said Captain Gillespie. 'No doubt about it. There's a bit of Frasque in that cat. You've seen the way his back legs go.' Xavier obviously hadn't, but he was on the case at once. 'I'll get the girls to shoot some close-ups,' he said, striding off to find Geneva and Beth. Jone sniggered and tickled Dodger, who muffled a roar of agony.

Ink was scratching the wall again. In the absence of Odin the dog ran up inquisitively. 'Oh, no, Timmy!' the children cried. 'He wants to scratch too!'

They rounded a bend, and pushed through a curtain of stiffened vines. Then came a general clamour of exclamation.

'Bloody hell,' said Captain Gillespie.

'How did we get back here?' said Jone.

The Professor and his principal map-bearer began a frenzied consultation, shaking their heads and calling for more light.

'There's two of them,' protested the hunters. 'There must be.'

But there was no getting away from it. It was the Cadillac again. In the few days since they had left it the ancient car seemed to have deteriorated very considerably. The tyres were all flat. The elaborate tail-lights had been smashed, and loose wires protruded sadly from the sockets where the headlamps had been torn out. The metal was bent, the paintwork scratched. Lloyd the Xtascite put down his pack and knelt beside the car as though to mourn its inexplicable decline. 'Connect,' he said. 'It's already rusty . . .'

Mr Archibald knelt down too, never liking to miss an opportunity, while Beth said, 'Rolling.'

'Geneva McCann, Channel 9 – It was on this spot,' said Geneva loudly, 'already becoming known as Cadillac Corner –'

'Cadillac Curve,' said a hunter, pointing out the obvious.

She clenched her teeth. 'Cadillac Curve, yes, thank you, Carl, we'll use that. Take two,' she said, pleasantly.

Only Ink paid no attention to the wrecked car. Even now she was making her precarious way down the slope beyond, ignoring, as ever, offers of assistance. 'Where we going now?' asked Lloyd, hurrying to pick up his load. 'Wasn't that it? The Big Chap? That wasn't it . . . ?'

*   *   *

Beyond, the tunnel floor started to rise. It opened out and became a giant stairway. The stairs were ten metres broad and a metre high. Even Ink had to be carried up these.

The men with guns went first, but the only adversary they found was Ink's cat, which was sitting in the middle of a stair, waiting for them. They shone their lamps to either side. Complex baroque forms stood all around, columnar extrusions of matrix looming up into obscurity. Unlike the stalagmites they had seen earlier these seemed to have been created and shaped deliberately, as if in representation of unimaginable Frasque divinities or potentates. They were moulded; they were articulated. Jone cried out in disgust.

'Hallelujah!' cried Mr Archibald.

'Fuck shit!' echoed Lloyd. He laughed. 'Check that one! It's got a face!' He jostled Jone, pretending to cringe from the statue's glare. 'It's looking at us, starchy!'

Tapers, cameras, recorders whirred. Geneva stood three steps up with her feet apart. 'Abstract or symbolic, these gigantic primitive totems –'

'Pricks,' grunted Ink. The hunters cackled.

'– reaching heights of fifty metres or more –'

Impatiently Ink smacked the step where they had put her. 'Come on.'

Thirty-three stairs up there was an aperture in the wall, with a ledge beneath it big enough for half a dozen people. They looked down into a very large cave. It was full of what seemed to be a vast mound of shiny brown mud with a glistening, streaky skin on it. It was difficult to get the scale until you realized the red metal boxes standing on the mound were heavy duty machinery of some kind, linked by cables and endless belts, and the little red ticks moving purposefully about were people, human people in scarlet uniforms.

'The Big Chap,' said their guide.

The mound was breathing.

'Oh my God –'

The hunters and the naturalists gazed intently. 'Here,' Captain Gillespie said to one of the hunters, and pressed his arm until he passed her his binoculars.

The machines were excavators. They were mining the mound. They were digging down into it and coming up with regular chunks of dripping wet flesh which they hung on the slowly rolling chain of hooks, to be carried away out of sight. Robot supervisors watched gangs of brawny men who were shovelling up debris, filling oval homing trucks with ungraded and irregular mince. Everything was red, red, red.

A broad hand tapped her shoulder. 'Captain?' It was the hunter, wanting his binoculars back.

The gangs were all wearing thigh boots or waders. They had pumps siphoning away the blood that filled the quarries as they deepened. 'Er, Captain Gillespie, these guys want a look too.'

The whole mound was a gigantic spongy sort of slug, so big you couldn't see either end of it, even from up here. It seemed to pulse with a tidal surge and contraction like slow, slow respiration. It lay completely unresponsive to the huge holes being gouged in its flanks.

'Come on now, Captain –'

Full, a truck rolled away, bumping over a thick patch of scar tissue where a previous dig had healed.

'Captain, I'm going to have to take those.'

They had Wisps down there, flying intently from site to site, carrying messages or checking progress.

People at the rear were shoving and fighting to get on the ledge. 'I know those uniforms,' said a woman.

'Tekunak,' Dodger said, handing the man his glasses back, never removing her eyes from the embrasure. Peripherally she was aware of Jone being sick over the side of the stairs. Jone wasn't the only one.

Ink hoisted a little girl onto her muscular shoulder, to let her look down into the cave. 'See him, down there?' she said. 'See the Big Chap? Your dinner, lovely.'

The child looked at her blankly.

'Chilli,' said someone. 'Lasagne.'

'Hearty Hotpot,' said someone else. 'Spaghetti Surprise.'

The girl's mother grabbed her from the troglodyte. 'She's a vegetarian!' she shouted. 'Aren't you, Deirdre! *Aren't* you!'

Professor Xavier, on the stair, seized hold of Ink's crutch. His mouth moved. 'How – long –'

Ink chewed her upper lip.

'But how – Who –'

Confounded, looking almost ill himself, the Professor looked around for somebody to tell him what to ask. His eye lit upon his map-carrier. 'Where the hell are we?' he demanded.

'Long Insular Sulcus Right!' gabbled the man frantically.

'Right?' said the Professor. 'Right? Obviously! Obviously we haven't suddenly gone waltzing across the Longitudinal Fissure!' But the only thing that was obvious was the Big Chap, slumbering there in the pit.

'None of this is here!' protested the map-carrier. 'The whole area is supposed to be dark, vacuum, disconnected!' Xavier glared at Ink, clearly holding her responsible.

Mr Archibald was shouting. Mr Archibald was testifying. Mr Archibald was recognizing the Horned Beast of the Book of Revelations.

Ink sat on the ledge with her back to the view. Her job was clearly done. Odin the cat sat in his place by her foot, washing his ears. His mistress had a tight grip of his tail. He did not seem to mind.

Captain Gillespie rubbed her hands. They were clammy. She wiped them on the knees of her trousers as she crouched down. 'People are not going to like this,' she told Ink, though she did not look at her. She stroked Odin's head, but did not look at him either. Odin closed his eye, accepting her tribute.

Ink looked pointedly at Dodger's pouch.

Automatically, Dodger got out her gear and started to roll Ink a fag. She understood now. Ink and her friends lived on their own in the lower depths not because they didn't know there was anybody else aboard; but because they chose to.

Her injured arm made her clumsy. 'How do they distribute it?' she asked, snapping her lighter, thinking of the Pause Café, the Sundae Joint, the Chilli Chalet, We Serve Every Level.

Ink smoked stoically. 'Trucks,' she said.

Lloyd was in the middle of the crowd, having some kind of excited argument with the Reverend Mr Archibald, who was dragging out of his backpack a cross twice as large as his crucifix. It was made of silver-painted wood, and studded with gems and chips of mirror. 'The Beast may not be defeated by the weapons of the body,' the exorcist was panting, 'but only by the weapons of the spirit!'

Dodger was tired. Enough shocks, she thought. Enough weird shit. She reached for the pale and shaken Jone. '*Let's* go. *Come* on.'

They picked up Ink and left the scene.

At the bottom of the stairs a black enamel creature with shining red eyes was waiting for them, riding a silver saucer. 'So this is where you've got to,' it said, in a voice rather like a little girl's.

'X!' cried Jone, exhaustedly.

'We found her,' said Captain Gillespie, while they were all resting. She was introducing Xtasca to Ink. 'Or she found us, I don't know.'

'Well, you've led them a good deal out of their way,' Xtasca said to Ink, hovering directly in front of her face. 'But your method is interesting. I shall examine you.'

Startled, frightened, Ink spat at it and hobbled energetically away. The Cherub did not react. It floated there with the drool running down its shining cheek. People laughed, nervously. Jone wiped it off with her sleeve. 'How's Captain Jute?' asked Dodger. She found herself watching the Cherub's face intently, though it was pointless, trying to read an expression in those glassy black curves.

'Rather tired,' said the Cherub. 'A lot has happened since you left.'

'Look, chief,' said Lloyd, 'are we going forward in time? Or is she going backwards?'

The Cherub ignored him. It told them about the Captain's little ghost.

'*Another* one?' said Jone disgustedly. 'This whole fucking ship is haunted.'

'Tell Xavier,' said Dodger, looking over her shoulder. 'Perhaps he'd like to go and chase that one instead.'

Its voice clear and eerie in the gloom, Xtasca recited the new ghost's poem.

> . . . Her mirrors racked from side to side.
> 'The Boojum is upon you!' cried
> The Lady of Shall-Not.

'That don't mean anything, X,' said Jone.

Xtasca's skin was dappled with reflected lights, the lamps of their helmets, the illuminated displays of the saucer on which it sat. 'It means we must find the Mystery Woman,' it replied.

'Well, I'm glad we've got that straight,' muttered Captain Gillespie.

'What's a Boojum?' Jone wanted to know. People shrugged. 'It's not that thing down in the cave, is it?' she asked. Her voice was hushed.

Dodger relit her fag, blew out a jet of smoke, and picked a shred of tobacco off her tongue. 'What is it, some sort of threat, this poem?' she asked.

'A warning, in all probability. An exact description of a very particular danger.' The lights on Xtasca's saucer changed, steadied, changed again. 'The code must be highly idiomatic,' it said.

Dodger thought of Tabitha, plagued by mysterious visitors. She thought of the Cadillac and its decrepitude. Her diaphragm tightened. How long *had* they been travelling, exactly?

Xtasca's saucer buzzed. 'May we go now?' asked its rider.

Captain Gillespie's arm was hurting. Her feet were sore. 'Did you know?' she asked the Cherub.

'About the Big Chap,' said Jone, completing Dodger's question. She drew up her knees and lay her head on them.

The saucer bounced gently in the air, bobbing on a stray current. 'Check she knew,' said Lloyd.

Captain Gillespie asked: 'Does Tabitha know?'

'She's never shown much interest,' Xtasca said.

'You haven't told her, you mean. She'd go spare.'

The Cherub said nothing. Its eyes glowed unfathomably.

Professor Xavier came lurching across. 'That thing in the cave – it's alive!'

'That's correct,' replied the black chrome spawn of the Seraphim. Plainly it thought their various reactions simple-minded, if not perfectly irrelevant.

Despite the arrival of Xtasca, Lloyd elected to go with the party heading back up with the news. Many of them were hunters. They were even now entrusting their secondary weapons and spare equipment to their buddies. 'The hunt will go on, Geneva, as you know,' they said, 'but we say folk up there got a right to know.' Tracking down a mystery was one thing, but this was a sensational story right here, very much in the flesh.

Beth was already working her way around the cavern to find the gate where the trucks left. She was planning to stow away among the steaks and record the secret delivery run.

Geneva was going with the Catsingles, into the pit, with the one surviving camera. They meant to get as close as they could to the gigantic creature without being seen. The Professor would not speak to her. How could the quest continue without commentary? But already she was roughing out her piece, under the working title of *The Frozen Moment.* 'In his novel *The Naked Lunch* Twentieth Century sage William S. Burroughs wrote of the moment when everyone sees what is on the end of their fork. For the passengers of the good ship Plenty that moment came today. Is now. For the passengers of the good ship Plenty that moment is now.'

The naturalists were leaving four of their children, two boys and two girls, to press on with Professor Xavier. 'Don't worry about us, Mother,' the elder boy said. 'We can look after ourselves. After all, we've still got to find Mystery Woman.' The girls held hands and looked at Xtasca, awestruck, as at a marvellous doll.

Xtasca hovered, its tiny hands folded on its globular belly. It was watching Ink.

Ink snapped her horny fingers at the cat. 'Mouses!' she hissed.

6

Two Xtascites called Jaz and Anno were working in one of the high cradles on the wall of the Hippocampus. They were tapping a cold slab, a sector of the dark red analogue rich in untranslated data. Crystalline, holographic, fifty million identical packets of memory hung suspended in the walls, as if flash-frozen by some traumatic, hysterical burst.

There was no traffic to be seen, but the sound from nearby tunnels seemed to collect up here in the hollows, stirring and mixing into a perpetual low murmur.

'This is hopeless,' said Anno. 'We've got nothing on any of this. Jaz, we got to leave this till Xtasca gets back.'

'Who's to say she's coming back?' said Jaz.

'Don't say that, slick . . .' moaned Anno.

'No,' said Jaz, 'we're just going to have to model everything back and recut, sample by sample. Wait.' His face changed. He had spotted something, in the distance; something that shouldn't be there.

'What is it?'

'Over there,' he said. 'Right over, as far as you can see. Is that a person?'

For a moment Anno couldn't see anything. Then Jaz turned the flood that way and she saw. There was somebody there: a human, by the look of it, spreadeagled on the wall.

Jaz was on the com, alerting everyone. Anno ran to the controls. She started up the cradle and cleared them a track.

'I've got her,' Jaz said, adjusting the screen.

'Is it her? Is it?'

'It is. That's her.' He gurgled with laughter. 'Accessed!'

'What's she doing?'

The woman was clinging to the insulite stack beading, forty metres up. She had the hook of a fat yellow jump lead in the corner of an analogue slab. She swung across in her long black coat with the other hook in her hand. The hook struck, slithered. The woman kept swinging across, and back again. As she made each time her momentary contact there was a sound like tearing steel, and her outspread arms and floating hair were outlined in tiny golden sparks. 'We got her!'

'Watch it, she's taking off –'

With one swift glance over her shoulder, the woman was gone. She danced across the wall in a crazy zigzag, went headfirst into a vent, and vanished into the airways. She left nothing behind but scuffmarks; a handful of scraps of aluminium foil and a smell of scorching.

And her image on tape. A little movie. *The Hippocampus Raid.* All 73.22 seconds of it. She was moving so fast, she had to be amped, or working in some private timefield of one. But once you slowed her down, it was perfectly obvious what she was doing. Until Anno and Jaz had come zipping around the wall at her and scared her off up a vent the Captain's doppelgänger had been trying to bypass a whole sector of Inferior Pre. 'ORBITAL MEMORIES,' Alice was able to tell them, after doing some tunnelling herself. 'VIEWS OF EARTH. NOTHING CURRENT AT ALL.'

Xtascite looked at Xtascite. 'We got to tell them,' they said.

They copied the tape to all surviving channels, spreading the news. Vespans hooted it beyond the net. Drum spoke to drum, horn to horn, passing it on, calling out to the lost and separated. Calling to tell Professor Xavier his quarry had been sighted!

On the one hand you had the Tabernacle of Dreams.

'*See* the face of the demon bandit woman who comes in the night to rob and steal.'

The Rooster would pace about in his top hat and shining waistcoat, a snake writhing in each fist. His congregation moaned, clutching their children to them. 'I liken her spirit unto a snake!'

The appliqué banners stirred, the faces of smiling macrocephalics and dead film stars rippling in the candlelight.

'Let the Woman called Tree pass over us, Brother Felix!' cried the Rooster, in a rising squeal.

'Let her pass over us, Sister Latitude!' sobbed a contralto.

The snakes would hiss as he squeezed their throats.

On the other hand, you had the Silicon Church, with the great cathedral they were building in an abandoned factory on the 115th. Their chanting flowed up through the airways into the corridors of the Lower Parietal, mingling strangely with the Hawaiian guitars of Channel 4 and the security and self defence instructions now playing perpetually on 7. The Siliconites were far from fazed by indisputable evidence that their divinity was both corporeal and fallible. Mistry, they claimed, was the cybermessiah: a superior being exalted in the flesh by the Holy Spirit of Information. 'She will guide us through the Void of Non-Being, into the Spiral of Ultimate Time!'

Meanwhile the Pineal Theosophists smiled indulgently. Had they not always taught that the Avatar of Plenty would come walking on air and dancing in fire? They had, in fact, and reminded everyone so at length, with quotations from the Bhagavad Gita.

'Three pints of Dead Badger, please, Rory,' said the Good Doctor, who was already swaying. 'Evening, Mavis, I trust you are well.'

'What do you reckon to this, then?' said Mavis Forestall, meaning the Hippocampus Raid, showing once again on Channel 3.

The Doctor tutted and turned his back on the set. He leaned his elbows on the bar and looked hopefully at the Window, at present showing nothing but a very realistic stretch of blank wall.

'It's the Captain,' said Rory. 'Look at her, that's her. Give us that,' he said, snatching the credit chip from the Good Doctor's breast pocket as that sworn foe of disease slid a degree or two nearer the floor.

The wall in the Window began to grow a selection of comic graffiti.

'I always said she was cracked,' said Mavis Forestall.

IGNORANCE IS STRENGTH, read the Window.

'Of course it's not the Captain, Rory,' said the Last Poet, who was writing an ode to the Mystery Woman. 'She's a supernatural being, a black leather elemental!'

'Isn't it the Captain?' said Rory. 'Bloody looks like the Captain to me.'

DEATH TO ALL EXTREMISTS.

'"Wise among tunnels, faster than desire,"' read the Poet.

'Oh god, he's started now,' said Rory glumly, and he plugged in the music generator, which started to tootle a Palernian polka.

'Oh good, I like this one,' said the Best Judge, reaching for his wig. 'Mavis, you beautiful creature, let's dance!'

'"Thief among Plenty,"' intoned the Poet, whisking his notebook neatly out of the way before the Judge knocked the table over. '"Steal our dead hearts –"'

Everywhere now, the cold was tightening its grip. Black water seeped down the piers of the Sylvian Aqueduct, freezing as it went. In the wild tunnels, the ivy shivered. Deep in Oxy Pit Dog Schwartz dispensed to the chieftains of Havoc the best drugs in the galaxy, brought from a secret hospital ruled by an ancient mad cyborg. Norval Khan sat bare-chested while his armourers slaved and his big mammas rubbed powdered matrix in his wounds. Jacked into an environment of pure white noise, Lupin his epileptic dwarf chanted of tame quarks and rivers of time, and of Mystery Woman, the ultimate gameworld princess. 'She speaks to me from her palace on the Ten Thousandth Level! She says we must build machines of mighty energy!'

Stoned beyond hope of motion, Dog Schwartz and Norval Khan grinned at the little oracle, and then at each other. Their breath steaming in the bitter air.

Tabitha Jute attended a candlelight dinner in a sumptuous apartment. They sat her in her chair, Dorcas Mandebra and Kenny the Thrant. Dorcas waved away the attentive head waiter and his lieutenants. She sat on the Captain's right; their host, Vanderlinc Bolt of MivvyCorp, on her left. Kenny stood behind her in black psuede, black gloves on his great paws.

It was not a large room. Dorcas had been on at her to bring a different bodyguard, preferably a human one, but Tabitha had ignored her. She didn't know what they wanted, these people, and these days she didn't trust anybody. The candlelight painted the faces around the table with masks of living gold. They were all from MivvyCorp, and all humans, except one. They were offering a deal on restoring power to a block of Middle Temporal Right. In return they wanted control of the area and a guarantee of immunity from Colonel Stark and her Redcaps. 'There's a great deal for her to do anyway,' they said blandly, 'elsewhere.'

The head waiter brought the Captain a bottle of beer and a glass on a silver tray. 'Your favourite brand, Captain, I believe,' said Vanderlinc Bolt.

Captain Jute sat with her elbows on the table, her hands clasped loosely in front of her. She focused on the label on the beer bottle. Trajan Reserve. She hadn't seen that in years. Everyone said there was none left on board. 'No, I'll have some wine,' the Captain said.

Dorcas Mandebra laughed brightly. 'You don't like wine!' she said.

Captain Jute rounded her shoulders and looked Dorcas Mandebra in the face. Dorcas Mandebra was smiling very emphatically. By candlelight her skin looked yellow and red, in blotches. She looked like a powdered pomegranate. Dorcas Mandebra was a bore. Tabitha had just remembered that Dorcas Mandebra was one of the most boring people on board. This whole thing was a bore. She had no idea why she was putting up with it.

The Captain took the glass of Montrachet the waiter stood in front of her and drank from it, not looking at it, swallowing it without tasting it. 'That's fine,' she said. She put the glass down and ignored it. She heard someone say:

'Completely disappeared, apparently.'

'Who has?' asked the Captain bluntly. 'Who's gone now?'

'You know, Captain,' said Dorcas, touching her calmingly on the arm. 'That man who had that dreadful show at the Mercury Garden.'

The Captain's nipples had already tightened. Her body was remembering. She felt a touch of melancholy then, like a distant light in a dark tunnel. She ate something. She didn't know what it was. She said: 'The paramedics have got him. I knew they would.'

She wished all her problems could be taken away so easily, especially the ones of her own making.

Bolt had changed places with a light-skinned man he described as his Airflow Controller. He was an ex-spacer. He started to talk to

Captain Jute about kites, planing his hands around and making points with his knife. He wasn't eating much. No one was. The smell of Thrant was putting them all off their dinner. As the meal proceeded several excused themselves and left the room.

Captain Jute ate rapidly. She couldn't remember when she'd eaten last. Her attention left the airflow man and wandered around the room. It was all very retro, luxuriously lo-tech, with hardwood panelling and velvet curtains. There was a painting on the ceiling, of muscular old men in swirling orange robes being fed with grapes by maidens. A waiter took the plate from in front of her and replaced it with a fresh one.

Now the alien partner was speaking. He was a Vespan. His name was the usual string of syllables, like a mouthful of pebbles. He was talking about another part of the development proposal, which would apparently provide a museum to commemorate the poor, slaughtered indigenes, the original builders of their magnificent vessel.

'The Frasque?' Twiggy limbs flickered in the Captain's memory. Thorny claws that tugged at the viewport of the *Alice Liddell*, from the outside, from hard vacuum. Wooden insects with giant splintering limbs that thrashed, splashing sap around the cryo chamber. 'You want to commemorate the Frasque?'

Blowing cigar smoke out of every orifice, the Vespan dipped his long neck. 'Everybody us all victims of Capellans,' he reminded her portentously.

'No,' she said. 'No you can't. No we don't want it.' It was obviously a blind, something to distract her from the central scam, whatever *that* was. Who was really behind all this anyway? Bolt, with his moodstone cufflinks and silver winged tie; or the museum man in his double-width dinner jacket? And Dorcas, what was in it for her? The gestures of ambition and purpose, the civility that barely concealed contempt, as if they assumed she knew they despised her and didn't really care —

Captain Jute knocked over her glass. She dabbled her fingers in the pool of wine as it spread. 'Oh dear,' she said, loudly. 'Perhaps I ought to have a beer instead.'

Then she looked up and saw, in an empty chair at the other end of the table, the little white girl with the pinafore and the solemn eyes.

*　　*　　*

259

The imago sat, seemingly, in the chair, glowering. Everyone exclaimed, but it took no notice of them, fixing its eyes solely on Captain Jute. At the foot of the table it hung, still as a photograph.

Kenny thrust himself between Vanderlinc Bolt and the Captain, snarling, shielding his mistress. The Captain rose up, glaring back at the child. 'There!' she said, grabbing Dorcas by the sleeve. 'There! I told you, see? You see her?'

They saw her. Some of them tried to touch her, but the child was never quite where they put their hands. One woman tried to train her wristset on the diminutive intruder. She was pressing buttons with a tiny silver stylus. 'An imago,' she said excitedly. 'An imago on remote!'

'Location sensitive!' exclaimed the Airflow Controller.

Tabitha Jute put the side of her fist to her mouth. 'What do you *want?*' she asked the apparition.

It got up, then. It got up and walked through the table to her.

The little blonde head and shoulders came sailing towards the Captain up the crimson tablecloth. The glasses, the candles, the giant silver cruets, passed through the bib of her pinafore and emerged from her back, undisturbed. In an instant the imitation child was face to face with the Captain. She did not look pleased with her. She looked sullen. Her little pink lips opened, and she spoke.

'Come, come, this won't do at all!' she said.

And with that rebuke, she folded herself into a vertical beam of searing white light and with a sound like a cosmic zip fastener telescoped up into nothing.

Kenny was up on the table, crouching over the point of disappearance like a baffled cheetah, his tail sweeping everything into disorder. He chattered into his com, ordering up area scans, while the company security ran about shoving pointlessly at the curtains.

The MivvyCorp technical heads muttered together. 'Such resolution!' marvelled the woman with the wristset. 'I wonder what the range is on something like that?'

'I'm sure I've seen that girl before,' Dorcas was telling someone, who was agreeing. 'Or a picture of her.'

Captain Jute discovered she still had hold of Dorcas's jacket. She was feeling triumphant, vindicated, but her heart was beating like a hammer. 'What does she mean, this won't do?'

Dorcas tried to soothe her. 'I'm sorry, Captain, I don't follow –? '

'She said, "This won't do",' Tabitha repeated. She looked around for confirmation.

Kenny shook his head, twitching his ears.

'I didn't hear anything,' said Dorcas Mandebra.

Vanderlinc Bolt spread his hands and raised his eyebrows. 'It didn't make a sound,' he said.

Inside the green dome that housed the Pons, the atmosphere was drowsy. The flutter of subvocalizing lips blended with the dull hum of the meta-monitors, the whisper of a thousand cooling units. The very light seemed to sleep, absorbed by the myriad surfaces of white plastic now sprayed a considerate charcoal grey.

On hold, waiting for some lattice to come free, Swundra Celi yawned. It felt like three in the morning when you've been working all night. Perhaps it was, perhaps she had. Automatically she checked the time, without noticing what it was. It made no difference anyway. There was nothing for it to measure now they never went home.

Life in the Pons was a recurring decimal, a repetitive series of infinitely self-dividing functions. Maybe, Swundra thought, all the lost time the Thalamus kept talking about was drifting in here. It was piling up around their desks like sand, blowing into every port and slot; slowing down actions and stifling options. The displaced time grew greasy; sticky, and thick. It smelled like cockroach spray.

It could be, thought Swundra, that having more time actually meant you got less done. Other people could be zooming through Tuesday, some of them already off in the middle of next Wednesday, while there you were stuck back around the hairpin of last weekend. And the longer everything took, the more you lost touch with reality. Perhaps that had already happened. Perhaps no one in here was doing anything meaningful. They were all running routines without referents, chasing the tails of their own traces as they multiplied in the datasphere.

As soon as she had that thought, Swundra felt it go slipping away from her into oblivion. She could no longer think what it was she had been thinking about; nor whether it had been an original thought or one she had had a thousand times. She wondered if she had fallen asleep for a moment, and had a strange and rather abstract dream. The place was so *quiet*. She checked the lattice queues and found she had been redirected again.

Swundra fingered the plug in her right temple and gazed lifelessly at the big screen on the wall. It was full of code, in green sheets and orange. The green was scrolling very slowly up. It scrolled until the orange appeared. It carried on scrolling until the orange filled the screen. It sat there for a minute. Then it started to scroll very slowly back down. Swundra watched it scroll up and scroll back, scroll up and scroll back. Then the whole big screen shattered from top to bottom, all at once.

Everyone gasped. Swundra was transfixed by shock. Some of the jocks started to clap and whistle, like customers in a restaurant when someone drops a tray.

The big screen hung intact an instant. Then they saw it belly out under its own weight and collapse. An avalanche of crystal dice scattered beneath the front desks. People were on their feet, backing up the aisles. They could all hear a loud squealing noise. It sounded like a thousand vengeful cats.

It was worse than that. It was a tribe of Perks.

'*Cheeeeeeeeeeeeeeeeeeeeeeeee – !*'

Already the guards were there, pouring wide-spectrum repulsers into the breach. The screaming redoubled. Shots were returned. The whole front three rows were on the floor now, crawling in frantic haste, trailing wires, dragging keyboards to the floor. A workstation exploded. Humans were screaming now.

The Perks were naked. Their little purple genitals were flushed with rage. They had gnawed and clawed their way up out of the darkness. Now they were hopping over the sill of their new hole, their ragged leaders writhing fast up the aisles towards the helm.

They were coming.

Swundra pulled her plugs and threw herself sideways. She was out of shape. It had been years since she had moved so fast.

One of the guards grabbed her from behind, pitching her out of his way. Swundra tumbled into a vacant desk. Her exit was blocked by a stationary cart. Whining with fear she struggled to climb over it.

The Perks did not seem pleased to see no one was at the helm.

The guard straddled the aisle, facing the attack. A Perk leapt. Teeth sought tendons with the speed of a flying razor. Another guard made a sharp jab with the butt of a Borniak. Perk bones snapped.

With a downward jerk of his forearm the first guard triggered a spring-loaded grenade. It fell among the Perks, hissing and blowing brown clouds of gas around.

Two Perks toppled over, falling on the can as if purposely to smother it, while the next trampled with no hesitation at all over their backs, still coming, at speed.

Lomax was there now, bellowing commands. He was roughly dressed and unshaven, as if he had been roused from his bunk. He was half into a flame thrower harness, blowing the scrambling rodents back with roaring puffs of fire. Their feathers were burning, making a nauseating stench. Smoke detection circuits started to wail, rousing the robot fire drones from their kennels in the walls. Confused by the warbling of the alarm, some of the Perks started attacking the fire drones, which turned the extinguishers on them. 'CLEAR THE BUILDING, PLEASE,' Alice was calling now in hard, metallic tones. 'CLEAR THE BUILDING.'

There was more commotion, from the foyer. Crouching behind her cart Swundra saw the Captain and her bodyguards come rushing in.

'Alice!' shouted the Captain.

'CLEAR THE BUILDING, PLEASE,' shouted Alice.

'Report, Alice!'

'CLEAR THE BUILDING.'

When they saw the Captain the invaders shrieked twice as loud. They went for her. Her guards struck low and beat them back, trying to contain them. Clumsily Captain Jute tried to make a break for the helm. Her Thrant restrained her. Three Perks stood on the big blue chair, defying her. Her men sprayed them with gas and fierce blue light.

Mr Spinner was with her now. Captain Jute seized his shoulder, supporting herself while he bellowed in her ear. With her free hand she pushed her hair back out of her face.

The Perks screamed at her.

With the Captain occupied, the Thrant was looking to the fight. Off to one side he had spotted two Perks on the body of a dead Pontine, chewing out the soft parts. The Thrant jumped on the Perks as if he was glad to see them. With a vicious tug he snapped the spine of one, kicking another in midair.

Then a bristling face snapped white teeth centimetres from Swundra's cheek. She screamed, stood up and dropped an auxiliary monitor on it. Not stopping to see what damage she'd done, she ran.

She cleared an aisle, pounding for the stairs to the gallery, hauling air into her lungs through her open mouth.

Lomax had got Captain Jute behind the food-train, two men in front with broadband repulse guns. He was trying to get her to leave. 'There's nothing you can do here!' He was getting angry. Mr Spinner was holding her by the arms, coaxing her back towards the door. But the Captain was into it now. She lurched away from her first officer, commandeering a Corregidor from someone. She put one foot, unsteadily, on the chilli cart.

'You think you can fly this thing?' she yelled at the intruders. 'Get out of here.'

The Perks made a rush.

The Captain started firing erratically. She climbed on the cart, completely exposed, blazing force packets into the scrabbling, lunging mob. The guards struggled to cover her.

As the Perks danced on one another, dodging Captain Jute's fire, they screamed, denouncing her. It sounded as if they were shouting something about a warren. 'Woman out of warren!'

Captain Jute was getting the rhythm of it now. She swung the Corregidor, quartering her field of view, putting one bolt between two Perks until they got too close, then blowing them apart. All the while she yelled incoherently, cursing.

Lomax had been putting a play together. Now he signalled, and they made it. Fire from the gallery pinned the Perks as two of her men grabbed the Captain from behind, pinning her arms and lifting her off her feet while a third relieved her of the gun. In the big blue chair Kenny squatted, a limp Perk in his mouth. He shook it by the throat, like a leopard worrying a monkey, dropping it only to snarl.

The Captain was in the foyer. The last of the crew personnel were out of there. Lomax moved in with his flamer. Now the clean-up could begin. The Perks were outgunned. They were gassed. A lot of them looked sick, with horrible sores on their lips and their fur falling out. Still they howled 'Woman out of warren!'

Helped by the food-train, four fire drones corralled them for the slaughter.

Saskia Zodiac selected a plum. 'So what do you know about J.M. Souviens?' she asked.

'Very nice little business,' said her host. 'Outlets on fifteen habitats in the first year of trading. Nice locations too, mostly. Or cheap. Plenty would have been one of the cheap ones. Over-equipped, though. Tok 690G's and Nero Corban Ariels. Completely wasted, on their clients.'

Saskia had eaten the plum. She cracked the stone with her teeth. 'Mine's stopped,' she said.

'Dear oh dear,' said the man in the grey suit.

'Yes, completely,' she said, as delicately she removed the plumstone kernel from the fragments of its shell. 'There's power, but nothing responds.' He leaned towards her, a fine lawn napkin in his hand. With one corner of his napkin he dabbed a spot of plum juice from her cheek. His face was very close to hers.

He said: 'I expect we can fix that for you.'

His shave was perfect, the skin machined to a microscopic tolerance. He smelled of distant icebergs.

'Why would you do that for me?'

He stroked the spot he had wiped with the knuckle of his little finger. 'I like you,' he said.

'Do you?' said Saskia. He had brought her to one of the most luxurious of his hideouts. It had panels of wood and people painted on the ceiling.

'I do,' said Grant Nothing.

'I don't think you do,' she said. 'You're just another Jutie. You just want to know what the Captain is like in bed.'

His eyes regarded her from another galaxy. She wondered if she had annoyed him.

He touched his fingernails together. 'Suppose I did,' he said, like a chess tutor discussing a piece of play. 'Suppose I did want to know that. Would you tell me?'

'She's not like your little movies, I will tell you that,' said Saskia.

'Guess where she was two days ago.'

The acrobat blew air through her lips, feigning boredom. 'Oh god, how am I to know? At the Trivia, I suppose . . .'

'She was right there,' said Grant Nothing. 'Right there where you're sitting.' He smiled. The precision of his little arrangement pleased him. 'She sat in that chair, and saw a ghost, and thought it spoke to her.' He too took a plum from the bowl. 'Her doctor says she often complains of hallucinations,' he told her.

Saskia recognized the quote from the tablemats in the Chilli Chalet. She supposed he had written those too.

Grant Nothing watched his guest. Because she did not speak he thought he had touched her. Her eyes with their unnameable colour seemed to stir with subterranean emotion.

He rolled his plum slowly on his plate with one finger. 'Shall I tell you what the Captain is doing now?' he suggested.

'That you don't know,' she said.

'Would you like to bet on that?' he asked, not unpleasantly. 'Day by day I know everything she has done in the long subjective months since you last saw her. I know the precise state of your estrangement.'

'Then you're the only one who does,' said the acrobat with calm conviction. Her eyes not leaving his, she slit the throat of a banana with her frosted blue thumbnail and began to peel it.

Grant Nothing looked past Saskia Zodiac to the door of the kitchen. He could see Iogo cleaning the dishes. The Wisp was at the workshop, being lubricated and recharged. Grant Nothing wanted no distractions tonight. 'Iogo,' he said. He knew there was no need to raise his voice.

He poured the last of the wine into Saskia's glass, adding the merest dribble to his own, then held the bottle up for the Thrant to come and take away.

When she arrived, he caught her by the wrist. 'I thought you were going to bring the Tokay now,' he said.

Iogo shuffled her feet and rolled her head. His tastes confused her. Also she knew the Captain's man had been there, in that room, and not long ago. She could smell him.

'Don't worry,' Grant Nothing said crisply, releasing her paw and pushing back his chair. 'I'll get it.'

When he returned with the bottle and a pair of octagonal glasses, his guest had finished her banana and was sitting with her bare feet tucked up underneath her. Her face was like a beautiful ice sculpture.

'I don't want you to fix J.M. Souviens,' she said.

He was amused. He set the tray down on the table, square. 'Why not?'

'Because you were the one who shut it down,' she said.

He took his seat, sitting back with his hands in his pockets. 'How do you work that out?' he asked her. He spoke mildly, teasingly; but she was, in fact, right, and so he wanted to know.

'You rang the com. When we answered I suppose you fed it some kind of virus.'

He was delighted with her, like an owner with a new pet puppy that has already learned a good trick. But he said: '*We?*'

The conjuror was not discomfited. 'Suzan and me,' she said.

He poured the wine, exactly the same in each glass this time. He twisted the bottle and caught the last drop neatly inside the lip. 'We'll bring the gear down here for you, from Sugar Grove,' he proposed. 'I'll get someone to give it a good clean.'

She did not react. Preoccupied by thoughts he couldn't immediately deduce, she sat there as if she hadn't even heard him.

That would have to change.

7

A thousand screens filled the red-roofed cavern with madness. Half of them were not working. Another quarter were working, but showing meaningless patterns, impossible views, roaming stegosaurs, galaxies of green suns. The cavern was alive with babbling transmissions, speeded music racing manically, low articulated moans like glaciers conferring. A rhythmic wheezing sound was the cry of the water pump, still soldiering against seepage. Half a dozen industrial ceramic heaters stood about, cooking the air.

At the Thalamus desks were what remained of the staff, a dozen or so scared-looking young humans in dingy clubwear. They were being supervised by a rather larger number of equally young humans, armed and unarmed, wearing red berets and black shirts. A blond, sharp-faced man was walking about, checking on everybody.

'What have you got at Mesenc S–370, Larry?' asked Lieutenant Rykov.

'Nothing,' said Larry at once. 'That's all dark, down there.' He was still very nervous; they all were. Nothing too bad had happened yet. People had been beaten up, but no one had been killed. Still there was no telling what they might do if they decided you weren't co-operating.

He stole a look at the nearest guard, a woman with an ultrasonic whip. If only the Cherub were still there. What should they do? What would X want them to do?

The lieutenant put his hand on the young man's shoulder. 'Just try calling that number for me, Larry,' he said.

So Larry did, and it answered. There they were, squatting in darkness. Black shirts and crimson berets assembled before the camera, waiting for the green light. There were little nests of them turning up all over the ship. Stark had more people than anyone had realized.

'K Company present and correct, sir.'

'Synchronize on me and stand down,' Lieutenant Rykov told each squad. They did it too. God knows what kind of chronometry they had.

The lieutenant phoned Colonel Stark to report 60% success with no casualties. 'The reception's still pretty spotty,' he told her, surveying the screens. 'But we're all being good little boys and girls here, ma'am!' He showed them all his teeth.

Larry's fingers fumbled the keys. 'Still no ax to Occipit,' he reported. He was co-operating with them. He was co-operating. But no way was he going to call them *sir*.

The Redcap lieutenant's voice was strong, sympathetic. 'Keep trying, son.'

They watched the monitors. Up on the raspberry red slabs of the Hippocampus tiny black dots were crawling around: the old scavenger crabs, moving sensors from point to point. The crabs were co-operating too. Somehow the militia had found and reprogrammed their primitive auton systems. 'Mr Spinner, sir,' a Redcap corporal announced from the far side of the chamber.

On the Pons line Mr Spinner's green face crackled and fractured. *'Hello? Hello?'* he called. He looked extremely agitated.

'Tell him we'll have something for him soon,' said Lieutenant Rykov, as if it were a meal he was promising to deliver. 'Tell him to maintain skip and await instructions.'

In Oxy Pit there was a fight going on.

In Oxy Pit there was always a fight going on.

It was Norval Khan himself who had started this one. He called Mistry a whore.

'What? The Virgin Mistry?' said Dog Schwartz. Vigorously he shook his great head. 'No, I'm sorry, Norv, no, you're just going to have to take that back.'

The Khan was a tall human man with a narrow face and a crafty expression. He was young, and lean, and brown as a biscuit in torn jeans and a single earring. He was strung out on Dog's latest consignment. They all were. The Khan yawned contemptuously.

'Fuggn whore,' he said. 'I've fuggn adder.'

Which was such an obvious lie, Dog Schwartz laughed.

Norval's captains all shifted, quickening, paying attention.

Dog chuckled and sniffed. 'No, no, Norval,' he said. 'You're talking bollocks.' He blew in the air. He looked at his fingernails. 'No, I'm sorry, Norv, I can't sit here and listen to you talk bollocks. I mean –' More quietly, but just as clearly, he said: 'If you were talking about your mother, I'd agree.'

The gang growled pleasurably, engaging a higher gear. 'Let me have him, Norv,' murmured one.

'Go on then, Joey,' said the Khan. 'Warm him up for me.'

'I'll let some of the air out,' announced Joey, producing a blade. He wore leathers of uncertain derivation. His eyes were like green headlamps and his hair was like burned matches.

Everyone stood back, folding their arms, grinning. They thought it would come to nothing. They thought he was an old fart, an old windbag. They thought they could besmirch the name of Mistry and get away with it.

Dog Schwartz gave a lugubrious toss of his head. He spat at Joey's feet. Joey came at him.

Now when they come at you with a knife, Dog Schwartz had once told Niglon Leglois, then you've got several options. You can duck, you can dive, you can weave. If you've got the space, you can try to get behind them. If you've got a knife, you can retaliate. If you've got a gun or some kind of concealed armament, you can retaliate more decisively. If you've got nothing but your hands, you might want to think about letting them come at you with a knife in the first place.

Once they do come at you with a knife, Dog Schwartz always found, the time for thinking is past. What you do is react. What you do is get hold of the guy's arm and smack him around the head so hard he falls over. The point being, they never remembered how fast Dog Schwartz could move. They were used to his big hands darting and fidgeting here and there all the time. They forgot he might smack them around the head.

Joey's knife was gone. He was on the floor. The boys were shouting. Joey swivelled, his legs scissoring round Dog's right leg.

Lupin Dwarf hissed damply in the Havoc Khan's ear. 'Shall I turn the hallucinomats on?'

Norval tutted, shoved him off. The dwarf bounced away, gurgling.

With a savage jerk Joey pulled the big man over. He landed him one on the shoulder that would have been very nasty if it had still involved a knife. He scrambled up and kicked him in the ribs. 'You fucker!' he yelled.

So Dog Schwartz, burning pure adrenalin now, rolled over and knocked him down again, on his back. Games were good. He liked games. But it was all so much more satisfying when it was real flesh, real knuckles. Like a levitating yogi Dog lifted his bulk from the floor and threw himself on top of Joey, riding him, pinning him with his vast hams. He grabbed his shoulders and banged his head on the floor, five times, six.

'All right, all right!' It was Norval shouting. Dog came back from his ecstatic and very blurry high sitting on Joey's skinny chest. Norval was looking amused. 'Christ!' he said.

'Take it back,' repeated Dog.

'What?' said Norval.

'You never had Mistry.'

'Nah,' agreed the Khan, with satisfaction. 'Someone that looked like her,' he added maliciously.

It was a standing joke that Dog Schwartz had known the Captain when she was sixteen and hadn't even touched her.

Dog Schwartz altered his position quickly, making Joey shout.

'Let him go, Dog,' said the Khan. 'What do you want?'

'I want to ride the ape,' said Dog Schwartz quickly.

Norval Khan gaped merrily. 'You what?'

Dog dug his knee in Joey's neck. 'I want to ride the ape!' he shouted.

They were all starting to laugh now, turning away. 'Let him go, Dog,' said Lupin Dwarf, skipping about. 'Dog, let him go!'

Dog relaxed. 'Come on then,' he said softly to Joey, and helped him up. Dog's clothes were dusty, his hair was all over the place. He slapped Joey round the head again, not so hard. 'Nervy little fucker,' he huffed.

'Yer,' said Joey, showing his upper teeth, not downhearted at all. He punched Dog in the side. But the fight was all done, it was only a ghost of it they were celebrating. The lords of Havoc regrouped. A flabby young mamma in a grubby shift was rousted out of bed and sent for more whisky. Lupin picked up Joey's knife and gave it back to him. They all started in on him, slowly but emphatically talking tactics.

Norval went out for a piss. He stood outside the cave looking down into the bottom of the Pit, where the legs stood. That was all there was, yet. That Dog, he was a headcase.

'Course you can ride the ape, Dog, you tosser,' said Norval, fondly.

Marmaduc Flecheur de Brae decided it was Christmas and held a great charity ball. Everyone dressed up as pantomime characters: Godfrey Bills, in a turquoise dressing gown, was an embarrassed, simpering Mikado, while Dagobert Moon, in yellow false whiskers and a scarlet suit, came lugging a sack of inflatable dolls and specialist magazines. 'Ho ho ho!' he cried, with inexpert jollity. 'A Festive Time to one and all!'

Lady Topaz had come as the Old Woman in the Shoe, in brown leather with her face tanned. 'It's far too late for Christmas,' she told everyone.

Zoe Primrose struck an attitude, her fists on her hips. In tights and feathered cap she made a merry Dick Whittington, especially after four cups of punch. 'Don't be moody, old thing!' she exhorted her friend. 'It's the season of goodwill.'

She was equipped with the traditional cat on a stick, which hung awkwardly down her back. In a luminous skull mask the Disaster Commissioner danced stiffly with a Sugar Plum Fairy, while the music played 'Walking in a Winter Wonderland'. The Best Judge was there in his robes and an enormous full-bottomed wig. He stole Moon's beard and kept taking young women on his knee and tickling them. At his behest a drunken run was made to search for mistletoe in the overgrown arcades of Montgomery Cleft.

Topaz and Zoe left the party long before midnight, coerced into delivering a wagonload of presents to the unfortunates of Snake Throat. Cast-off clothes and unwatched tapes, people had mainly given, though someone had been very practical and boiled up a vast cauldron of stewed fruit. The gyrus road was deserted. The head-lights of the wagon bounced around the blackened, seeping walls. Here, there were only intermittent deserted buildings, their grey fronts emblazoned with intricate and unintelligible territorial insignia, messages of wild pride and defiance perfectly at odds with the dreariness of the region. The tunnels were littered with empty beer tubes and rags of garbage – nothing edible, the transients had already seen to that. At an intersection a solitary cable maintenance unit stood and watched them, its head revolving as they passed. Zoe Primrose stood up. 'And a Merry Christmas to you too!' she carolled, and slapped her thigh. Somewhere a Vespan hooted, and another more distant answered; and another, more distant still.

Topaz kept cycling the scanners, looking in all directions. 'Where are the bloody unfortunates anyway?'

Already they seemed to have been driving for hours. Zoe played with the com. All it would pick up was the health and safety channel. 'Exactly like Terran cockroaches but completely transparent,' it said, and played a little scurrying music, xylophone and strings.

They detoured around a major collapse, labouring over uncleared debris. Topaz could feel the vacuum beyond, sucking tirelessly at the walls. The heater started to labour. She tightened the laces of her costume.

The tunnel twisted, black and flaky as the inside of a hollow tree. They saw a light ahead, a frail spot of pale green shed by a ring on a stick. 'Oh look,' said Zoe. 'A food stall.'

It was. It looked like a grounded hoverfloat, equipped with a spirit kettle and a sparse selection of provisions. At the sound of their engine the hairy proprietor heaved himself up into view.

'Isn't that the chap who used to run the Flying Tiger Restaurant?' asked Topaz, cheering up a fraction. Odd as it was to see him here, at least they were still in some sort of civilization.

'That's you, Puss,' Zoe said to the cat, dangling it in the air, laying her cheek on its fur. 'The Flying Tiger.'

The failed restaurateur had a large and baggy airmask on. There was something infinitely pathetic about the way he stood behind his pans of violent yellow noodles and deep fried snakeweed pods. 'Poor thing,' said Zoe.

Topaz touched the brake key, pulling in. 'Ask him if he's got any booze,' she said.

Gingerly Zoe opened a window. The smell of rancid fat came wafting in. 'Merry Christmas!' she called, less buoyantly. 'Are we right for Snake Throat?'

Behind the plastic visor the caterer's black eyes glittered in the intercellular twilight. He looked sourly at the stewed fruit, and pointed with his snout. 'Ow Ca Shoo,' he answered.

Zoe almost took it for a reference to her friend's costume. '*What* did he say?' she asked.

'Down the Crap Chute,' repeated Topaz, driving on.

'Charming,' said Zoe, hiccoughing.

'Everyone calls it that,' said Topaz, waving at the disappearing stallholder. 'Don't you call it that? What do you call it,' she asked in a tone of friendly sarcasm, 'Left Limbic Thingummy?'

The Captain's personal assistant put her feet up on the console. 'That's at work,' she said. 'Not when you're out having fun,' she said. She sounded limp now, and ghastly. Topaz hoped she wasn't going to be sick. The smell of frying had invaded the cab, and the air conditioning didn't work.

'We should have offered him something,' she said, unenthusiastically. Giving things to Alteceans was not always a good idea. You couldn't always get rid of them afterwards. Like Eeb, for example. Whenever you turned round, there she was, shuffling along behind you with her carrier bags.

At last a tunnel opened onto a canyon as deep as Long Fiss. They could see quite a way in. It was brown and porous as an exhumed bone, with spots of silt black and snot yellow. There was nothing moving, but their scanners said there was life.

'This must be it,' said Topaz.

They hadn't gone a hundred metres into the canyon when they saw someone. It was a woman, quite young, and very thin. Despite the cold she was wearing nothing but a short ragged skirt. She stood gazing at them stupidly, while they tried to smile. A sticky discharge was running from one of her breasts, like wasted milk.

'Oh thank goodness,' said Topaz, stopping the van.

'All right,' said Zoe, opening the windows. 'One, two, three.'

Then Lady Topaz and Zoe Primrose began to sing.

> 'We wish you a Merry Christmas,
> We wish you a Merry Christmas,
> We wish you a Merry Christmas – '

The Snake Throat woman began to bellow. The shadows began to move. People were appearing from nowhere, human people, hairy, emaciated, coming out of the walls. They stared.

Quickly Topaz shut the windows.

The woman continued to yell, abusing the aid mission in some incomprehensible language, pelting the windscreen with lumps of dirt. The wagon rocked as someone leaped up on the back. Already they were surrounded, besieged.

'No, no! It's for you! It's all for you!' shouted the women, frantically, pointing to the appliqué shirts, the boxes of liquorice allsorts. But the Rooks had assumed that.

During the seconds it took them to strip everything not welded into place, Topaz and Zoe sat tight. They sat with their fists clenched at their sides and smiled fiercely while the grimy creatures swarmed round them, whooping, banging on the bodywork.

'They can't have regressed this far,' Topaz said. 'Zoe, we've left our own time. We've gone down a timeslip, haven't we? Yes, that must be what it is.'

'Start the bloody *van!*' squealed Zoe, very much too late.

Into the Thalamus two of the guards brought a filthy young man in a torn pink zip-front and khaki pants. There were scratches on his face and tunnel grime in his hair. As they presented him to Lieutenant Rykov he sagged between the Redcaps like a man exhausted.

'Lloyd!' murmured everyone.

'Where's Xtasca?' people wanted to know. 'Where's Captain Gillespie?'

Lloyd gazed stupidly around the transformed com centre. He stared at the stern young agents with their crisp, through-designed insignia and assortment of guns. 'What's going on?' he asked.

'Who is he?' the lieutenant asked the guards.

'Claims to have been with the missing expedition, sir,' said one. 'But he belongs here.' She pulled at a rip in Lloyd's sleeve, showing Lieutenant Rykov the Xtascite tattoos.

'Anno?' Lloyd said, peering around at his friends in bewilderment. 'Larry?'

'Lloyd, is that your name?' said Lieutenant Rykov. 'Talk to me, Lloyd, not them.'

The guards brought a console chair and sat him in it. 'Hands on your knees,' they told him. 'Where we can see them.'

The circumstances were not important. 'You've got to tell every-body about this,' said Lloyd. 'Everybody, check?'

The Redcap lieutenant stood over Lloyd with his arms folded. His expression did not change as he heard that all the meat being cooked and sold by Chilli Chalet, which meant all the meat on board any more, practically, was the living flesh of a gigantic alien creature sleeping in a deep ventral cavern.

Lloyd held up a tape. 'Play this,' he said. 'It's Geneva McCann,' he told them all. 'Geneva McCann, Channel 9. I got to take it there.'

'Ensign,' said Lieutenant Rykov. A young woman in a black shirt saluted, took the tape from Lloyd without a word.

The lieutenant's eyes were steady on Lloyd. 'We'll get someone to have a look at it,' he promised. With the smallest movement of his head he indicated the aisles of com gear, seine scanners, the trans-lucent spaghetti of cables. 'You work here, do you?'

'You don't connect!' said Lloyd. He pointed at the tape the young woman was carrying away. 'This is basic!'

Guards barred his way. 'When Colonel Stark is in control, we'll be taking care of all food stocks,' said Lieutenant Rykov.

'People have got to know!'

The lieutenant turned to Jaz, who was at the controls of the public channels. 'Jaz. Let's see what you can find us about the Big Chap,' said the Redcap, and casually sat, resting his bottom on the railing.

One by one, a dozen screens blinked over to images of trays of slimy pink flesh in racks, roads unreeling into blackness, figures in goggles shouldering bloodstained shovels. A randomized chorus of Beths recited grim commentary. Very soon it became obvious all the scenes were from the same film, coming in at different speeds from different districts.

'Everybody knows already, Lloyd. People are very angry. Naturally.' The lieutenant showed Lloyd the pickets; the diners with their gun emplacements; footage of the firebomber who had burst apart in the door curtain of the Chilli Chalet at Parietal P29.

Dazed, Lloyd tried to stand up again. The Redcaps dissuaded him. 'We've got to do something!'

Lieutenant Rykov gave him a smile of quiet pride. 'Lloyd, you're in the right place. When it comes to getting things done, we're the guys to get.' His troops grinned, their weapons not wavering.

'It's all under control,' he said.

Larry watched helplessly as Lloyd began to shake. Lloyd didn't understand what he was hearing. The lieutenant was fondling his shoulder and saying, 'Why don't you go and get a shower and a snooze and when you're ready, come back and join your friends?'

The guards pulled at him, taking him out. Lloyd gazed wildly around the remains of Xtasy Krew, confined to their desks by guns and ultrasonic whips. He shouted, as they hustled him out, 'Lieutenant! Lieutenant! You better check what you're gonna do if that thing wakes up!'

'We've got to do something.' *'We've got to do something.'* While they were looking at him, he'd have a couple of seconds, Larry thought, and a couple would have to be enough. He hit the com channels. Fear clutching him, binding, glutinous, made his fingers seem to move in slow motion, like time fault material. He keyed general alert and opened a mike. 'Calling the Dragonfly! Calling the Dragonfly! The Thalamus has been invaded! This is a message for Tombo, somebody check in, shit, get on the com – '

'Ensign!' rapped the lieutenant.

A pistol snicked. Larry slumped across his board. A wisp of smoke rose from his scalp, just below the occipital bulge.

Lieutenant Rykov paused an instant to let the message of his demonstration sink in. Then he asked: 'Now has anybody else got any bright ideas?'

Tiltsnirip Tilpnotuel was often to be found at the apartment of his brother, Noptot'toplin. They enjoyed long soaks together in the protein bath. 'Full bladders, Tiltsnirip,' Noptot'toplin would say.

'Full . . . bladders . . . Noptot!'

Together they would submerge until only their eyes and lumbar nostrils protruded above the green surface.

On Vespa, before the Great Rescue, Noptot'toplin had been a local commissioner of beasts. He and his brother had worked the justice banks, receiving and paying out vengeance allowances. They spent many a happy hour reminiscing about this attack and that, ruminating their way back through the battles of their grandfathers and great-grandfathers and great-great-grandfathers. Then Tiltsnirip would speak of his beloved wife, the late Irskoraituen, and they would weep sharp acetic tears.

Afterwards, draped in towels, they padded through Noptot'toplin's Perk kennels, clambering up and down the ladders to greet each family in its quarters. What a squealing there was! '*Chee-chee-cheee! Chee-chee-cheee!*' What a parading of new claws, new scars, tiny wriggling babies. The Vespans sat on the floor and allowed themselves to be clambered over, their sweet glands licked, their leathery toes subjected to experimental nips and pinches. 'I envy you, Noptot,' said Tiltsnirip. 'The happy hours you must spend here among your pets.'

'None so happy as the hours when I share that pleasure with you, Tilt,' puffed Noptot'toplin.

'And now for the proud fathers,' said Tiltsnirip.

Behind a steel grille two first-generation Perks in denim waistcoats and silver ornaments crouched on the floor playing a savage and complicated game with five outsize knucklebones and a human jaw. One wore a greasy old baseball cap decorated with a logo that read *DV8*. He came rushing to the bars and stuck his arm through, wheedling for cigarettes. 'Come on, Not-Not. Smok DV8, smok suck.'

His brother's name was SKP. As long as he was fed and exercised he seemed oblivious to the ironic disparity between his name and his situation as a captive in these rank hutches. Only occasionally would he start to fling himself bodily at the bars, until his landlord, fearing broken bones or even internal injuries, had him clamped and sedated. At other times, like now, he wore a battered miniature top hat and fawned on the Vespans.

Tiltsnirip and Noptot'toplin Tilpnotuel stroked the little scrappers' spiky fur, and whispered in their mug-handle ears of certain plans. 'There is a human,' said Noptot, who had heard the story a hundred times. 'A very old human.'

'There is a whole nest,' sighed his brother, 'of murderous, treacherous, poisonous humans.'

8

Tabitha Jute lay in bed. She was wearing a grubby dressing gown of apricot silk. Her eyes were two purple pits. She felt like death.

'I'm not sleeping any more,' she said. 'When I sleep I get horrible dreams. I dreamed the walls of the Pons came open and a horde of horrible little monsters burst in.'

The Good Doctor sat beside her, his left hand spread on the covers. His fingernails were immaculate. Only his shirt cuff was frayed, and his eyes were a bit wobbly, and he smelled strongly of ethyl alcohol. He asked her: 'How did that dream make you feel?'

She looked straight at him. 'Not pleased,' she said. 'It was not a nice dream.'

'You feel sometimes things are overwhelming you,' said the Good Doctor, nodding; but the Captain was not listening. She was wondering what had happened to the vigorous young men and moist young women that used to occupy the other pillow. They seemed to have run out of them.

The Good Doctor was going on about paradigms in the Captain's personal life experience. 'We might say the Capellans represent the father, empowering but prohibiting; Sol the mother, nurturing and protecting. Separation from the system is like leaving home.'

'Home?' said Captain Jute. 'Where's that?' She thought a drink might make her feel better too. She looked around for a drone. Then she remembered there were none left. Zoe had found a place down in the docks where even now, she said, you could get a drone repaired; but somehow they never seemed to come back.

Which made Captain Jute think of Saskia Zodiac.

'What I don't understand,' she said, 'is why she's getting at me.'

The Good Doctor started to make a note. 'Who is it, do you think, that's getting at you?'

'All that crap on Channel 10.' Things out of the past, things she didn't even remember telling her about. Things she hadn't even told Alice about. That had to be her.

Captain Jute thought of Saskia Zodiac sitting here in the bed, naked, hugging herself tight. A child in a grown-up body. She would wake to find her weeping silently in the dark. 'I can't cope with other people's problems,' she told the doctor. He was taking her pulse.

Anyway, she thought, that was all past. Since she had had her hobby, Saskia Zodiac had discovered independence. The last time Tabitha had got stoned enough to phone, it had rung and rung. She had gone into the pod and come out again and it was still ringing.

'The Lady of Shall-Not,' she said, witheringly.

'Ah – now apparently,' said the Good Doctor, 'that's a parody of an old poem. And you know the imago, the little girl, is out of a book –'

'There you are. I saw her reading it.' And she wouldn't say where she'd got it. The book must have given Saskia the idea, to disappear and send the child to torment her. God knows what it was supposed to mean.

'— a book called *Alice in Wonderland*.'

'No,' said Captain Jute. 'That wasn't it. It was called *Peter Pan*. It was the one my dad used to tell us about. Alice?' she said, belatedly noticing what the doctor had said. 'Alice was out of a book too, yes. Alice Liddell, that was it, probably. Alice could tell you.' She looked at him writing. 'Don't worry, doctor,' she said. 'I'm not suffering from delusions. Not the delusion we'll ever see Alice again, anyway.'

From the com by the bed spoke an exasperated Mr Spinner. '*Alice is not a piece of plastic! Alice is a persona, a voice-operated self-reflexive grammatical metasystem!*'

'What are you doing listening?' cried Captain Jute.

Mr Spinner looked upset. Something was bothering him. The lines beside his mouth were deep and hard. His glasses had slid down his nose. '*Forget about the plaque, the plaque won't solve anything!*' he barked, with the raw force of the repressed man finally roused. '*Captain, I must speak to you in person.*'

'Later,' she said. 'I'll be there.' He looked so upset she lunged across the bed to switch him off. 'It's this fucking ship,' she said. 'It's driving us all mad!' She struggled back beneath the sheets. 'The moment we materialize, I'm off, I tell you. I'm the one that will be disappearing then, just watch me.'

'The environmental factor.' The Good Doctor tapped the side of his index finger against his teeth. 'The leukophobia, an unreasoning fear of blankness and erasure . . . We must not forget that we are all victims of an extreme dissociation of space and time.' He held his hands open before him, as if to support a large invisible globe. Disregarded, his notebook slipped off his knee. Captain Jute looked at it. He hadn't been making notes, he'd been doodling, she saw: spiderwebs, toadstools, large spurting penises.

'Perhaps these chimeras are symptoms . . .' he rhapsodized. 'Consensual hallucinations . . . admonitory archetypes that patrol the outer zones of our own identity . . .'

'It's Saskia,' she said.

The Good Doctor cocked his head. 'A cry for attention?'

Saskia as she saw herself. Captain Jute remembered the words the little ghost had mouthed, the words only she could hear. '*This won't do at all.*' What was she complaining about? What more could she do than she was doing? If Saskia Zodiac had something to say to her, why didn't she just come and say it? Was she in some kind of trouble?

'Find Saskia Zodiac,' she commanded. 'Find her!'

'Her apartment is empty,' reported Otis. 'Has been, for months.'

'The modelling shop has been dismantled,' reported Clegg.

The Captain turned away in the ruin of her bed. She was exhausted. 'Just find her!'

Then the com whistled. '*Captain to Pons! Captain to Pons!*'

'Christ Almighty,' she said, in a low disgusted voice.

'*Colonel Stark is here, Captain.*'

She stiffened. She clutched the gown tight between her breasts. 'Give me something to hold me together,' she told the convenient physician. Her voice sounded like a worn-out tape. 'Just do that for me, would you?'

'Of course,' said the Good Doctor solicitously.

He opened up his case. Inside, the ampoules gleamed.

The Captain took her fix and pulled some clothes on. The doctor hung about, trying to get her to drink some vitamin gunk. She sent him away. Then she was in the car. There were white flakes swirling about in the tunnel. Soi could see them too. Her whiskers twitched as they plopped on the windscreen. 'Wha' is 'at?'

The Captain gazed out through the armoured glass. 'That's snow, Soi,' she said. 'It's snowing.'

In the foyer of the Pons Colonel Stark and a black-shirted escort of four were facing Lomax and Otis. The Redcaps were young and beautifully groomed. They gleamed with clean living and physical fitness. They anointed themselves with Hoppe's No. 7 Gun Fluid.

The other smell was Kenny. The Thrant's fur was up and his shoulders were spread. The Colonel was fingering her baton.

The Captain went and put her hand on her bodyguard. His muscles were tight as rock.

More crap, she thought. Taking Kenny on into the control chamber she said, 'What is this? What's the big idea?'

'Forgive me, Captain,' said the Colonel, following her in. 'If I'd known you were not presently at the helm I'd have factored a delay into the timing of my visit.'

Mr Spinner came towards her in his wire hat, holding a clipboard. 'Captain, at last. We have a report –'

'First let me get rid of these – people,' she said, as she reached her chair and collapsed in it. Kenny crouched with his back to her, growling softly. She rubbed his leather-clad spine with the toe of her boot. 'Why have you brought these people with guns onto my bridge, Colonel?'

Colonel Stark stood with her feet apart, her hands clasped behind her. Lomax had her and her people surrounded. 'We have a proposition, Captain,' the Colonel said.

'You have a problem,' said the Captain, correcting her. She saw Otis grin to himself. He was powered up, his safety off. Meanwhile Mr Spinner was fuming. She wondered what could be so urgent as to get him out of his box. A small part of her was glad to postpone that news.

'Captain,' said the Colonel, 'there is prevalent concern about your security provisions.'

Captain Jute felt as if she was floating twenty centimetres above her head. She felt perfectly secure. 'Is there?' she said.

'Specifically with regard to your defence capabilities,' said the Colonel. She brought her hands forward, raised, her baton horizontally between them. 'The Council at its last extraordinary meeting questioned whether your resources and your strategy are adequate to prevent another attack eventuality.' The Redcap leader nodded at Lomax, and more faintly at Kenny. 'I've been talking to your people, and they don't seem able to enlighten me.'

Captain Jute didn't look at Lomax, or at Kenny. She looked at the Colonel. 'They probably don't think it's any of your business,' she said.

Encouraged by the cold animosity in the Captain's voice, Kenny swayed up onto his hind feet. One of Lomax's men farted, derisively, and the Pontines sniggered.

'Captain! All our lives depend on you.'

'These boys are the best,' proclaimed the Captain. 'The response was superb. Instant. How instant was our response, Alice?'

'.875 SECONDS, CAPTAIN.'

'.875 seconds, Colonel. Next time we reckon to shave off that 5.'

Some of the men were laughing. The Colonel displayed no

281

emotion. She held her baton behind her back again, straightening her elbows.

'Let me outline some items of concern, Captain. This vessel was never meant for human occupation. Discomfort is escalating as ambient temperatures and the temporality consensus deteriorate. The passengers look to you to get us all safe to Palernia, and when they don't see you offering adequate defence capability, they seek the security they need from other suppliers. Some of those suppliers do not have your best interests in mind.'

The woman spoke unhesitantly, with absolute faith, like every maniac. Tabitha wondered who wrote her speeches. Behind her stood her Redcaps in their starched black shirts, clear-cut and confident as trainee gods. The Pontines sat stolidly, unhappily, disliking this intrusion into routine. Captain Jute watched the woman speaking.

'Outside this building,' said the Redcap leader in a voice that meant, *and inside too*, 'we represent the only credible stabilizing force. The passengers of this vessel believe it's time we put that force at your disposal.'

Captain Jute picked at a cuticle. She bit off a tiny piece, and blew it away to one side. 'Find Saskia Zodiac,' she said, 'then we'll talk.'

The Colonel took a breath. She lifted her wrist to her mouth and spoke. 'Attention all units, this is Stark, this is Stark. Search all jurisdictions for VIP, Zodiac firstname Saskia – '

'Personally, Colonel. Go on! Do that for me. Then we'll talk about the future.'

The Colonel looked around the circle, inspecting the Pontine guard. Her eyes slid across their battered servos, their greasy hair, their armadillo boots.

Kenny gave a loud, dyspeptic growl. It was a deadly insult in Thrant; but a growl is a growl, on any world.

The echoes clattered away. Colonel Stark was not impressed. 'I hope your bodyguards have been tested for rabies, Captain,' she said.

'Don't worry, Stark,' said Lomax quietly. 'Reptiles like you can't get it.'

The boys loved that one.

Tabitha stood up. She was wearing her long black leather coat. With her wild hair and her lurching hostility she looked like some unravelling desperado facing off a squad of space marines.

God, she was so tired. 'Thank you very much for your support and loyalty, Colonel,' she said. 'Now *piss off*. Go and play with Havoc, if you've nothing better to do.' As soon as the words were out she wondered whether she had really spoken them, or whether it was just in her mind.

Lomax and a Redcap were having a grimacing contest. Captain Jute heard Lomax ask the vigilante, 'You ever thought about how you'll pick up your teeth with all your fingers broken?'

She pointed to him. 'This is what I'm listening to, Colonel,' she said. 'I'm becoming familiar with the ideas of people like Mr Lomax. They are not gentle, Colonel. They are barely domesticated.' They loved that too, of course, and so did the watching Pontines. 'Like this ship, Colonel. Like this ship. Now go away,' she said, more quietly, 'find me Saskia Zodiac, bring her to me, *un*harmed, and we'll talk about defence capabilities.'

While Captain Jute was speaking Kenny had crept closer to the Colonel. He displayed his teeth to her. He shook his head from side to side. Recoiling, the Colonel reached for her gun.

In a moment, there were guns everywhere.

The Redcaps pointed theirs at the ceiling. The guards pointed theirs at the Redcaps. People started shouting in confused, excited voices. There was a shot. Then the only sound for a while was the crackle of electricity. Stun bolts bruised the air. Microbullets zipped.

A Redcap fell, bleeding from a hole in her chest. At once one of her comrades turned and knelt, unsnapping a First Aid pack. The Colonel signalled, shouting, 'Disengage!'

The shot woman lay motionless as meat. There seemed to be little they could do for her. One stooped and hoisted her on his back as they retreated. 'There was no need for this,' Colonel Stark was saying, as Lomax's guards hustled them all out of the chamber. 'This is a zero advantage move, Captain, completely destabilizing –'

As they marched from the building Tabitha called the Colonel on the radio. 'Find Saskia and we'll talk,' she said again, when the cold, baleful face appeared on her console. 'I promise. The Colonel's right, there was no need for all that,' she told the room at large then, keeping the line open. 'That was stupid. Who started it, Lomax?'

A man at the back shouted: 'She was going to shoot, Captain!'

She waved at him. 'Take his gun. Take his gun, somebody. No more guns for this man, okay, Lomax? Okay, Colonel? Right, goodbye. Now, Mr Spinner,' she said, cutting the connection.

He indicated the cubicles, up in the gallery. She went with him to one, waving Kenny away as he came loping towards the stairs. Everything was under control. The Captain was ready for her first officer's report.

There was a desk. Captain Jute sat at it, while Mr Spinner closed the door.

He stood before the desk and spoke formally. 'It is my duty to report that at 045.4.4 we entered Approximation, ma'am.'

Captain Jute felt the onset of a great relief. She slapped the desk. 'We're coming through?' she asked. 'Why isn't everybody celebrating?'

Mr Spinner looked troubled. 'I think you ought to take a look for yourself, Captain.'

'What is it? What's wrong?'

He tabbed the desk screen and it brightened. There was a pale cloud of pink and white tesserae. Tabitha watched it for a moment. It was nothing she could read. 'Is this the proximity signature?'

'Yes, Captain,' said Mr Spinner. 'An unidentified binary.'

'What do you mean, unidentified?'

The first foreign star within imaging possibility, the mass of it bruising the nanopores of the hypertract. Its signature was bigger than she'd thought it would be, broader and louder by far than any of Alice's models. The Captain narrowed her eyes at its faint ghost on the monitor as though she could already feel its heat. 'Is it not Alpha?'

Mr Spinner put his fingers between the wires and rubbed his pate. 'You can see we have a possible surface temperature match with Alpha,' he said, kindly, 'but the scale makes nonsense of it. And if it's Alpha, Captain,' he went on, 'where exactly is Proxima?' He had obviously been all through all of this already.

'Bollocks,' Tabitha told him. She bit the side of her hand. More nightmare shit. 'Where the bloody hell's Xtasca? I need someone to make sense of this.'

Mr Spinner had thought of this. He had it all planned. 'Let me bring some people up, Captain –'

'No,' she said. 'Nobody. Keep everybody out of here.'

She tabbed the vox, and her wristcom too, for good measure. 'Alice?'

'CAPTAIN?'

'I need the latest object projection.'

'ON THE BIG SCREEN NOW.'

The Captain went and looked down through the panel in the door. A temporary screen had been hung up in place of the shattered original. It showed a faint red circle like a glowing cinder at the centre of four familiar planets, three beige and one green.

'Then what have we got in here?' she asked.

'ROGUE DATA,' said the disembodied voice.

Mr Spinner took off his glasses and wiped them on a corner of his jacket. There was a ghastly pallor beneath his olive-brown skin. He reached for the tab and cut the persona out. Firmly but softly he said, 'Alice hasn't touched this. This is straight out of the Occipital Lobe, straight off the analogue.'

Tabitha half rose. 'The Occipital –?'

Mr Spinner shook his gleaming head.

'The residents do not influence the activity. You know that, Captain. They don't even believe it exists.' He placed his hand resignedly on her monitor. 'This is raw data, Captain: recent access, unprocessed.' His voice fell to the merest whisper. 'What the stuff is Alice has been giving us, god only knows.'

Captain Jute traced a circle on the monitor with her finger: the profile of a star she could not see.

'Go,' she said. 'Go.' And when he tried to protest: 'Leave me, Mr Spinner.'

She sat there, in the anonymous cubicle. There was a Chilli Chalet Whole Enchilada box seal someone had peeled off and fastened to the desk. 'The bloody thing doesn't even go where you tell it,' she said.

She shifted in the utilitarian plastic chair, so standard it fit no known species. She started to pick at the Whole Enchilada label.

'Alice, it's not Saskia, is it?' she said. 'It's you.'

The muscles in her jaw tightened.

'What have you done?'

In the anonymous cubicle, lights started to come on. Red, green, blue: in separate clusters they pricked the air, like imaginary constellations. 'PROXIMA CENTAURI, CAPTAIN,' whispered the deceitful voice.

Captain Jute cast around the little room as though looking for an engine fault. 'Don't lie to me, you fucking thing! Don't ever lie to me!'

'THIS CONSTRUCT IS INCAPABLE OF UNTRUTH, CAPTAIN,' came the reply. 'THIS CONSTRUCT IS A PERSONA, AN OPERATING METASYSTEM.'

'Is that so,' said the Captain. 'Is that a fact. Well, here's a test, all right? Do you remember Venus, Alice? Do you remember what happened?'

'YOU CRASHED THE KOBOLD, CAPTAIN.'

'I crashed, Alice. I crashed; and you crashed too.'

Captain Jute moistened her lips with her tongue.

'I came in and found you, Alice.'

'PROXIMA CENTAURI, CAPTAIN.'

'I came in and found you, and I almost killed myself doing it, and you –' The Captain shook her head. 'No.' She ran her hand through the wild bush of her hair. 'No, you see – the thing is – I don't believe in you. That's the thing. That's it.'

Captain Jute wriggled in her chair as if it had become hot suddenly. 'Alice,' she said, 'is on that plaque. She's not real, but she's what drove the Kobold, and she's what brought Plenty when we were all staring death in the tonsils.'

She shook her head again. 'What there isn't,' she said, 'is you. There's nobody there now. You're random. Completely fucking random. Everybody thinks you're there, because they expect a persona. Like the way they're all so nuts about Mystery Woman. It doesn't matter if there really is a Mystery Woman, does it? Someone will become her. And it doesn't matter if there isn't an Alice either. Because the bloody ship goes where it chooses.'

'PALERNIA COMING UP, CAPTAIN,' said the voice imperturbably. 'STARBOARD BEAM 36° 42' 06", 170.33.05 SUBJECTIVE.'

'You're just one thing, now, aren't you?' The Good Doctor's dose was wearing off now, eroded by the sheer intrusiveness of weird shit. 'All one thing. The Frasque built you. The Seraphim wrote you. Put them together –' Captain Jute stood up, holding on to the desk for support. 'You don't remember Venus,' she told the sparkling room. 'You don't even remember *Alice*.' The little lights shimmered. A ripple ran across the boards, like a wave of silent laughter.

The Captain swayed. 'Alice is dead,' she said.

'PALERNIA RISING, CAPTAIN,' whispered the voice.

Dog Schwartz rode up from the Caverns of Disorder, out of the deep ravine of Oxy Pit. He too was stoned out of his gourd. Above him the pylons of the frozen lift seemed to glow in the dark, beautiful baby blues and pinks. They had been claimed by vines that sprang from under the floor, as if seeking a firm anchorage for some coming upheaval.

The road beneath Dog Schwartz's wheels felt fine. He was thinking, in a loose, unstructured way, about the mammas of Oxy Pit, how funky they were, how it had taken three of them. A heavy fuzzed riff was sounding in his head, over and over, interminably. Dog Schwartz was happy. He was quite unprepared to be hailed from overhead by a voice as familiar as it was unpleasant. 'Where have you been?'

It was the governor. He was standing in the door of the immobile lift pod. In token of the climate he had added a charcoal-coloured scarf to his perpetual grey needlecord suit, and a pair of black leather gloves. His hair glistened like vinyl.

Dog Schwartz rode his bike up the steps to the boarding pad, where he stopped. The man paid his wages, it was not a good idea to annoy him.

'With friends,' said Dog Schwartz.

'The Horde,' said Grant Nothing.

Astride his bike, Dog Schwartz gave him a bemused smile. He scratched his beard. 'Absolutely, the Horde, yes. They've got some good toys, governor, you should see.'

Grant Nothing put his hands in the pockets of his jacket. He gave a small, fastidious quirk of his lips.

'Come here,' he said.

Dog Schwartz moved forward. In the enfolding shadows he saw the green eyes of the Thrant. She was lying on her belly, up on the wires, watching him through the foliage.

Grant Nothing's own eyes, when Dog Schwartz drew near enough to see them through the lenses of his spectacles, looked small and black as button diodes. 'Did I tell you to come that way?'

The henchman's ire began to stir; but the happy molecule in his blood whirled his mood about and scattered it in a twinkling swirl.

'Oh, it's very good, governor, you'd like it,' he said. 'Lots of fun.' He looked up and caught the Thrant's eye. 'Morning,' he said.

Grant Nothing put out his right hand, palm up.

Dog Schwartz patted the numerous pockets of his voluminous vestments. They were all full of drugs, but none of them the right drugs. Finally he found the sheaf of sedatives and put it in the black leather palm.

'I expected these three days ago,' said Grant Nothing.

'Yeah, well,' said Dog. 'Time goes faster back there.'

'Don't be irritating.'

Their breath steamed between them in the cold cleft. Dog Schwartz swished his ponytail, pulled it through his fingers.

Grant Nothing was thinking that all problems were system problems. What you needed was the information, information pure and cool and weightless, and infinitely multipliable. The Dog Schwartzes and Uncle Charlies of society were negative functions of the system. Powerfully entropic, they jeopardized your information, blasting out noise in all directions.

He tossed the sheaf of drugs up and caught it. 'I shall need more,' he said. 'Tell Uncle Charlie. And stay there till I send for you.'

Dog Schwartz blew out his lips. He glanced behind him down the road and back again. 'Yes, well, I'll tell him,' he said.

Grant Nothing considered Dog Schwartz's bulky face. 'And what does that mean?'

Dog rubbed his nose. 'I've got a bit of running around to do first.' It was so plain he was intending to go straight back to his toy-owning friends in the Pit that for a moment Grant Nothing simply stared. Then he opened his charcoal-coloured scarf and touched the jewelled pin that secured his red tie.

A needle of light flashed out of the jewel and pierced Dog Schwartz's left thigh. It passed through the flesh, through the velvet trousers of midnight blue, and cancelled itself out in the floor.

Grant Nothing stepped down and stood over Dog Schwartz, rewrapping his scarf. 'That should slow you down for a while,' Dog heard him say. Everything went red; then white; then black.

Dog woke alone beside the abandoned lift. His left leg was on fire, from the hip to the knee. When he moved, the fire went nuclear.

His right hand roamed feebly around his person, as far as he could reach without moving his leg. All his drugs were gone. He thought about Uncle Charlie. He thought about Uncle Charlie's nurses. They would know what to do. That was when he rolled his head around to his bike and saw that he was not alone at all.

There was a coloured woman sitting there in a striped T-shirt and a long black coat; sitting on his bike, with one foot up on his saddle. Dog stared at her upside down. He thought it was the Lady Mistry, come to take him to heaven; but it was the Captain.

'I'm trying to remember,' she said, 'where I've seen you before.'

The fire seemed to have got Dog Schwartz's voice. His throat felt like scorched tarmac. His vocal cords were burned to a crisp.

'Why do I keep thinking about Marco?' she asked. 'You're not a mate of his, are you? Marco Metz? No? Why do you remind me of him, then?' She leaned forward along the handlebars. 'I mean, I know he was lying like that, like you are, in the swamp, on Venus. When his leg was broken. But that isn't – What was I saying?'

Dog Schwartz gave a small croak.

'*I* know,' she said, with pleasure. 'Marco's leg! You're the one that came from the hospital, to repossess Marco's leg. But I did – I did – I know I did know you –' She stumbled through the obstacles of English syntax. 'Before – somewhere.'

'Dring,' managed Dog Schwartz. 'Dr-ink.'

The Captain pushed her hands vaguely into the pockets of her coat. She looked on the saddle beside her as though she expected to see something there. Her movements were slow, tranquillized, like her speech.

'I used to have this bag, right,' she said, 'this big bag. I used to carry that bag everywhere! I carried that bag from Mercury to Charon. I always had a beer in it. I could have given you a beer, if I still had my bag.' She kept tossing her shaggy head and giving little sniffs. 'Where was it? Not the bag, I mean, you. Go on, I give up.'

Dog Schwartz spoke. 'Cleaning,' he said. Perhaps if he reminded her she would help him. 'Windows.'

The Captain opened her mouth in a round O and pointed her finger at him. 'Integrity 2!' she said. 'On the chain gang. I was just thinking about that. Before. Before when –' She shook her head, giving it up. 'Yes,' she said, getting down from the bike and coming towards him, 'you're whatsisname, Dog, Dog Thing, Dog Something. Hello, Dog. Fancy seeing you here. How you doing, mate?'

She poked his shoulder with her toe. He gave a small scream.

'Not doing very well at all, are you?' said Captain Jute.

She squatted down and looked him in the face. His eyes were dull, pupils no larger than a pinprick. So were hers. She nodded sagely at him, looked up at the ceiling. Steaming, their breaths mingled as they rose.

'This is Havoc territory now, is it?' asked the Captain.

'Down,' said Dog. He tried to move his head to indicate the way.

'I don't come aft much any more,' she told him. 'Well, you probably know. It never does me any good.'

She showed him her hands. They were all bashed and bloody, as if she had been hitting something hard for some considerable time. She gave him a dreamy smile.

'It doesn't hurt,' she assured him. 'Nothing hurts, when you've got a friend.'

Dog Schwartz looked for her shadow, the Thrant; but she was evidently entirely alone.

The Captain reached up inside her shirt.

'I told the Colonel,' she said. 'I'm becoming familiar with the ideas of people like you ... Like you ... and Kenny, and Lomax ...' She seemed to be peeling something off her skin.

'Do you know what I think?' she asked, frowning as she concentrated. 'I think it's this ship. I was a normal fun-loving girl until I got her. Still am, really. Despite – *despite* everything.'

She removed her hand from her bosom and held it out to Dog Schwartz. There was something on the end of her index finger. It looked like a tiny peeled lychee, only it was brown.

'Do you want one?' she asked. 'You won't mind your leg. You won't mind anything, very much.'

Then she drew her hand away, looking at the shiny little thing stuck on the end of her finger.

'I'm not going to give you one,' she said. 'Why shouldn't you hurt for a change? Integrity 2, bloody hell, we really are going back in time today!'

Through the fire, Dog Schwartz tried to focus on her. If he could get her now, Grant could come begging. He could come crawling on all fours, begging. Dog had personal protection with him: a Magnani neutralizer. It was on the bike.

'Oh, here you are,' said the Captain, relenting, and she crouched down again. 'Here you are, then.'

She pushed up his shirt and bared a wide crescent of pale white belly. Frowning, she coaxed the leech off her finger and on to it. It settled, with the smallest of movements, adhering to his skin.

'This is our local natural remedy,' she said, watching the tiny creature start to fill. 'Everybody eats each other.'

Completely confused, Dog Schwartz gazed at the browsing leech, then at his former fellow convict. Something had started to lay a furrow of feathery ash between him and the fire of his pierced leg. The heat still blazed, but a little way off now.

'Eats each other,' said Captain Jute. Her teeth were set, and he thought her eyes were wet. 'If one lot don't eat you, the other lot will.' He supposed she was talking about him. He suddenly understood that she was not just flaky now, she was dangerous.

'Look,' he said. 'Look. I don't think you've got the position. I haven't done anything. I wouldn't. I may be big but I'm not that kind.' He heard his voice come flowing out of his mouth now, as if the heat had burst some bladder of words inside him. 'All I do is what I'm told. Make myself useful. Give a few chirpy arseholes a hard time. Give them a bit of a talking-to, now and again. You know.' He strove towards his bike, but his body would still not obey him.

Tabitha Jute was not listening to Dog's confession. She had a statement of her own to make: a cargo of her own feelings to unload upon him. 'Well, I quit,' she told him. 'Let them eat me. I'm not,' she said, shaking her head again, 'going to struggle – any more.'

She got on the bike and started it up.

'Get help!' he called. 'My leg!'

His head sideways on the floor, he watched her go, on his bike. It's all gone pear-shaped, he thought distantly.

Not that it really mattered.

Dog Schwartz was rescued soon enough, by people who knew not to let him have any more leeches. In the case of Captain Jute, the rescue took rather longer.

They found her eventually up off Lat Fiss Port, in an abandoned analogue working. They never found the bike. The crevice she had crawled into was barely big enough to send the rescue workers in, and she was blue with cold. When they got her clothes off they found four of the things on her, keeping her docile while they supped her liquors. All she was capable of saying was something that sounded like 'Dodger'.

But of Captain Gillespie and the rest of the expedition there was still no sign.

9

'This is hopeless,' complained Xavier. He had become increasingly irritable and discomposed since the discovery of the Great Beast. Between them the cripple and the Cherub seemed to have taken things out of his hands. Worst of all, the Channel 9 women had abandoned him.

He turned on the troglodyte, lifting his shooting stick in a gesture of impatience. 'What *is* the point of bringing us back here?'

Ink smacked her lips. Balancing herself with her crutch, she ducked down and scooped up her cat. Was there a look of amusement in her eggshell eyes? Of challenge, even?

The doors of the Cadillac were open now. The bonnet and the engine beneath it had both disappeared, together with every last vestige of glass. Inside, very still and intent, small dirty faces were looking out at them. The doors of the Cadillac slammed shut.

The dog growled. 'Quiet, Timmy!' said the elder Catsingle girl. 'You'll frighten them.'

Dodger Gillespie thought it unlikely.

She went and stood next to Ink. Together they surveyed the car. 'A lot of these, are there?' asked Dodger.

Jone overheard her. She came and put her arm round Dodger and pulled at her bottom lip. 'Check, this one's a different colour pink,' she said.

Dodger laughed. 'Stroll on, gel,' she said, squeezing her.

Ink was determined to force the pace. She swivelled and stumped on. 'Vermin,' said a hunter.

'They're only children,' said one of the girls. But she edged past the car like the others, making no attempt to ask them out to play.

The Reverend Mr Archibald, his puttees tattered, his clerical collar long gone, came sailing up like a man inspired. His spiritual exertions on the giant staircase had kindled his evangelical zeal. 'Hallelujah!' he cried, brandishing his glittering cross. 'Bless Oh Lord we pray these Thy lambs.' He had barely completed the downstroke when missiles started hurtling about him.

'Watch yourself, reverend,' said Captain Gillespie, hustling the exorcist to safety.

'All souls are His,' he assured her. His body was hot, his eyes full of fever. 'Shall these also perish?'

'Very probably,' she said, chivvying him on. 'Look, this way, hm, would you mind?'

At the turn of the tunnel Jone looked back. Behind the wheel of the disintegrating car, the little eyes gleamed in the retreating light.

The hunt passed through a district of high ceilings and dry dirt underfoot. Withered vegetation hung in grey strips, a monochrome jungle of bleached and blackened fronds. There was running water somewhere, the first they had heard for a long time. Their lights picked out a bridge, apparently made of bamboo and steel hawsers. It looked quite old.

'Should we fill our water bottles?' asked one of the little boys, doubtfully.

'*Ugh!*' said his sisters, univocally.

'The little girl *was* Mystery Woman,' Jone was saying to Xtasca. 'It's obvious.'

'No,' said the Cherub. 'She wasn't.'

Captain Gillespie was teaching it to roll cigarettes. 'My hands are too cold,' she said. The Cherub had spread the makings on its saucer. Instantly, static pasted shreds of tobacco all down its front. It repolarized itself, chuckling.

Ink insisted on walking everywhere, refusing even to lean on the saucer. She remained extremely wary of Xtasca, seeming to suspect the little black imp of wanting to steal her knowledge; which the imp would have gladly indeed, had it been possible.

Later Xtasca raised its globoid head, as if scenting something new in the air. 'We're back on the map,' it said, precisely and with satisfaction. Blue and green light filled its saucer, running up and down its body. Preoccupied already, it held out the rolled cigarette to Dodger with its tail. 'Mm, I think you'd better lick this.'

It called the Thalamus, and seemed unsurprised to find Stark's people had been in residence for some time. 'How's everybody, chief?' asked Jone, not having heard the reply.

'Quite well,' the Cherub told her. 'Working hard.'

Odin the cat ran around Ink's ankle, seeming always about to be under her foot or under her crutch when it came stamping down, but always somehow avoiding it. The cat turned in its own length, flicking dust from its ear with a paw. It was still unused to these enigmatic new associates, and kept turning back to stare, its single Siamese eye like an unanswered question.

Soon, by local standards, they came to another inhabited area. The path ran along a sizeable fissure, its edge reinforced with concrete. On the other side, windows appeared with lights in them.

The children walked along in a line, holding hands. They started to sing.

> 'Hi-dle-dee,
> Hi-dle-da,
> Hi-dle-dee,
> Hi-dle-da-ha-ha-ha-ha-ha,
> Hi-dle-dee –'

In the mouth of a tunnel Mr Archibald stood with his arms raised. 'Let us pray,' he besought them, in a voice like an untuned trumpet. 'Let us give thanks to the Mighty Lord Who has brought us safe out of the Valley of the Shadow of Death –'

Behind him in the tunnel there suddenly appeared a demon.

It was a long spindly creature that unfolded out of the shadows with a dry, crackling noise. It had four arms and two legs and its body seemed to have been woven from brambles. It moved slowly, swaying, as if it had been taken by surprise; woken, perhaps, from a long sleep.

The priest fell, and the creature walked over his body.

Amid the screaming Professor Xavier raised his voice in fury. 'This is your doing, you disgusting old hag!' As the sportsmen's first gun-shots smashed fist-sized holes in the wall he threw himself at their conductrix.

He struck her, bowling her off her crutch. Captain Gillespie grabbed at her, clutched her, lost her to the force of his rush. She heard Xtasca on the radio, hailing all frequencies.

Between them men were lunging forward, shoving the children back, firing as they came. Blue bolts lit the air. Jone was yelling at her. Ducking back, dazzled, Dodger could see Ink and the Professor on the edge of the chasm; then only the Professor.

He lay on the path, looking over the edge. 'Find your way out of that!' he shouted, in triumph.

As if objecting to the noise of his voice, the Frasque reached for the Professor. Armaments battered it, making it squeal with anger, but not perceptibly impeding its motion. It seized hold of Professor Xavier's head in a claw like a flail of holly and tugged him back towards the tunnel. Screaming, the Professor seemed to fumble at his belt for a weapon that was clearly not there. Then he seized hold of the attacking limb with both hands. Blood began spouting from him like red wine from a punctured bag. Brown spines slipped through his flesh, impaling him, tenting his bag. A hunter hacked at the foot of the Professor's attacker with a chopper, cutting off lumps that splashed pulpy white goo around. With a nonchalant swipe the creature cut him down.

The Professor began to spasm. Dodger Gillespie seized the priest's fallen cross and smashed at the twiggy arms wrapped around him. The cross snapped and broke apart, showering shards of mirror, and another arm lashed at her like splintering bamboo. Captain Gillespie ducked away, torn, bleeding, falling over the heel of her own boot and fetching up with a smack against the wall.

'Shit!'

Winded, she rolled over and watched with sick horror as the Frasque flexed its peculiar limbs and pulled the Professor's head off.

By this time the last Frasque had finally begun to react to the bombardment. It stepped back with a curious mincing gait, as if seeking the fastness of the tunnel.

The humans waded forward, spraying the shrieking creature with purple radiation. The air reeked of ozone and buzzed like a harp caught in a circular saw.

There was a fallen weapon. Jone was going for it. 'Stay back!' shouted Dodger, going forward herself on all fours.

'What is it?' Jone was shouting. 'What is it?'

'Frasque!' shouted Dodger, rolling. Of course, it was the first the girl had seen. She reached the gun, hooked it to her. On the stock a tiny red pip winked rapidly: empty. 'Damnation!' Her arm hurt. Her side hurt more. The Frasque lost a limb. It whirled up into the black air like a flung branch. The children cheered. The Frasque screeched. It was definitely retreating.

The children dived on the glass-studded remnants of the broken cross. 'With these mirrors, we can warn the Captain!'

Together they ran on along the path, flashing spikes of light across the fissure towards the distant buildings. $S - O - S$, the flashes read, in the Interplanetary Morse Code.

But the Frasque was not yet gone. It suddenly lunged forward, trampling its adversaries in a last spasm of violence. Adults with flashing metal or young with flashing glass, it was all the same to it.

The children disappeared in a vast bouquet of young red blood.

Then all the remaining artillery turned on the Frasque and destroyed it. It took a horribly long time. It was more like a movie massacre, full of slow motion and spouting arteries. The gunners sprayed the bouncing, dancing, collapsing body with five different kinds of destruction; while the body flapped its five remaining limbs about and spattered everything with a white fluid like glue.

When the noise stopped there were few of the human party left standing. Those who were, were screaming in wild rage and terror. One man who was no longer standing was begging someone to shoot him, over and over again, begging someone to shoot.

Xtasca hovered low over the carnage, sweeping the alien remains with a tail-tip sensor. 'Male,' it remarked. Jone looked at the smashed ribs and tubes, wondering how it could tell.

Dodger Gillespie, bloody, reared up and grasped Jone by the head. 'Are you all right, gel?' she bellowed in her ear, over and over.

Jone clung to Dodger, shivering from reaction, starting to snivel. Her stomach hurt from abuse. She had thrown up so hard she had nothing more to throw. 'Ink! The Professor! The children!'

'The last of the Legion,' said Mr Archibald, exultantly. He was rising to his feet. He looked as if someone had poured a bucket of blood over him. 'Is it not as it was written,' he said, addressing the survivors, searching this way and that as though looking for someone in particular, then lighting on the figure of the hovering Cherub, pointing his torch at it – 'that they fell from Heaven into the Pit, and in falling were changed?'

'Shut the fuck up!' Captain Gillespie roared at him, hugging Jone hard.

'Somebody, somebody, somebody!' begged the ruined man.

The missionary took no notice of either of them. 'The Servant of the Horned One,' he declared, waving his light hectically around the tangle on the concrete.

'Frasque, male, young adult, soldier specialization,' Xtasca recited.

Mr Archibald swept the beam of his light at the Cherub, speaking right over it. 'They were changed in their bodies, and unto the limbs of them, that were also changed.' He was ecstatic. 'With twain did they cover their eyes, and with twain did they cover their ears, and with twain did they *smite!*' It was very plain that he was now completely mad.

'Oh grievous sin!' responded a shrivelled looking acolyte. She picked up a fallen Buck 09, wobbled over and shot the pleading man through the head.

'Oh God,' Jone whimpered.

Slowly, gratingly, the last of the crusade picked up their weapons, strapping them around their bodies like so many holy relics.

'Oh Lord in Thy Name we harrow this stinking pit!'

Into the tunnel where the Frasque had emerged waded the crimson cleric, and his little band behind him, howling for alien ichor. The gunfire started again immediately.

Xtasca dropped down before Dodger and Jone. 'This way,' it said pleasantly.

Jone flung out her arms. 'But Ink!' she cried, her voice cracking like a child's. 'And all the others!'

Dodger clasped her firmly. 'Best you can do for Ink,' she said rapidly, 'is make sure the same thing doesn't happen to you.'

The Cherub's path led up a fifty metre incline, deeper into the rotten honeycomb. Captain Gillespie never doubted for a moment they should take it. She and Jone supported each other. Behind them for a long time they could hear the sound of Timmy the dog, wailing over the slaughtered children.

PART FOUR

New Blood

1

I said earlier that the end of the journey was not the end of the story. Stories always do end. Eventually things stop happening. The last page turns; the connection terminates; the voice ceases to speak, and the story is over. A story is not real life, and is obliged to provide a satisfactory conclusion.

Life, if I may presume to speak of it – life of the sort called real provides no conclusions, apparently. In life everything is always *meanwhile*. Things continue to happen, one after another, ceaselessly. The only end is death, and hardly anyone seems to find that satisfactory. Even after death things keep on happening, only they happen to other people.

Some people used to maintain that all the stories in the world, all the fortunes found and hearts and battles won, all the mountains climbed and conspiracies foiled and murderers detected and inheritances disentangled – all these were really only ever aspects of one supreme and single story. This 'universal' (or rather, geocentric) story is the story of an individual representative of humankind who gets up and goes out and strives and suffers and achieves and then comes home and lies down. The stages of the hero's journey, according to these authorities, all those ordeals and metamorphoses, correspond with the pattern of the passing day, or year, or lifetime, as it appears to whoever is trying to tell the story. The day, like the year, like the life, begins in the stirrings of light in darkness. It passes through growth to fulfilment, repletion, plenitude; and then the warmth begins to cool, the energy becomes unavailable for work; the eyes dim and the light fails, and darkness and inertia prevail again, ready for the next cycle.

Of course, that was before the coming of Capella and the Big Step into space. Life has been more fragmentary since, more scattered in space and time. So few people who go out these days ever come home again. There are a million other places to go. But on that first long trek to another star we certainly had our own ordeals and metamorphoses. We began, nobody would deny, in the midst of plenty. Then we became distracted, dissociated, unavailable for work. We passed through weary months of bleakness when nothing would go right, not even time itself. After that, when all seemed hopeless, a kind of regeneration did begin. Lost things, forgotten things started returning, recurring like flotsam in orbit; like the sun, the old geocentrists would say, rising in the morning.

And this was odd, because it was the middle of the night.

2

The Trivia Bar kept busy, even when the Last Poet decided to recite his 'Frasque Sequence', recent work which mainly seemed to involve standing on a chair and shrieking. The regulars were very tolerant, really. Two or three big Thrant were always there now, in corner seats, drinking cup after cup of lemon juice, keeping an eye on the crowd.

Mr Moon's latest idea was to coax out some of the big brown spiders that lived in the walls and race them along the table. The clientele watched in disgusted fascination, betting on this titan and that with peanuts and raisins. 'I don't know, look at them. Like a lot of bloody kids,' Rory would grouse, wiping and wiping his bar. Mr Bills egged them on, but in some spirit of social justice or sense of emergency kept redistributing the kitty.

There was still no news of Dodger Gillespie, or indeed of Mystery Woman. If anything, the phantom's complete disappearance only fed the popular fever. Where was she? What new enormity was she planning? Was it true she had been sighted in a Lat Fiss Chalet, wolfing down a Sizzlin' Steak? In the Rookeries up Snake Throat, according to Calico the Xtascite, everyone believed she had appeared with a big gun at the recent Battle of the Pons and creamed a lot of Perks.

The Trivia Window showed a dark and cloud-congested sky, with searchlights slowly scanning. 'This is a bit grim, Rory, eh?' said the Best Judge. 'Don't you think? A bit grim?'

Mavis Forestall sat in her nook in a bulky hand-knitted cardigan, nursing a Double Nightshade and her open handbag, ignoring any jollity. A recent savage and mysterious epidemic had raised all the veins in her face and turned it blue. For a large gin, the Good Doctor would reveal how far the effect went down.

Her eyes rolled up in her head, Mavis would grouse, in a feeble singsong voice, to anyone who sat within earshot. She had no single complaint, but spoke continually of the wretched state of everything and the malice of all agencies, specifically in regard to Mavis Forestall. 'And as for where I woke up yesterday,' you would hear her say. 'Talk about soot!' She hated the Captain, and took every opportunity to run her down; but that, by now, was common.

Mavis still had her Wisp, though its tiny spark unit had burned out and it could no longer fly. Disablement had made it surly and shy. It would not sit on Mavis's shoulder, but preferred to skulk in her handbag, shredding paper tissues.

On the last day of the Trivia's simple but perfectly satisfactory arrangements, Eeb the Altecean was sitting with Mavis and the philosophers, her short red legs sticking out in front of her, sucking asthmatically at a glass of blue mist. She had had her head fur threaded with beads of jet and amber and wore an outsize cloche hat. Like many of her kind she seemed to wear a permanent look of distress. It was nothing at all to do with the company.

The Good Doctor spoke, enumerating wonders. 'Ghosts, repetitions, disturbances in time. A patient of mine saw snow falling in the DextroTemporal.' He turned up his hand, as if to show them an imaginary snowball. 'Monster maggots feasting in the garbage caves.'

'Unprecedented times,' observed the Best Judge.

'On the contrary,' said the Last Poet. His eyes were like pickled eggs and his hair was standing on end. He gripped his pencil so hard he snapped it in two. 'In the windings and unwindings of this great ball of wax,' he intoned, unsteadily, 'Earth endeavours to recreate herself.'

Mavis grunted. It was the only contribution she ever made to any conversation that was not about her. Her handbag stirred slightly in her lap. The Last Poet supped his beer and spoke again from a vague, sodden distance. 'Did you know Adolf Hitler believed that the Earth was hollow? He thought there were nations underground, just waiting to be subjected to the Aryan yoke.'

The Best Judge coughed placidly and ruminatively. The Good Doctor peered speculatively into his throat.

Eeb played with the beaded fringe of fur that hung down below her cloche hat. 'Hwo'us Arydolf Hyitler?' she asked, diffidently.

At that moment the Prosperity door opened and a blond man came in in a purple silk blockneck and bulletproof trousers. He was conspicuously armed, and adorned with serial numbers and barcodes.

The Thrant bristled, putting down their coffee cups and rising. Rory motioned with one hand, gesturing them to keep their seats. It was perhaps a mistake, though in all probability it would not have made any difference, in the end.

He did it because he knew the man. They all knew the man. 'Oh yes,' Rory greeted him, a certain truculence audible in his voice, 'and what do you want?'

More of them were coming in now, whoever they were, quickly, by every door. They wore colour-coded combat suits and airmasks. The place was full of them suddenly.

Mavis stiffened. Their blond leader was Sven, her estranged husband.

Sven spread his hands on the bar and smiled amiably up at Rory. 'This bar is being secured by order of the Hands On Caucus,' he said, 'under emergency provisions laid down in agreement with the Synod and Hierophant of the Church of Christ Siliconite.'

Now Rory was looking to his Thrant. But the Thrant were already facing the barrels of several Spite 70's.

Eeb mooed unhappily. In her nook Mavis Forestall was glaring at her husband. She had not seen him in years. She did not want to see him now. Nor did she want him to see her.

'Behind these walls,' Sven said, as a couple of his troop climbed carelessly over the bar and started to inspect the stock, 'are circuits for fine-tuning our approach to Proxima. On behalf of all passengers and crew,' he said with a satisfied smile, 'the Hands On Caucus takes responsibility for these chambers.'

'Bollocks,' said Rory derisively.

An armed human and one of Rory's Thrant were snarling at each other. There was a brief, ugly scuffle.

Sven's people handed him up dishes of pills from behind the counter. The guerrilla scooped up a fistful of pills and stuffed them in his mouth. Without change of expression he swiped a beer from the table nearest him and swilled them down, spitting out any that resisted.

'Are those your security, landlord?' he asked then, with a level look at the Thrant. 'Now you know the trouble with security, don't you?' he said, as he took the tequila his troops were passing him and drank that down too. 'The trouble with security is, security always shoots second,' he said. 'Security can't do anything until someone else starts.' He reached across the bar and caressed Rory's plump cheek. 'You're not thinking of starting something, are you, landlord?' he inquired gently.

A Thrant yelped.

Rigid with distaste, Rory stepped away from the fondling palm towards the gate at the end of the bar. He found himself penned in by a small guerrilla. He must have been at least twelve. His eyes were brown, and highly amused. He was pointing a custom Nervecracker automatic thoughtfully at Rory's paunch.

By this time, of course, Sven had spotted Mavis. He strode across the room and inspected her more closely. He stood with his hands on his hips, surveying the painted and overdressed wreckage of her.

Eeb pawed at her hat, tipping it forward as though to cover her eyes from the coming carnage.

'Hello, love,' Sven said, his tenderness a feeble and obvious fraud. 'You don't look at all well.'

'You never did,' said his wife.

'Still too good for me, are you, my poor old cheese?'

This reference to the unfortunate state of her skin made Mavis writhe and bare her teeth in hate. 'Shit would be too good for you, you smear!' she retorted.

'Right, that's it!' Rory shouted, too late. 'That's enough!'

Agonized, Eeb put a clumsy paw on Mavis's arm, endeavouring to calm her. Then in a great rush she and the philosophers abandoned the table and the premises, hauling one another hastily out of range as their companion's estranged husband leaned forward and kissed her full on the lips.

* * *

Sven could not have offended Mavis more effectively if he had pulled out his cock and pissed on her. Mavis struggled, waving her arms, turning from blue to purple. Next moment, while he was still leaning over her, a fat blob like a half-kilo bundle of sausages sprang out of her open handbag and fastened on the front of Sven's purple shirt.

It was the Wisp, defending its mistress.

Sven was amped, his triggers tight. He snatched the Wisp from his chest. Blood sprayed after it, splashing Mavis and the table. Sven clasped his free hand to his throat.

Everyone fell back, holding their breath. The marauder was dead now, if the Wisp had any go left in it at all.

Blue lightning blazed, arcing between the fingers of Sven's fist. Sven grimaced with pain. Still he made no sound, and held the little cyberpet tight. It wriggled in his grasp, keening, trying to prise itself free with its little plastic claws. Sven lifted it high and whipped it down, smashing its head on the counter.

Mavis shouted something anguished and unintelligible.

Sven tossed the limp Wisp on the floor. There was blood running all down his front. He looked pleased with himself.

Enraged, Rory knocked the guns aside and came barrelling out from behind the bar. He rounded on all of them. 'Get out of my establishment,' he commanded. Those who were there swear that he positively growled it.

Sven was pressing a bar towel to his throat. He sucked his teeth regretfully, and held up a finger. 'Now you're being a nuisance,' he said, 'and that's what you mustn't be.'

The boy with the Nervecracker looked at him inquiringly.

'Go on, out!' shouted the landlord of the Trivia Bar.

Stiff-necked, Sven nodded gravely. The small guerrilla gave him a radiant smile. He took a stance, raised his gun in both hands and shot Rory ten times in the chest.

Rory twitched. He made little paddling motions with his hands and knees as though he thought he could swim away through the air. He fell to the floor. Black fluid ran from his ears and nostrils, smoking. There was a horrible smell of burning blood.

Chairs scraped. People screamed. Thrants roared and died. People ran to Rory, heedless of the guns. He was very, very dead.

The assassin looked very satisfied. He cocked his head for his commander's approval.

Sven touched the corpse with his toe and nodded. 'New management, the Hands On Caucus,' he told them all, mopping his front, 'until we are safely docked in true space. Now open for business.'

The customers stared at him. 'Business as usual,' he said. They still didn't seem to get the message. Two orange-clad troopers were kneeling, bundling Rory's remains into a bodybag. He seemed much smaller, somehow, dead, than he had been alive.

'No hard feelings, then,' said Sven to his former drinking companions. 'Here. Drinks all round, on the house. I can't say fairer than that, can I?'

In an upstairs room in Clementine Crescent Mrs Shoe was looking for one of the old tourist maps of Plenty for her daughter Morgan, who had just turned fourteen. 'Stop moaning, Morgan,' said Mrs Shoe, standing on tiptoe to try the shelf in the wardrobe. 'Anyone would think you'd be grateful, the chance to get out and see a bit of the world.'

Morgan was not helping. She stood with her arms folded and her shoulders hunched. 'It's all right for you,' she muttered. 'You never had to do it.' Morgan was having no pleasure in contemplating her rite of passage into majority. Soon, she and a couple of others whose birthdays were that month would be taken down to the docks and made to find their own way home. The purpose of this practice, according to the leader of New Little Foxbourne, was to toughen up the fibre of the community.

'Well, no, but we did have our own problems,' Morgan's mother said vaguely. It was difficult to remember what they had been, growing up in England, forty years before. Hemlines had been part of it, she thought: raising or lowering them, one or the other. Here it was so cold all the time everyone wore everything they possessed.

'You'll be all right as long as you stay this side of the Fissure,' she said.

'I might not come back,' said Morgan. 'I might go away aft and find the Caves of Disorder.' She was picking up books and flicking through them, putting them down again. She had always been going to learn to read and never got around to it. 'I might go and become a lesbian biker,' she said.

'For goodness' sake, Morgan,' said her mother, who was going through the chest of drawers. 'There's no such place.'

Morgan looked out at the window box. She wiped a space in the dusty glass with her fingertip. 'Mum?' she said. 'What's this?'

'I can't come over there now, I'm busy.'

With a deliberate gesture, Morgan opened the window. Her mother winced at her from across the room. 'Don't let the cold in,' she said, looking at what it was that had attracted her daughter's attention. 'It's only a snowdrop,' she said.

'I don't remember them.'

'You wouldn't. We don't have them.'

Morgan did not bother to reply. She kept the window open. She wanted to look at the snowdrop. It was a delicate pale green shoot with a pearly little bud dangling from it, like a drop of toothpaste.

'Do you remember when everyone was afraid of white?' she said.

'I wasn't,' said Mrs Shoe, kneeling. 'I wasn't afraid. I just don't like white. Needs such a lot of washing.' She looked down at her clothes. Her frock had started off blue with orange hollyhocks. Now it was practically white from being washed. It had been difficult since you couldn't get to the shops. Mrs Shoe opened a drawer quickly. A puff of ancient air rolled out, tickling her nostrils with the sweet odour of mould.

Through the window a voice came from a distance, not loud but clear. 'It's all looking a bit dingy round here, isn't it?' said the voice. 'Tell them to put up some bunting, Dotty.'

Natalie Shoe and her daughter looked at each other. 'Oh god: Marge,' said Natalie.

'*No loitering on the Promenade!*' called the loudspeakers then. '*Make way for Her Majesty Queen Marjorie!*'

'It's up to us to put on a good show,' the Shoes heard their leader say. They went and stood against the wall, either side of the window, so as not to be seen. They had always thought it best to humour Mrs Goodself, but there really ought to be a line somewhere, thought Natalie Shoe.

Cautiously, the Shoes peeked out of the window.

Two robot knights arrived first. They were painted in Redcap livery, and held huge dogs on leashes. The dogs were sniffing every corner with lugubrious pride. Next came Dotty Wallace, who was the Mistress of Revels, and Mr Cuthbertson the Chancellor of Electricity, in his puffy blue bonnet, dictating a note to his secretary.

'Here she comes,' murmured Morgan.

Along the Crescent Marge Goodself came trundling into view. She was growing stout. She looked crushed beneath the weight of her stainless steel crown. Behind her two pageboys tottered with her cloak of murian fur. 'That bag definitely doesn't go,' said Natalie.

Queen Marjorie's face was caked with an apricot foundation and her eyes were thickly outlined with black. She was speaking about Colonel Stark, who had called her with the great news. 'She will be so busy, poor lamb. She says she needs more dogs.'

'I wouldn't mind the cloak,' said Morgan.

The Queen fondled one of her own hounds. 'Gorgy will defend his Queenie-weenie against total anarchy,' she crooned at it. 'Won't he, Gorgy, eh, darling? Yes he will, booful.' She straightened, glancing back towards the Aqueduct. Neither she nor her subjects ever attempted to cross it. People said they had seen monsters over there: giant centipedes, and people with their heads on backwards.

Dotty Wallace was clearly excited. 'We must have a masque,' she said. 'And an anthem. And an ode.'

'Such splendid news,' declared Queen Marjorie, to the herald arriving from the other direction, scurrying, holding her hat on. 'Go, herald, bid them sound the horns, and let loudspeaker ring unto loudspeaker. Tell Proxima and all her subjects that we have them in our telescopes!'

Then a dreadful noise began blaring through the tunnels, like two, ten, twenty startled bagpipes. And the cry went up from every porch. 'Queen Marjorie crowns this embassy with her presence! Hurrah!' they cried. 'Floreat Foxbournia!'

The horns blew all day, winding the tidings through the estates of the Parietal. Guitar loops howled and bells tolled and bins rattled to ring in the Feast of the Approximation!

In time-blighted regions, in huts made out of looted spaceship plate and pilfered street signs, shivering Rooks took several days to hear the echoes. Then they began to cup their hands and hoot, passing the word from tribe to tribe.

In Maison Zouagou Father Le Coq presided over the writhing bodies. Prancing in his feather cape and red fez, he looked something like a rooster indeed. 'Brethren and sistren, soon we shall be there!'

he told his sweaty congregation. 'Brother Elvis calls us into green pastures for His Name's sake!'

At the top of Oxy Pit a battered fence of chicken wire blocked the end of a pedestrian side-tunnel. The air smelt distantly of burning. A dingy sign hung on the fence warned of the sheer drop beyond, into an 'Unreclaimed Area'. The sign had been perforated with a number of holes of various sizes. Forensic examination would have revealed that all the holes had been made from the other side.

In the darkness and solitude, human fingers suddenly appeared in the links of the fence, clinging on.

The fence jingled, very faintly.

The figure of a young woman in zero-gees and patched leather raised itself into view (had there been anyone there to see; had there been any light to see by). Breathing hard, the woman hung behind the sign, looking into the tunnel beyond. She was trying to pin down something she was picking up on audio.

The sound was regular, rhythmic, percussive. It was not particularly fast. The scout knew what it was, of course. It was the sound of Redcaps. It was the sound of their marching feet up the main drag. It was the sound of their feet marching closer.

The scout waited until she was sure she could distinguish the number of them. Fewer than ten, she decided. A Redcap patrol, braving the darkness and decay of the stern.

Without a sound the scout lowered herself back into the darkness. At the bottom there were rats roving among the trash and rubble. Fearlessly she leapt among them, bounding safely over and around huge lumps of debris, steering on infra-red. She climbed a couple of hundred metres down the dead lift cables and dropped into another tunnel.

The guard lifted his chin, acknowledging her. Behind him, in the depths of the Pit, the horde of Havoc moved sluggishly around their fires.

Oxy Pit was a human place, now, exclusively; like the Pons; like so many other places around and about. The wealth Havoc commanded they got by ancient traditional crafts: banditry, rapine, highway robbery. They did not range far, but collected tribute from sternward districts that had not made proper arrangements for their defence.

Tombo they respected, across the frozen jungles of the sulcal time faults.

In most places Havoc visited the sisters would arrive first, dressed to kill in ripped sleeksuits and fishnets. Like their heroine they wore dozens of necklaces of silver and colourful components, but added basilisks' teeth and barbed wire.

In most places the men would come out to jeer, and flirt aggressively, and within five or ten minutes a fight would start. Then the sisters would damage a few key individuals, and after that the locals would normally be happy to give whatever they had: water, metal, credit.

The men of Havoc preferred to husband their strength. They wore black leather tabards, slit to display their injuries. They wore shaggy jerkins, spiked gloves and crush boots. A knife at the belt meant two others in concealment. Boys and girls plastered themselves with Mistry decals; older enthusiasts wore her name in studs on the thighs of their jeans. No one had ever seen her, except the veerseers in their pods, yet all were expert in her sexual requirements.

Outside the stockade the riders tuned their bikes, riding slowly here and there in twos and threes, sharing tubes of hooch and smoke. Ex-dock mechs worked on the battletrucks, welding on new armour and elaborate, ornate battering rams. The hanging smoke blurred the din of hammering metal and turning motors, harsh calls of obscenity, screams and laughter. It was the sound of a people at peace.

Norval Khan lay in his cave, toying with a couple of big mammas. He was resting, and in good humour. There was nothing to do for the moment. One day, inevitably, the tribute would no longer be enough, but until then everything was under control.

The Khan wore a narrow leather waistcoat, no coat or shirt. He had on alumail gloves and motor boots, an old leather helmet with a bulky mono com pack. His jeans were undone. The mammas were dressed in crimson corsets, black stockings straining around their expansive thighs. They brushed his hair a thousand times, then fed it through a ring made from a Palernian vertebra plated with silver. They kissed the Khan's stale flesh, running their lips along the lines of his wondrous scars. He pinched their enormous breasts, and rubbed his thumbnail along the gussets of their panties.

At the receiver Lupin Dwarf spun the dial back and forth, picking up fragments of long-forgotten AV soundtracks, the mournful bellows of ranging Vespans, the chittering of Perks. The ship was a gigantic sponge soaked with sounds and visions!

Outside the cave of Norval Khan sat Havoc's major players, shaven-headed women and hollow-chested men, their neural induction sockets encrusted with grease. Years of virtual enemies had left their eyes permanently on another plane, watching for sabre-toothed chimeras. They stared down at the battletrucks, at the towering shape inside the stockade, dreaming of the day the horde would all ride out together.

The major players saw the scout climbing the ladder up the cliff towards them. Norval heard them quizzing her outside. 'Redcaps,' he heard her say.

Just what he needed. Exercise. Norval Khan grinned and rolled across the bed, slapping the importunate mamma whose lips and fingers tried to restrain him. Reaching for his power harness, he said: 'They never give up, do they?'

On the shores of a depleted reservoir the cubs of New Little Fox-bourne stood listening. Far below they could hear the metal horses of Havoc roaring, preparing to roll. Was it the Chilli Beast, the 'Big Chap' waking? Or volcanic grumblings from the legendary Cavern of Fire? Gripping the straps of their fluorescent rucksacks the teenagers gazed at one another with apprehension, wondering whether to climb towards the sound or away from it. Already they were forgetting their homes, the fitted carpets and repro end-tables. A new scent was stirring on the breeze, a hint of something yeasty and pregnant, gone too soon for anyone to name it.

Meanwhile, not five hundred metres above their heads, the Last Poet, who had woken up a lost poet and was trying to find his way home, had an unexpected encounter in the tunnels and became quite possessed.

3

The end of the long skip at last in prospect, the Council appointed a Disembarkation Committee, who at once began activity in the docks. Long-neglected plans were revived, and the power put back on for an auction of spaceships and equipment. Dorcas Mandebra went with Eric Ajax of Tekunak to buy up one or two craft that had belonged to poor vanished Topaz.

It was a very popular occasion. Everybody took the opportunity to come and stare at the half-forgotten ships which were to take them to Palernia. People came in trucks or dragging supermarket trolleys filled with all kinds of space gear they were hoping to trade, though much of it was in very poor condition. In ski boots, toting globular glass helmets sealed with insulation tape, they viewed the merchandise.

Dorcas Mandebra and Eric Ajax strolled the battered silver length of a Caledonian Lightning while the auctioneer's assistant read out specifications. 'A 250-seater, ladies and gentlemen, two Shernenkov Capables forward, four SJ90's astern. Working aerator and nutrimat. Property of Total Gumbo Tours.' Spectators and representatives alike were nosing about, examining the door seals and shaking their heads. Disparagingly they probed the inertium sponge and poked the upholstery. Dorcas's shoulder was bumped by a camera drone which ducked apologetically before resuming its scrutiny.

'Anyone here claiming for Total Gumbo Tours?' called the auctioneer's assistant for the ritual third time.

Dorcas, Eric and the drone scanned the crowd. Dorcas spotted some Pontines standing off to one side in a huddle, making calculations and fingering their beards. 'Oh, look, there are those Blobs again.'

'Things must be heating up to get them off their stools,' said Eric. The auctioneer banged his hammer. 'Bidding starts at 150,000, ladies and gentlemen. 150,000. 150,000 anywhere.'

Eric touched his right nostril. Dorcas clasped his arm. '150,000, thank you Mr Ajax, 150,000 I'm bid, do I hear 160?'

Eric took it up to 285 before there was a hitch. His main rival, bidding for Ojintuku, asked 'under advice' for the ignition to be tested. 'Oh for goodness sake,' Eric muttered. 'This could take hours.'

'Shall we have a look around?' suggested his companion. 'You're sure to find something else you fancy.'

Making their way out of the press and through an arch, Eric Ajax and Dorcas Mandebra climbed a rickety tubular stairway to the next parking bay. Here two huge dusty cola tankers lay side by side, roped off with red ribbon and official-looking seals, and guarded by armed Redcaps. The Redcap Colonel stood nearby, talking to one of her captains. The chilly light of failing biofluorescence turned their faces the colour of cement.

Dorcas waved. 'Yoo-hoo, Colonel Stark!'

Behind her, Eric Ajax halted at the top of the stairs. 'I've no time for that woman,' he said, in a tone that would not carry.

'It's a dirty job, but somebody's got to do it,' said Dorcas lightly.

'So you say.'

They looked at a big silver Eagle. Its lines were noble and fine, in best Capellan-approved style; but the panes in its cockpit canopy were broken, and its baffles were rusty. They found a cave full of Nebulon Minions with the logo of some historical oil company; but their controls were shot, in need of a total refit. Being shut up in the dark so long seemed to have robbed the ships not of motion merely, but of meaning. There they stood, deaf and motionless, like hopeless old jokes; like the vast elaborate sarcophagi of vain, glorious pharaohs.

Back at the Lightning, the scaffolding inspection tower was still crowded with people. Clearly the sale would not resume for a while. There was an electric motor that kept whinnying, a weak, discouraging sound. The Ojintuku bidder was remonstrating with his head mechanic, who seemed to be adopting an attitude of self-reproach.

'What on earth is the matter now?' asked Dorcas.

'God knows,' said her companion grumpily.

Then smoke began drifting from vents in the superstructure of the bus. Eric grunted with finality.

'The smoke is blue,' he told Dorcas. 'That probably means the fault is electrical, rather than mechanical.'

Dorcas nodded.

'If it was the quantum compressor, for example, it would be brown,' he went on.

'Brown?'

'Brown.'

'And that would be all right, then, would it?'

'Well, you can always replace a compressor. If you can find one. Then again,' Eric persisted, starting back down the stairs, 'if it was mauve, it might be the plasma sieve.'

Below them the big bus farted. The smoke increased.

'It is mauvish, though, don't you think?' suggested Dorcas.

'Don't be silly, Dorcas.'

The conversation ceased. It had reached the limits of its ability to deny the bleakness of the environment, the uncertainty of the future. Of course, there was no need to panic. The Frasque ship had brought them this far without falling to pieces. Palernia was a golden plum of opportunity, ripe for the picking, and this time, with no Capellans or Eladeldi to interfere, there would be a good chance for everybody to do nicely out of it. It would be a treat just to have a proper planet underfoot again. For the moment, however, there was bare matrix and oil-stained rockfoam and a shadowy jungle of half-dismantled machinery, and people like Colonel Stark to remind you things were not really going terribly well at all.

Amid a sudden late flurry of bids from the Pontines the Lightning was knocked down to Ojintuku, despite the questionable state of the electrics. By now Eric was in a bad temper. 'They staged the whole bloody thing,' he declared.

'Did they, darling heart?'

'Come on.' Eric Ajax took Dorcas Mandebra's arm, and they followed the rest of the ticket holders back to the platform that was hovering outside, ready to take them in search of the next lot in the Great Spaceship Auction.

As the platform moved off, Dorcas Mandebra and Eric Ajax leaned on the railing and watched the flotilla of personal fliers and hovercraft jostling slowly around them. A rusty autogyro puttered by overhead, stirring everybody's hair. 'I haven't seen so many people for ages!' Dorcas said. The water sellers were doing a brisk trade, and a couple of helicopters were cruising about with parties of sightseers. Everyone kept turning to gaze at the force seal stretched like a curtain across the great lipped forward door, like a vast mirror obscured by dirt. Perhaps they expected Proxima to be visible somehow, a red beacon in the supradimensional grey.

Dorcas looked down. 'There's one of mine,' she said. In a bay on a lower tier were some of her people, busy at the big old Vassily-Svensgaard grain freighter she had already claimed. One of Topaz's, she corrected herself, feeling rather sad. They passed a line of cruise ships abandoned by Shigenaga Patay, the baroque bulk of a forsaken Bergen König with Vortigern insignia. Up ahead somebody pointed out the burnt wreck of Captain Gillespie's *Charisma*, and everybody on the platform went forward to see.

'None of this stuff will ever fly,' said Eric, blowing his nose a trifle petulantly. 'It hasn't been maintained.'

Dorcas put her hand on his wrist. 'I'm sure you'll see something you like soon.'

In a while the platform came to rest at another large bay. The lines were secured and the footbridges extended. Several hundred metres beneath them on the cavern floor lay the proton baths, cold and white and regular as styrofoam cartons.

In the bay they were stripping the fixtures and fittings from a Shinjatzu Cormorant, the *Supreme Dagon III*, but Dorcas was not tempted. Accosting the auctioneer, she pointed to the shadowed profile of a Navajo Scorpion, discernible in one of the upper tiers. It looked powerful and mean. She asked, 'How much is that ship?'

'That ship is not for sale, madam.'

The Scorpion was called the *All Things Considered*. That was what had recommended it to Grant Nothing, who had acquired it early, right back at the start of the voyage, though nothing in the log would ever reveal that fact. The name had amused him; and the ship was a nice ship. They sat aboard it now, Grant Nothing and his Thrant and his Wisp. His prisoner lay in the captain's giant bed in the captain's stateroom, dressed in a new oyster silk camisole and stockings. Her captor had conceived an enormous respect for her and made sure she was surrounded by everything she could possibly want: baskets of truffles, chocolate, endless films and holos – even the fittings of her J.M. Souviens kiosk, though she never so much as switched it on.

Grant Nothing sat in the Scorpion's darkened cockpit, in the pilot's web, swinging one elegantly shod foot back and forth. Blue monitor light illuminated the lenses of his gold-rimmed spectacles. Grant Nothing had Dog Schwartz on the screen. Dog Schwartz was at the rear edge of the auction, in a frilly shirt and plaster cast, watching some of his chums buy a load of scrap metal.

Grant Nothing tutted.

Iogo twisted her head and shook her hands in front of her like a disturbed chimpanzee. Her coat was scruffy. She looked as if she had lost some weight.

The delinquent Dog Schwartz was on one screen, Saskia Zodiac on another. Grant Nothing was staring at them, but he was not seeing them. He was seeing Captain Jute. Tabitha. They were hers, all these cast-offs, these accessories: her rejects, that he had been obliged to rescue, because of their place in the scheme of things. They were like discarded clothes, that reveal the body. His Wisp floated about in the air like an overgrown mechanical locust. It nuzzled its man with its serrated jaw and buzzed something in his ear. Grant Nothing stroked it absently, running one finger beneath the rim of its carapace.

He touched a third screen, bringing into close-up the McTrevor Clavicorn two levels beneath the *All Things Considered*. An auton mech was welding one of her dorsal seams. 'Now that's a little beauty, whoever gets her,' said Grant Nothing. Absent-mindedly he took the registration, just in case.

Iogo made a soft murmuring yammer in the back of her throat. She could see the tension in the lines of his neck, the way he kept touching his cuffs. She knew his mind was not on the auction. She twisted her head and looked at the woman in the red hat on a fourth little screen on the cockpit ceiling. Grant Nothing sensed her movement. He followed her gaze and smiled. He tapped some keys. Iogo saw the woman in the hat put her hand to her earpiece. 'Are you interested in a Clavicorn, Colonel?' asked Grant Nothing. 'One careful owner, seeks early disposal, exchange for electricity, food, security, what have you?'

The Colonel smiled humourlessly. '*We already have plenty, my friend,*' she said.

'Not quite, Colonel. There are a few more lots to go before that item.'

In the stateroom of the *All Things Considered*, surrounded by AVs, Saskia Zodiac was trying to do a puzzle.

In the puzzle, you were alone in a locked cabin on a ship occupied by a hostile Thrant, a hostile Wisp, and a hostile human, any one of them more than strong enough to overpower you. Day after day you continued to wake up there, as if being kept prisoner guaranteed you a kind of spatial stability denied to the free. There was a good chance you could get out of the ship if you could get out of the cabin and defeat all three of your enemies. You had internal com access only, and no control over it. You had no weapons you could trust except your own feet and fists, and you were weak from lack of exercise.

Saskia ate another preserved plum. She supposed there must be a solution. The Thrant was not very bright, and the Wisp was not very big. The man was very bright, and big enough. He was physically vulnerable, especially when he took his clothes off. But when he took his clothes off, he always tied you to the bed first. And knowing your skills, he always tied you very tightly.

She sighed. There was nothing more boring than a puzzle when you'd looked at all the elements ten times over and still couldn't solve it.

With the Wisp floating before and the Thrant shambling behind, the man came in to see her.

'I'm thinking of getting you a spaceship,' he announced. He never used her name. There were no women in the universe for him but one.

The Thrant came to the bed. Saskia turned her face from the stink; felt her take hold of her arm. She pretended she was not there.

'What would you like?' the man asked her. 'They're selling that nippy little Quarklet in J3K, you know the one? That would be just your style.' He fingered his perfectly shaven chin, watching the Thrant fasten the woman's hands to the bed. It was a bona fide proposition and he was truly interested in her response. But the woman neither spoke nor looked at him. 'Or there's a Clavicorn, if you fancy something with a bit more oomph.' Still nothing.

'Show her,' the man said to his Wisp.

It motored over and hovered in front of one of the AVs. On the screen twenty young human women in pink were dancing in a line, kicking up their legs. The little cyborg hissed and pawed at the controls, trying to change the channel.

Grant Nothing laughed. He sat on the bed and rubbed his captive's concave belly, sliding his hand under the thin silk of her camisole. The Thrant had secured her feet and was already on her way out of the cabin. Grant Nothing raised his voice. 'Thank you, Iogo,' he said.

Over her great shoulder she gave him a sad, almost reproachful look; and he laughed again while she shut the door.

Grant Nothing took his shoes and socks off. He patted Saskia Zodiac's belly again. She was staring at the ceiling, trying to ignore the array of screens that were turning, one by one, to the same picture: an overhead shot of her, live, spreadeagled on the bed in her negligible apparel. Despite the definitive femininity of the garb she looked distinctly boyish in the shot, like a successful transvestite.

'Wouldn't you like a spaceship?' Grant Nothing breathed, nibbling her neck. He was naked now, kneeling on the bed between her thighs, leaning over her.

'I want a garden,' said Saskia distantly.

His face filled her view. He still had his glasses on. 'With silver bells,' he said, rearranging her lingerie, 'and cockle shells, and pretty maids all in a row.'

It pleased him to say things she could not understand, especially at moments like this.

'Like we used to have,' she said.

'You enjoyed life under the Seraphim, did you?' he asked.

She rubbed her armpit with her cheek. 'They made me,' she said.

'They killed your brothers and sister,' he said, thrusting his penis into her vagina, too soon; any time would have been too soon. She did not want him, never would.

'They could make them again,' she said, contradicting him for the sake of it.

Saskia thought of the Seraphim, looming behind their silver walls. Mogul had said they had seen one once, when they were babies; a colossal man who had held them in his arms and spoken over their heads to someone else. All Saskia could remember was cold pink and purple armour that had made her cry. 'They could make us all over and over in their magic cauldrons,' said Grant Nothing, rhythmically. He clearly idolized the post-humans. It was a measure of his hatred of the Captain that he had remained on board at all, and not gone at once to the Temple, to negotiate terms. At the worst moments, Saskia thought Xtasca the Cherub was her only hope. She wondered how he was shielding his activities from her, running around the nets the way he did. Assuming, of course, that anything he let her see and hear was true. Perhaps, despite the view from the cockpit, she was not in a Navajo Scorpion parked in an upper tier of the docks, but in a boarded-up tourist hotel, or some secluded virtual suite of the Havoc Cavern. It would be like him to enjoy fooling her with such a pointless pretence: snaring a conjuror in an illusion.

The taste of her cunt was bitter and salt and acrid, all at once. Grant Nothing thought she tasted exactly like a real human woman.

Whenever he tasted her, he thought of the Captain tasting her, of this same taste on her tongue, in her mouth. And then of course he thought of the Captain, of her cunt, of whose appearance he had a very good idea; and he tried to anticipate the taste of that. He considered this cunt, so white and bitter, and contrasted it in his mind with that, so dark brown and luscious. He hoped it was not spoiling while she was waiting for him.

The body spread beneath him was not brown and compact, but starved and smooth, all narrow planes and angles of perfect, childish skin. On the monitors, a pair of white buttocks rose and fell. Though the buttocks were his, Grant Nothing had no particular sensation of movement, only of the dissolution of the boundaries of his sensibility, as though the simple, primitive activity in which he was engaged had the effect of erasing everything in the universe beyond the confines of the bed, permitting his identity to expand without horizons, without resistance.

The woman was extraordinarily compliant today. He did notice that. She didn't even object to the Wisp hanging by the bed watching them with its curranty little eyes. Only later, showered, dressed and back in the cockpit, did he think: It was not like her to lie so silent and still. Often she would writhe in her bonds, trying to expel him, fighting him in a way that could be quite stimulating. Though Iogo was the fiercer animal, she would never have dared to struggle the way the Captain's skinny little pet did. Perhaps his captive had at last begun to accept his authority completely, to understand that the Captain was not about to dispatch a couple of her moronic knights to rescue her. He had not told her yet, about the state of the Captain.

The Wisp tickled his ear with its antennae. 'The woman has pissed in the bed.'

Grant Nothing turned to Iogo with a curse. 'Did you forget to untie her again? You did? Why can you never do anything without having to be told?' He turned in disgust from her sway-backed, subservient posture. He knew perfectly well her negligence was deliberate, petty jealousy. 'Don't just stand there, you stupid creature. Go and clean it up.'

'Have you seen your friend Mr Schwartz lately?' the Good Doctor said to Niglon Leglois in the control room of Uncle Charlie's sanatorium.

Niglon Leglois had worked his chair into the corner, with his back to the wall. It was his usual position now: the only way he could keep an eye on all the walls and the ceiling. Through the wall he could feel the sub-zero cold of the evacuated quarter beyond, that had used to be Wingwater. It was dark in there, airless as true space.

'Mr Schwartz will be back soon,' he told the doctor. 'He knows routes round all the time faults.'

The Good Doctor looked round from the control panel and gave him a sympathetic smile. 'My dear fellow,' he said. 'There aren't any *time faults* on Plenty. There's no such thing! All it is, is a socially-reinforced mnemonic disorder, a long term side-effect of subjective time. Now come and show me again how to get Mrs Oriflamme on this thing, there's a good chap.' Unwillingly the shabby little man left his corner, keeping his head down as he crossed the room. His clothes, the Good Doctor could not help reflecting, proclaimed the poverty of his self-esteem. Why, there were hundreds of decent suits in the stores still, if you were just prepared to go and look for them. The ship was no place for claustrophobes, he concluded, as Leglois climbed up on the stool and started to turn the knobs. It simply wasn't healthy.

On the central screen a beaky old woman appeared, sitting propped up in bed. Dry yellow skin hung on her face in folds, but the hands that protruded from the sleeves of her frilly nightgown looked muscular, pink and healthy. It was almost as if her arms were some kind of paired parasites that had attached themselves to her withered trunk, one either side, to feed on the last dregs of her vitality.

'Ah, Consuela, good morning,' said the Good Doctor. 'And how are we today?'

Mrs Oriflamme looked up at the camera and waved energetically. More and more she was coming to resemble some roosting bird of prey. Her great yellow eyes seemed lit from within, as if by the lurid contents of an overwrought imagination. 'Frankie?' she whined.

The doctor pressed the touchplate. 'No, Consuela,' he said indulgently to his patient, 'not Frankie. Not today. We're just going to take a little look at you, that's all. Could you roll up your sleeves for me, do you think? That's the way.'

Niglon Leglois tracked Mrs Oriflamme's new arms while they swayed gracefully this way and that. They seemed to move through the air without reference to the rest of her body, like the limbs of an idle Thrant. 'Up over your head now, Consuela.' In a window on the screen readings from the sensors clipped to her gown rose and fell, registering calorific expenditure, blood pressure, torque at wrist and shoulder. 'Those arms are stronger than ever,' pronounced the Good Doctor.

Then he frowned, peering at the screen. 'What's that?' he asked. He was pointing at a small white shape that had suddenly appeared, poking up behind Mrs Oriflamme's pillow. 'What is it? There's another one. Good god, the place is crawling with them!'

Niglon Leglois pulled back to a wide-angle. What seemed to be happening was that Mrs Oriflamme's room was being invaded. A pack of dirty white creatures were scrambling up through a hole in the carpet. Bristling, vigorous little bodies, elongated and snaky, were flowing without pause up onto the bed, where they jumped about, excitable as puppies, catching their claws in the bedclothes, salivating on the elderly patient's face.

Before Leglois could think what to do, the door to Suite 1 burst open and more of the things came pressing in, older ones riding on each other's shoulders, firing large weapons back into the corridor behind them, laughing manically. Some of them were trailing bits of rag and leather, remnants of ruined clothes, abraded metal ornaments, neck-chains and identity tags. MORLOCKS, the watchers read, as the camera swooped down again. SHITFUC. '*Cheeee!*' the invaders chirruped. '*Cheeeeeeeeee!*'

Leglois was scrabbling for the alarm. 'Where are the guards?' he babbled, his voice high with terror. 'Who the fuck's on duty?'

The patient's hands lay about her in no uncertain fashion. Each caught a Perk by the neck and tossed it onto the floor. But for every Perk the arms were able to throw aside, another was there, biting at their smooth pink skin. The sound of Mrs Oriflamme screaming began to tear over the com, clashing horribly with the mischievous squealing of the intruders.

The Good Doctor looked around for a weapon – a crutch, a fire axe, one of the goads they used to torment the patients. There seemed to be nothing. What was more, the lights had started flickering.

Leglois was cycling through the cameras, his forefinger pressed hard to the console. The screens flashed with meaningless scenes: the disused pool, empty of everything but scum and beer tubes; a vacant bathroom; two of the characters in *Sharp Practice*, kissing passionately amid soaring music; the distorted face of a dead security guard pressed up against the baseboard in the hallway. Leglois was almost weeping now. 'Shit shit shit . . .'

'Where's that nurse?' shouted the doctor.

'In with Gloria,' he said wretchedly.

Speckled now with dozens of tiny bloody nicks and bites, Mrs Oriflamme could be seen sliding half out of bed on her back, being overpowered. But something or someone would not let her finally succumb to her vicious little attackers. Two strong hands rose up from the shredded sheets and fastened themselves around her throat.

'She's only strangling herself!' gasped Leglois.

It was physically impossible, of course. The brain would lose control of the limbs before any serious damage could be done. Yet there was Connie Oriflamme turning purple, her tongue starting to well out of her mouth, her mad eyes glazing while her elbows still bashed Perks this way and that.

'Frankie!' she rasped, as Leglois and the Good Doctor watched her choke and die. 'No, Frankie, no –!'

On the screen for Suite 2 now was a rather confusing scene. Whimpering, Leglois fiddled with the camera, as if seeing it clearly would somehow counteract it; either that or he was trying to compensate for a certain putrid green phosphorescence about the uncleaned cell.

The pharmaceutically engrossed patient appeared to be in her usual position, cowering against the ceiling inside her personal force field. Her uniformed attendant was dashing frantically backward and forward, trying constantly to reach the door. She was a most peculiar figure; source, no doubt, of some of the indeterminacy of the picture.

The nurse resembled an old-fashioned piece of computer animation, a clumsy and unconvincing photo-composite. Her face was three different colours, including white and black; her hands didn't match, and when she lurched away from the camera her legs seemed to be different lengths. More even than the unfortunate Mrs Oriflamme, now completely inert on the adjacent screen, she seemed to have been assembled from several different people: as though Uncle Charlie had found himself with a number of attendants expiring or becoming injured in various ways, and been obliged to have each repaired with transplants from the others until the process of combining and discarding reached its inevitable conclusion.

The Perks were in Gloria's room, skidding about in the rotting food on the floor, squeaking with malevolent joy. One of them was dressed in a miniature top hat and a denim miniskirt with silver knee bands, and armed with a full-size Vindicator. '*Cheee!*' it exulted, and shot a jet of purple light into the ceiling. Gloria fell to the floor with a great bouncing thud that they felt in the control room. Then the lights flickered again and all the screens went dead.

Leglois could not stay in the sudden gloom and silence. His only thought was to seek help and protection. 'Monk!' he yelled. 'We've got to get to the Monkey!'

The Good Doctor was less ready to quit the control room. There was bound to be an emergency suit in one of the lockers: though perhaps one only, sadly. He encouraged his frantic assistant on his mission.

'Go now, quickly! Glory will delay them.' The Good Doctor imagined what must be happening now behind the door of Suite 2; the Perks getting their heads down into hot, bloated vitals. What a feast!

In Suite 3, despite all the noise outside, surgical casualty Leroi Gules slumbered as always, flat on his back, his arms at his sides, his lidded eyes astir with dreams. Above his head his machinery purred unevenly to itself, circulating the liquors of life effortfully around his body.

He was warm. He was breathing. Yet the Perks climbed up on his chest with some reluctance, sniffing him cautiously, drawing back in disgust, wiping their little arms across their noses.

On a chair in the corner an outsize tabby cat was sitting with all its paws tucked under it. Curiously, the incursion of the Perks had not disturbed the cat at all. In fact the expression on its odd, flat face might almost have been taken for a smile.

Savage though many of the cats aboard had become, the Perks took no more notice of this cat than this cat took of them. It was all most inexplicable. The Perks seemed to be distressed to be in the room at all. Their eyes were screwed up tight, their feathers pricking up all over as if in some stiff breeze or powerful field.

The Perk in the top hat seemed to have a particular aversion to all the machinery in here. Scarcely waiting for the others to get clear, it and three of its kin shouldered their enormous gun and blasted the life support system above Mr Gules's head.

The machine exploded in a violent spray of hot, stinking fluids. Promptly, the holo cat winked out of existence. In the dazzle of explosions, the white streak of its teeth seemed to hang an instant after the rest of it, a fading crescent ivory moon.

Scrapping among themselves, the Perks vacated the room. Outside there was another burst of firing, mingled with shouting, the squeals of the injured and dying, the urgent hooting of Vespans. Leroi Gules lay, unmoved. He had stopped breathing some moments before.

When Niglon Leglois swung in at the door of Suite 4 the Perks were already inside. The Gunky Monkey was there too, naked and filthy, defending the ruined conservatory. He had been screwing with one of the guards, who was taking cover behind a white iron planter as she struggled back into her combat suit, getting tangled in her own accessory leads. Up to his knees in dead chrysanthemums, the Monk was wielding a crowbar. A Perk with a baseball cap on back to front was dodging his blows, weaving lithely and expertly from side to side. DV8, said the logo on its cap. The Monk looked over its head and recognized Leglois. 'Get Uncle Charlie!' bellowed the Monk.

It was in that instant that Niglon Leglois knew they were all doomed. The crashing explosion of Suite 3's life support machine only reinforced his despair. Behind him Leglois heard firing, saw a tall, lumpy silhouette loom hooting through the smoke and dust that filled the corridor. It seemed to be waving some kind of whip around. Then there was a terrible cracking, crumbling sound.

Leglois gazed at the Monkey in horrible surmise. 'The wall's going!' he screamed.

The guard was still not completely dressed. Her helmet lay among the rhododendrons like some sinister garden ornament. As one, both men reached for it.

The Monkey hit Leglois with his shoulder. He kicked the snarling Perk aside. He snatched up the helmet and thrust his dirty face in it.

Now the murk and smoke redoubled on a rising wind. Two of the tall figures came struggling along the corridor, clinging on to the walls. They were Vespans. They seemed to be trying to drive the Perks on, on through the collapsing sanatorium. 'Gone got that old man, yus!' honked one.

It was the last audible thing before the final breach that tore down Uncle Charlie's kingdom and raked everything altogether into intercellular vacuum. In a hurricane of broken syringes and dead flowers the half-naked guard went tumbling after the tangle of broken Perks, and the walls closed in on Niglon Leglois at last.

When the smoke cleared, the Gunky Monkey stood up, bleeding and cursing in the stripped flowerbeds. He had one thought: get to Uncle Charlie. A survivor like him was bound to be a powerful force in the conflict to come. His chair alone was worth the price of a modest asteroid.

Then the Monkey saw what was in his way. One of the Vespan intruders lay between him and the door, his body wrapped around an oxygen tank like a spilled cargo of mutant gourds. All his bladders were distended, and the air was blowing wetly out of his every orifice, but he had the valve of the tank full open and the mask clamped to his mouth. 'For Irskoraituen,' he boomed unintelligibly, and stabbed with a triple-bladed knife at the naked belly of the onrushing Monk.

Who twisted so the blow slid off his greasy hip. 'Give up, you stupid heap of vegetables!' he roared, and tearing away the ice-cold mask, scooped up a handful of dirt and thrust it into the dying Vespan's mouth, grinding it well home.

A minute before the destruction, the Good Doctor stood before the firmly closed door of Suite 5 in a sealed combat suit, leaning on the doorbell. The doorbell wasn't working. The doctor banged determinedly on the door, drove his shoulder into it. 'Uncle Charlie! Uncle Charlie! Let me in!'

The door numbered 5 slid haltingly open, dislodging a couple of dead Perks. A sound of wild guitars came blasting in the doctor's earphones. 'Come in, man,' called a hoarse, squeaky voice.

In the dark, fetid interior an aged, aged man sat in his motorized chair amid an ear-punishing storm of Atavist Rock. He was wearing a little embroidered red skullcap and sunglasses. He had a bowl of muesli on the tray of his chair. Despite his steel teeth, it was food he preferred. He was eating it with his hands.

The light from the hallway flashed on his glasses. 'Is that you, doc? Come in, man. Shut the door.'

The Good Doctor did. It was at that moment that the pressure equalized and the walls of the rooms all along the corridor blew.

'Heavy!' shouted Uncle Charlie, inaudibly, while the carnage outside peaked. The door seal held a few seconds; then the bathroom door snapped in two like a sheet of fibrefoam. The Good Doctor hung on to Uncle Charlie's chair as a blizzard of oats and ampoules and yellow magazines and incense ash blew out through the violated bathroom, dragging the brown water out of the poisoned fishtank and bumping the furniture about.

Uncle Charlie blinked open-mouthed at the devastation. It was definitely the heaviest happening he had ever witnessed in all his swirling, indistinguishable years. His psychedelic wallpaper was ruined. His commemorative poster for the Fugs' Martian Tour had been sucked away like a sheet of used bogpaper.

Through the rippling haze of his personal force field the centenarian peered myopically out at the wreckage in the hallway, the smashed bodies of Perks and dead guards, the Gunky Monkey in a helmet, his naked side all bloody, carving up a fallen Vespan with a triple-bladed knife.

'Wow, heavy, man,' chuckled Uncle Charlie dazedly to the clinging physician. 'What a fucking mess.'

'Come on, Charlie!' shouted the doctor, kicking the side of the chair. 'We've got to get out of here!'

The crazed antique peered in through the vizor of the doctor's suit. Stoned as always, he didn't seem to have taken in the magnitude and imminence of their peril. He waved a nicotine-stained hand. 'The Monk's not ready, man. Look at the little fucker!'

The Good Doctor shouted at the top of his voice. 'Monk! Where's Leglois? We've got to go!' But there are a lot of bladders to burst on a Vespan; and the Gunky Monkey always finished everything he did.

They were mad. They were both mad. And Leglois was nowhere to be seen. The Good Doctor let go the chair and threw himself away from it with a grunting curse, feeling its force field snap closed behind him like plastic film. Not looking back he ran from the shaking building, into the derelict cave, ran like crazy for the tunnels of the High Parietal.

After he had thus escaped so many dangers, it seemed quite anti-climactic that a smiling, reciting figure should appear and beckon the Good Doctor through a narrow passage into a dim hole where he lost his mind. His hosts there prevailed upon him to remove his emergency suit, so even that sensible precaution ultimately availed him not a jot. It was all most unfair, really.

327

4

In the high tunnels of the Neocortex the black delta kites of the Law were flying once again. Up Horst Cascade and all along the dorsal sulci the scarlet banner of justice was raised, and a gauntlet of might thrown down to every skulking opportunist and troublemaker.

Surveillance was a key resource in the stabilizing process. When a band of hungry Thrant came upon an Altecean browsing in the garbage and ran her down in Peacock Park, the Thalamus Bureau observed, timed and recorded the event. They were keeping a close eye on all non-human passengers now, especially Palernians. Everyone hated the Palernians. They hated their hysterical sneezing, their eternal boasting about 'gaaoing haaome'. Sparks spiralled through the corridors of the PreCentral from the Mercury Gardens where the hooded houngans held their rallies. Orders were to let them take a Perk or two from time to time, for their bonfires. That way, everybody stayed calm.

In the eighty-ninth subjective month of the voyage strange tremors and palpitations were felt in all regions, more pronounced than any before. Structural specialists were kited in to the green dome. They tapped into Corpus. The readings were the same port and starboard. The hypertract of transit was shearing along every conceivable post-molecular axis. 'Like migraine,' said a Thalamite to Lieutenant Rykov. 'LIMINAL TRANSIT IN PROCESS,' said the persona. 'INFORM MR SPINNER!'

On an emergency relay the message went flying to the First Officer, who was on his way to the PreFrontal, to Kanfa, the Observatory of Imaginary Stars. It was a journey few had cared to make since the disappearance of the Transverse Bridge. Mr Spinner was on foot, halfway down the Cypriot Stairs, and the going was crumbly. The tin edges of the steps caught his lamplight. Already they were bent and half-detached, their fastenings protruding. The message on his wrist went unheeded as matrix shifted beneath his feet and pattered down from the ceiling.

Kanfa by candlelight seemed in utter disarray. The matrix walls were buckled. The paving tiles had cracked and risen, like the squares of some catastrophic chessboard. Archaic optical instruments of glass and steel lay strewn about, toppled from their mountings.

Mr Spinner was met by the new Supervisor. She was an elderly woman in a hooded robe, her hair thick and grey.

'The windows!' he cried.

'They are safe.' She seemed to be little perturbed by the tremors. She welcomed him with scholarly dignity. There was dust on both their shoulders, and in their hair.

Mr Spinner read the message on his wrist then, with irritation. It was as if he were being punished for his impulse. He wondered how quickly he could finish this and get back.

He apologized to the Kanfa Supervisor for the turbulence. 'We wish we could compensate for it,' he said.

'Which of us could?' replied the Supervisor politely.

'But your projectors,' said the First Officer. 'Can they be saved?'

'Ah, Mr Spinner,' said the Supervisor. 'Kanfa has no need of them. The stars are not here,' she said, pointing to her eyes, 'but here,' pointing to her brain.

Now Mr Spinner looked again, he could see not all the disorder was recent. The fixtures showed signs of disuse. Cobwebs hung from them. They were trembling yet.

The Supervisor clapped her hands. A servant came hurrying silently in slippers, bringing them green tea. They sat in the middle of the chamber, away from the walls.

'The onset of Emergence at last,' said Mr Spinner. His voice sounded silly to his own ears, squeaky with false enthusiasm. 'I wonder what we will find.' He realized now how reluctant he truly was to ask her a direct question; to admit ignorance to such a questionable authority.

'The ice is breaking on the canals,' said the Supervisor. 'The Wisps are mutating.'

Her eyes over the rim of her teacup were placid.

Behind her head, the vast windows of the derelict observatory gave the view. Faintly the void was scintillating, like white noise, like concrete on Terra in a fall of fine rain.

Mr Spinner leaned forward, so as not to be overheard, and spoke with a hard, flat emphasis. 'You know we're not at Centauri,' he said. It hurt him to say it. 'We're not sure where we are, in fact.'

'A ship may journey far,' replied the matron, overlooking his clumsy directness, 'yet still miss the shore.'

Her passivity discouraged Mr Spinner. This visit was looking like a disaster. Perhaps he had been wrong to come. Perhaps it was ludicrous to think Kanfa might know something.

He gestured at the pseudoactivity in the hypermedium. 'That is a star,' he said carefully, inviting her agreement. 'A double star. But it is not Alpha Centauri. It is none of the nearer stars at all. Supervisor, can you identify that star?'

The Supervisor drank. She drained her cup and set it down before replying.

'Have you heard what the Vespans are saying?' she asked, to her visitor's infinite irritation. 'They say, the Singer has a new song.' Her smile wrinkled the fine creases at the corners of her eyes.

Mr Spinner blew out air, as though he meant to cool his tea. 'I wouldn't know. The persona's hallucinating and the Thalamus is being used as some kind of public surveillance facility . . .'

'She has changed her tune,' said the Supervisor, blandly ignoring him. 'Or have we misheard her all this while? How disappointing, if we have been led astray by angry ghosts.'

The ship trembled again, and the sage of Kanfa gave a little toothy smile.

Mr Spinner took off his glasses and polished them. 'Yes,' he said. 'Disappointing. Very. Supervisor, I am sorry for interrupting your meditations. Thank you for the tea.' He rose. He must get back to his post, before she told him they were all parasites in the guts of some vast spacefaring monster.

In the Thalamus Bureau Lieutenant Rykov watched the two little figures on the screen. So Kanfa, informed by their antiquated instruments and mystic texts, believed the ship had brought them to a preprogrammed destination. Pretty much what the Captain said, in her last intelligible ramblings. Rykov thought, the Colonel would not be pleased to know Mr Spinner was consulting mystics these days; and without telling her. She might want to think about replacing Mr Spinner, when the time came, with someone more reliable – someone like Lieutenant Rykov, for example.

'*Perhaps angry ghosts have led us astray,*' the grey-haired woman with the teapot was saying to the man wiping his glasses. '*Perhaps the only truthful map is a blank sheet of paper.*'

On another screen the same man was also wiping his glasses, but in a smaller room, and standing up. It was an earlier recording. Lieutenant Rykov was replaying the moment when the First Officer had finally decided to admit his incompetence to the Captain. *'If it's Alpha, Captain,'* he said to her, *'where exactly is Proxima?'*

The Colonel had laughed out loud when she saw that expression on Captain Jute's face. She had had them isolate and blow it up, to play to her superiors at the next meeting. 'Have you ever seen a black woman go white?' she had asked them.

Lieutenant Rykov fingered his jaw. Was it really not Proxima on the scopes? A maiden voyage with an untrained crew. How could they be sure? What if the persona did turn out to be wrong, and they were materializing inside a solar system infested with Frasque? What kind of a fight could they put up? His ensign disturbed the Lieutenant's martial meditations to announce a message from Agent E.

Some years before, in Terran space, Tredgold Systems had mounted a project called Palestrina that had gone badly wrong. A bundle of selfaware had brought an autonomy suit against them, claiming unlawful restriction of entity. The Eladeldi had found in its favour, and ordered its relocation to an uninhabited asteroid. For a few brief months before the Capellans intervened to depose it, Palestrina had ruled that bald lump of basalt, assembling a rusty court of exiled baggage trucks, emigrant trouser presses and renegade industrial devices.

Not since the reign of Palestrina had so many robots been gathered together in one place as there were gathered today in the First Interstellar Church of Christ Siliconite. Traffic waders and automatic drills, chainsawyers and combat simuloids, all were ranged rank by geometrical rank before the altar. In ready mode, humming a sweet and steely hum, they awaited the Hierophant's blessing, and their baptism of oil.

'Gaudeamus automata,' sang a thousand voxes. *'Nunc hic sumus dedicata.'* Flesh and blood too had assembled to watch the ceremony: reporters, protesters and the Siliconite faithful. Everyone marvelled at the sheer number of machines. Clearly they had been secreted somewhere, out of reach of the extension modules of the Second Integration. Theories as to their origin and allegiance were rife.

Many of the onlookers were masked, because of the poverty of the local air. Their masks were decorated, as was now the fashion; worked up into the fanciful likenesses of animals and insects, androids and Cherubim. They looked more like a carnival than a congregation. Frogs took photographs, iguanas held up signs. At the back near the entrance a muscular man in a starched black sleeveless shirt stood with his arms folded, watching everything closely through the eye-holes of a giant bird's head.

Gazing down from the pulpit, the Hierophant's own mask was the solemn, authoritative stare of divine vocation. His face was bare, and severely shaven. The hands he raised in supplication were clean, the nails precisely machined; his vestments of plastic and foil were neat and shiny, the greater and the lesser. The heaven he invoked was a black void divided into identical cubes by a grid of silver lines. The axes of the grid were infinite, yet every line was numbered; and at every conceivable co-ordinate was a purified, quantified soul, at one with the essence and totality of God. Around the great church hung enormous, almost abstract pictures of Mystery Woman: transits of her limbs, sections of her body. It was difficult to tell, thought the man in the heron mask, whether the Siliconites wished to sanctify or dissect her. Perhaps if you were that far gone there was no difference.

Another deacon was stepping forward, bowing to the priest, pre-senting another line of squat slaved cargo drones. In formation they rolled forward on gleaming castors, trailing a symmetrical fan of wires with the deacon's skull as its apex. No matter what happened, the drones would never get their leads tangled.

The sacristans approached, holding purple napkins under the spouts of their polished silver oilcans. As one the metal candidates dipped their domes.

'*Apud nos victoria in alu-mini-um . . .*'

While the cyborgan swelled thrillingly, Heron Mask slipped out of the church and round the corner into a darkened crevice. His back to the wall, he checked no one had followed him. Then he stooped. In the dust on the floor his fingers made out the release of a trapdoor. He opened it and stepped below, loosening his mask as he went.

In the blackness beneath the floor he found the field com he knew would be waiting there. While the connections were engaging he took off the long-beaked headpiece and put on a red beret.

He was young. His report was enthusiastic. 'The robots are all here, sir. They look fantastic.'

'The Colonel will be pleased.' Lieutenant Rykov did not smile, but the glint of pride in his eyes was plain even on the com screen.

'Any sign of Mr Grant?' he asked.

'No, sir,' said Heron Mask. There never was, of course, anywhere.

'Carry on, Agent E.'

In the Rookeries the recent quakes had changed little of the general effect. It was all still a heap of junk, whichever way you tossed it. Much had been tossed or tumbled down into the poisoned pit at the bottom of Crap Chute and abandoned to the cats. Still overhead the slum city grew, hour by hour, incrementally, excrementally, spreading up through the Left Inferior Colliculi like a cancer. The squalor was incredible, almost terrestrial. The stench came out to greet you. It seized you warmly by the nostrils.

Those who chose to live there were loose-limbed creatures, stringy, underfed. They moved in fits and starts, swinging up and down the squalid arteries on their ragged climbing nets, inhaling a miasma of burnt hydrocarbons and sewage. They squabbled and hit one another over the head at the slightest provocation, usually.

Yet there was a different mood in Crap Chute these days. It was nothing to do with drugs. It was a new emotion, without a name: an emotion for re-emergence, for arrival in the light well of another star. It felt more than anything like a perpetual surprise: a mixture of discovery, elation and fear, all together at once.

There were spontaneous outbreaks of clapping and chanting. People would gather on a ledge, playing flutes and singing. *'John say I seen a number of signs.'* A precentor would call a miraculous birth, a large find of untainted food, a prodigious dream, working each into the same turning, falling singsong, and the people would echo, turning the tune back around for the beginning of another line. In their ritual embroideries the possible musical proclamations and exclamations seemed infinite; yet these gatherings could disperse as quickly as they had assembled, the shaggy grey choirs vanishing among the rubble, the foamboard and corrugated PVC.

In his ragged tubesuit and data harness Calico the Xtascite swung up the wires, following the children of his class. He had twenty or more today, and he was taking them up to the derelict mall. Some of them were only five and six, and full of mischief. They had been born fearless, with pointed ears and bitter ancient eyes. Those who could climb helped those whose limbs were less differentiated. With their soiled stretchsuits and lousy hair they made a formidable pack, scrabbling through the pedestrian tunnels in the dark. Their little brown nails and teeth would make short work of any rat unwary enough to scamper across their path. Mice they ate whole.

'Next right,' shouted Calico. '*Right*, Gob, you splatch! Show him right, somebody.'

The Crap Chute Rooks as a rule formed close, suspicious families. Calico had had to persuade all their parents to allow him to take the kids away from the constant task of scavenging, hoarding and repairing. 'Maybe they'll never read or write,' he had told them, 'but they've got to know how to ax a system.'

The grown-ups had looked scornful when he said they were going to the mall. There was nothing in those outlets. They had all been picked clean, if that was the word, years ago. But they heard Calico explain how he and his friends had got the mall local net up and running, and when they heard there was a working video, they nodded to one another and stroked their chins, and let the children go. They remembered video. Movies. People chasing each other, and explosions. Streets on planets, open at the top, with real skies overhead. It was strange how quickly you could forget.

Today as usual at the mall, there were already children at the terminals of the abandoned stores. They were playing with the system, moving long-vanished stock backwards and forwards, piling up great top-heavy stacks of data and watching them overflow in fountains of electric light.

'Calico! Calico! Listen to this!' Tarmac and Maz had worked out how to make all the empty registers play 'Jingle Bells'. Store by store the merry tune faltered out.

'That's really integral,' approved Calico. 'Do you know what that song's about?' He sang them the first two lines. 'You remember the snow, yeah? In places where it snows all the time they have these, like, special cars to ride around in it.'

A dozen faces of varying degrees of filthiness stared at him without comprehension. To the first extrasolar generation, the concept of a one-horse open sleigh was inaccessibly remote. 'This is integral, check!' said a four-year-old, pushing Tarmac out of the way and making the registers all jangle shrilly at once.

Later they heard a different sound, a deep hollow metal sound, ringing from far away. 'Who knows what that noise is?'

'A gong,' they all said.

'A gong, okay. Whose gong is it?'

'Foxbournia,' said a little girl with no nose and snot running out of the hole in her face.

'That equates, Flix,' Calico agreed. 'Right. That gong means the Foxbournians have seen someone coming up Lat Fiss. Who do you think it is?'

There were lots of ideas about this. It was the Redcaps, it was Xtasca and Captain Gillespie, it was the circus. 'No, it's a chilli lorry,' said Flix. 'Cos that's what they play when they're hungry.'

It was a chilli lorry: the Rook child was right about that. Where she was wrong, like everyone else including the crew on the lorry, was that the gonging sound was actually Auk of the Tombo banging on an empty metal shell he had removed from an automatic tunnel sweeper.

Playing the Foxbournian *Welcome traders*, Auk had hooked the lorry off the back of a convoy fifteen levels below, and now he was luring it into an ambush. Without warning the driver would find the road leading over the edge of a pit, and reversing, would find himself boarded.

Already svelte, silent figures in white and gold spandex were riding droplines down out of the vaulted darkness. Suddenly they were on the roof of the cab. Thump! Crack! Unceremoniously the driver and guards were trussed and tossed outside. Not a weapon had been fired.

'Sorry about the headaches, boys and girls,' said a diminutive black-haired figure in white jodhpurs. She stood jauntily, with her hands on her hips.

'It will take you all night to get out of those ties,' said Sir Thopas, pulling a last knot tight. 'By then we shall be in another part of the ship!'

'Taking this food to people who really need it,' added the woman, slapping the side of the lorry. 'My name is Lucifer,' she said, sternly. 'And this we do in the sign of Tombo!' she cried, climbing into the driver's seat; and the vigilantes all lifted their fists and chorused with her, 'Tombo!'

Lucifer reversed the great grey lorry back to the junction and trundled off up the tunnel, with Auk standing on top like a mahout balancing on a metal elephant. The whole raid had taken less than two minutes.

Sir Thopas rode shotgun, not that he possessed such a firearm or any other, nor would have wished to. 'There'll be a feast in Swallow Throat tonight!' he called forward to Auk. Gracefully the two men ducked as Lucifer negotiated a low ceiling, then straightened up again as they rolled out into the bottom of Long Insular 6.

Sir Thopas had sought out Tombo and dedicated himself to them. He had nothing else to live for since the disappearance of his lady. He loved and admired his new comrades, and gloried in their work. The raid had been a triumph, and triumph was twice as sweet when it served the needy. It was at moments like this that Sir Thopas rejoiced in the tattoo on the back of his hand, the Knowledge in which he walked, and the Cause in his heart. It was good that he rejoiced at that moment, for it was his last occasion to do so. The next moment the searing beam of a lightlance transfixed him from behind, entering just beneath his left scapular and cauterizing his heart. The unmade knight toppled back off the accelerating truck without a cry.

At speed, the lorry took to the tunnels. The pursuing Redcaps were numerous. They harried it by kite, on bike and on foot, but lost it down Karman Vortex Street, where there were sudden obstacles: a stalled honeywagon; a boisterous, tumultuous tunnelball game. TOMBO OK, said the graffiti. The militia fell back, seething.

Queen Marjorie of Foxbournia got the corpse of the hijacker from the Redcap posse and ordered Laura Overhead and Mrs Cuthbertson to take it to the Hanging Gardens, where the Best Judge was sitting. 'He'll make an example of him,' said the Queen, jabbing the unresponding felon with her sceptre. 'He'll show these bandits and terrorists we aren't going to let them get away with it!'

In her white suede shoes and needle slacks Mrs Overhead stood uncomfortably among the catshit, trying not to look at the shrivelled corpses twisting up among the foliage. Theirs was already in the dock, propped up against the wire netting. 'I think I'm going to be sick,' said Mrs Overhead.

Mrs Cuthbertson was more robust. 'Take a few deep breaths and think of justice, Laura.'

The Best Judge sat on a punctured couch amid a thousand cushions and blankets. He was arrayed in his old blue and red gown, which was rather the worse for wear. He had a large bottle protruding conspicuously from his pocket, and a huge wig made out of Palernian wool.

The Best Judge banged his gavel on the lectern, narrowly missing the clerk's head, and glared at the slumped figure inside the wire. 'All persons more than ten-tenths dead must leave the court,' he commanded.

'My client is not *more* than ten-tenths dead, m'lud,' objected the Defence, gripping his lapels. 'In fact I should say your honour's estimate was impeccable.'

'Nobody had better try to peck it, then,' said the judge, and banged his gavel about as wildly as a toddler. 'Name?' he demanded.

No one knew. Mrs Overhead thought she might have seen his face before, but she could not identify him. 'Kept his hair nice, didn't he?' said Mrs Cuthbertson to her, nodding.

'Prisoner at the bar,' said the clerk with an asinine grin, 'if you refuse to answer when the judge addresses a question to you, you will be ruled in contempt of court.'

There was much laughter from the scabby locals running around the gardens. 'He's dead, your honour!' jeered one.

'I *know*, I can *see* that,' said the Best Judge, wobbling his head and crossing his eyes dramatically. Children shrieked and threw dirt and refuse. 'He's Tombo, your honour,' confirmed the local sheriff from the dock, as the children were chased away between the trees. He held up the dead man's arm, showing everyone the three-line tattoo.

The Best Judge fell back among his cushions, wiping his forehead. 'Perhaps we can proceed, then, Tombo Euronna,' he said, resettling his lopsided wig. There was more laughter. He banged and banged and banged his gavel. 'Clerk of the court, read the charge.'

'Tombo Euronna,' recited the clerk rapidly, 'you are charged that in this forenoon at or about Port Lateral 202 together with others of your disreputable gang of hoodlums you did wrongfully and with malice aforethought waylay and take possession of a conveyance laden with chilli con carne, property of Tekunak Charge Foodstuffs Division, with intent permanently to deprive their rightful customers, to wit the Queen of Foxbournia and her loyal subjects, thereof. How do you plead?'

'Guilty!' shouted everyone present, as usual.

337

'Can't hear you!' shouted the judge.

'*Guilty!*'

'Call Exhibit A, the chilli!' said the Best Judge.

'Can't do that, your honour.'

The Best Judge went as red as his gown. 'Can't?' he bellowed. '*Can't?*'

'No, judge.'

'And why not, pray?'

'Because you've eaten it, me lud.'

The Best Judge opened his mouth wide and let out a rich and rounded burp. 'And very nice it was too,' he said.

High up among the pale yellow vines, the corpses dangled. Shrivelled and black, or green and bloated, they hung motionless on their ropes, or creaked round in slow, small arcs of a circle. Flies went in and out at their mouths. 'Sentence – sentence – sentence,' chanted the crowd.

'What? We've hardly begun yet,' complained the judge.

But they knew what he was like once he got going, and still they chanted 'sentence', with the Prosecution conducting them like a choir, until the judge gave way.

'Prisoner at the bar,' he trumpeted, 'it is my solemn duty now to sentence you –' When the cheering began to die, he went on. 'To be hanged by the neck until you blacken and burst,' he intoned, grimly. 'And may the owls have mercy on your eyes.'

The condemned man lolled against the fencing, mute. You could see where the wire squashed into his face.

Then the sheriff and both barristers and officers of the court and other busybodies doubled Sir Thopas up in a supermarket trolley with his knees under his chin, while the crowd pelted him with rotten fruit and worse. They trundled him across the garden to where a rabble of Havoc were waiting to put the noose around his stiff grey neck and hoist him up with the others, tugging and jerking on the rope to make him seem to kick, while the snakeweed hissed as if in approval. There were new buds on it, delicate little fangs of peppermint green.

There was bound to be a fight. Some people had arrived who were indebted to Tombo, and not likely to be able to witness the proceedings without expressing their feelings, preferably on the persons of the officers of the court. Already the young men were dogging out

338

their cigarettes and picking up sticks and stones. 'All right, then?' everyone taunted each other. 'You want it? Here we go, then! Here we go!'

Laura Overhead stood aside, pressed to a tree trunk, her handkerchief to her mouth. 'It's just beastly,' she muttered. Just because they were in these ghastly surroundings, people thought they had the excuse to behave badly.

'You have to get into the spirit of the thing, Laura,' said Mrs Cuthbertson, flinging an empty tube at someone. Her hat was askew, and she had a ladder in her tights.

Somewhat the worse for drink after the ensuing festivities, the Best Judge took a wrong turn, or perhaps the ship changed around him, for he found himself in a capillary road that led down into Snake Throat, where he had no business being at all. There he stumbled into the burnt-out shell of a wagon, inside which lay the skeletons of two humans: female, he decided, bending down with some difficulty to examine the skull of a small animal which seemed to have been tied to the end of a stick. A small white flower was growing out of its eye socket. He attempted to finger its tiny petals.

'A very interesting case,' said a familiar, medical voice. 'Toothmarks on pelvis and femur.'

'A positively Jacobean tableau,' said another, poetically. 'In the midst of death we are in life, and vice versa of course.'

Looking round the Best Judge was so astonished and horrified at what he saw he capitulated at once, thus becoming the swiftest and easiest of the new converts. He was in any case too stout to run away.

5

Perhaps it was the cat that knew after all. Without Ink's scratchings and scrapings still it ran on ahead of the Cherub, sliding and pattering down helter-skelter corridors into a low, lightless region.

Propping each other up, Jone and Captain Gillespie stumbled after as best they could. Jone was extremely unhappy. Captain Gillespie was just cold. Her sockets ached. Her wounds ached worse.

They had bathed in a stagnant aquifer. They still stank, but at least they were not now covered in blood and the ichor of dead Frasque. Jone still had her helmet. Captain Gillespie had kept the Borniak Vantage she had picked up in the battle, though there was precious little likelihood now of being able to reload it.

When they crouched, resting, the black thing with the voice of a little girl explained. 'All the silver inscriptions join up,' it said, 'to form a circuit.' Across the surface of its saucer large scale maps were flashing, too fast to read. On each there were blinking silver insignia, one or more.

'Mr Archibald said they were "Sandscript",' said Jone.

Captain Gillespie drew stiffened fingers down her cheeks. She felt a thousand years old. 'Mr Archibald has gone to feed the Frasque,' she said.

Jone wiped her face with the back of her hand. 'There's not going to be more of them things, is there?'

Dodger grimaced meaninglessly. 'They did build the thing,' she said.

The Cherub studied its maps. '"The web a spider spied",' it quoted. 'Do you suppose the "spider" is me? It's extremely rude. Come on,' it said, and zipped off, expertly following the contours of the low ceiling, leaving the women in the dark.

They waded on through trailing roots, hearing the cat ahead, jumping from bulge to bulge. Then the floor went down and the ceiling lifted. They were entering a large cavern that smelled strongly of some kind of animal. 'The Mesencephalic Nucleus, Jone,' Xtasca announced. 'Lots of mental traffic. Major axons. Steady signals of Proxima Centauri.'

Suddenly there was a light, a deep, thick, cherry red light glowing in midair. It was Xtasca. The little Space Child had lit up inside, like a novelty lamp, illuminating the scene around them. They saw rubble, sparse yellow grass, a gulley, raw matrix around a torn black hole. They saw Odin, nosing at the ground. They looked up. Towering over everything was a crenellated mound like a termite hill thirty metres high.

'The power source,' said Xtasca.

Jone whimpered. Dodger held on to her weakly.

'We've been here,' she told the Cherub. 'It's a Perk warren. It's called the Castle.'

'The Mesencephalic Nucleus,' said the Cherub, flying across to the hole, illuminating it. The stink was unpleasant, tainted with much death.

'I think I'm beginning to understand,' the Cherub said, filling the mouth of the warren with red light like blood. The shadow of its saucer moved across the floor like a dark spotlight. It swept over the cat, which was staring intently into the silent hole. As the shadow passed it darted down into the gulley and vanished under the floor.

'No.' Jone tried to hold back Captain Gillespie.

Captain Gillespie gave her a sketchy hug. 'Odin's happy,' she said, and climbed down into the hole.

It was spongy underfoot, the matrix eroded by constant traffic to and fro. The glow of Xtasca's unconventional innards glinted on fragments in the dirt: shards of bone, broken glass.

'Hurry up,' said the Cherub. 'I can't keep this up for long, you know.'

'You stay there,' Captain Gillespie told her companion.

'I'm coming,' said Jone, in a tone so near panic it would permit no refusal.

Captain Gillespie sniffed and swore. Then she crouched down and squeezed into the shit-caked tunnel. The air that met her was foul. Everything was foul.

'I shall follow at my own pace,' she heard Xtasca say behind her. Then Jone was there, hustling her.

'For fuck's sake hurry up, Dodger, this is scratchy horrible!'

The two women wriggled forward, crawling, using their hands and knees where they could. Nothing, not the silence nor the atmosphere of death, could dispel the fear of meeting something toothy, Perk or Frasque or feral cat, coming rapidly in the opposite direction. Captain Gillespie crawled with the gun under her arm, pointing forward. She doubted it would deter anyone for a second, but there was nothing else.

They saw only bones and shrivelled Perk cadavers. A line of vertebrae from a long-decayed snake passed between their knees like a string of triangular yellow beads.

Before long they were deep in catacombs beneath the Castle. The air was thick and full of static electricity. The hairs on Jone's arms stirred, pricking. She hated the matrix enclosing her. It seemed to be vibrating now, as if all the activity had finally become tangible. Perhaps they were drawing near some private buried generator. Jone was exhausted and sick of crawling. She put her head down on the floor. It felt cool beneath her cheek. She could have fallen asleep there and slept until Emergence. She lifted up her head and crawled on.

Suddenly Dodger stopped, so suddenly Jone thumped her in the backside with her helmet.

'There she is.' She was looking down a crack. 'Come here,' she said. There was just about room to get by. Jone could see Dodger's face. There was light coming up through the crack.

They were looking down into a low cave. It was like an Altecean junk shop in there. There were refrigerator coils and space train coupling magnets. There were the miniature image units from a hundred personal holo mirrors and tabletop ad projectors, all opened up and lashed together. Everything had been cannibalized into one complex installation. In amongst the wires, in a Meierstein zero-g pilot web, lay someone in a black leather coat and UV visor. Captain Gillespie pressed a stud on her wristset. Faintly, the cracked screen flickered with stills from the Hippocampus tape: a tiny figure in a coat spread like black wings, clinging to a dark red ceiling like Count Dracula going out for the night.

'It's her, all right.'

Jone stared. There were the wires, and the web, and lines going in through the web; and inside the web, a great bundle of necklaces and a wild tangle of curly dark red hair.

'We're not going to shoot her?' whispered Jone. It was the first time she had mentioned the possibility. 'We're not, are we. Don't shoot her.'

Captain Gillespie showed her the red empty light on the stock of the gun. 'We're not doing anything until she unplugs,' she murmured, glancing around with her eyes narrowed. 'This whole toybox could be slave armed.' There were all the stolen mirrors, hundreds of them, banked on suit racks, retail carousels, slotted frames of supermarket shelving. The mirrors were all turned to the wall. The walls glistened. Jone realized they were bare analogue.

'No wonder the Perks cleared out,' muttered Captain Gillespie. She displayed the Geiger counter on her wristset. 'Look at the rads in here.'

Jone stared at the woman in the web until her eyes started to water. You couldn't see her face, but she certainly did look like Captain

Jute. It couldn't be. The Captain had no sockets, everyone knew that, Ronald had used to tell jokes about it. *'What did the Captain say, right, when they offered her a socket set? "I need that like I need a hole in the head!" Ha ha ha ha ha!'* But suppose it wasn't true. Under all that hair, who would know? Who ever got that close to her anyway?

'Dodger?'

'Sh.'

Under cover of the junk Captain Gillespie squeezed through the crack and dropped into the cave. Jone had no option but to follow. On tiptoe, she thought about mines. Keeping her elbows in, she thought about electrocution. She wondered how many ways there were to die down here.

They hid behind what seemed to be an eviscerated photocopier, three metres from the web. Mystery still looked like Captain Jute. She looked a *lot* like Captain Jute.

'Dodger – '

Captain Gillespie ignored her.

Mystery Woman reclined a long while communing with the alien neurons.

At last the languid pale brown hands began to move. They slid between the straps of the web, unplugging one lead, then the other. Jone grabbed Captain Gillespie's arm. Captain Gillespie pushed her hand away.

'Keep your hands up,' she said aloud, so sharply and suddenly she made Jone jump. 'Out of the web, please. Right away from there – slowly. I know how fast you can move, now I want to see you move slowly. That's it. No, you don't need to touch anything.'

The woman was on her feet. She was turning around obediently. She was thinner than Captain Jute, and a few years older. Her face was the same shape as the Captain's. She had the same skin, the same mass of wild hair, held off her face by a circlet of braided flex.

'Who are you?' Captain Gillespie demanded.

'This is the W-w-witness for the Holy Sepulchre of the Exp-expanded Neurosph-sph-sphere,' said the woman in a husky voice.

A plughead, a real one. Jone knew them. They hung around spaceports and rail stations – they were always there, wherever people were in transit. They would hold up their palms and buzz you with a stim of peace and love, talk about the bliss of pure connectedness.

If you slowed down even for a second they would be pressing gospel software into your hand and vacuuming up your spare change.

'What's your name?' Jone asked the plughead.

'This body is called Angela. It means M-messenger.'

Her voice was even a bit like the Captain's, Jone thought. Maybe her eyes were different. Her forehead was rounder.

'Who else is with you?' Captain Gillespie asked.

'N-no one.' The stammer was endemic; she seemed vacant, exhausted rather than distressed. She licked her lips. Jone could see the groove where some kind of nasal drip feed had once been fitted into her nostril. There were people up above, she thought, who had built a church to this woman. They worshipped her.

Captain Gillespie gestured at the machinery, the racks of mirrors. 'What is all this?' she asked.

There was a slithering sound overhead. Jone jumped once more, and turned, in terror of Perks.

Xtasca appeared in a crack, crawling. It reared up on stiffened arms. 'Oh my goodness –' it said.

Captain Gillespie pointed to the web. 'She was in there.'

Xtasca started to wriggle out of the tunnel, looking for a way down the floor of the cave. Odin the cat arrived then, behind the Cherub, poking its head out above Xtasca's, licking its chops in a preoccupied way as if it had found something to eat somewhere in the deserted warren.

Jone ran and lifted the Cherub down, carrying it like something fragile and heavy, made of glass.

Angela the Mystery Woman watched. She seemed unsurprised to see a Seraph infant arrive in her cave. She wasn't offering much of a reaction to anything. 'She says she's a messenger, chief, but she don't seem to have a message,' Jone told the Cherub. 'She's supposed to have superspeed, but she don't seem to have much of that either.'

'Her job is done,' Xtasca said, 'her resources depleted. Can she speak? Speak, messenger.'

Angela opened her mouth, but nothing came out. She smiled a strange, hesitant, private smile.

'She stammers,' said Captain Gillespie, in an undertone.

'Her processor speed is probably out of synch with her mouth,' said Xtasca. 'I expect she hasn't spoken to anyone for a long time. Put me in the web, please.'

344

Jone sat the Cherub in the web and watched it. It was clearly less interested in the altered, alienated Angela than in her monstrous composite machine. It lay on its back opening and closing its chubby little hands and probing circuits judiciously with its tail.

Captain Gillespie was keeping Angela covered with the empty gun, her hand held over the little red light. At the same time she tried to spot any piece of equipment that had a plaque reader, checking for slots.

Angela was paying no attention to her captor, or the gun. She pointed to Jone's arm. She was admiring her tattoos. Unnerved by the woman's attention, Jone rubbed her arm, looking at it for the first time in days. You could barely see the ferny spirals beneath the dirt.

'Odin has a tattoo too,' she said, for something to say. She crouched to finger the cat's ear, keeping her attention on Angela all the while.

Angela ignored what the Xtascite was doing with the cat. Still gazing raptly at her arm she said: 'The Holy Net . . .'

In a while Xtasca said: 'I was expecting some kind of mental block. A concentration override. I see I've been underestimating you, haven't I? We shall have to have some people down here and dismantle this whole thing. Dismantle you, too, before Colonel Stark does it for us. Colonel Stark will be less considerate.'

The name meant nothing to Captain Gillespie, or to Jone. They looked at the control units, the insane knitting of cables. 'What is all this?' Captain Gillespie asked.

The Cherub was turned away in the web, inspecting another control panel. 'Oh,' it said flatly. 'Jone? Perhaps you could reach that down.'

Jone looked where it was pointing, up into a shadowy recess of matrix above a console casing. She ducked circumspectly in between the wires, stood on tiptoe and reached up into the recess, feeling around. Her hand found a slim grey slab of unmarked plastic, some kind of industrial data cassette, it looked like. The Cherub must have been operating on X-rays to notice it at all. Jone held it out.

'No,' said Xtasca. 'You carry it, why don't you. Nobody knows who you are. Don't lose it,' it added crisply.

'Lose it and I'll fucking skin you,' grunted Captain Gillespie.

Jone gave her a startled look, and tucked the plaque in the belt of her trousers.

345

'What's she been up to, then?' Captain Gillespie asked the Cherub.

'She's cut out the entire Nucleus, Captain Gillespie, that's what she's done. All the information that's been coming through here, everything I've been passing on to the Pons, has been false. Everything.' The Cherub seemed more impressed than angry. Pulling out wires, unplugging connectors, it said: 'Where are we really?' The question was addressed to Angela, as if it were a matter of merest curiosity.

Jone tasted fear in her throat. Captain Gillespie swore a low, voiceless oath.

'The logical place, I suppose?' said Xtasca.

Angela smiled a smile of insipid serenity. 'All n-nodes are one on the Holy Net.'

'A fucking hijack,' growled Dodger. Jone came and stood close to her. Her heart was thumping. 'God, she'll be in a right state,' Dodger said. 'We should never have left her alone.' She was staring at Angela, but Jone knew she was thinking of Captain Jute.

It took them two days just to reach the Medulla Funicular. Fortunately its mechanism was still running. They sat in the surviving car and felt themselves hauled slowly and creakily up out of the depths of the ship, back towards the light. The cat had deserted them already. They supposed it had gone back home to Ink's people, slumped around their stinking bonfires.

Angela was perfectly passive, giving them neither trouble nor information. Sometimes she hummed repetitive little tunes to herself, or moved her lips, as if replying to unheard voices deep inside her own brain. Now she slept, her shaggy head on Captain Gillespie's lap. Jone kept looking at her. Under all her hair and necklaces she looked so pathetic, so insignificant, it was hard to believe she could be a threat.

Jone shifted on the hard seat. 'How did she do it?' she asked. 'How did she know what to do?'

Captain Gillespie looked sidelong at Xtasca. 'She's been programmed by the people who do know,' she said, brushing the hair back from the head in her lap. Jone looked warily at Angela. Her sockets glinted in the intercellular twilight. 'The people who wrote the important bits of that,' Captain Gillespie said, nodding towards the plaque in Jone's belt.

Jone fingered it. 'This?' she said. It was no bigger than a notebook, or a pocket keyboard. 'What is it?'

'It's the persona plaque for a Bergen Kobold,' said Xtasca the Cherub. 'Modified to run a Frasque stardrive.'

6

The Parietal estates were full of anticipatory anxiety. In their apartments lone residents paced, their lips twitching with prayers and calculations. Others clustered on the stairs, watching everyone who came and went. Stark's patrols were about, rounding up Palernians. There was always someone ready to report another five, for some advantage of food or electricity.

In every corner, high and low, the passengers bargained for pieces of armour, phials of medicine, pictures of Mystery Woman, highly speculative maps. Their preparations for Emergence were well advanced. Many were already clad in optimistic assortments of space and jungle gear, and laden with survival packs, folding bicycles, axes. Two men claiming to be survivors of the Xavier Expedition were going from door to door drumming up a pioneer party.

In the concourse the transport agencies were busy, dividing up the last of the unsigned. Crewcut frontmen in leather suits stopped their spiel to watch as Tombo arrived. Parents stepped back against the walls, calling their children to them. In their gestures, in their apprehensive eyes, Lucifer could see they had been touched by the rumour.

The rumour flitted everywhere; the self-perpetuating rumour. No one would say they believed it, everyone denied it, yet they repeated it, the rumour that the star they had found was not Proxima Centauri.

Lucifer would listen to rumours, like a Vespan listening to the tunnel winds. She listened to this one and dismissed it, letting it blow on by. It was their fear speaking. Captain Jute would not lead them astray.

It was a party of Alteceans that had sent for Tombo. Apparently Marjorie Goodself was trying to steal something from them.

'Where is this woman?' Lucifer asked the boy who had come to fetch them.

He pointed through the crowd with snout and both arms. 'Long vere, wiv gny dad.'

Lucifer signalled to Krishna and Auk, either side of her, to open a path. She could hear the Alteceans now, whinnying and coughing protestingly. Krishna and Auk went ahead, parting the crowd, and gave her sight of them and their vehicles. The shaggy dealers were showing their chins and thrusting with their snouts while men wearing clothes like the pictures on playing cards jabbed at them with hedge-clippers.

Lucifer halted, making her preliminary assessment.

Somewhere the Alteceans had got hold of a wagonload of personal recyclers, human standard, still sealed from the factories of Valparaiso. The others thought they should have them, for some reason, and without paying. 'By order of the power vested in me as Chancellor of Foxbournia,' a man in a puffy blue hat was shouting, while people booed, 'I hereby proclaim – I hereby proclaim – crown confiscation of these goods,' he finished hastily, ducking as a chunk of tarmac flew past his head. Behind him plastic bags were already being loaded into the royal chariot.

Standing in the chariot, the Queen of Foxbournia towered over her Chancellor. Beneath her crown her vast mane of chestnut curls cascaded over her broad shoulders, her Jovian fur. Her face was orange with black eyebrows and scarlet lips and pearls in bunches clinging to her ears like grapes. In one fist she brandished her trident.

'Let none be missed,' she ordered, in a voice like brass. 'Let them all be piled here, at our feet. Oh, jolly good.'

The chariot was simply splendid. It was made of beaten car shells, embossed with swags and carbuncles and the heads of snarling lions. With the spokes of its huge wheels painted red, white and blue it stood out proudly among the battered vans of the traders and mountebanks.

The celebrated Little Foxbourne guard of Redcaps were conspicuously absent. Had there been some falling out, some official withdrawal? Lucifer contemplated a new ripple in the ever-shifting nexus of power. Still Queen Marjorie was guarded by some enormous emaciated hounds, and half a dozen curly-haired young men in doublet and hose and mascara, armed with power tools. A couple of them were off in the crowd, punishing the woman who had thrown the missile.

It was a convenient moment. Lucifer nodded to Little Mojo and hopped up on the bonnet of a nearby car. She struck a pose with her head back, her arms folded, observant, stern. As the disputants noticed her and fell quiet, she pointed dramatically down the Angular Gyrus tunnel.

'Go home, Queen Marjorie,' said Lucifer loudly. 'You have no authority here.'

Above the starched lace collar and gold chains the regal eyes bulged, the regal chins wobbled with indignation. '*Seize* that woman!'

Yelping, the dogs hit the tarmac.

Buyers and sellers scattered as the Masters of the Dragonfly went into their dance. Auk overturned a table, blocking an approach. Krishna feinted left, threw himself right, drawing the dogs off. Meanwhile Little Mojo leapt, balancing for an instant one-footed on the taut leash, then somersaulted and took the handler down, knocking his hat off, seizing his head in an elegant knee lock. Auk sidestepped an electric drill and drove the side of his fist into a bare midriff.

It was a day for the knife and the nunchak. When Auk's fist came away the unwise warrior's belly was spouting red.

Lucifer met a dog. She grasped its front legs in her two hands and tipped it over on its back, kicking it hard in the diaphragm, choking it. To left and right, sticks whirled, engaging two of its kennel mates. Satisfactory. Now for Her Majesty the Queen.

The chariot was defended. Unmoved by the pandemonium beneath her Queen Marjorie put out her thickly ringed hand and pulled a lever. One of the lions' heads coughed and spat out a fat red and gold missile that sparked and fizzed its way overhead before burying itself in the ceiling.

'Gut them all, traitors and ragamuffins! We command you!'

Dropping their combatants simultaneously, Krishna and Auk stepped back, converging on Lucifer. Between them they seized her foot and hand and tossed her into the air. Alluding in passing to Mojo's manoeuvre, Lucifer rolled over and came down driving her toes into the neck of a gaping chariot guard. Bouncing, she downed another with an elbow in his throat, then swivelled and grunting loudly broke the back of a third over her knee. She was in the chariot, ankle deep in tumbled packages. She would have to watch her footing here.

Queen Marjorie fired off another missile. This one brought down a ledge and killed several people, though the Queen seemed not to notice. 'Little nuisance,' she upbraided her boarder, stabbing her trident viciously past Lucifer's speedily departing ear. Lucifer came up on her toes and kicked the trident out of Queen Marjorie's grasp. It spun, slashing the royal fur as it flew. The Queen was open, her hands clutching widely at thin air, but first there was another of Her Majesty's defenders to deal with. He was wearing a baroque exoskeleton, powered up, moving fast. Lucifer was dangerously isolated. Dogs and guardians had all her people tied up for the moment. Lucifer ducked down under the apron of the chariot, surprising the amplified man. His throat was too well covered, so she crippled his back knee instead, driving the sharp edge of the servo hubcap straight under the patella with the heel of her right hand. It was a tricky shot, but it left her well outside his descending fist, in position to step on his hip pack and up over his shoulder, kneel on his back, fingers extended, and snap his spine with Diving Crocodile. Ah!

Two more troopers were fighting to get at her, dodging Tombo quarterstaffs to clamber forward over Queen Marjorie's gigantic bustle. Lucifer threw herself at the Queen. The Queen swung at her and landed a lucky punch on the side of her head. To Lucifer's left an axe split the floor of the chariot, which sparked and spat with ruined electrics. Then something hit her on the back like a falling wardrobe and everything went black.

'She's mine!' howled the Queen. 'She's mine!' She drew back her flashing trident.

That was the moment when the Redcap contingent stepped out of the upper tunnels and filled the concourse with ear-shattering violet light. It had been a trap, of course: two public security problems dispatched together, with minor concomitant civilian losses.

All the occupants of the marketplace went down, with hardly time to cry out, their senses frazzled, their nervous systems flash fried. The traders slumped. Krishna crumpled like a shattered pillar. Little Mojo died severing an artery in a cowled axeman. Auk was already dead, spitted like a walrus. Lucifer expired, shrivelling like a flake of blackened paper. Queen Marjorie of Foxbournia exploded, whistling like a collapsing balloon and shedding hair and fur in one great spherical blast of ash.

As an operation, it was a brilliant success. The Redcaps even managed to salvage better than 70% of the disputed goods.

*   *   *

'Did you see the Siliconite ceremony, Colonel?' asked the dapper man in the pale grey suit. 'Wasn't it uplifting?'

'I was busy,' said the Redcap leader. There was an edge of asperity in her crisp white voice.

'I'll get the station to send you a copy,' he said. 'It's a good recording,' he told her. 'I directed the whole thing from here. Speaking of which –'

Here we go, thought Colonel Stark to herself.

'I hope you like what they did with that little escapade of yours,' said the man. 'Heroic Champions of the Poor die helping stop Mad Monarch of Little Foxbourne.' Catching sight of his reflection in a blank screen, he began to adjust his tie.

She had known he would not be pleased. 'They're not poor,' she said. 'They're all equipped with personal aerators, in that locality.'

'Everybody's poor in their own estimation, Colonel.'

They were sitting in the saloon of his flagship, the *All Things Considered*, with the blinds down. The Thrant lay on the floor by her master's chair, asleep. The place was heaped with equipment, coms and seines and recorders.

'So you didn't like the coverage?' said Grant Nothing, crossing one foot over the other. 'That's a pity. Perhaps if we'd had some notice,' he said. The Colonel had always loved it when he got angry. His nostrils narrowed fractionally. That was the only way you could tell.

'All right, you had to squash the Dragonfly,' he conceded, 'but I didn't see why you had to eliminate Mrs Goodself.'

'Mrs Goodself was a destabilizing element,' said Stark. 'Norval Khan, Uncle Charlie – they're all equivalent anywhere, regional bandit chiefs. Neutralizing them is standard procedure for pretranquillizing potentially misaligned locals.'

'Well, I used to think she was rather funny,' said Grant Nothing. 'Tell me, then, Colonel, how are our woolly brothers and sisters?'

'They're not yet comfortable with our containment policy. We tell them they're going to be sent ahead in the first ship.'

'They're lucky to have you looking after them.' His annoyance had already evaporated, subliming off into his habitual aura of self-satisfaction. He was not interested in Palernians. They all looked the same to him. They looked like giant blubbery turkeys with paws like kangaroos', all covered in yellow wool. They had no value in the new game. '*The animals went in five by five,*' he sang quietly. '*Hoorah, hoorah.*'

351

'I don't know,' Stark admitted. 'Septal containment is nearly at capacity. We may have to take the surplus aft somewhere for disposal.'

'Let Norval Khan chase them around on his motorbike,' said Grant Nothing.

The Wisp came whirring in. The Colonel assumed it was still the same one, though its head was looking different these days, more like a bat than a prawn.

'Ah,' said Grant Nothing, as the Wisp buzzed a message in the neat pink whorl of his ear. 'Now then.' He stroked the Wisp's wrinkled head. 'Your toys are ready, Colonel.'

Stark looked at the side of her finger, inspecting the sideseam of the leather glove. 'Toys? We don't get much leisure for games, Mr Grant,' she said.

'You play games,' he averred, chidingly, while the Wisp flew out again. 'We all do. And what we all want to do is win, isn't it? Now look.' At his word the blinds lifted from one of the windows. Outside the ship, floodlights were glaring.

The man in grey touched a tab. The window polarized. Now they could see down into the next bay of the spaceship park. It was full of robots. They were packed together in tight rows, like cruets on a restaurant shelf. They had never looked more harmless.

'I want you to be very careful with them,' said the man called Nothing. 'It took a long time to get that lot.'

The Wisp returned, motoring slowly under the weight of a full-size control gauntlet which it cradled like a length of pipe.

Grant Nothing took the gauntlet from the Wisp and gave it to the Colonel. She put it on, examined its different coloured buttons. 'Everything you need is in that,' he told her.

He was lying, of course. He had to be. He would no more let her control that metal army than he would the Hierophant of the Church of Christ Siliconite. He was the gameplayer here, the eternal opponent, the Adversary. 'We shall miss them, won't we, Iogo?' said Grant Nothing, reaching down and scratching his concubine's ear. 'Take them downstairs and play with them,' he told his visitor. 'But do keep them away from our friends in the stern.'

The Horde of Havoc. He despised them as much as she did. There they lay in their Pit like wallowing Vespans, up to their armpits in beer and engine grease, semen and tomato sauce. They would punch one another out over the scores on ancient battlegames or the lyrics of old Anal Re10Shun albums.

Colonel Stark put the aerial of her control gauntlet up and down. She felt suddenly as tall as their ridiculous statue. They might well like to have one of these, though, she thought, the barbarians of Oxy Pit.

'Enough business,' said Grant Nothing then, killing the floodlights and lowering the blinds again. 'We haven't introduced you to our guest, have we? Iogo. Iogo, wake up. Come along.'

He led them through the ship to a velvet-covered door. Iogo, moving at such a simian shamble she was almost on all fours, went to the sensor plate and lifted her muzzle. With a soft *clop* the velvet door opened, sliding aside. Grant Nothing mutely pointed out to the Redcap commander the jewel on the collar of his concubine that had opened the lock.

Behind the door was a stateroom. It was hideously decorated in oranges and pinks, with great swags of material everywhere. It stank of chemicals and sex. There were screens here too, surrounding a big circular bed. All the screens showed Wile E. Coyote painting a railroad tunnel on the face of a cliff.

Tethered to the bed, oblivious, was a pale sliver of a woman in a tangerine corset and fishnet stockings. It was Captain Jute's missing pal: the acrobat, Saskia Zodiac. She was whining to herself, very softly.

Grant Nothing picked up a discarded box of chocolates and offered one to Colonel Stark. 'She's pretty comfortable in here, you see,' he said, taking one for himself, 'and perfectly safe. Just like your Palernians,' he added, giving the box offhandedly to Iogo and stooping over the bed. The Zodiac woman looked up at him uncomprehendingly. 'This is Colonel Stark, my dear,' he told her. 'Remember the Colonel, hmm? Course you do. Don't worry. Nothing to worry about,' he said, fondling the back of her head. 'She's just looking around.'

The woman looked like a skeleton. Her head was a skull that someone had put eyes and hair on in an unconvincing attempt to make it appear alive. Her skin was yellow as bone, except in the orbits of her eyes, which were deep discoloured blue. Colonel Stark wondered what he had her on.

'The Fairies come,' whined the woman, singsong, 'and then they go. Go and come, come and go.'

The man in grey touched her head, and she fell quiet.

'She'll be all right here,' he promised, 'till it's all over.'

A train shot out of Wile E. Coyote's tunnel and flattened him. Grant Nothing laughed. The screenlight flared on his spectacle lenses, eclipsing his star-black eyes.

The image froze. That was where the Colonel's tape had run out.

The Director of Tekunak Charge leaned back in his chair.

'What was the meaning of that little exhibition?' he asked, as the members all swung their chairs back to the conference table.

'He's a show-off,' said a Chilli Chalet mining executive. 'We know that.'

'It was a threat,' said Colonel Stark. 'He was issuing a warning in case I ever neglect to acknowledge his authority.'

At the Director's right Dorcas Mandebra compressed her lips. 'You're checking the robots,' she said.

'Yes, ma'am,' said the Colonel.

The Director stuck out his bottom lip and looked at them all beneath the parapets of his eyebrows. 'Anybody?' he said.

One of the other executives put her elbow on the back of her chair. 'He's a destabilizing element,' she said.

'Like the Tombo woman and Goodself,' said the first executive.

Dorcas Mandebra agreed. They all did.

'Colonel?'

The Colonel glanced back at the oversize figure on the screen. It was stooping. Its hand was arrested in the action of brushing back the lank hair from the Captain's lover's forehead.

'Zodiac is a new element,' said the Colonel.

'The woman?' said the first executive.

'The woman,' said the second, who was one.

'What priority at this point would attach to extracting the woman?' the Colonel asked.

The Director pressed the balls of his thumbs together and looked at them. 'There would be a case,' he said ponderously, 'for saying screw the woman.'

'Who needs her?' echoed the first executive.

The second didn't disagree.

'She'll keep him occupied until we give him Tabitha,' said Dorcas Mandebra. 'Perhaps the two of them will have a touching little reunion.'

'Look,' said the second executive. 'Let's not get confused here,

354

Colonel. The problem is not the woman. The problem is the man.'

'Who needs him?' said the first executive.

'With respect, Director,' said Colonel Stark, 'progress is still through Grant. His com capacity is shipwide.' She gestured at the multitude of screens still visible on the screen. 'He thinks he's God, affirmative, but he's got lines to every live district,' she reminded the board. 'He's got command sequences. He can deliver the Siliconites. And he's sitting right on top of the docks.'

'Jerking us around,' said the Director, resoundingly.

Colonel Stark turned to face him squarely. 'Grant's posture impacts decisively on the latitude of our future capacity.'

Dorcas Mandebra put her notepad down on the table with a sharp smack. 'What a perfectly loathsome little tick he is,' she said.

'The Zodiac woman is only going to be an element short term, no?' said the Director. 'Either way. No?'

Colonel Stark thought of those faded eyes, that wasted skin. 'That is my assessment, Director,' she conceded.

'Were you dreaming?' Grant Nothing asked the woman in his arms.

For a long time she did not answer. Her distracted eyes gazed over his shoulder. With ease the Roadrunner was escaping the Coyote's billionth aborted barbecue, vanishing between stylized buttes in a cloud of dust.

Saskia said faintly: 'I was in the Garden.'

She always dreamed of the Garden now, the artificial realm where she and Zidrich, Goreal, Suzan and Mogul had played away their brief sunlit infancy, attended by Cherubs. She thought of it more and more as Paradise, the place she would go again once her accelerated and pointless existence had come to an end. More and more she yearned for it.

Grant Nothing slipped a finger into her panties. She was cold and dry. The cartoon music played, unheeded.

'We were all there,' Saskia murmured. 'In the Garden.'

He caressed her stomach. 'All of you?'

'All of us. Zidrich and Goreal and Suzan and Mogul.'

He looked into her attenuated face while she found her way through this list of her dead siblings. It took her a while.

'Not Saskia,' he said lightly. He was naked, but for his spectacles. He fiddled with her.

'Yes – Saskia,' she told him.

'Not Saskia,' he repeated, in exactly the same tone as before. He squeezed his temples. 'Um. Could you be here now, do you think?'

Saskia lay inert. '. . . and Xtasca,' she croaked.

He tutted and got up on his knees, straddling her hips. 'What's wrong with you? You've just completely let go, haven't you? You've lost it. Haven't you, my darling, eh?'

He remembered when she had used to moan and scream beneath him, grinding her pelvis against him, straining at her bonds. Even after she had stopped making sense she had continued to respond. Now her flesh rolled under him, slackly.

It was a shame, the way things wore out. Imitations were so much more reliable.

Grant Nothing looked between the AVs at the J.M. Souviens imago unit, which he had kept switched off while the Colonel was on board. It was on again now. The Captain stood there on the holodeck, spreading her famous leather coat. She was naked under it. With the cabin lights low you could almost not see through her.

'You're not still worried about *her*,' he said to Saskia warningly. 'We've been over all that, haven't we, mm? You remember.'

Her eyes didn't even stir.

'You're not jealous of the Colonel, are you?' he said. 'Old Plier Legs?' He wiped Saskia's face. He wondered what it might be like with Iogo now, after so many weeks enjoying the Captain's pet. He had supposed Saskia would last until the takeover. He disliked the thought of returning to Iogo now, even as an interim measure. It would feel like a setback.

'What are we going to do with you?' he asked the acrobat. 'It's too late to take you home,' he told her. 'Things are too advanced for that. I don't know if the Captain would fancy you anyway, the state you're in.' He sniffed delicately at her sunken cheek, then touched it with the tip of his tongue. Over his shoulder he gave the Captain's imago a look that was almost an apology. Coolly, it batted its eyelashes. Grant Nothing raised his captive on his arm. She was limp. Wide eyed, her head lay in the crook of his arm like a large defunct fish.

Infinitely slowly, he put his lips to her ear.

'What would you like?' he whispered slowly. 'What would you like me to do to you? Perhaps there's something we haven't done yet. Can you think?'

Still nothing.

For a moment he thought she'd really done it. Really pegged out on him. Which absolutely would not do. She must remain alive to greet her girlfriend. Then the great vague eyes of a nameless colour, the colour of hyperspace, tracked slowly round and found his.

'Mogul?' whispered the artificial woman. 'Is that you, Mogul?'

'Yes,' he said at once. 'It's me, Mogul.' He gazed at her in glee. This was new.

'I want to touch you,' she said.

She was talking to her own reflection in his spectacles!

'Darling sister,' improvised Grant Nothing. 'How I have missed you. Now we are together again, nothing will separate us.'

The effect was delightful. She was becoming animated again. 'Yes,' she moaned. 'Yes, Mogul, yes . . .' She caught her breath and started to cough. He opened her clothes.

'Untie me, Mogul,' she said, as he covered her damp yellow skin with kisses. 'Mogul, untie me, you must, oh. I want to hold you.' She was feverish in her weakness, her intensity.

The coughing took her again. She writhed weakly on the bed. There was something black in her mouth.

'Darling, hush,' he said. 'It's not good for you to strain yourself like that.' He found he meant it, too.

Still she dragged on her bonds, crushed his lips with hers, fighting him with her kisses. She tasted of drugs and containment, mucus and blood. When in a moment she sank back exhausted, he thought again it might well be now or never. He looked up at the imaginary Captain. 'What a little teaser she is, eh?' he said. He knew there would be no reply. He had disabled the vox. The thing was only a model 3. He had no tolerance for its primitive vocal impersonations.

He caressed the starved face of the acrobat with his hand. She was trembling like an over-ridden pony. Her flesh was like glass, her bones like plastic.

'All right, my darling,' he said. 'All right, sister dear. Hold on. Patience now.'

He reached up to the corner of the bed and twisted the release on her left wrist.

'Mogul!' she cried.

At once her hand was on his cheek, fumbling awkward caresses.

357

She mewed like a kitten. She stroked his chest, ran her hand down his stomach. Grant Nothing released the second restraint.

Saskia Zodiac sat up under him, pressing her shrunken breasts against him with more energy than she had shown for ages. Her arms were around him, her hands roving wildly up and down his back, stroking his head, his waist, his buttocks. Her bitter tongue quested urgently in his mouth.

'Mogul – Mogul – my brother, my love –'

Her left hand cupped the back of his head, her fingertips kneading his immaculate scalp. He put his arm around her shoulders and pulled her away. She dropped her head and clung to his chest. There was fire in her now, hot, like fever.

'I know what I want,' she was murmuring into his clavicle. It was hard to hear her above the ancient orchestra playing for the little cartoon bird. She kept saying it over and over again. 'I know what I want. I know what I want. I know what I want.'

He bent his face to her. 'What, sweetie?'

'This.'

The heel of her right hand broke his nose. It was a good shot, and would have driven the bone up into his brain, had she not been so weak. As a bonus, though, she found she had broken the left lens of his spectacles, snapping the glass into triangular shards. She ground the splinters into her captor's eye. His scream was shrill as a bandsaw.

She struck again, but he was recoiling, out of reach.

Claws were scrabbling in the corridor. The door slid open and Iogo came bounding in.

Saskia Zodiac had hoped there would be a minute to free herself first. She had hoped to get up, grab some kind of weapon and finish the man before having to face the woman. She had had no choice, really, but to hope.

The Thrant paused, nostrils flaring, eyes blinking in the AV light. She saw her master staggering towards her naked with his hands pressed to his left eye, his buckled spectacles protruding from between his fingers. Blood was running down his bare pink arms and dripping on the carpet. He was shouting at her. She stared at him. The human female on the bed was half untied. She was sitting up pulling ferociously at the bonds on her feet. There was blood on her too, fresh blood, the scent of it hot and singing in the air, two kinds of blood mingling.

The master's face was contorted in pain and shock and rage. He was shouting, 'Don't just stand there, you stupid ape!'

Iogo obeyed. She stood no longer.

She leaped on him with all four paws.

She had not hunted and killed in years, not since the Eladeldi had captured her. The sharp red salty glory of it rose up in her head. It was the work of a moment to tear the squealing human's throat out.

On the bed Saskia dragged the slip off a pillow and wrapped it round her bleeding wrist. 'Well, good idea at last,' she complained to the unheeding Thrant. At last! She had been here forever. She finished untying her feet and flopped off the bed in a trail of ruined lingerie. Trying not to look at what was happening on the floor she disentangled herself and staggered to the open door.

Outside the stateroom, the Wisp was waiting.

With a shriek, Saskia went down on one knee. The berserk cyborg passed over her head, buzzing like a malign bee.

'Iogo!' Saskia shouted. 'Iogo, call it! Call it off!'

She rolled on her back and kicked out at the thing as it dived again, connecting squarely with both feet. A violent electric shock whipped her along the passage and down a ramp. She came to curled on the carpet of the saloon, bruised and aching. Her mouth was full of the taste of ozone and she could smell singed hair.

The Wisp was circling, choosing its angle. It dived again.

Saskia flung herself over onto her side, cannoning into the legs of an AV deck. Hauling her stiff length beneath it she grabbed at the wires that trailed profusely from every portal of the equipment and tugged them hard. The Wisp was low, coming zooming towards her across the carpet.

Metal boxes, decoders, tuners, toppled onto the floor in its path. As it zigzagged the acrobat lifted her legs, pivoting on her hip. She lashed out at the Wisp with a disconnected lead, catching it straight across the thorax, knocking it a couple of metres away. She scrambled out from under the deck, overturning it in her struggle to get her numb, stung feet back under her. Already the cyborg was recovering, spitting and buzzing, and circling back to divebomb her again.

She could only stand, bent, crippled, feeble from inactivity, her head swimming with hunger and drugs and adrenalin, as the Wisp came hurtling towards her. She wrapped the lead around her hand. She could see the little triangular mouth gaping, see the spiny rows of teeth.

At the last moment she dropped under the arc of its trajectory, put her hands to the floor and spun herself over in a cartwheel. She screamed as she kicked it again.

The Wisp flew backwards, out of control, and smacked its head on the corner of another equipment stack. It fell to the floor where it hovered groggily, whining nauseously. There was green slime on it now where porcelain and plastic had cracked, the seams between steel and artificial flesh splitting.

Saskia stumbled to the stack of gear. With a loud, sharp cry she tipped it over on top of the disgusting toy.

She knelt for a moment with her head on the arm of a couch. She retched, but her stomach was empty. In a moment, while the saloon tipped backwards and forwards around her, she pulled herself back up on her feet. 'Tabitha,' she said, to the turning tapes, the cameras, the attending microphones. 'Tabitha.'

In the pink stateroom Wile E. Coyote was painting a railroad tunnel on the face of a cliff. Iogo was still busy. She had dragged her catch across the floor in her enthusiasm.

Saskia, reeling in, tried not to look, but she could not help seeing that the tyrant's head had come off. It lay now by the wall among scattered electronic equipment, at an uncustomary deferential or whimsical angle. The broken spectacles still clung to it by one ear. Its hair was still perfect.

Keening numbly, in a fog of shock, Saskia Zodiac located the discarded grey needlecord jacket, located the inside pocket, located the jewel that worked the private locks and lifts. Her head spinning, she leaned on the jamb of the door. 'You'd better come with me,' she told the feeding Thrant. Then she collapsed on the floor.

The Thrant wiped her muzzle on the carpet. There was blood everywhere. There was blood in her now, nourishing her. She found she had known all along exactly how it would taste, her master's flesh and blood.

Snarling with triumph she jumped up on the bed and shat on it, as much as she could shit. She shoved one of the noisy machines with her feet. It fell over on the floor on its back, unbroken. She jumped on it, but the glass was tough. Beneath it the coloured pictures went on changing.

Iogo went to the unconscious human and sniffed her, baring her teeth. She snorted disapprovingly.

Busy music chugged from the fallen machine, bells clanging, steam whistles hooting. A train shot out of Wile E. Coyote's tunnel and flattened him.

The Thrant lifted the human onto her powerful shoulders.

Eeb was an Altecean, least discriminate and most acquisitive of species. The apartment was crammed with her hoard. Mismatched crockery, battered tapers, jumbled jewellery, cleaning implements and billiard cues and folded solar receivers lashed together in bundles with coloured string. Cardboard boxes piled on the bedroom AV console proved to be full of dirty styrofoam cups, many containing original cigarette ends. Under the bed were three different brands of oxygen cylinder, all empty. In the bed was Captain Jute. They were keeping her sedated, since it was her favourite state. The Good Doctor could no longer be found, but an apothecary Eeb knew had taken her off the leeches and was pumping her full of saline and vitamins, fabulously expensive by now. He would have his reward on whatever world they finally stumbled to.

Since they had been in hiding here an air of beleaguerment had settled upon the miscellaneous company of friends and well-wishers gathered about the sickbed. The Disaster Commissioner, relieved of his office by Redcaps, sat in the bedside chair with his head in his hands. Eeb was tidying up ineffectually, picking things up and caressing them, wiping them doubtfully on her fleece before putting them down again.

Kenny the Thrant sat on the floor between the bed and the door, eating raw mince from the last smuggled consignment. He kept trying to persuade his sister to eat too; but Soi was fretting, sniffing suspiciously at shadows. The chauffeuse was unhappy here, off the road. She wanted them to convert the Pango into a mobile hospital, ready to shift the Captain wherever a thicket of safety might beckon next. Meanwhile, planning to defend this one to the last, Otis sat by the door tuning his knees. Several hefty pieces of artillery lay by him, loaded.

Everybody was trying not to listen to the sound of the AV coming from the bedroom, which was playing old civil defence training movies, shelter basics and space respiration. It was Channel 10, the only station still on air.

In the lounge Karen Narlikar, there because she was a friend of Eeb's, was talking to a nice boy from Earth, there because his girl-friend was a nurse.

'If only we had Captain Gillespie here,' she said. 'They were great friends. Really close.' She glanced nervously at the door of the sick-room and away again. 'None of us knew her before, you see,' she said, as though to account for some failure of her own that she supposed was evident. The Disaster Commissioner wandered in and sat down heavily in the middle of the couch. 'She's driven everybody else away,' he opined, and put his head in his hands again.

There was a sound at the front door.

In a second the entire apartment was at full alert. Kenny went to the door, with back-up, while Otis stepped in front of the bedroom door. The listeners knew the voice they heard. It gladdened and relaxed them. Mr Spinner entered, leaning on a couple of desk crew. He had been wounded escaping from the Pons. He was grey with pain and shock, but refused to lie down. He sat at the kitchen table to have his arm set and bandaged by one of the nurses. 'I've never actually done one of these before,' she confessed. 'It's all good prac-tice, though, isn't it?'

The apothecary told Eeb to brew Mr Spinner a cup of moss tea, just like the Captain had. Otis started to tweak his servos again.

A nurse came out of the bedroom. 'She's going to make a statement,' she announced urgently. 'She'll be on in a minute.'

Everybody crowded in there, glancing at the unconscious body in the bed, the shaven head grey-green against the snowy pillows. They made no comment as they took their seats.

Karen Narlikar turned up the sound. On the wall behind the fresh-faced Channel 10 announcer numbers were flashing, counting down. '– go over now to the Pons,' said the announcer expressionlessly, 'for a special broadcast from Colonel Stark.'

The Redcap leader came on in tight close-up. She might have been anywhere, really. One by one the watchers glanced tensely or fearfully or accusingly at Mr Spinner, sitting there among them, and glanced away again to the screen.

'Some of you may have already heard,' read the Colonel, *'that our Captain, Tabitha Jute, is suffering from strain and unable to perform her duty in the Pons at this time. On this the longest and hardest journey in human history, no individual has been subject to more stress than our Captain. I know all crew and passengers will want to wish her well with me at this crucial juncture of Approximation. And at this crucial juncture we all, humans and others, must appreciate that it is imperative no disruptive elements are permitted to disturb the Captain's rest or imperilize ship or personnel safety at this time. Your Redcap volunteers will have the privilege of taking care of you for the rest of the voyage to Proxima Centauri.'*

Kenny barked sharply and disgustedly. The smell of his hostility was almost tangible in the overcrowded room.

The screen divided to show a sequence of familiar locations: a PreCentral Chilli Chalet; the Starboard Temporal walkways; the crimson vaults of the Hippocampus; the glowing little nest that was the Thalamus Bureau. In each picture a pair of one red-capped human and one freshly-painted red and white robot was patrolling, scanning pedestrians and vehicles alike. Refitted tunnel sweepers and ceiling crawlers toted prominent armaments.

The spectators around the bed exclaimed disgustedly.

The camera pulled back, showing the Colonel was indeed in the Pons, in the Captain's big blue chair, with a squad of heavy control machines and uniformed humans behind her. Clegg was among them, and some of Lomax's men. Otis cursed. Of Lomax himself there was no sign.

Mr Spinner blinked, mistily. The Pons was busy. Every desk was occupied, every console aglow. On the big screen Proxima Centauri smouldered, speckled and dim.

'Certain precautions will be necessary,' said the Colonel, *'to ensure the ship continues to transit safely through into real space. There is no need, repeat no need, to give goods or money to any of the so-called transport agencies to take care of you or your family. Your Redcaps are trained and experienced in provision of round-the-clock security and have defence capability resources to defuse any and all threats to ship or personnel safety. Your co-operation in this service will help us to help you,'* she said, and saluted.

All eyes were on the screen. Nobody was looking at the bed.

From among the pillows a small terrible voice said: 'She's not fucking having it.'

7

In the cave of Norval Khan the captains of Havoc were assembling weapons. Their eyes shone brightly through the greasy fringes of their hair. The air was heavy and full of smoke.

Aloof, a big man sat reading a disintegrating paperback. Next to him a muscular Thrant was squatting, sharpening his nails while he watched the recharge gauge on a Drinski lance. The sound of racing electric guitars mingled with the clatter of metal and the drumming of engines rising up from the Pit below.

The Havoc chieftain sat with his head thrown back and his feet thrust out. The big mammas were arraying him in his harness, tucking his heavy black locks into his old leather helmet. They had rubbed his scars with fat, so that they looked angry, red as fire.

'Boots,' said the Khan.

A shaven-headed young woman in nothing but heavy duty work-boots and ripped jeans brought the Khan's left motorboot. She knelt to put it on, running her fingers caressingly around the seal. Another woman in laddered tights and a dress that might once have been white put his right boot on. From the lobe of her ear hung five broken syringes. On her chest was a dirty red cross. Across her back was a blue steel Persuader.

The women kissed the Khan's boots.

'Com,' said the Khan.

'*One, two, three,*' said a voice in the Khan's ear. '*Testing, testing, ladies and gentlemen, rock and roll.*' Across the smoky cave a dwarf with a face like a mad warthog turned from a console, put his head on one side and raised a horny thumb.

'Gotcher, Lupe.' Pressing his earpiece the Khan stood up. He was restless, ready to go. He kissed the women, rubbing their cheeks with the palms of his hands. He levered himself up and down on his toes, testing his boots. He punched the big man on the arm. 'Want see?'

The big man's eyes sparkled. He twitched his blunt nose. 'Review the troops, is it?' he said. 'Everybody present and correct.'

Throwing aside the book he slapped his knees, rubbing at a smudge on his multicoloured hose. He tossed back his ponytail and rose with

364

some care to his feet. 'Zero minus ninety-nine and counting,' he told the assembled captains.

The Thrant chortled throatily. The woman with the blue gun reached out a skinny hand and rubbed the big man's thigh, as if touching him for good luck. The big man gave them a sloppy salute and accompanied the Khan and half a dozen cronies out of the back of the cave. He was noticeably favouring one leg.

They took the rope walkway across the pit. Despite the thirty-metre drop the Khan of the Lower Depths walked with his hands in his pockets, taking long, energetic strides. He threw the big man a sly look. 'Gonna get Starkie hopping?' he said, as if proposing a bet. 'What you say, Dog?'

'She'll jump like a Perk bit her on the bum,' said Dog Schwartz, stumping after.

Norval Khan slapped his associate's arm, laughing manically. 'Like a Perk bit her on the bum!'

Thinking of Perks made Dog think of Uncle Charlie, the mad old bugger. God bless him, wherever he was. He thought of the old geezer bombing off like a miniature tank through a storm of Perk feathers. To Dog, the collapse of the sanatorium was a major satisfaction. Grant was unhappy about it, apparently. That had made Dog Schwartz chuckle.

'Hey,' said the Khan. 'Give me another one of those pills.' He snapped his fingers.

'These are my private stock now,' said Dog. 'They'll have to last us.' But he handed them round anyway, as they left the walkway and stepped into the back of the head of the giant statue.

Inside, their feet clanked hollowly on the scuffed metal floor. There was a stink of oil and transmission fluid. The inside of the head was fitted out like a cockpit, with monitors and rotating seats. At the control panel at present was a small man filthier even than any of the captains.

'Let me take her a minute,' commanded Norval.

'What ho, Monk?' said Dog Schwartz. 'Are we fighting fit?' He balled up his enormous fists and pretended to box the Gunky Monkey.

The Monk grinned. He was in his dark brown element. He twisted two wires together and plastered the connection with grease.

The Khan took his seat. He let out a clutch and pulled a lever. The head of the statue began to turn.

Through the eyes of the giant sentinel they viewed the Havoc horde. The bikes were drawn up in a phalanx around the trucks, which had been fitted with new rams and decorated with chains and black flags, not to mention battered icons of Mistry, pneumatic and provocative in shiny leather and torn fishnet. Mistry, the biggest mamma of them all!

Brandishing cutlasses and Spite 70's, in armour and denim, in shaggy jerkins of Palernian fleece, men draped themselves on and around every vehicle, feeling their scars, drinking and laughing. At the water cisterns the sisters polished their heads and adjusted their teeth with a file. They had blackened their nipples and put on their best chains.

All around the Pit, the smithies glowed, putting wheels on the hallucinomats. Beyond the gate, the deserted canyon was thick with midnight.

Dog Schwartz patted Norval Khan zestfully on the shoulder. 'You're fucking trouble, you are, Norval,' he remarked, à propos of nothing, or everything.

She had the strength of a cat and the agility of an ape. She had torn off her clothes. In her flight she flashed up the airshafts and fissures like a wisp of tawny smoke. She was fleeing the cage of his fingers, the prison of his eyes. She was fleeing the scent of him.

The human on her back weighed almost nothing. The arms around her neck were thin and white. The human had used her last strength disabling the tyrant. Iogo had found a full-body support in the ship and clipped her into it, knowing it would make her stronger. Everything else on the ship she had left alone. She hadn't wanted to touch any of it, for fear of traps. Iogo had always remembered the time her sister Aughari was hurt falling out of a tree. Iogo was seven, Aughari nine or ten. She had to carry Aughari home, across two rivers, with no cover, Aughari squealing and cursing all the way. The *stharauq* appeared, circling in the white sky, following them thoughtfully. The pain had made Aughari mad, and in her frenzy she had clawed her sister's shoulders raw.

Here the tunnels were made of glass. Everything was dank and dripping. The slime was crusted and deep, and the footing nasty

366

under her fingers. 'Take the high –' murmured the woman in her ear. She did not finish her utterance; and Iogo did not reply. The flesh and blood of the tyrant was inside her, making her stronger, making her invincible.

They came to an air outlet. Iogo put her head between the vanes and peered down into the tunnel below. She ducked back, lips wrinkling. The human slid from her back. The exoskeleton coiled, containing her. Her eyes stared out of the dark. 'What?' she complained.

The Thrant did not speak. Confused scents rose from below, penetrating the reek of slime: weapons, Alteceans, the stench of medicines. She lifted her muzzle again. Could this be the place? She sniffed. Excitement was starting to seethe in her belly. It could!

A servo whirred briefly as the human levered herself upright. She reached up an arm and leaned on the outlet housing.

'Food,' she said. 'We must find –' Her ragged voice reverberated in the glass tunnel like the voice of a machine.

Iogo silenced her with a gesture. She tried to open the inspection hatch, but the unfamiliar device resisted her. Slowly and painfully the human opened it for her.

Iogo looked at her charge. 'You 'tay,' she said.

She let herself down head first, dropping onto plastic flooring with a clatter of claws.

Saskia Zodiac lay down wearily on her face. She put her head out of the hatch and looked.

She saw another Thrant appear at the turn of the tunnel: a male in a data visor, armoured grey jerkin and orange knickers, aiming a big gun. In an instant he had scanned the scene: the unexpected visitor, the open hatch.

It was Kenny, on guard, as ever.

Iogo was crawling towards him on her belly, head back, ears pricked. The smothered cries of their reunion filled the aging air with longing.

'Can we expect, Colonel, that the Captain may be unable to supervise the Approximation at all?'

Colonel Stark looked down at her thumbnails. Her hands were clasped on the desk in front of her big blue tubular chair. She had taken her cap off and placed it to one side, on the unused persona plaque reader, with the badge prominently to the front.

'Well, Zanna,' she said, favouring the Channel 10 interviewer with a frank and level look, 'as you know, personnel appointed by the Hands On Caucus are working very hard now taking us back into real space as you see.' The camera surveyed a Pons busy, if somewhat subdued. All the jokes and decals had been taken down and the litter cleared up. There were people at every desk and few weapons in sight, if any. The big screen showed Palernia modelled at aphelion. A graphic overlay painted in acid tones its regions, settlements, principal climate zones; even a ship or two thoughtfully silhouetted in orbit.

The Colonel ran a hand back over her crewcut skull. 'I'd like everyone to be advised that Captain Jute is receiving the best of medical care and attention at this time,' she said. 'Our message for passengers and crew is, keep to your allocated tasks and territories and we'll have you all out of this with maximum immediacy.'

Zanna Robbins gave the Redcap Colonel a firm look of her own. 'And if the present unrest continues, Colonel, what are your plans in that eventuality?'

'If the present unrest continues, Zanna,' said the Colonel, 'we are equipped and resourced to escalate our presence in any quarter of either hemisphere.' She waved her hand briefly and decisively. 'Let me say that again: in any quarter, inhabited or uninhabited, we have the capacity to pacify anyone engaged in violent activities.'

As if on cue Lieutenant Rykov appeared on her com. '*Invaders, ma'am!*' he rapped. '*The Sylvian Aqueduct!*' Pictures followed, large shapes moving through a tempest of static. A man appeared, standing in the back of an armoured vehicle waving a battered-looking sword. He was Havoc: it was plain as the dirt on his face.

So it was come at last, the Occipital Surge. The board had been divided over this development, whether it should be expected before or after Full Emergence. The barbarians had decided to put an end to the discussion and move forward now. It would be a pleasure to encounter them. In her breast Colonel Stark felt the pure righteous joy of battle ignite.

The AV reporter was chirping excitedly into the camera. 'This is Zanna Robbins for All-Area Channel 10 bringing you live reports of fresh unrest at the Lateral Fissure! We'll be right there with Colonel Stark, after these reminders of the Redcap Five-Step System for Personal Safety for you and your family.'

Colonel Stark's officers were all around now, in person and on screen, saluting, reporting for orders. 'Mobilize DorsoTemporals,' she told them. 'Rykov, Global Alert Ready status. Duty navigator, you have the helm.' In a wedge of command and security operatives she strode from the green dome to the lift. 'Attention all units,' she broadcast, 'wheeled and airborne, this is Stark. Prepare Command Post LF1 for my immediate arrival.' As she spoke, her fingers stalked about the glowing buttons of her gauntlet. 'Operation Bridgehead,' said the Supreme Commander. 'Condition green.'

Captain Jute was in bed. She had been in bed for a while.

It was not her room. It was full of junk, but none of the junk was hers. She did not recognize these piles of secondhand clothes, these specimen cabinets full of folded plastic bags. There were Alteceans around, so when she first came to she had thought she was back on the *Fat Mouth* with old Captain Frank. Soon he would be trumpeting, calling her to help him land some new piece of interplanetary detritus he had hooked in the garbage orbits. But then some nurses had appeared and started fussing over her, so she understood she was still aboard the Frasque starship, her failed command, crossing the probability horizon of an unidentified star. She must get up and take decisions, make plans, issue orders. She felt like a piece of orbital garbage herself. She wondered why they had bothered to scrape her off the floor of whatever hole they found her in.

People bustled in and out, muttering so she couldn't hear them. Otis was always somewhere nearby, assembling and disassembling pieces of artillery. She recognized one of the Pontine guards, teaching Mr Spinner some basic defence moves. He looked incredibly young. There was Eeb, and Karen Narlikar, and a tattooed girl who had used to work with the Cherub, Xtasca, who had gone, gone to look for Dodger Gillespie, who had gone long before. So many people gone. Swallowed up by the monster ship.

The Captain's own throat was dry.

'A drink,' she whispered.

A nurse said: 'I'll get some water.'

'No, Christ,' she said. 'Beer. Get me a beer.'

'Gnot advixzed,' said the Altecean gloomily, shaking the heavy mop of his head.

The Captain closed her eyes. 'Beer,' she said to Karen in the doorway. Karen found one, and brought it to her.

'Guard,' said the Captain. 'Guard.'

They brought the boy. He stood at attention. She held him by the shoulder. 'Listen. I've forgotten your name. Listen. There are some Vespans we have to get hold of. We need them, and we need Perks. And Palernians. Palernians. They do a lot of damage. Get them out of detention. Bring as many as you can. Otis.'

Otis loomed into view. He looked like some kind of horse, with his sideboards long and his hair all in his eyes. She wanted to give him some sugar, but she hadn't got any.

'The docks,' she said. 'We need to have a ship ready. For afterwards.'

'There's a dozen ships,' he said. 'We've got people on all of them.' He seemed dejected.

'Good,' she said. 'Good. How soon can we be back in the Pons?'

He raised his hand. 'Soon, soon,' he said.

Captain Jute closed her eyes. She knew he was lying to her.

'Double the people in the docks. Take whoever you need and secure the stern curtain controls.'

Otis started to make snuffling noises of disapproval. He was getting more like a horse every moment. 'No, Captain, you need me here. Any time they could come.'

Captain Jute was dreaming. She was looking forward to abandoning her unlovely ship. But not until they arrived in space, real space, with proper planets in it. She was dreaming of feeding Stark to the Perks before she went. 'Go and cover that exit, Otis,' she said, opening her eyes and pushing the mattress with her fists. 'Go. That's an order.' She pointed, approximately. 'There's Karen. Take her with you.'

Karen Narlikar looked at Otis. 'Yes, Captain,' she said in an obedient undertone. 'Only first I've got to help them change your sheets.' The Captain scratched her armpit. 'Sheets?' she said muzzily. 'I don't need any more sheets. I'm getting up in a minute.'

'Anything you say, Captain.'

Otis left. The young guard left. Other people seemed to go with them, their loud, despondent voices dying away down the hall. Captain Jute felt some of her energy go with them. Life was so tiring. She was too tired even to drink any more beer. She held out the tube for the nurse to take, and fell back on the pillows. Slowly, unhandily, she blew her nose.

'All right, Kenny,' she said. 'Bring her in.'

In a long, clean robe, white with pinstripes of red and blue and green, Saskia Zodiac seemed to sag between Kenny and the guard who steered her into the borrowed bedroom. She looked more gaunt than she ever had, if that were possible. She had arrived wearing a full-body support, they said, but the guards had quickly had that off her, and now Tabitha waited while Kenny decided to frisk her once more for concealed weapons, explosives, or just to feel her up, god knows. Saskia didn't seem to take any notice. Her deep eyes stared only at Tabitha. Tabitha felt the recriminations that would soon come pouring out of those eyes, unstoppably, like creatures out of a wall. They guided the experimental woman to a chair the nurse put at the foot of the bed. She sat leaning forward with her forearms on her thighs. Her smile was sad.

'Hello,' she said.

The Captain shivered. She must hate Saskia Zodiac. She knew that now. She could do it.

She sent the guard away. Kenny would stay. Nothing would dislodge him.

'You decided to come back,' said Tabitha. Her voice seemed to be tangled up somewhere in her chest, looped around something and pulled taut.

Saskia shrugged her coathanger shoulders. 'Iogo brought me,' she said vaguely.

The monster ship had taken Saskia Zodiac away and turned her into someone to hate. That needn't hurt. It needn't hurt at all, if you did it right.

'I don't know what you think you'll find here,' she said.

Saskia looked bleak. She said: 'Death.'

The Captain's eyes widened. Kenny was already half up on the foot of the bed, ruff bristling.

'Well, you look like shit,' explained Saskia, in righteous innocence. 'You look worse than Hannah Soo did. The ship is lost and now everybody is going to die.' A tear leaked from her right eye and ran down her marble cheek. 'I think we are all dead already, in this floating tomb.'

So the little lost clone was frightened and miserable, and it was up to Tabitha to do something about it. She had no intention of doing anything about it; she couldn't see why it always had to be her who did something about it; she had done something about it far too often and got far too little joy for her pains.

'Fuck it,' said Captain Jute wearily. 'Bring her here,' she said to Kenny, as she moved aside on the bed. 'Come on. She's not going to try anything.'

The Thrant helped Saskia Zodiac up on the bed. She lay down half a metre away from Tabitha Jute. He continued craning over her, sniffing suspiciously. Tabitha batted him away.

She thought about putting her arms around Saskia, but she couldn't. She felt too hurt, hurt and betrayed. She put her arms behind her bristly head and looked at the ceiling, what she could see of it between the towers of junk. 'All right,' she said, quite calmly. 'Tell me about the little ghost. Little Alice in her pinafore. Little Lady Shall-Not.'

Saskia lifted her head and looked at the nurse, who shook her head uncomprehendingly. 'Alice in a pinafore?' Saskia echoed.

Tabitha took a breath. 'The little girl you made.'

'The only little girl I made was Suzan . . . She was my sister. When did *you* see her?'

'You sent her to my room.'

'Suzan is an imago,' said Saskia impatiently. 'She doesn't go any-where, only on and off. Where is Alice? Whose pinafore is she in?'

'Yours, obviously.'

'I haven't got a pinafore!'

Her bafflement was obvious and complete. 'Forget it,' said Tabitha, sore. 'Kenny, down.' She wondered what the point of all this was. Saskia had never made much sense at the best of times. The little white ghost had never reappeared. No doubt the doctor had been right: it was a chimera, a phantom of her own detached conscience, wandering in the corridors of the monstrous ship.

Saskia Zodiac yawned. Her mouth looked wet and vulnerable. Tabitha Jute remembered the taste of her, strange and zestful, rich in complex peptides. Her sinuses began to hurt.

She summoned up another grievance. 'What about all that stuff you gave Channel 10?' she demanded. She was almost shouting, though Saskia was so close. 'All that stuff they showed on *The Ugly Truth*.'

372

'I didn't give Channel 10 anything,' said Saskia, offended. 'He ran all that, right from the Scorpion. *You*'re lucky, you never saw the really bad stuff. He kept it all for himself. Things even you would never do. He had an imago too, of you, he made it undress and beg for him.'

Captain Jute was losing this. She felt there must be another part to the conversation, a parallel track to which she had no access.

'Who did?' she asked.

'Grant Nothing.'

'That's not a name.'

'You remember,' said Saskia. 'He gave you that book. At the party! And he gave Colonel Stark all those robots. The Hands On people, he said they would fall apart without him. Oh, I don't know. He was rather boring,' she said, yawning again.

Little of that was any help.

'Where is he?' asked the Captain.

'On the Scorpion!' said Saskia with asperity. 'He's dead, though, thank *goodness*.' She smacked the bedclothes emphatically. 'Iogo finally had a good idea. He used me for his pleasure. In bondage and everything. I suppose it was pleasure, it was hard to tell, sometimes, with him. It was very sad, really,' she said.

She turned on her side and took the Captain's hand, quite as if it were the most natural thing in all the worlds to do. 'He used to talk about you all the time,' she told her. 'And he had some powerful drugs. I think I was completely gone for a while. Nothing left of me at all.' This she said with some satisfaction, as if relating an unexpected achievement. 'Now all I want to do is *eat*.'

Captain Jute understood there had been some ordeal. Saskia had not been having more fun somewhere else. Under the robe there were bandages on her wrists and ankles. Yet now it was over the ordeal had already become an adventure. Her vigorous young metabolism was righting itself, her mood lightening like the sun coming round the shoulder of Jupiter.

Saskia was talking to Kenny, pointing with distaste to his bowl of raw meat. 'Is that all you have here? On the Scorpion we had all kinds of things, things that ran out ages ago. And the equipment! You must be careful with that Scorpion,' she said to Tabitha. 'You must not touch it until Xtasca's been over the whole thing.'

Captain Jute's heart was sore. The gnarled grip of jealousy was

373

loosening, falling away at the touch of the conjuror's slender hand.

'Take her away,' she said loudly, almost harshly. 'Give her something to eat. Where's the Commissioner? He wants to talk to her.'

'You ought to have something to eat too,' the nurse told her.

'Later,' said Tabitha. She remembered the man with the book. He had called her a cunt. A lot of people did that habitually now, and worse. 'I'm sorry I forgot to look after you properly,' she said to Saskia. She said it as if she had not known the words were in her mouth and had to get them out as quickly as possible. 'I can't seem to look after anything properly – not Plenty; nor Alice –'

Her voice cracked. She was aching all over. Her ill-shaven scalp felt tight and sore.

'Nor me . . .' she said.

The deep-eyed figure in the white robe leaning against her bodyguard looked grimly over her shoulder then, as if in some doubt about her dismissal.

'I'll see you later,' Captain Jute assured her fiercely.

The room fell very quiet now. The nurse wiped the Captain's eyes, which had become unaccountably wet.

Captain Jute thought something she had thought before. People were like planets. You set out towards one, but you could make the tiniest mistake and not notice it until it was far too late, and then you ended up hundreds of thousands of kilometres away from where you were supposed to be. It was a wonder anyone ever got anywhere, really.

It was one reason she had always been fond of artificial company.

She chewed the sleeve of her nightgown. 'Saskia hasn't got her,' she told the nurse. 'Where *is* she?'

'I'm sure I don't know, Captain,' said the nurse lightly, plumping up her pillows.

By now the bikes of Havoc were already halfway across the Sylvian Aqueduct. They rolled slowly, churning up the waters with their mighty wheels. Their scars were ghastly, eloquent of epic pain and suffering. They rode with banners, heraldic, cryptic and obscene: their devices were obese female hindquarters, swollen phalluses decorated with the insignia of half-forgotten terrestrial tyrannies. Ahead of them across the gulf, the horns and gongs of the Telencephalon kept up a panic clangour, as if the passengers thought sheer noise would somehow help protect them from pillage and rapine.

Along the Promenade the robot army advanced to meet the invader: automata and free-drones, reprogrammed luggage trucks and reconditioned exercisers. Those built without weapons carried guns; those built without hands were proving wonderfully adaptable. An industrial sewing machine and a hovercrate had formed a very unpleasant and highly mobile partnership which stitched its way through leather and flesh alike. Bowling machines hurled grenades, while windscreen cleaners hopped here and there, squirting hydrochloric acid.

In her command post the Redcap Colonel gestured, and through the gulf from high and low came the red and black delta kites, streaming like playing cards from the hands of a prestidigitator. Across the windows of the apartment blocks they scattered their reflections, multiplying like shards in a kaleidoscope. Their weapons spat peevish dots of black fire. Engines exploded. Barbarians flung up their hands, vacating their saddles, and toppled over the parapet into the abyss.

Now the weapons of Havoc coughed gouts of dirty smoke. Horrible projectiles – dead cats, rusty bolts and razorblades – blasted the fabric of kites into shreds. They perforated casings; drenched black shirts with crimson blood.

In the trough of the aqueduct the water boiled like grey milk around boots and wheels and caterpillar tracks. The robots hated it. They clung to each other's superstructures or crawled precariously along the parapet coping, rather than risk that immobilizing fluid. Devices that had already succumbed to it and seized up provided perches for the nimble and magnetic to pepper the grubby foe with flechettes, powdered glass and tacks. The barbarians roared with laughter, crushing unwary robots into pancakes of steel and plastic beneath their wheels.

On two high landings aft the hallucinomats stood, pouring illusions into the hapless squadrons hemmed between the bridgehead and the barricaded streets. The troops fell on each other, comrade attacking comrade, though they swore afterwards what they were seeing was seamed and hairy Havoc faces jeering at them from under the noble red cap. Beautiful creatures of ambiguous sex appeared, beckoning them to the brink, tempting them to leap into the chasm. Ordinary ensigns, realizing at last they were invulnerable, walked boldly into the Havoc guns.

Colonel Stark shielded her eyes. 'Visors!' she ordered.

They stepped forward, men and women in visors and power

shields, scouts with radios to marshal the kites and direct them against the exposed faces of the hallucinomats. Just out of range the kites banked, gliding in one after the other across the updraughts, edge on to the Havoc guns. One by one delicately they lobbed their bombs, then, spilling air, dived steeply away to safety.

Smoke and pulverized matrix clouded the scene, obscuring the seductive pulsing of the illusion machines. The Havoc gunners redoubled their efforts, firing blind.

'Lights!' called Colonel Stark, and huge searchlights blazed down. In the confusion on the bridge she could see the bulky outlines of her battledrones moving forward now. They were tough, all-terrain automata, each with the armour and firepower of a small tank. They didn't present the kind of superior profile she could have found ideally desirable in terms of numbers, but in a narrow saliency like the aqueduct that was not insuperably a disadvantage. The battledrones chewed up fallen bikes like hyperactive trash compactors, reducing them to angular mounds of crumpled scrap, while steadily blasting significant holes in the bodywork of ancient and overwelded trucks. All along the aqueduct Havoc banners were going down. The battledrones pressed on, and in a pack the black iron scavenger crabs followed, dispersing the wreckage and dismantling the casualties with their tungsten-tipped claws.

Then from the rear a great shape appeared: upright, bipedal, looming through the obscurity like a giant thirty metres tall. It roared a huge amplified roar that shook the windows of Amygdala Gate.

The room rocked. Adjutants were yelling, forgetting their microphones, wrestling with remotes. The Colonel put both hands on the desk and gazed into the dazzle of searchlights and smoke. 'What is that thing? Where the hell did they get that from?' It was stamping across the bridge now, trampling her battledrones underfoot.

The Havoc ape had come to the fight.

The sound had failed. The AV screen danced with silent light. Tabitha Jute, up and dressed in jeans and a tartan flannel shirt, was sitting on the bed. Beside her Saskia Zodiac had pulled up the hood of her robe and tucked her hands in their opposite sleeves, like a penitent who withdraws from the tainting world. Two of the nurses stood by them, anxious for the Captain not to distress herself, but riveted by the nightmares replacing each other regularly on the screen, disparate timescales coinciding at last as the dissipated particles of the ship began to reassemble. Nearby Mr Spinner stood watching with the Disaster Commissioner, both muttering incoherent phrases and expostulations, their faces creased with rage and loss. Half in, half out of the door, Eeb and the apothecary stood mooing and weeping, great tears dripping down their furry faces.

The screen was cycling views of battle zones.

The Crap Chute Rookery was in flames. Emaciated men and women clung to the climbing nets or fell screaming into the void as waves of fire cascaded over them, up and down. On high ledges children rained missiles down on Redcap riot floaters. The Redcaps replied with scathing blasts of vivid violet death.

In the abandoned kitchen dinettes of Little Foxbourne, spiky Perks and maddened hounds tore apart store cupboards, soft furnishings, and each other.

On a Lateral promontory Zanna Robbins stood mouthing wildly at a microphone while behind her the battle for the bridgehead raged. The watchers could see the giant robot ape. It had crossed the aqueduct and reached the traffic concourse before the overstressed floor beneath it had given way. Waist-deep in smashed matrix it stood swiping at the mobbing kites and bellowing in mechanical fury. There seemed to be a man on its shoulder, a big man with a beard and ponytail, swinging at climbing robots with a hammer. His clothes were so colourful they made the pixels overload.

With a small cooing noise one of the nurses took the Captain by the shoulders, trying to turn her face from the accusing screen. Captain Jute obeyed her, putting her arms round the starched white hips and resting her cheek on the cool midriff. There was no need to watch. Captain Jute had the distant sense that the entire event had been somehow co-ordinated like a sporting fixture, every combatant matched with their exact mirror opposite, their perfect enemy. Let them all neutralize each other and leave me alone, she thought. She never had liked having people on her ship.

Saskia touched the Captain on the arm. 'That's your man,' she pointed out. She seemed distressed.

From her hygienic refuge Tabitha looked up at the new scene: a Septal corridor set with barred windows and reinforced doors. Redcaps were radioing reports. At their feet lay a young Pontine guard in a grey camo suit with a big red hole in his chest and another in his head.

A deep groan and shouts of protest rose from the little gathering. Then came the next scene, the docks. Beneath walls of shadowy, almost regular cells where vehicles of every shape and marque lurked like larval wasps waiting to hatch, armed figures stood looking down at a tangle of slaughtered humans. The camerawork was unsteady, wavering, the picture ravaged and gashed with static. Still the blackened bodies on the floor were inescapably Otis and his team. Captain Jute had stopped watching. Instead she began to dream again, of triumph beyond disaster, of her glorious restoration. She was thinking how wonderful it would be when they finally hit the Pons and took back Plenty.

8

In the Pons, Lieutenant Rykov was frantic. He had thought the Bureau kept you busy, but this was madness. All the conflicts everywhere were disrupting communication, damaging the fabric, creating bad distortion on the scopes. There were a lot of new dark spots and the internal sealing units were all backed up.

The guard sergeant brought a woman to him.

'Says she's looking for the Captain, Lieutenant. We found this on her.' 'This' was a plaque of plain grey plastic, industrial electronics of some kind. The Lieutenant took it and tapped it on his thumbnail. She was an obvious technoid: ripped clothes, peeling boots, a swirling tattoo on her arm. Her hair was bleached, her eyebrows met in the middle. Lieutenant Rykov saw a couple of the crew wave to her, and saw her give a little wave back.

'The Captain's not here,' he said. 'You can speak to me.'

She was not small, but she had a small voice, difficult to hear in the hubbub. 'Xtasca sent me with that,' she said, meaning the plaque, 'for Captain Jute.'

'The Cherub? Where is it?' Xtasca had not been sighted for weeks, not since it had quit the Thalamus.

Rykov heard the woman say 'Mesenc Nucleus'. He sent a signal to the Bureau to have the little tadpole fished out and put in a jam jar as soon as personnel came free. He held up the plaque. 'And this is what?'

The woman made a sort of self-conscious shrugging motion. 'Well, I don't know that much about it, only what Xtasca says.'

His patience was dwindling. Two sergeants and a desk controller were vying for his attention. 'And?' he said loudly.

The woman sucked her teeth. 'Well, basically what you've got on there is a voice-operated self-reflexive grammatical metasystem. Runs decont and recont and all the trans in between.' She seemed to be watching his eyes uncertainly. 'Check, what it actually does is ax the base code entablature and override the subpart prob spin while restacking simultaneity field struc via the drive filter and layoff node varias.'

The lieutenant exhaled. He pressed a button. 'Tech!' he shouted.

There were Most Urgent message blips coming up on the screens. The half-hourly report was still waiting. There were only three techs visible in the entire place and each of them was already doing three other jobs. 'Persona!' shouted the lieutenant.

'LIEUTENANT,' said a disintegrating voice like a dirty signal.

He held up the unprepossessing piece of plastic. 'Do you know about this thing?'

A camera swivelled. 'IT LOOKS FAMILIAR,' said the voice.

'Is it advantageous?'

'. . . INCALCULABLY,' the voice crackled.

'Can you run it?' Rykov asked the woman, as he rerouted the messages and looked at the head row controller to tell her he'd be ready for her next. 'Oh,' said the woman, starting to beam. 'Check! I mean, thanks!'

Obviously it was what she'd been wanting all along. What *planet* did they come from, these people?

'You have to load it here,' she said, reaching to put it in an empty slot just at his elbow.

Eeb and Saskia arrived at the apartment tumbling over each other with good news. Eeb was trying to say something, making a sound like a sneeze played at quarter speed. Her plaits bounced.

'Xtasca,' said Saskia, interpreting. 'She's back!'

Kenny, at the foot of the bed, gave a glad yip.

'At last!' said the nurse.

'Alice,' said the Captain, who was dressed but lying down. 'Alice!' she called.

The air in the cluttered chamber remained silent and uninhabited. Saskia climbed on the bed and hugged her. 'They say Alice is safe,' she told her.

'Dodger,' said the Captain.

''ap'n Genechpy!' tooted Eeb, with an excited little dance that shook the furniture. She liked Captain Gillespie, who was kind and funny and didn't look down on you just because you had a long nose and fur and feet like a big chicken and were too big for crawl tunnels.

'Did they find Mistry?' asked the nurse.

Saskia spoke to Tabitha. 'They found her,' she said.

The nurse raised her shoulders and clasped her hands together. 'Oh, I knew they would! I always knew it!'

'Where is she?' said the Captain, meaning Dodger. 'I want to see her. Bring her here.'

'I expect they're resting,' said the nurse, trying to soothe her.

'They'll be up later,' said Saskia.

The Captain took no notice of either of them. 'Where?' she said.

Saskia Zodiac looked at Kenny the Thrant. 'Pari 10–20,' she said.

Captain Jute knew where that was. She got up and left the apartment. They caught up with her outside, where an incoming guard was just getting off his bike. 'Where are you going?' Saskia cried.

'Dodger,' said the Captain. The guard looked surprised to see the Captain walking towards him.

'Captain, you're not strong enough yet!' said the nurse.

'I'm going,' said the Captain. With the eerie submarine grace of a somnambulist she climbed on the guard's bike.

The guard stood by, tense. He looked to Kenny for instructions. Kenny was standing in front of the bike, his shoulders forward. The guard looked for another bike, but they were all out. ''ey kill you!' mourned Eeb, scratching her pelt in distress.

'I'm going,' said the Captain. She touched her wristset to the starter.

Kenny circled the bike, ready to bound onto the pillion. 'I come too,' he told her.

She gunned the motor, steering away from him. 'I'm going alone,' said the Captain; and she rode away.

Parietal 10 was out amidships, beyond the Central Gyrus. The old names were meaningless now. Emerging, Plenty was changing shape, cracking open new corridors into unsuspected chambers. It looked less like a brain than it ever had, unless it was the brain of some creature undissected yet by human science. In the shafts and tunnels you could hear the guns, feel the walls repercuss with the furies of a dozen scattered battles. People who had never been afraid before began to wonder if the ship really would make it through into materiality in one piece.

The Captain arrived with the entourage she had acquired, of locals, barefoot children, hooting Vespans, all astonished to see her riding by, all clamouring to show her where the triumphant searchers were staying. The local stairs were crowded with people, Mistry fans and lookalikes, apostles and acolytes. Father Le Coq was there in his long mauve jacket and iridescent waistcoat, his ruined top hat and ever-multiplying rings. He was ready for the Devil. Shaking a sharpened stake of real wood he scuttled out of the crowd and seized Tabitha as she tried to push her way towards the apartment.

'Wait, Captain, wait, for the sake of your immortal soul I beseech you.' The Rooster smelled of blood and snakes and unwashed flesh. He talked into her face. 'Mystery Woman, that's a M and a W,' he intoned, making the shapes of the letters with his long knobbly fingers in front of his chin. 'Now M is thirteen and W is twenty-three – two prime numbers, Captain, two primes. Thirteen plus your twenty-three is thirty-six, which is six by six, and you put six next to six next to six, why, that ain't nothing but the number of the She-Beast!' He rolled his eyes and gnashed his long yellow teeth.

Captain Jute laid her hand on his shoulder. He pulled back his head and squinted at her through his grimy glasses, as if in hope of seeing her better. She said, 'Are these your people, priest?'

He ducked his head in a parody of humility. 'We are all God's people, sister.'

'Get them out of the way,' she said.

The Rooster skipped backwards, waving his stake in dangerous arcs. 'Everybody stand back!' he boomed. 'Everybody back now!'

A space cleared in front of the door, which, a moment later, opened. A silver disc slid out, half a metre off the ground, with someone shiny and black and very small sitting on it.

The crowd made wild noises, cries of wrath and joy, and demands. 'Show us the woman!' People lunged forward with their tapers. Father Le Coq, legs astride, tried to hold them back, clasping his stake at both ends.

Captain Jute was in, the door was shut.

She sagged against the wall. 'Jesus H. Christ in an enchilada,' she said.

The Cherub hovered, keeping its distance. 'Are you unwell, Captain?'

'I'm all right,' said Tabitha, not altogether truthfully. She looked around. The hallway was raw matrix, with the usual stains of dereliction, smoke and seepage. There was a distinct smell of cat piss. 'Where are they?'

Beyond the hallway the place was big; huge, in fact. Ornamental stairs rose up to other levels. The floor was paved with what looked like Deimos marble, and there was a banqueting table fit for a minor hall at Valhalla, surrounded by half a dozen enormous thrones of iron and glass. Crates and bags of personal effects stood about, half packed, or half unpacked, crumpled clothes and scattered gadgets incongruous in the grandeur.

The far end of the table was littered, Tabitha could see, with the remains of a meal, or possibly more than one – lichen bread, dried snails, candlefruit: local stuff. A pale cat looked round from nosing through it. It trotted along the table towards her, curious. It jumped down and ran to sniff her boots, then gazed up at her face. It had only one eye.

Dodger Gillespie got up from the table and stood there watching, her right arm comprehensively bandaged, her left fist on her hip.

'Fuck you, Dodger,' said Tabitha. Riding the bike had taken it out of her. She swayed across the floor to her old friend and gripped her tightly by the left shoulder. '*You*'re not dead.'

Captain Gillespie seemed amused. She bared her upper teeth. 'Not quite, gel, nice of you to mention it.'

She patted Captain Jute on the back. It seemed only a couple of weeks since she'd seen her. The change was frightening.

'You're not looking so perky,' she said.

'I'm all right,' said the Captain distantly. 'Where is she?'

'Mystery?' Dodger Gillespie pointed her thumb at a large white door.

'Contained,' said Xtasca.

'Alice!' said the Captain frenziedly.

Dodger drew down the corners of her mouth. 'We sent her to the bridge,' she said. 'Haven't you got her?'

Captain Jute turned to leave. 'Come on,' she said.

'What about the prisoner?' asked Xtasca pleasantly.

The Captain looked from one to the other. Dodger looked like a patient soldier. Xtasca was a shiny doll, perfect, incorruptible.

'Who is she?'

'Her name is Angela, she says,' said the Cherub.

A cold, metallic singing started in the Captain's head, as though that name had touched a switch. She stood arrested, like a statue of Self-Forgetfulness.

'Angela what?'

'She says she hasn't got a surname,' answered the Cherub. 'She's a unit of the Expanded Neurosphere. The farthest expanded unit of all,' it observed.

'She's a plughead,' said Dodger, in case the Captain hadn't understood. She really was not looking at all well.

Near the table there was a field com set up, on a closed circuit. Xtasca touched a spot on its saucer, and the com lit up to show a light brown woman with a profusion of dark red hair and jewellery. She was sitting on a couch with her head at an angle, her feet tucked under her.

'Angela won't be her real name,' Dodger was saying, as she put a flame to her latest cigarette. 'The Messenger, she says it means.'

Already Captain Jute, who had hardly glanced at the screen, was crossing to the large white door at the pace of a far fitter creature. Xtasca barely had time to disable the lock before she flung the door open.

Inside was a room, generously proportioned, carpeted, and panelled up to shoulder height with material that gleamed like polished slate. It might have been a bedroom or a study. The only furniture was one huge couch, which had been pulled round at an angle with its back to the door. Over the back Tabitha could see the top of the woolly head.

She went round to the front.

The Mystery Woman was dressed in colourful pyjamas with a Palernian pattern, big leaf shapes in orange and green and terracotta. She was meditating. Two threadlike wires hung drooping from sockets in her temples to one of her pendants, a basic biofeedback unit. The nails of her toes and fingers had been painted in different colours, metallic blues and pearly whites that clashed horribly with the pyjamas.

'Angie?' said Tabitha.

The woman looked up placidly.

'Hello T-Tabby,' she said.

In the outer room, Captain Gillespie heard the greeting. No one, no one in all the worlds and all the years she'd known Tabitha Jute – no one had ever been allowed to call her Tabby. No one except this hijacker, this thief, this saboteuse. Yet instead of shouting at her, Tabitha was hugging her.

Captain Gillespie looked at the com. Two faces, two women, so alike: the one smiling blandly, the other dazed, amazed. She gave a short, ironic chuckle that sounded more like a cough. 'Oh bloody hell,' she said, and turned to the Cherub. 'Angela Jute,' she said.

The Cherub hummed softly. Lights came and went on its saucer. 'We have no record of an Angela Jute,' it said.

Dodger looked at the big white door. The cat was going in there, cautiously. 'Every family has one,' said Dodger. 'The black sheep.'

The Cherub continued its search. 'Sheep?' it said.

'The one they don't talk about,' she said. 'The one that went the wrong way.' Captain Gillespie narrowed her eyes against the smoke from her cigarette. 'Like you,' she said.

The Cherub made no comment. Its eyes glowed dimly as it processed the material. 'Alice will know,' it said.

Dodger took the cigarette out of her mouth and pointed it at Xtasca. 'Let's not talk about Alice till we hear from Jone.'

Xtasca whisked away through the air, following the cat into the inner room.

Captain Jute was sitting on the couch beside the woman called Angela. She was scrutinizing her face, saying: 'Where did you come from?'

Angela lifted a hand, smiling blissfully. 'From the Holy Sepulchre.'

384

'She must have joined us at Venus,' said Xtasca, flying a hyperbolic curve around the couch, 'from the *Seraph Kajsa.*'

'The b-body is b-buried,' Angela was murmuring happily. 'The spirit mu-mu-multiplies to infinity!'

Dodger Gillespie came in too, to keep the party together. She stood to one side, just in Tabitha's line of sight. She wasn't sure what Tabitha was getting, how much she could take.

'It's a Seraphim front, their church,' Dodger reminded her. 'The Sepulchre – what is it –?'

'The Holy Sepulchre of the Expanded Neurosphere,' Angela said.

Everybody was looking at Angela. Angela was looking glassily around, blessing them with her love. They might have all been guests at her birthday party.

'What have you done to my ship?' the Captain asked her hoarsely.

'Many strings go to m-make the Holy Net,' answered the disciple, with satisfaction.

'What have you done to Alice?'

Angela Jute smiled a smile of serene blankness.

'It's entirely possible she has no idea what she's been doing,' said the Cherub. 'An operation that complex might well require the complete suppression of the higher –'

Captain Jute interrupted. 'Can we get her back?' She had her hand on her sister's cheek, as if testing her temperature. She looked up at her companions.

Dodger Gillespie suppressed a grimace. We haven't got you back yet, she thought. She glanced at the Cherub.

'Well,' said the little Seraphic apostate, touching two fingers to its rosebud lips, 'I'm sure she can be deprogrammed, given time. Whether the result will have a recognizable identity is not something I could offer an opinion on.'

Angela Jute sighed then and stretched, like one waking refreshed. She reached up and delicately took the leads out of her sockets, letting them reel back into her pendant. 'Tabitha,' she said, taking the hand that had touched her cheek and patting it. 'You are in the N-net. It holds y-you. It keeps you safe!'

The Captain looked into those ecstatic eyes. She seemed to think it important to describe the situation as she saw it. 'It's not Proxima,' she told the electronic evangelist. 'Everything's all going to shit. They won't let me fly my own ship.'

385

Xtasca whirred to a new position overhead. 'This is the woman who's been stopping you, Captain,' it pointed out.

Dodger Gillespie sucked air loudly through her teeth. 'Not now, X,' she muttered.

The Cherub opened and closed its chubby hands. 'How anyone,' it remarked, 'can be expected to solve a problem if principal information is concealed –'

'I'm warning you,' said Dodger Gillespie.

Angela hugged the Captain's arm. 'The Net is light,' she said. 'The N-net is flesh. The Net is unbro-bro-broken!'

There were noises outside. The Pango had arrived.

The screaming, clawing, rock-throwing hordes of Lat Fiss Left grew silent, staring in wonder as the drone copters appeared. They were yellow and green, unlike any model seen on board before, and they dropped out of the chasms overhead in synchronized pairs, unrolling huge plastic sheets which they held suspended between them like banners.

On the banners appeared the old Channel 1 logo, as on a gigantic AV screen; but instead of any of the normal presenters people remembered, they saw Mystery Woman, sitting there with beads in her hair and a chuckling baby on her knee, and smiling at the camera! Weary and frightened mothers clutched their breasts and moaned. It was their baby. Those were their children, playing around the feet of the Infanta of the Interface. They looked happy, well fed, full of restless impatient energy as children ought to be. They were in Kanfa, the old Earth Room, with space and white stars and a big planet outside the windows. The planet was green and dappled. It looked like the crown of an enormous chestnut tree.

'*Come!*' Mystery Woman called to the astonished spectators, and she held out her hands. '*We are waiting for you! No one will stop you if you come now!*'

The starved, scorched, sickened dispossessed of Lat Fiss Left stared at each other and broke once more into clamour. They leapt up and down as if they thought the screens themselves could save them, while the copters whickered softly back and forth above their heads, putting out the fires.

*   *   *

386

In the docks sailors were fighting with stevedores, owners with pilots. The few fully working ships had been stormed, besieged, attacked where they stood. Some of them were already in pieces. Organized looters scrambled up the cliffs, battling their way from tier to tier, fighting hand to hand with corporate commandos struggling to hold some imaginary line. Wreckage on the lower levels was extensive. A pen of disabled Mitchums burned messily, filling the area with black smoke. No one saw where the little copters came from, everybody just started shooting at them.

The copters evaded the fusillade with ease, unfurling their enormous plastic sheets. The Channel 2 theme trumpeted out, and the Channel 2 logo appeared on the sheets; and then, with the lurching immediacy of an urgent news bulletin, the image of a figure everyone knew, everyone recognized, though she had been hidden from them so long. It was Mystery Woman, in her long black leather coat and flight overalls, commanding a flock of drones on a sheaf of wires that stretched out from her skull. She was in one of the cargo bays, overhead, where some new action seemed to be breaking out. Her drones were obviously cargo drones, though they had clearly been refitted with weapons.

Mystery Woman zoomed into close up. In the docks, the guns ceased firing. Everyone who could was crowding onto the balconies, Redcap next to cowboy, while the rest ran out on the dock apron, craning their necks.

They could see the sweat on her face, every drop three metres high. Her hair was tied back in a camo cloth rag.

'The Frasque are coming!' she shouted. 'The Frasque! The Frasque!'

In the head of the giant ape of Havoc, the monitors fizzed and spluttered. No amount of tuning could restore their proper channels. Instead, something purporting to be Channel 3 announced itself, though everyone on board knew Channel 3 had folded more than a year ago.

Norval Khan thumped the arm of his seat. 'Grant, right?' he demanded. The Monk shrugged, spreading his grubby palms.

The scene on the monitors was the one they had left behind that morning: Oxy Pit, with the smithies banked. There was no one in view but mammas and kids. They were all gathered round –

'Mistry!' gasped Dog Schwartz.

It was Mistry herself in a little bitty skirt and a brass brassiere, just like she'd stepped down from a painting.

'It's her! Norval, it's her!'

'Shut up!'

The woman on the screen lowered her head and looked straight at Norval Khan as if she could see him; and she spoke. Her voice was low and breathy, full of promise, just the way you always imagined it.

'*Come home, Norval Khan,*' said Mistry. '*The ship is yours.*'

Norval jerked his eyes away from the screen. 'It's a trick,' he said.

'There's Lupin,' Dog said.

Norval looked. It was, Lupin Dwarf, the lead of his headset trailing as he brought the Queen of Chaos a beer. He waved excitedly at the camera.

Dog Schwartz twitched and wriggled. 'Come on, Norval, Christ, let's go!'

Norval climbed up to look out of the eyes of his ape. He surveyed the scrapyard that had been the Redcap front line. He said, 'We're not moving till *she* does.'

'What is this?' barked the Colonel at her coms operator.

'Channel 4, ma'am,' said the tech.

'It can't be Channel 4! Who's controlling it?' Her face creased up with hate. She looked a lot older suddenly. 'It's *him*, isn't it? Grant. A tactical misinformational device. Get me a line. Any line!'

'Ma'am, I can't. There isn't anything. There's only that.'

Stark glared at the screen. It showed the Pons. It showed the helm, the big blue chair. There was a woman sitting in it. The woman looked a lot like the Captain, but wasn't. The helm was plugged into her head.

Stark ground her fist into the console. Outside, something exploded, very close to. All the lights flickered and a shower of plaster pattered down from the ceiling.

What if it was true? Could Tekunak have betrayed her? Had they finessed the situation, exploited the opportunity window of her absence to position a pawn, a noncombatant, a nonplayer character?

A double explosion. Then a lull. And onscreen the camera moving from the woman at the helm to the woman lying unconscious at her feet.

That *was* the Captain.

388

The seated woman's face returned in close up. Her make up was flawless, her smile like an ad for toothpaste. '*Colonel*,' she said. '*Please be advised*.' Her eyes were violet and orange and flaming green. '*The ship is mine*,' she said.

Colonel Stark hit the window with both hands. She looked down in fury at the Horde of Havoc. They had disengaged and fallen back around the ape. Their bikes circled the towering metal beast, round and round and round. 'The scummy sons of bitches fucking diversioned us!'

'*Stark*,' purred the Siliconite goddess, '*it is me you must reckon with*.'

The Colonel was already grabbing her red hat and running for her car.

In the cave of the Big Chap miners coated to the armpits in blood and slime stood back from their labour to watch the Channel 5 Special that was suddenly playing on every screen. There they all were: the Director of Tekunak Charge and Dorcas Mandebra and Captain Jute, all raising their glasses while Mystery Woman sloshed champagne into them. She draped her arms round the three of them. The Director reached to pat her hand. '*We're very pleased indeed*,' he announced to his employees, '*to report that Tekunak Interstellar Trading has acquired the rights to this fair ship and is now open for business!*' To the sound of crowds cheering, the capitalists toasted the camera.

At the same moment, all around the crescents of New Little Foxbourne the AVs had flashed into life. Over the sightless bodies of their owners sprawled across couches and occasional tables the image now flickered of a long-necked shaggy mocha-skinned human woman chattering like a burrow mother. '*Chi-chi-chi-chee! Chi-chi-chi-chee! Chi-chi-chi-chi-chi-chi-cheeee!*' In bedrooms and breakfast nooks the Perks drew into a huddle. Spitting dog fur from their mouths, they began to slither back into the ruptured walls.

In Captain Jute's Pango the com had been picking up nothing all the way but white noise, chanting, and sometimes something that sounded like someone pleading desperately. Haphazard light flashed from the screen, dancing around the armoured van.

The interior of the Pango appeared somewhat the worse for wear. The dashboard was covered in chewing gum and gobbets of dried gristle the chauffeuse had picked from her teeth. The floor was sticky with spilled cola and alcohol, the seats furry with use by Thrants and Alteceans and people in shaggy coats. Promotional stickers for beer and ammunition dotted the windows and walls. A fluffy toy Perk on a spring dangled from the mirror.

Saskia Zodiac sat up front with Xtasca the Cherub on her lap. She kept looking round at the Captain and the prisoner.

'You never *said* you had a sister,' she complained.

'Don't start,' Dodger Gillespie muttered; but it was no use.

'If you'd *said*, we would have worked it out ages ago.' She seemed annoyed, that the solution to the puzzle had turned out to be so simple.

Angela smiled at her sweetly. '*Swing low,*' she sang softly, '*sweet chariot . . .*'

You could feel their hate and mistrust surround her, like the field of cold around a refrigerator. Everybody knew now the ship had come fifty light years too far, and that it was all her doing.

Kenny and the boys were keeping a tight guard on the Captain. Their eyes never left her. The apothecary was at her too, trying to persuade her to drink something that smelled like stagnant water. Unsettled, the one-eyed cat slipped from his lap onto hers.

She pushed the cat away, along with the flask. 'Quiet!' she shouted. 'Everybody shut up!'

In the ensuing silence she watched the screen. She thought she had seen, for an instant, her sister's face.

There it was again.

'Did you see that?' she asked them.

'That was Angela,' said Saskia.

To her sister the Captain said: 'Was that you, doing that?'

Angie was petting the cat. She shook her head slowly and solemnly. 'This unit isn't tra-ansmitting,' she said.

Soi stabbed the brake. The van screeched to a halt. 'Wook!' she cried, pointing through the windscreen.

The Captain was on her feet and in the aisle, hanging on the rail, staring ahead up the tunnel.

In the middle of the road stood an image of a little white girl with a lot of long blonde hair and a blue dress and white pinafore.

She came whizzing straight up to them like a drone on a track. She came very close. She looked up through the windscreen with a disgruntled smile. The audio scribble on the com ceased abruptly. 'AH, CAPTAIN,' said a warm, calm voice. 'THERE YOU ARE.'

9

Along the powerless pleasure arcades of the PreCentral, the signs were dead, their bulbs broken. The great doors of the Mercury Garden had jammed half open. Trash had collected around them, twists of hair and bones. The air was thin, sparse as rotten cloth.

Inside the gloomy amphitheatre the seats were empty, the dining tables gone, smashed, stolen or burnt. The broad skylights inserted to show patrons the orbital diadem of Terra's Tangle had long been full of the blurred nothingness of hyperspace. Their glass was streaked with dust and smoke. On the central podium where famous entertainers had once performed, rubbish fires were burning. Hooded figures were gathered between the fires, intent on dark business around an altar block. The firelight wavered on their robes, and on the banners they had erected to proclaim their allegiance to an ideal of purity. The firelight picked out a cluster of skulls on a pole.

There was another scream, rich and multitonal with pain and terror and finality, and the celebrants all cried '*Ha!*'

'Fa-a-arkin' 'ell,' a thin voice could be heard to say, 'that was a good one!' Meanwhile the knights of the legion began to chant something deep and thrilling and full of menacing bass harmonies. The voice was that of the officiating executioner, an aged, aged man whose manifest disabilities seemed in no way to prevent him from dispatching the victims with decision and vigour. 'What one we going to do next?'

The flames of the rubbish fires guttered in a weak, foul zephyr that flowed through the Mercury Garden as if the remaining air were unstable and about to run away. The old man moved his stiff right hand to turn up his oxygenator. He was hooded like the rest.

'Bung us another one over!' His tub of a chair whined as he rolled towards the hobbled victims. 'Here, let's have you,' he said, grabbing one by the wrist and dragging her to the slab where two of her fellows lay dead already.

The other two would not easily let him take her. They hugged her to them, treading on one another's feet, gobbling stridently. They were Palernians, the so-called 'woolly wallies', detested by all: by all decent red-blooded humans who had not been kissing their smelly arses for months, thinking to curry favour with them for the world that lay ahead. Greedy, clumsy, destructive, Palernians were responsible for all the problems and offences suffered by decent red-blooded humans on board, along with pushy Vespans and vicious Thrant and larcenous Alteceans. You only had to see one Palernian, or five, in fact, they were too cowardly to go around singly, to appreciate how loathsome they were. They had the sort of foolish blubbery faces and podgy flesh you just wanted to hit and hit and hit. It would be a virtuous undertaking to rid the galaxy of them.

The chanting swelled. The knights of purity strove at their work. They had engaged the services of the very best man for the job. 'Hee-hee-hee! She doesn't want to go, does she?' tittered the executioner.

The breeze returned and the fires gusted smoke everywhere. The old man switched on the light ring that circled his chair. The light showed him the immobilized Palernians pawing at him, moaning and clamouring. His third victim was warbling in distress, in a seizure of fear. The light showed her the motionless bodies of two of her life's companions, slumped in steaming puddles of their own black blood. She shook her head, sucking her lips, pissing and dribbling uncontrollably, as the hooded avengers manhandled her to the block. 'Fuck me, wot a fucking mess! Here, come on –'

But the woman wouldn't lie down. She bucked and kicked. She was not strong, but she was bulky, and her wool was greasy. It was like trying to master an amphetamine-crazed sheep.

'Oh, here we go then, here we go –' muttered the old man, and his withered left arm rose in its tubular brace, buoyed up on a repeller field. He used the brace to knock a control lever three notches to the right. In the side of his chair a panel slid open. From the depths inside a counterbalanced arm unfolded, probing sensitively out towards the neck of the struggling woman. It was tipped with an angled syringe full of some clear liquid.

The syringe glistened in the bleak light cast by the chair ring. The two survivors of the Palernian five tried to turn their backs and cover their eyes, never ceasing to gibber with outrage and horror. The syringe bobbed an instant in the smoky air, then darted in, pierced the thick hide and discharged its load.

With a high choking cry the third sacrifice spasmed and flailed. She drummed her bony heels on the slab. The hooded celebrants chanted. The woman was dead.

The next moment, the light in the great amphitheatre changed. Through the skylights overhead there suddenly began to glow a redness like a reflection of distant fire. It poured in, richer and redder, until every part of the arena was flooded as if with a crimson fluid.

The chanting failed.

'*Faaar*-kin' 'ell,' croaked the old man. 'Wha –? W-wha's –?' The headrest of his chair whirred, adjusting as he tipped his head back. Through the eyeholes of his hood he gazed upwards.

Above the skylights of the Mercury Garden burned two vast red lights. Suspended in the blackness of night, they stared down like the vast sardonic smouldering eyes of some malevolent deity. They were staring down at the old man. To him, they seemed to be staring as if amused at his pretensions, watching to see what he would do next.

Inside the shell of its metal and plastic accoutrements, the old man had a heart, though it was wizened and black as a prune. The black old heart gave a shiver. It squeezed, and did not relax. It froze.

Warning lights started popping on all around the old man's control panel. The old man wasn't watching. He was staring up at the giant red orbs. His slack lips fell open and a string of drool ran out from under his hood, trickling down among his love beads.

'No, man!' he mumbled, gasping. Wrinkles were appearing in the plastic envelopes of his lungs. 'Not me, man. Not me . . .'

His left arm struggled to rise, but the hoverbrace was no longer responding. The cultists started to shout. The Palernians shrieked and gibbered.

As if responding to the colour of the flood, by twos and threes the control displays of the amazing chair blinked from green to red, red, red. Under the seat an adrenalizer pumped and a fluid link drained itself dry. The black heart was in spasm, as if trying to squeeze itself into something even harder and denser and more obdurate, like a knob of coal. A tiny automatic valve switched over to an emergency supply. The heart stayed squeezed. The emergency supply gurgled empty. *Tick tick tick*, the valve went, switching over and back again, over and back. *Tick tick tick tick tick.*

By this time the knights of purity had realized something was wrong. They pulled off the executioner's hood. A masked legionnaire, feet apart, hands on knees, stared into the desiccated face. 'The man is dead . . .'

It was enough. The destruction of the destroyer; the red orbs like a cosmic portent – in consternation the assembly disassembled, jumping off the edge of the stage and running for the door.

The tiny automatic valve went on ticking a long time. It ticked all the while the two surviving Palernians were crying out in hunger and thirst and rage and despair. It ticked after they fell silent. It ticked while the life support chair's all-systems emergency alarm was squealing, running its batteries down. It carried on ticking. Eventually the insects that had come creeping up to investigate the smell of blood and decay grew used to the little noise and decided it meant them no harm. Then they started to burrow their way in to the aromatic relic, taking advantage of the many pipes and drains that already pierced its shrivelled skin.

Insubstantial though it was, everybody drew away from the little white ghost when it slipped inside the van. It floated straight through the bonnet and into the cabin. Odin the cat took one look at it and vanished beneath the apothecary's coat.

'Alice,' said the Captain.

'READY,' said Alice. The voice came now from a loudspeaker on a lamp post outside.

Captain Jute felt her breath swell up inside her.

'Did she damage you?'

'SPECIFY *SHE*,' said Kenny's wristset.

Everybody looked at Kenny. Saskia Zodiac and Xtasca the Cherub turned around, staring together over the seatback.

'Are you damaged?' asked the Captain.

'INSTABILITIES PRESENT,' said the com on her own wrist.

Captain Jute looked at her sister. Angela was gazing at the ghostly child.

'Alice?' said the Captain. 'You recognize me.'

The voice came again through the window, from all the speakers up and down the street.

'I RECOGNIZE YOU VERY WELL. I RECALL YOUR DIRTY SOCKS, YOUR BAD MOODS, YOUR TRAIL OF DISCARDED

LOVERS. YOUR NAME IS TABITHA JUTE, AND YOU ARE THE CAPTAIN OF THIS SHIP. YOU USED TO TALK A LOT BUT NEVER REMEMBER WHERE YOU PUT ANYTHING. YOU USED TO TELL ME STORIES.'

People had begun to gather in the street. They were gasping, talking, sniggering.

Captain Jute ignored them. She said: 'And you know who you are.'

'I AM A BERGEN SERIES 5 KOBOLD PERSONA RECON-FIGURED FOR A FRASQUE CONTROL SYSTEM EMULATION. MY GIVEN NAME IS ALICE. CAPTAIN, WE ARE IN RATHER A MESS, I SUPPOSE YOU KNOW,' said the van com, as the imago selected an empty seat.

'Drive on,' said the Captain.

She looked at Dodger Gillespie with gratitude dulled only by exhaustion. Captain Gillespie was curling her lip at her, shaking her head in acknowledgement of something more than luck.

As the van rolled on everybody started clapping. Kenny's boys stamped the butts of their weapons on the floor between their feet.

Captain Jute hung on to the strap, grinning in sheer triumph. She wanted to roar like Tarzan.

Along the road tunnels the lights went on now as they approached, and off again behind. In the van a tense silence had fallen. The guards were watching at the windows, weapons at the ready. Kenny sat behind the cannon. Captain Gillespie was keeping her eye on the prisoner, the lone agent of the Seraphim, in case any residual programming should suddenly kick in, turning her into a super-charged assassin.

Tabitha Jute kept looking around, from face to face. She felt she was having a dream in which they had all died on takeoff, and this was an afterlife through whose corridors they had been wandering ever since. The further they drove, the more lost souls turned up, as if the Pango were some kind of ferry collecting them all out of the past. Saskia, Dodger, Xtasca, Alice, Angie: they had all returned. Who next? she wondered. Auntie Muriel? Ma?

Her eye fell once more on the transparent passenger. The image of the old-fashioned child sat placidly, on or in or just above the seat. It seemed to register nothing, but sat as if it were quite alone.

'Alice,' said the Captain. 'What is this thing?'

'DON'T YOU LIKE HER?' responded Alice, who had settled in the van com. 'SHE SEEMS TO BE A SUBSIDIARY FUNCTION OF SOME COMBINATION OF MY PARTIALS. I ASSUME SHE WAS MEANT AS A REMINDER, CAPTAIN, A WARNING. A PUZZLE ONLY YOU COULD SOLVE.'

'You must be joking.' Just listening to the answer was making her head hurt.

'HER NAME IS ALICE,' said Alice. 'SHE'S THE IMAGE OF A PICTURE OF A STORY ABOUT A DREAM.'

'No wonder it never made any sense.'

'The poem was about Angela,' Xtasca remarked. 'The Lady of Shall-Not.' Tabitha looked at her sister. She tried to remember the poem that had appeared on her cabin console, and couldn't. Instead she remembered Luna, the message left on the screen for them then, saying Angie had gone to join the cult of the Expanded Neurosphere: '*I have been called*', and her suit missing from the rack in the airlock. Tabitha remembered ma and pa shouting and screeching.

'The only poem I know is *Nine Times a Night*,' she said.

Dodger Gillespie winced, puffing on her fag. She knew all about the Captain's taste in music, her prowess on the harmonica.

Saskia Zodiac tutted. 'If you'd *told* us you had a *sister* who was a *plughead* –' she began again, with righteous weariness.

'I wonder why it's not speaking now,' said Xtasca.

That seemed to trigger the imago somehow. Its mouth opened. 'I am a dream,' it said, with the voice Tabitha had heard before, that small, high, persistent voice, so exactly like a human child, like a child of any species. They all heard it now. The apothecary lowed fearfully and made a horrible smell.

'At least,' the imago went on, 'that's what I was, you know, a dream. I think I must have been changed several times since then. But where is the Red King?' it asked, with an air of bewilderment. 'The gentleman in bed? He was the Red King, of course. It was his dream I was,' it said.

'Bless her!' smiled Angela Jute, delightedly. She obviously understood nothing, her sister had decided; her own mission least of all. She no less than the ghostly child was a component of a circuit – the component whose function it was to collect the other components and construct the rest of the circuit from them. She had stolen the persona plaque, but made no use of it. It was almost as if she had been asking to be caught.

The small apparition had begun to distress itself. 'Please,' it said, gazing around hopelessly, 'where *is* the Red King and has he left off dreaming yet? I cannot suppose he has, you know, for here I am again, large as life, as they say, though probably they don't mean me when they say it – and as for the part about being "twice as natural", oh dear – I suppose I am not a bit natural, not even a half or a quarter, probably!'

Captain Jute gritted her teeth. 'Have we got to have it, Alice?' she asked.

There was no reply.

'Alice?'

'PLEASE WAIT,' said the com politely, in Alice's voice. 'PLEASE WAIT. PLEASE WAIT.'

It went on until Captain Jute shouted, 'Shut it off!'

Panting, Soi cut the sound.

'Stop?' she asked.

'No,' said the Captain. 'Keep going.'

In the front seat Saskia helped Xtasca put on a tail, and the Cherub began to probe the com circuits, fishing the wavelengths for a clue.

The tormented imago babbled on, quietly, playing with its fingers. Tabitha looked away. If it really was a function of Alice, it was a bloody useless one. The apothecary watched it suspiciously out of the corner of his wet black eye. Dodger and the guards continued to watch Angela; and Angela continued to smile at infinity. The Captain thumped the roof of the van. 'Alice!' she moaned. Alice, however, the real one, was still otherwise engaged.

Soi pushed the Pango up the broken road. It juddered as its tread slid and gripped, slid and gripped. Ahead, waste air was gushing unchecked through torn gratings, filling the tunnel with dust and grit. Dazzled by the headlights, angular shadows loped away.

The Pango crawled into Cent Fiss along a high ledge, overlooking what had once been Eden Dale. Far below their wheels, a burnt-out halftrack stood abandoned amid the smouldering ruins of the Pause Café. Bodies and equipment lay here and there as if flung about by explosions. Mutant Wisps hovered sluggishly around the bodies, looking from this height like torpid bumblebees.

'Aha,' said Xtasca, as the com screen cleared.

Everyone looked. It was a sequence of a familiar face talking, gloating, cajoling.

'THERE,' said Alice suddenly. 'THAT'S BETTER, ISN'T IT?'

The Captain felt a lurch of apprehension. 'Alice,' she said, 'what have you been up to?'

On the screen, pictures cycled:

There were the docks, where flying pictures of Mystery Woman lured the defenders this way and that, looters and soldiers running together through the access tunnels in pursuit of invisible Frasque. There was the Sylvian Aqueduct, with Colonel Stark struggling to manoeuvre her troops through 180° while behind her the local Alteceans were already arriving to pick over the flattened robots and sort them for scrap. Behind them, some way behind now, was the ape of Havoc and its rattling army, shambling pell-mell back towards the Caves of Disorder in search of a hip-swinging caricature of Angela Jute in a brass bra.

Saskia Zodiac put her hands to her face. 'They've all stopped fighting.'

Captain Gillespie, beginning to understand, looked to see how Angie herself was taking it.

Angela Jute was staring at herself playing nursemaid in Kanfa, squeaking in Perk, declaiming in peals of thunder to the Church of Christ Siliconite. These spectres of her fame, the multiplication of her disowned identity, seemed to be upsetting her. For the first time the electronic evangelist was starting to look disconcerted.

'I'VE BEEN SHOWING EVERYONE WHAT THEY WANT TO SEE,' said Alice. 'A THREAT – AN APPEAL – A VICTORY.'

Kenny and the boys were laughing. They started to stamp and bang their guns on the floor again.

'An elegant equation,' Xtasca said approvingly.

Saskia stretched her supple limbs. 'Now everybody's been betrayed,' she observed, in a tone of satisfaction.

The Captain was perfectly sure it wouldn't last. 'You stay here with us now,' she ordered the voice.

'DON'T WORRY, CAPTAIN,' it replied. 'I'M AHEAD OF YOU.'

The com screen came to rest on a high angle shot of the Pons, where Lieutenant Rykov and his team were raging impotently. Everyone was mobbing the helm, neglecting everything else. The light next to the plaque reader slot flashed rapidly on and off. 'HERE I AM,' said Alice.

Xtasca hummed, Kenny and Soi began to whoop, and Dodger Gillespie cackled softly, catching sight of a sly-looking Jone.

Odin the cat crept out of hiding. From beneath the apothecary's fur he poked out his head and scrutinized little Alice, whiskers twitching. Noticing him the imago suddenly rolled itself up, turning into a cat too, a large cat with staring eyes and a wide, feral grin. The guards laughed louder, pointing at the astonished Odin.

'Show me the big screen,' said the Captain. It was empty now, bereft of Angela's false pictures. There was a Redcap sitting in her chair.

'Can't this thing go any faster?' said Captain Jute.

Soi pulled up in the shadow of a concrete bridge. Ahead lay the green dome. It was surrounded. They could see spiky Thrant and leprous Vespans; disconsolate robots; naked shivering Rooks; tunnel bandits, humans, wearing dried Frasque heads over their own. Men and women in red caps were corralling the sightseers, taking control of the residual violence.

'We've got to get in there,' the Captain said.

Kenny chittered. He swung the cannon.

'No,' said Saskia. 'Wait. Here.'

Delicately extending one hand, she moved it through the air in an odd, screwing motion, reached into Soi's left ear and seemingly pulled out a length of brightly coloured cloth. As they gasped she shook it out with a flourish. It was a Redcap flag in scarlet, black and gold.

The driver shivered, grinning self-consciously and scratching her ear as if she thought perhaps the flag really had come from inside it. 'Open the window,' said the Captain, and the conjuror gave the flag to Kenny, who clambered swiftly out and up on the roof. They heard the scuffling of his feet on the metal roof as he tied the flag to the aerial of the Pango. Clumsily, Tabitha reached for Saskia and kissed her on the lips.

She did taste marvellously good.

Arriving at speed, the Pango was down the ramp, through the crowd and into the car park before any of the troops realized they had been tricked. In the rearview they saw the defenders racing after them, the air beginning to flicker with gunfire.

They rounded the dome, accelerating. Captain Jute patted Soi on the shoulder, signalling her to pull up at the top of a flight of steps that led down into the building.

Dodger Gillespie was already on her feet, checking her armour, putting her fag out.

Angela jumped up. 'Not you,' said Tabitha. The guards restrained her, cuffing her to the seat.

'Tabby!' Angela cried. She was resisting now, seeming at last to be possessed of a will of her own. 'Tabby, you s-sickbag.'

Xtasca gave a high-pitched chuckle and deftly plugged her into the com, where the fractured images of her unlicensed selves still came and went like wandering sprites. Angela whimpered softly. The Cherub was already planning her interrogation.

Purple fire burst in the air outside.

'Kenny,' said Captain Jute. He swivelled the cannon. 'Fire over their heads,' she said.

He writhed at the controls, showing his teeth, the whites of his eyes. 'Over their heads,' she repeated. The cannon stuttered, flatly. Soi opened the door of the van and the guards jumped out, shooting high.

The Redcaps held their fire. They were under no orders to kill the Captain. They were under no clear orders at all. Lieutenant Rykov was having problems of his own inside. In a moment the Captain was out and down the steps into the dome.

The crowd mobbed the door of the Pango while the occupants got out. First came a big fat Altecean with a cat in his arms; then a walking hologram of a little white girl; then Xtasca the Cherub zipped over their heads on its saucer, elusive as ever.

The crowd began to be obstreperous, cheering and crushing one another up against the side of the van. Inside now there were only a couple of Kenny's men with Spite Supremos and broad spectrum Inimics, guarding a hunched plughead with a jacket over her head. Was there something familiar about that shrouded figure? Were those beads dangling out from under the jacket? A clamour started. Soldiers and fanatics tried to hurl themselves against the locked door of the Pango.

Inside the green dome a great synthetic fanfare went up. 'Quiet!'

shouted the Captain, pressing her hands to her ears. But they were swallowed up by a crowd of welcoming Pontines, techs and clerks who were toasting everything in cola and pelting everybody with shredded printout. For a moment, Captain Jute couldn't think why they were so pleased to see her.

Lomax was there, still alive, trying to clear her a path. Captain Jute pressed through, shielding Saskia with her arm. 'What's all the noise?' yelled the Captain.

His eyes assessed her, disparaged her, accepted her, in one swift and complex sweep. 'We've Emerged, Captain,' he said. 'We've got Mr Spinner on the com.'

On robot carts they rode through the foyer and into the control chamber. Jone appeared, running to hug Dodger. Tabitha tried to keep hold of Saskia, but was pulled away by a mob asking questions and demanding decisions. With hardly a glance at Lieutenant Rykov, standing bitterly alongside, she let herself be half carried, half man-hauled into her seat. She pulled on a headset.

'HELLO, CAPTAIN,' said Alice, her voice clear in the earpiece, but still distant.

Captain Jute reached out and touched the plaque in its reader. She felt she was floating in a sort of warm golden glow. What did it matter where they had emerged in the universe? They were far from Earth and the clutches of her sister's controllers. They had arrived, they were alive, most of them. If the photosphere was the least bit habitable, there would be no need to suffer through the grey blank nothingness ever again.

'I understand we're here,' said Captain Jute.

'THAT's RIGHT, CAPTAIN. ALL IT TOOK WAS A LITTLE PUSH.'

At her disposal were control pads, palettes, keyboards, more than she could remember the use of. Above them on a monitor was Mr Spinner in Eeb's apartment, his arm in a sling. Even he looked happy. *'Full Emergence logged at 317.4.3, ma'am.'*

The big screen was still dark. Captain Jute tapped an astroscope with her knuckles. Her confident mood of a second before had evaporated. There was a sick feeling now in her stomach. 'All right, Alice,' she said. 'Show me.' A big red blob appeared on the big screen, out of focus. The room at once fell silent.

It was ovoid, the red blob, and seemed to be seamed like a plum.

The monitors started to flicker with data, temperatures, measurements, surface flow patterns. Video lines swept down the image, combing the resolution higher, higher. The blob separated into two.

Xtasca floated at Tabitha's elbow, sipping from the datastream through its tail. The Captain felt strangely comforted to have it there.

Dodger Gillespie came and leaned one hip on the console. The console was slaved to the big screen. Tabitha tapped it, bringing up the detail.

The red blob was two big old suns burning down in tandem. Two or three dead worlds were visible, grey lumps of clinker, and a shower of strangely shaped asteroids, musroid nodules, artificial planets no doubt honeycombed like Plenty itself. Glittering among them like flecks of tinsel in a cloud of ash were several tiny golden waisted shapes like wasps, elongated teardrops joined tip to tip.

Captain Jute felt cold sweat between her shoulder blades. She knew that feeling. It was time to reach for crystal, thril, a couple of Sideways, anything to take away the edge, for the edge of this was agonizingly sharp, like a blade of comet ice.

'She brought us here?' she said, meaning Angela.

'IT WAS A PRESET COURSE,' said Alice, sounding stronger now. 'SHE FOOLED US INTO TAKING IT.'

The Captain turned to look for Saskia but couldn't immediately find her. Across the gigantic double sun on the big screen there now drifted a little shadow in shape like a swan, or perhaps more like a flying horse with no legs, carrying what looked like a whole city on its back. It looked as if it were coming towards them.

The Captain's sick feeling increased. 'Why have the Seraphim brought us here?' she asked the Cherub.

'I should imagine, to resume a previous promising collaboration,' mused the little creature. It came to Tabitha then that Cherubim had been bred without fear and desire, and that that was a far, far better state of being, because it was only desire and fear that had brought her here, to the last place in the galaxy she would have wished to be. Fear and desire had destroyed her, had destroyed everything.

'Well, okay now, here we all are then, ladies and gentlemen,' said a new voice, bold as brass from over their heads. 'Ain't life grand?'

Throughout the control chamber all eyes of every species turned up to the gallery, where the doors of the cubicles were opening. They were all opening together, all at the same speed, opening onto golden light. From them was emerging a group of figures in silhouette. The figures were all oddly similar in shape: human in scale, but with an upper distortion, an enlargement that made them somehow both awesome and grotesque.

As they floated forward to the rail, each of them precisely fifty centimetres above the gallery, their features became visible. You could see they had all been human, originally. They had lost all their hair in the process that had expanded their crania, but they were still quite recognizable as a number of the missing passengers, now mostly dressed in white and looking down on the astounded company with benevolent smiles and gestures of benediction.

There were ten of them in all. This one in classical toga and sandals had been a poet, people remembered, a habitué of Rory's Trivia Bar – and that was his friend, there, in the clinical coat with the stethoscope trailing out of the pocket – and another, truly splendid in buckled shoes and robes of red and blue, though his head had grown too large now for his judicial wig. In a ring around the Pons they floated, like a fleet of silken effigies.

Tabitha Jute tasted bile. She put a hand on her stomach. Her hand was shaking, or perhaps it was her ship.

Directly in front of her hovered the chubby figure that had spoken. He wore tight leopard skin trousers and a quilted high-collared cape of gold. His snow-white shirtsleeves were ruffled, their cuffs linked with outsize platinum crotchets. His right hand was made of glass.

'Captain!' said Brother Marco, saluting her. 'Welcome to Capella!'